"Mrs. Bevis told me the war will be over by Christmas," she said.

"It's more like a hope than a prediction," Mom told her.

More code that grown-ups used. "Okay."

"It can't go on forever, honey. It'll stop one day, and then we can go home. We'll all be together again."

Mom always talked about Hannah's dad as if he were still alive and as if her older brother, who'd disappeared, had made it back to their house in Sterling.

"I can't wait," Hannah played along.

"Until then, we're doing okay. All we have to do is keep going."

Praise for

OUR WAR

"Brutal, unflinching, mesmerizing."

—Peter Clines, *New York Times* bestselling author

"An instant classic that will join the ranks of dystopian futures that at times feel all too real."

—Nicholas Sansbury Smith, *USA Today* bestselling author

"An unflinching look at what happens when politics fail and war truly comes home, powered by the narrative shock of truth-telling."

—Christopher Brown, author of *Tropic of Kansas*

"Presenting a dark alternate reality that touches the seams of current events and a possible future, DiLouie offers an uncompromising view of child soldiers and patriotism in conflict."

—*Library Journal*

"DiLouie brings depth to his dark vision of America with a story that draws parallels to the sad reality of conscripted children fighting in real wars around the world today."

—*B&N Sci-Fi & Fantasy Blog*

"This may be one of the most important books you'll read this year....Craig DiLouie has written a heart-breaking, terrifying novel."

—*Cemetery Dance*

"*Our War* further solidifies that Craig DiLouie is not only one of the best fantasists working today, he's one of the best writers out there, period. This novel is harrowing and heartfelt, upsetting and, most of all, utterly compelling."

—Bracken MacLeod, Shirley Jackson
Award–nominated author of *Stranded*

OUR
WAR

By Craig DiLouie

Our War
One of Us
Suffer the Children
Tooth and Nail
The Alchemists
The Great Planet Robbery

CRASH DIVE

Crash Dive
Silent Running
Battle Stations
Contact!
Hara-Kiri
Over the Hill

THE INFECTION WAR

The Infection
The Killing Floor

THE RETREAT

Pandemic
Alamo

OUR WAR

CRAIG DiLOUIE

orbit

www.orbitbooks.net

Copyright © 2019 by Craig DiLouie
Excerpt from *One of Us* copyright © 2018 by Craig DiLouie
Excerpt from *A Boy and His Dog at the End of the World* copyright © 2019 by Man Sunday Ltd

Cover design by Lisa Marie Pompilio
Cover art by Trevillion and Shutterstock
Cover copyright © 2019 by Hachette Book Group, Inc.
Author photograph by Jodi O

Orbit
Hachette Book Group
1290 Avenue of the Americas
New York, NY 10104
orbitbooks.net

First Paperback Edition: February 2020
Originally published in hardcover and ebook by Orbit in August 2019

Orbit is an imprint of Hachette Book Group.
The Orbit name and logo are trademarks of Little, Brown Book Group Limited.

The publisher is not responsible for websites (or their content) that are not owned by the publisher.

The Hachette Speakers Bureau provides a wide range of authors for speaking events. To find out more, go to www.hachettespeakersbureau.com or call (866) 376-6591.

The Library of Congress has catalogued the hardcover as follows:
Names: DiLouie, Craig, 1967- author.
Title: Our war / Craig DiLouie.
Description: First edition. | New York, NY: Orbit, 2019.
Identifiers: LCCN 2019000763 | ISBN 9780316525268 (hardcover) |
    ISBN 9780316525275 (trade paperback) | ISBN 9780316525251 (ebook) |
    ISBN 9781549171536 (downloadable audio book)
Classification: LCC PS3604.I463 O97 2019 | DDC 813/.6—dc23
LC record available at https://lccn.loc.gov/2019000763

ISBNs: 978-0-316-52527-5 (trade paperback), 978-0-316-52525-1 (ebook)

Printed in the United States of America

LSC-C

10 9 8 7 6 5 4 3 2 1

*For my children, with hope we leave
the world a better place for you.*

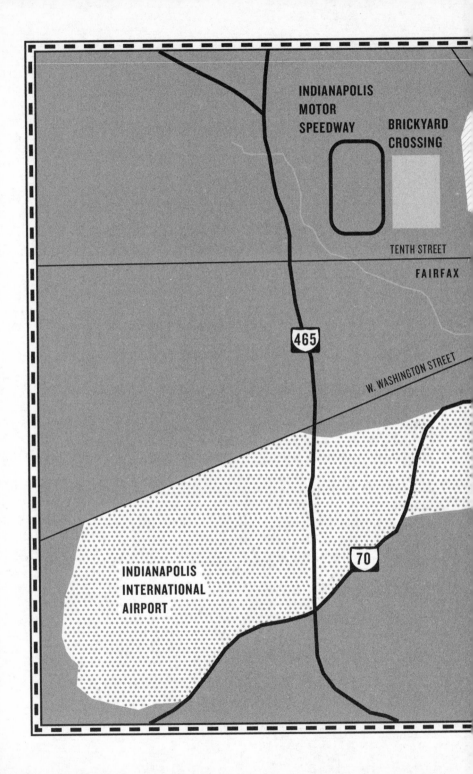

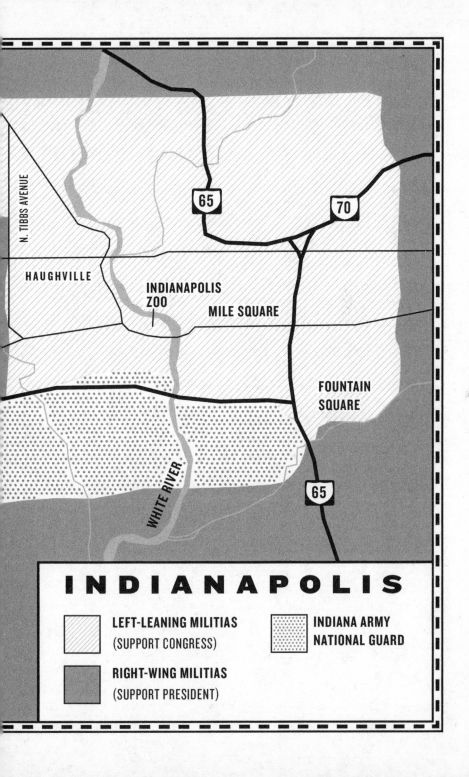

And the rocket's red glare, the bombs bursting in air,
Gave proof through the night that our flag was still there;
Oh, say! does that star-spangled banner yet wave
O'er the land of the free and the home of the brave?

—American national anthem

ONE

Every week, Hannah asked when the war would end.

Soon, Mom always said, which her child's mind translated as, *Longer than you want.*

The war had taken her home, friends, and family. If it didn't end soon, it might take everything.

Ten months ago, Hannah and her mother arrived at the refugee camp set up at the Indiana Convention Center. They'd settled in Hall D, a vast space sectioned off by metal pipe and dark blue drapes into rooms ten feet square. Rough living, the days suspended between tension and tedium, but it was safer than outside.

Now Mom sat on her cot and inventoried their weekly aid package. Spam, rice, cheese, beans, sugar, powdered milk, soap, cooking oil. The bland basics of survival.

Before the war, she'd been an accountant. Now she added up calories, while Hannah counted the hours to their next meager meal.

Mom licked her finger and dipped it in the sugar. "Taste test?"

They used to bake together in their kitchen back in Sterling. Cookies and cupcakes and scones. Hannah helped out, knowing she'd be the official taste tester.

She licked the sweetness. It only made her hungrier, but she didn't ask for more. She already received more than her fair share of the food. Once a plump woman, her mother had wasted away to gauntness.

"We have enough to get us to Friday," Mom said. "Except water."

"Okay." Hannah looped a belt through three plastic gallon jugs.

"Why don't you stay here and play with your friends?"

Mom always said this before they went outside. The streets were dangerous now with muggers, bombs, and rebel snipers who'd infiltrated the city.

"I want to go with you," Hannah said.

She'd already lost Dad and Alex. If Mom went without her, she'd go out of her mind waiting. She hated being alone.

Mom understood all this. "All right, honey."

They left their tiny room and closed the drape behind them. People traded rations and gossip in the aisle. A couple was having a loud argument. The air smelled like pee and frying Spam. Smoke from cooking fires hazed around the dead ceiling lights high over their heads.

Mrs. Bevis yanked her drape aside. "Did I hear you're going out for water?"

Mom pursed her lips. "You did."

"Because my back is still killing me." She was already holding out her jug.

Hannah took it. "We can fill this up for you, Mrs. Bevis."

"My waste bucket is getting full too."

"Some other time," Mom said before Hannah could say anything.

The old woman shot a look down the aisle. "Listen to them. Arguing again. They go at it all day and then again all night."

Mom said, "Well, we should get going."

Mrs. Bevis regarded her with a judgmental frown. "Don't let me hold you up."

They walked down Aisle 1500. War news droned on a portable radio. A swarm of kids ran laughing through laundry hung on lines spanning the aisle. Hannah sometimes joined in the fun but more often stayed close to Mom, an oasis of warmth and love in a world that had otherwise turned against her.

"Mrs. Bevis told me the war will be over by Christmas," she said.

"It's more like a hope than a prediction," Mom told her.

More code that grown-ups used. "Okay."

"It can't go on forever, honey. It'll stop one day, and then we can go home. We'll all be together again."

Mom always talked about Hannah's dad as if he were still alive and as if her older brother, who'd disappeared, had made it back to their house in Sterling.

"I can't wait," Hannah played along.

"Until then, we're doing okay. All we have to do is keep going."

Outside, bright sunlight washed the cold street. Dirty snow covered the ground. Bicycles zipped around dead cars. Gunfire crackled at the front line a few miles away. A band of militia walked past, hard men and women wearing ratty uniforms and carrying rifles.

The water tanker was three blocks east. They waited in line until they could fill their jugs. Hannah shuffled her feet to stay warm and read political graffiti covering the wall of a nearby building. FREE INDY, THIS GUN KILLS FASCISTS, RESIST.

At last, it was their turn to fill their jugs from the spigots, and they started home.

Mom gave her a sly smile. "If Christmas is coming, you know what that means."

"Hooray for me," Hannah sulked.

"You only turn eleven once. I'm going to make you a cake."

Hannah understood grown-ups told white lies to protect their kids, but this was going too far. "We don't have any flour or butter. We barely have any sugar."

"Then I'll have to make something out of nothing."

She shot Mom a warning look. They'd once had an imaginary dinner, where they'd pretended to eat a sumptuous feast. "Okay."

"It's a real thing, honey. I got a recipe from another mom."

Hannah believed now. The women at the refugee center were like mad scientists when it came to making new meals from the monotonous aid packages. They knew how to turn rice, vinegar, water, and powdered milk into cheese.

"What's in it?" she said.

"It's best if you don't know."

Hannah laughed. "Like a hot dog."

"It'll be yummy," her mother assured her.

"I can't wait." She was still smiling. "It's gonna be awesome."

"When the world goes back to normal, we can have a proper birthday party."

The grown-ups always talked like that, how nothing was normal, as if the war was an embarrassing mistake. But this, talking about a birthday cake. This felt normal, even after everything she'd lost. Something out of nothing.

"I love you, Mom—"

Blood sprayed across her cheek.

Bikes crashed in the roar of the rolling gunshot. The street emptied.

Mom shuddered on the blacktop.

Hannah blinked in shock. "Mommy?"

"*Sniper!*" a woman shrieked.

A large man scooped Hannah like a football as he charged past. She screamed and clawed at the air as Mom dwindled with each step.

The man set her down behind a burned-out bus but kept a tight hold of her arm to prevent her from bolting. Other people had sought safety here in a gasping huddle.

Crying, Hannah watched her mother struggle to rise.

"Stay down," the man hissed. "Don't move."

Mom freed herself from the belt and its heavy water jugs. She heaved onto her elbows. She started to drag her body off the road.

Hannah was wailing. "Mommy."

Their eyes locked. A smile flickered across Mom's face.

The second shot rammed her back down. The crowd screamed.

Hannah howled with them. *"MOMMY!"*

Nothing out of everything.

TWO

The Canadian Air Force transport plane trembled on air pockets at fifteen thousand feet.

Gabrielle Justine sat clenched in her metal chair attached to the bulkhead. She wore a blue helmet, flak jacket, parachute, and around her neck an oxygen mask. To her left, tarpaulin-covered wood crates filled the cargo hold. Twenty tons of milk and cheese. Cold air whistled through the compartment, bringing a strong whiff of fuel and canvas.

Corporal Kassar smiled at her from his seat on the opposite bulkhead. Goggles and a dashing red scarf complemented his uniform. The other crewman chewed gum while reading a paperback.

"You're UN, right?" the corporal shouted over the propeller hum. "UNICEF."

She didn't trust herself to speak. She nodded.

"But you're from Quebec," he added. "Your accent."

Gabrielle spoke French as her first language. "Yes."

"Here to help the children. Very noble. First time in the jungle?"

Booms sounded far below. They were getting close now.

Gabrielle turned to look out the nearest window. From way up here, Indianapolis appeared peaceful through a smoky haze. *Indy*, the locals called it. *The crossroads of America.*

Then she spotted the scarred ground marking the contact line, battlefields and trenches among houses and strip malls. The city and its population of some nine hundred thousand people had been under siege for nearly a year.

No sane person would come here by choice.

The gum-chewing crewman called out without looking up from his paperback, "What's the difference between a smart and a stupid American?"

Kassar rolled his eyes at the old joke. "The smart one is watching the war on TV in Canada."

Gabrielle flinched as light flashed on the ground.

The crewman set down his novel and threw her a sharp look. "The same joke now goes for Canadians, it looks like."

Two years ago, the Democrats retook Congress and impeached President Philip Marsh. After the Senate convicted him, he refused to leave office, and in the end, it was the bulk of Congress that fled Washington, DC. The military wavered as massive protests swept the country. Armed groups seized government buildings and TV stations, triggering a civil war.

When UNICEF put out a call for field operatives to go to America, Gabrielle quit her safe job buried in a humanitarian relief organization and took a contract. In Indianapolis, she'd evaluate the needs of the city's children. It promised to be hard work, and dangerous. But worthwhile.

Her friends worried she'd lost her mind. Her parents had begged her not to go. Dad told her she was smart and young and had a long life filled with choices ahead of her. She was already helping children at her current job. Why risk life and limb?

She could do more good in the field. She wanted to take part in history. Gabrielle gave him every answer except the truth, which was long ago, if a single man hadn't taken a risk on her behalf, she'd be dead.

She was tired of helping from a safe distance. It was time for her to pay it forward, take her own risks, and try to make a difference.

Now that she was here, she wondered if she'd made the right decision.

Gabrielle sighted the sprawling airport. So close. Then the plane tilted and cut off her view. "Why haven't we started descending?"

Kassar grinned. "Because we don't want to get shot down."

He leveled out his hand and angled it toward the deck. The plane had to maintain altitude to avoid ground fire and then plunge for a rapid landing.

She grabbed onto the canvas webbing and prayed. *"Dieu nous protège."*

The C-130 Hercules dropped out of the sky.

"Here we go," the corporal said.

Alarms shrilled from the cockpit. The plane screamed in its descent. Corporal Kassar reached into the folds of his scarf, found a talisman, and kissed it for luck.

"Hey, UN," he said.

Gabrielle stared at him, unable to speak. The airframe was shaking.

"Hey!"

"What?!"

"Are you seeing anybody?"

"Are you kidding me?"

"Can I take you to dinner sometime?"

"No," she said. "Maybe. I don't know!"

Anything, she prayed. *Just let me survive this.*

Her stomach lurched as the transport plane leveled out. Giant wheels slammed asphalt, carbon brakes screeching. Gabrielle gaped out the window at the blessed ground. Armored personnel carriers flashed by on the tarmac. Hesco walls surrounded the airport like a medieval town.

She prayed again—this time that she hadn't made a huge mistake coming here.

THREE

For a half hour, they huddled behind the abandoned bus as gun-fire popped in the distance. Apartment buildings loomed over boarded-up retail stores. Surrounded by water bottles, Hannah's mother lay facedown in the empty street.

Get up, Hannah prayed.

The shooting stopped.

"We got him," said the man who saved her. "I think we're safe now."

Nobody moved.

"Screw it," a woman said. "I'll go first."

She snatched up her discarded bike and started pedaling. She didn't look at Hannah's mother lying in the street.

The onlookers tensed, but nothing happened.

The man turned to Hannah. "Do you have somewhere you can go?"

She began to cry. Mom lay in the road, and nobody was doing anything. They didn't care. They were all leaving.

"Oh, man," he said. "I can't. I mean, I'm not..."

"Mom," she screamed. "Mom!"

Willing her to get up, though she knew she wouldn't.

"Mommy!"

A wailing ambulance turned the corner and screeched to a halt.

Men in blue jackets jumped out. After checking for a pulse, they took hold of Hannah's mother by the armpits and feet and tossed her on a stack of other bodies inside.

To Hannah, it was as if she were being taken out like trash.

"Don't touch her like that! Hey!" She ran into the street as the vehicle sped off.

Only a red stain on the road remained. The rest of her mother was headed to a mass grave at the American Legion Mall. Exhaust hung in the air like a ghost.

"Are you all right? You shouldn't be out in the open like this."

The man who'd saved her was gone. A skinny woman with a bandage taped over the left side of her face towered over her.

Hannah wiped her eyes and shied away. She wasn't supposed to talk to people she didn't know. One couldn't trust anybody or anything these days. People were always looking over their shoulders for a reason. They slept with one eye open.

The woman scratched at her bandage. "Is this your water? It's a lot for just one girl."

Hannah heaved the belt over her shoulder, but the load was too heavy. She unbuckled the belt, looped it through a single jug, and started walking. Mrs. Bevis would get upset if Hannah didn't bring back her water.

The woman scrabbled the rest into her arms. "Bless you, young lady!"

Hannah didn't answer. Still in shock, just trying to think.

Images flashed through her mind. *Convention center, Hall D. Red Cross packages. Bulldozers digging a trench at the American Legion Mall.*

Mom knocked to the ground still wearing a loving smile.

"No crying," Hannah yelled. Not this time, not ever again.

She did anyway. She was going to cry forever.

She found herself near Victory Field. Merchants had converted the baseball diamond into an open-air market. As she grew close, the city's smells thickened. Waste, burning, death.

Mom had taken her here before so they could look at all the nice things. Back in Sterling, they'd once had everything. A heated home and plenty to eat. School and clothes and summer camps.

And after they lost it all, Mom said: *Now we know what's truly important. Now we know how to live in the moment.*

Something out of nothing. Hannah had no idea where to even start.

If the worst happens and I can't take care of you, you have to survive.

Mom hadn't taught her how.

If she went back to the refugee center, the aid workers would put her in an orphanage. She'd seen war orphans roaming the streets like packs of wild dogs, fighting over territory and salvage.

The idea of living with them terrified her.

Hannah veered into the bustling market and walked through the crowds in a daze. It was the first time she'd ever wanted to become lost.

People hauled old and useful things to and from sellers standing behind plastic picnic tables. A man grunted as he pushed a shopping cart filled with firewood across the cold, rutted ground. Everybody looked skinny and tired. Vapor puffed from open mouths.

She stopped to warm herself at a burning trash can. Nearby, a seller had connected a car battery to a TV tuned to CNN. She watched it for a while, mesmerized. The handsome newsman wore a grave expression. The scrolling caption read, PRESIDENT SUSPENDS OTTAWA TALKS.

Always this stupid war.

"Hot cocoa, kid?" a man said. He'd set up a hillbilly coffee shop at his table. Balanced on bent coat hangers, Campbell's soup cans boiled water over fires burning in other containers. She spotted jars of instant coffee, packets of hot cocoa.

Hot chocolate. It made her think about all the little things that were gone. Ice cubes tinkling in a glass of lemonade on a summer day. Bologna and mustard sandwich in her lunch box. Warm sheets just out of the dryer. Cartoons on TV. A text from a friend on her phone. Fragments of a long dream, already half-forgotten.

Back then, her biggest worry was math tests.

Thinking about the little things made her forget, if only for a second, what she really missed. Mom, Dad, Alex, her friends and teachers back in Sterling.

Now we know what's truly important.

Hannah shook her head at the man. She had no money.

One of his fires burned out, and he bent to relight it. This was the new math. The precise amount of heat it took to boil a cup of water. How to make an aid package provide calories for two people for a week.

"I'll trade you," he said. "Half what you got in that jug for a cup of hot cocoa."

It seemed a fair deal. "Okay."

Careful not to spill a drop, the man measured out half a gallon. Then he filled a Styrofoam cup to the brim with hot chocolate. It steamed in the cold air.

"This'll warm you right up." He smiled. "I gave you a packet that had marshmallows."

Hannah sipped. The cocoa scalded her tongue, but she didn't care. Its heat flooded her chest. Her taste buds sang. "Thank you."

He dabbed a napkin and offered it to her. "You have some . . . red on your face."

Hannah took it and balled it in her fist.

"Indy is one of the last places in Indiana that is still America," a stout policewoman cried from a nearby table. She wore an impressive uniform that included ballistic armor. Behind her, a blue banner displayed an eagle, gold stars, and the roman capitals IMPD, which stood for the Indianapolis Metropolitan Police Department. "We must defend ourselves. We can't do it alone."

Hannah gazed at her with wide eyes as she sipped her hot cocoa. The woman appeared confident, well-fed, and tough.

"Do you want to suffer wrongs or right them?" she said. "Do you want a democracy or a dictator? Do you love the Constitution? Step right up and do your part by joining the Metro Police. Three square meals a day! Signing bonus if you have military experience!"

Food, Hannah heard. *Power and control.*

The police would teach her how to survive. She wanted to be this woman, standing strong in armor and being able to protect herself.

She approached the table. "Hey, can I join your police?"

The woman sized her up with a glance. "Too young."

"I don't have anywhere else to go."

"Sorry, kid. I can't help you."

"Do you know where the front line is? The one facing Sterling?"

She pointed. "That way."

"My brother's on the other side. He'll take care of me."

She started walking again, this time with purpose.

Alex was all she had left in the world, unless the war had taken him too. She'd cross the front line and find him.

"Wait," the policewoman said.

She wrote in her leather notebook and tore out a sheet. Hannah frowned as she inspected it. Traffic summons. It said she had to go to court.

Then she read what the woman had written. An address. Prospect Street.

"Why do I have to go there?"

"It's what you're looking for, and it's safer than where you were going."

"Did you find my brother?"

The woman turned away and called out, "Indy is one of the last places left in Indiana that is still America!"

Hannah scrubbed her face with the damp napkin and returned to the coffee seller, who smiled and said, "How's your cocoa?"

"Good." She showed him the traffic ticket. "Do you know where this is?"

He scrutinized it. "You going there?"

"Yeah."

"It's in Fountain Square. A bit of a walk. I'll draw you a map."

It was in the opposite direction of where she wanted to go. So far in the opposite direction, it was near a whole other front line.

She finished the last of her hot chocolate and handed the cup back to the man to reuse. Then she left the market and walked along the route he'd drawn.

Each step took her farther from the refugee center. Ahead lay a long, cold trek. She had no idea where she was going or how long it'd take to get there.

The freezing wind tugged at her, as if it too wanted her to go back.

She kept going.

Hannah was mad now. Mad at the sniper shooting her mom for no reason. The policewoman sending her on a wild-goose chase. This whole stupid war.

Anger felt better than helpless despair. She held on to it. She was going to walk until she discovered what the policewoman said she was looking for.

Hannah had been trying to become lost. This was as good a way as any to do it.

FOUR

The C-130 taxied on the runway before parking near an aircraft hangar. Corporal Kassar heaved Gabrielle's duffel bag over his shoulder and offered his hand. She took it and stood to stretch aching muscles battered by the rough flight.

He said, "No offense, but you don't seem cut out for this line of work."

"My first time in the field," she admitted.

"I got out of Syria during the civil war against President Assad. You might say I grew up in a place like this. You want some advice?"

"Sure."

"Watch out for the kids," he said. "They'll rob you blind."

Gabrielle threw him a warning look. He grinned.

"Okay, okay," he said. "Here's my advice. Keep your idealism in check and take your time."

"What do you mean?"

"The United States is no longer united, right? Neither is Indianapolis. There are at least a hundred major militias in the city, some just armed gangs."

"I don't care about the sides. I'm here for the children." She looked around the cargo hold as the ramp dropped. "These supplies will do them some good."

As long as the humanitarian aid kept flowing, the innocent majority might survive.

"All I'm saying is get to know the players and how things work before you try to change things. Allow yourself to accept small victories. It's the trying that counts. I've flown out enough burned-out aid workers to have learned this much."

Maybe spending more time with Kassar wasn't such a bad idea. "So how does one date during a siege?"

He laughed. "I was trying to take your mind off the landing."

"It's too late to back out now, *mon cher.*"

"I'm not authorized to go into the city," he said. "And if I did, somebody would think I'm an Arab terrorist and shoot me. The whole country has lost its marbles. When you get home, look me up and I'll buy you a drink. You'll need it."

She smiled. "It's a deal."

"Here, take this too. For good luck."

He removed his talisman and gave it to her. It was a gold maple leaf on a chain, symbol of Canada and its multicultural unity. Where Kassar had found a safe place to call home after fleeing his own civil war.

"Thank you," Gabrielle said, touched by the gesture.

She took her duffel bag and walked down to the tarmac, enjoying the feel of solid ground again. Forklifts converged on the plane to offload its precious cargo.

A slim young soldier with big ears met her at the bottom of the ramp. "Pleased to meet you, ma'am. I'm Lieutenant Douglas. I'm your liaison officer."

She shook his hand. "Gabrielle Justine, UNICEF."

He reached for her bag. "Let me get that for you. That's my jeep there."

Gabrielle had expected this reception based on her briefing. Units of the Indiana Army National Guard held the airport southwest of the city, along with a narrow strip of land between West Washington Street and I-70.

The jeep sped off toward a hangar, where Lieutenant Douglas had arranged safe transportation into Indy. He sat rigid behind the wheel, polite but distant. She sensed he'd rather be doing something else.

Soldiers smoked cigarettes around a burning barrel by a drab utility shed. An impressive armored vehicle rolled past. She wondered why these men weren't out there trying to put an end to all this. They didn't seem to be doing anything.

"I hope you won't mind a word about your helmet," he said.

She reached up to touch the cold metal dome. "Did I put it on wrong?"

"It's blue."

"The press and UN wear blue helmets," she said. "It means I'm neutral."

"Yes, ma'am. Not everybody sees it that way."

"I don't understand."

"For some folks here, the UN is the enemy. They think the UN wants to strip America of its sovereignty. They hate you more than they hate the press. I'm trying to tell you your helmet might as well have a bull's-eye on it."

"I came here to help the children," she said.

He shrugged. "Make of it what you want."

Gabrielle studied his neutral profile and wondered about his motives telling her this. "What about you? What do you think of the UN?"

"My orders don't include thinking about the UN, ma'am."

The liaison officer parked the jeep and hopped out. She didn't press it further. The short jaunt across the windy tarmac in the open-top jeep had her frozen. She followed him into the hangar on uncertain legs.

"Make yourself at home," he said. "We're waiting for one more passenger, and then the APC will take you all to Indy. Good luck, ma'am."

"Lieutenant Douglas." Her voice sounded loud in the cavernous space.

"Ma'am?"

Gabrielle gestured around her. "What are you doing here?"

"Our priority mission is to provide security for the airport and aid shipments."

"I mean, why don't you stop the fighting?"

He smiled. "Do you want the response I'm supposed to give or the real answer?"

"The real one."

"The real answer is it's complicated."

The liaison officer set her bag on the floor and left her standing by a big armored personnel carrier. Its crew clambered over it like monkeys, performing maintenance. Technical exchanges and ribald asides echoed off the metal walls. The soldiers paused to nudge one another until they were all leering at her.

Gabrielle shied away toward a coffee service set up against a wall of sandbags. She steadied herself with a deep breath and poured a steaming cup. Her stomach growled, though she had little real appetite. She popped a bagel into the toaster anyway. She'd force it down.

The military had Wi-Fi. Her cell started pinging, texts from home.

"Haven't seen you before." Two men lay on nearby cots, blue helmets by their feet. One sat up. "Hello. Who are you with?"

She sipped her coffee, savoring its heat. "United Nations Children's Fund."

Shoulders sagging and his face weighted down by jowls, the middle-aged man was built like a melting iceberg. His eyes, however, glittered with energy and intelligence, giving him a cunning look. "I'd heard they were letting UNICEF into the country."

"I'm Gabrielle Justine."

"Pleased to make your acquaintance. Terry Allen, *The Guardian*."

"The British newspaper."

"The very same. I'm doing the full tour. Hitting all the big cities."

The other man waved from his cot. "Walt Payne. I'm with the Gary municipal government. Here to see the governor. Welcome to the Alamo."

Like Indianapolis, Gary, Indiana, was under siege. Population eighty thousand, the city protected Chicago's eastern flank.

"You may as well settle in," Terry said. "It's always hurry up and wait with military types. We've been sitting on our arses all morning watching these blokes get their vehicle sorted. How did you get in?"

"I hitched a ride on a shipment of humanitarian aid from Canada."

The man snorted. "Investment is more like it."

She blinked. "Why do you say it like that?"

"Canada is being overrun with refugees who riot if they can't get a decent cheeseburger. The Canucks figure if they feed the Yanks here, they'll stay put."

The soldiers had stopped working on the APC and were listening.

"I don't think you're being fair," she said.

He was showing off by playing the cynical journalist. In her view, Canada's desire to help was earnest. The whole country felt like children stuck in their room while their alcoholic parents beat the crap out of each other downstairs.

"Look," Terry went on, "most of the aid doesn't even reach the people for whom it's intended. The city government puts the lot in warehouses, where most of it mysteriously disappears and ends up on the black market."

And certain men profited from the misery. Gabrielle sensed this was just a taste of what she was up against. Nothing about this place appeared welcoming.

She said, "How do you know all that?"

"It's been the same in every city I've visited. Why should Indianapolis be different? There may be seven basic plots in literature, but in real life, there's only one, and it is always explained by following the money."

Her bagel popped in the toaster.

Crump, crump.

The soldiers dove to the floor. "INCOMING!"

Gabrielle dropped her mug, which shattered.

Terry was already on the ground pulling on his helmet. "For Christ's sake, get down!"

She landed hard with a cry. Mortar rounds shrieked as they tore the air overhead. Muffled explosions vibrated through the cold concrete. Coffee soaked into her sleeve.

"If you hear the round, it's not going to kill you," Terry said.

"Okay," she gasped.

"If you don't hear it, well, you're fucked."

The soldiers got to their feet and pulled on their gear. Their hairy sergeant growled, "Mount up. We're moving out now."

Terry heaved his bulk off the floor and grabbed his luggage. Walt was already jogging to the APC's rear door. Gabrielle followed.

"You forgot your kit," Terry said.

She ran back for her duffel bag as mortars thudded in the distance. She threw herself down again to wait out the barrage. The APC's engine roared to life.

Get up, she told herself, though she remained glued to the floor.

The engine revved like a warning. She picked herself up and raced to the vehicle's protection with her bag.

Terry was inside next to Walt, who said, "You still with us, Gabrielle?"

She sat trembling in the cramped compartment. The ramp closed.

The reporter chuckled. "They don't teach you much at UN school, do they?"

She'd received a crash course on the political and military situation in Indiana, the local population and culture, and her humanitarian responsibilities.

They hadn't taught her how to survive.

FIVE

Anger kept Hannah moving, but it couldn't keep her warm. The cold seeped into her bones. The sloshing water jug grew heavier with each step. The napkin in her pocket had her mother's blood on it. She broke down outside a boarded-up pet store, eyes flooded with tears.

The few people on the street ignored her as they went about their errands.

Mom is gone, I'm all alone, and nobody cares.

In Hannah's imagination, the whole city was packing up and leaving her behind. Abandoning her just as her mother had.

If something bad happens to me, do whatever it takes, Mom had said.

"You left me alone," Hannah cried.

She knew she wasn't being fair, but she couldn't help herself.

"You said everything was going to be okay, but it's not."

Her brother's voice intruded. *You can't always cry to get your way, brat.*

"Screw you too, fart-face." Nobody was here to tell her to mind her language, so she added in a quieter voice, "Friggin' ass."

Alex abandoning her was the greater sin, since it had been his choice.

Her big brother had always known how to make her mad. *He*

knows how to push your buttons, Mom had described it. Hannah had pictured having a real button on her forehead, which was where she always felt her anger start.

Now, she was almost grateful for it. The anger felt good.

Do whatever it takes.

Maybe what Mom meant was surviving wasn't a list of things to do. Maybe it was how you looked at things. How hard you tried.

Mom was telling her she had to be strong and make her own decisions like a grown-up. Should she keep slogging forward, or go back and register at the orphanage?

Hannah had wanted to get lost, only to revisit how horrible being lost felt. Every step just got her more lost. Turning around, however, meant going to a terrible place. Going forward offered a chance. *What you're looking for*, the policewoman had said.

Maybe there was food awaiting her. A hot bath and a soft bed.

That settled it.

Hannah set the water jug on the sidewalk and started walking again. *Sorry, Mrs. Bevis.* Her legs protested, but it felt good to be journeying toward something rather than escaping. That would come later, when she'd leave this nightmarish day with a long sleep.

The road turned into an overpass over a highway, which the map said was I-70. Below her, the highway stretched south until it curved around a hill covered with the stumps of trees cut down for firewood. She couldn't see the siege line from here, but she knew the rebels were out there, trying to get in and run things the way they had at Sterling.

By the time Hannah crossed the overpass, her face ached from the cold, and she was dragging her numbed feet. She didn't stop. She kept her head down and stared at her boots, taking one step after another until she'd banished all sense of time.

Finally, she looked up to take in old brick buildings. A theater, a bookstore that was still in business, and several art galleries stood side by side. The windows of a closed clothing store were covered in propaganda posters, protest signs, and lurid graffiti declaring, NOT MY PRESIDENT, PRO-AMERICA/ANTI-MARSH, WELCOME TO THE RESISTANCE.

Prospect Street. Her face was so cold now, she couldn't even smile as she approached the address on the ticket.

At the top of the stone steps, the sign read, DOMESTIC VIOLENCE COLLECTIVE.

A security camera perched over the doors. She waved at it, but nothing happened. The city only had electricity a few hours every evening.

This wasn't what she'd expected.

As she reached to knock, two women came out and almost walked into her. Both wore brown wool coats belted at the waist. The younger woman carried an automatic rifle slung over her shoulder.

The older one sized up Hannah. "A cat left a bird on our doorstep."

"Can we help you?" the younger one said.

Shivering from the cold, Hannah eyed the rifle. "I'm sorry to bother you. A policewoman said I should come to this place."

"Are you an orphan?"

"Yes."

"Then you should go to an orphanage."

"I don't want charity," Hannah said, repeating something Mom said often enough since they'd come to Indy. "I was trying to join the police."

"We aren't the police. And you're too young, anyway."

"Perhaps not all that young," the older lady observed. "This is Sabrina. I'm Abigail."

"I'm freezing."

Abigail laughed, though Hannah hadn't been trying to be funny. Her eyes turned hard. "Tell me your name, please."

"Hannah Miller." She garbled the words, her face numb. Talking was like trying to speak while wearing a rubber mask.

"Nice to meet you, Hannah. What happened to your folks?"

"They're gone."

"Dead?"

"A sniper shot my mom this morning." She winced. Saying it out loud made it real again. "My dad died months ago. IED in the road."

Abigail nodded as if it were normal such things would happen to a ten-year-old. That it was normal a girl would know what an improvised explosive device was. "You look frozen to the bone. Where did you come from?"

"The refugee center."

"You walked a very long way to get here."

"The policewoman said what I was looking for was here," Hannah said.

"And what would that be?"

"I told her I was looking for my brother."

"I understand. You're looking for family."

"Is Alex here?"

"No." Abigail said to her friend, "We've taken young ones before."

"They're from the Square," Sabrina said. The fighter had elven features accentuated by rectangular glasses and red hair that hung in long braids. "It's sad what happened to this girl, but we can't take care of everybody. She belongs in an orphanage. We should let her warm up and then send her on her way."

"Hannah, do you know what we do here?"

Her eyes left Sabrina's rifle to again read the sign next to the door, but what it said wasn't true, not anymore. "You're militia. You fight the rebels."

"What do you think about that?"

Hannah thought about her mom toppling over from a sniper's bullet. The IED blast ripping through the car. The strong and confident police officer barking at the crowd to sign up and resist the dictator who'd caused all this.

"I think the policewoman was right," she said. "This is the place."

Abigail turned to her friend. "You go on ahead. I'll catch up." After Sabrina left, she bent to look Hannah in the face. "Would you like some hot food?"

Hannah grimaced. She was shaking now from the cold. "Yes, please."

"Then let's get you inside before you freeze to death."

Hannah trudged after her into a reception area, where an old woman smiled from behind a desk. Then through a room with Ping-Pong and card tables, a dining hall, a spacious living room with a TV. Everything drab but comfortable as an old sofa. Two women walked past, guns holstered on their hips. Another stomped a pedal to stitch a uniform on an old sewing machine.

Double doors swung open to reveal the kitchen. Abigail and Hannah went inside, where a team of women worked at preparing some kind of stew in a giant oven jury-rigged for wood fire.

Abigail took off her coat and ladled a bowl. "Sit."

Hannah sat at a small card table. Her entire body ached as it began to thaw in the kitchen's heat. Abigail placed the bowl in front of her and took a seat herself to watch her eat.

Hannah spooned some broth and sipped it. Scalding but delicious. She blew on it a few times before slurping the rest.

Abigail folded her hands on the table. "We are the Free Women Collective. I'm the commander, but everything you see here was built by a community."

Hannah began to shovel her stew as hunger overtook her.

"If women ran the world, do you think we'd be having a war? Hannah?"

She perked up at her name. "I don't know. No, I guess."

"A year ago, we were a women's shelter offering second-stage housing for victims of domestic violence. They lived in fourteen apartments over our heads. Eat a little slower."

Hannah paused and studied the woman's face. Abigail was thin like everybody else, and younger than she'd thought at first. A strong woman, though worn down by hardship and care. Past Abigail's shoulder, another woman gave a massage at a table. A rifle stood propped against the wall.

"Women and their children would come here and live for as long as two years," the commander went on. "We provided food, childcare, counseling, life skills. When the troubles started, the police couldn't protect us."

She said they cowered inside during the big demonstrations, the bombings and barricades, the police engaging in house-to-house fighting against right-wing terrorists. When they peered out the windows, they saw men flashing victory signs as they drove past in trucks.

A man came to collect his wife. He yelled, "This place is under Marsh-al law!" Marsh-al law, not martial law, a different kind of law, one that let him do whatever he wanted.

He found his wife in her room, seized her by the hair, and told her he was taking her home. This time, he promised, she'd behave herself.

"We grabbed any weapon we could find and helped her," Abigail said.

Hannah's mouth fell open. "You hurt him?"

"I'm not going to talk to you as a child. You earned it."

"Good." Hannah hated when grown-ups lied to avoid a hard truth.

"We beat that man until he could barely walk and dumped him out on the street," Abigail said. "You could say the Free Women started that very moment, in a collective act of self-defense."

"Oh." It went against everything she'd been taught. "You couldn't just talk to him?"

"You ever have an imaginary friend, Hannah?"

"When I was little." When Alex wouldn't play with her, she always had Bekka.

"Well, the fascists out there, they grew up having imaginary enemies, boogeymen under the bed they never outgrew. Immigrants, Muslims, gays, you name it, even women. They're scared of everything and want to control it by hurting us. If they win, we'll lose everything. No, we couldn't have just talked to him."

Hannah regarded her empty bowl and nodded. She didn't want anybody to talk to the sniper who'd murdered her mom. She wanted him arrested and put in a jail forever, and too bad for him if that hurt his feelings.

"This war has given us sadness and hardship we'd never imagined," Abigail went on. "Just like you. But here, we've done better than survive. We built the Free Women. We fought back. We stopped the fascists at Pleasant Run. We're holding our ground. And more, we built a community. A community based on equality, empowerment, and protection. For the first time in their lives, a lot of these women feel like they're in control."

"It's good here," Hannah agreed. She felt safe in this warm, busy kitchen with Abigail, surrounded by the smells of food and the chatter of women.

"I'm telling you all this because you need to know who we are and what this is," Abigail said. "What we're fighting for and why it's important. If you didn't like anything you heard me say, you can leave tomorrow with a full belly. If you did, you can pitch in. Fair enough?"

"Yes."

"It's a big decision. Best to sleep on it."

Hannah smiled at the idea of sleep. Her eyelids were already getting heavy.

Abigail gazed around the room crowded with women working together to prepare the next communal meal. "You know, as horrible as it is to say, when this war is over, I think a lot of us are going to miss it."

SIX

A lex Miller jerked awake in his tent. "What?"

"Get your ass out here, that's what," Mitch said.

"Coming, Sergeant." The boy emerged groaning from his warm sleeping bag and pulled on his uniform and boots over his thermals. After watch duty last night, he was tuckered. But when Mitch said get your ass outside, you did it.

He crawled out of the tent and stood blinking in morning light. "Reporting."

Mitch eyed him with his thumbs hooked in the load-bearing vest of his woodland camouflage uniform. The sergeant was a large man, broad-shouldered and muscular, his only concession to middle age a soft gut and some streaks of gray in his beard. He was a combat vet who'd served two tours in Afghanistan.

The rest of the squad stood grinning behind him. They were either going to beat him up or give him a Christmas present. You never knew with these guys. Alex fidgeted from nerves and an urgent need to pee.

"How old are you again, son?"

"I'll be sixteen in March."

"You've been with us awhile now. Through the whole show, almost."

Ten months ago, Alex asked the wrong men for a ride. The men were with the Liberty Tree militia. They'd handed him over to Mitch to break in. Since then, Alex had worked as a runner, cook, porter, and sentry for the patriots.

"Yes, Sergeant," he said.

Booming gunfire to the north. The libs were making another push against the siege line at the Brickyard Crossing golf course.

"The Liberty Tree got its name from the elm in Boston where the colonists made their first stand against the British king," Mitch said. "Do you understand what we're trying to do here?"

"Sometimes, you have to break it to save it," Alex recited.

The patriots held an iron-clad, black-and-white view of the world. They exalted America, the Constitution, and the role of the average citizen in safeguarding the republic from tyranny. They weren't destroying America. They were protecting it. To them, overthrowing the government wasn't treason but the height of patriotism.

"Good boy." Mitch held out an AR-15 rifle. "This is for you."

He hesitated before taking it. "Thanks, Sergeant."

"You're a fighter now. You ready for that?"

For nearly a year, he'd been helping them because he'd had nowhere else to go. Now they wanted him to fight at their side.

He thought about pointing out he was only fifteen, but Mitch already knew that. The militia had other teenagers fighting with them. Boys became men early these days.

He gave the only answer he was allowed. "I sure am."

"That's good, because I have a job for you." The sergeant put one thick arm around Alex's neck and pointed with the other. "Walk that way about two hundred meters until you spot the enemy's forward posts. Then hustle back and report what you saw."

A solo recon patrol in urban ruins infested with snipers, armed with a rifle loaded with a single thirty-round magazine. It was a simple test. To join the Liberty Tree militia, a man had to follow orders. Then he had to prove his courage.

The pressure in Alex's bladder became unbearable as he imagined it. "You can count on me, Sergeant."

"Then get to it. Holler at me when you get back. And don't get shot."

He wondered if it was okay if he hit the latrine first, but he was too scared to ask. Best if he just took off and made a show of it.

The front line lay a block away. During the siege, the Liberty Tree had dwindled to company strength, about a hundred fighters. These men held a mile of trenches and fortified houses running down the west side of North Tibbs Avenue. Concrete barriers and sandbags straddled the cross streets.

"Hey, fag," Sergeant Shook called to him. Wearing ballistic armor, the giant left his campfire. "Look at you. My little boy is a man now."

Alex grimaced. His bladder was about to burst. "Mitch gave me recon duty."

"Not until you give me ten. Ten push-ups or ten free punches."

He did the push-ups. Shook was a psycho. Before the war, he'd drive to protests wearing homemade armor and wade into antifa with a club. In his simple ideology, you were either a patriot or a pussy. He called himself an intellectual and the "last man." Fierce, though he struck Alex as more jackal than wolf.

Stroking his goatee, Shook walked off bored before Alex finished. He got off the ground and started running, ready to explode. He raced past the trenches on the front line.

"Get some," somebody yelled after him.

Shrapnel and vehicle wreckage littered the street. He bolted across and into the backyard of the nearest house. There, he tucked the rifle in his armpit, unzipped his fly, and blasted the wall with a satisfied moan. His shoulders sagged.

"Thank God," he gasped. It felt like victory.

Snow covered the ruins and muted the distant crackle of gunfire. Pretty in a way. Christmas soon, and a white Christmas from the looks of it, the first in years. Alex had grown old enough to find the holiday boring, but now he missed it. He'd been part of a family once.

Now he was in the patriot army.

Zipping up, he checked out his surroundings. Alex was alone at the edge of No Man's Land. So quiet, though he knew the enemy was out there. Across the alley, a house stood with the corner of its roof blown off and covered in tarpaulin that rustled in the breeze. He imagined a sniper nested up there, drawing a bead on him. He shrank back out of sight.

Alex was a fighter now, a big deal in the militia, but he was no soldier. He was a teenager who liked skateboarding and online games. The war had turned him into a LARPer playing with real bullets.

Two hundred meters, Mitch said. Alex had no idea how far that was. He was more afraid of going back than forward. The militia had kept him alive this long, but now it dawned on him he might not survive this war. There were people on both sides all too happy to get him killed. He made up his mind to give himself up the first chance he got.

He spotted a Venus symbol spray-painted on the wall near his head. The militias tagged houses Mars, which meant friendly, or Venus, which meant liberal. The Liberty Tree guys were always going on about how feminine liberals were. Alex remembered seeing that symbol painted on his own house back in Sterling. That night, Dad loaded up the SUV, and they made a run to Indy.

He wondered what his dad felt while loading up his bewildered family to flee his own home. Alex had been too absorbed with his own troubles to notice. He wished he'd paid more attention. That night was the last time they'd seen each other.

No doubt, Dad had been very scared, even more than Alex was now.

Similarly, he'd soldier on and hope for the best. He too had no choice.

He tucked the AR-15 against his shoulder and crossed the back-yard. There, he made another mad sprint across the alley into another yard. He cleared it the way they'd trained him. Check the corners and blind spots. Entrances and exits. Stop, look, listen. He saw a kid's rusting play set blanketed in snow. Stump of a tree cut for firewood. A gap-toothed fence.

Across the next street, he'd start approaching the Blue line. Then he could either hightail it back or figure out a way to surrender.

He flinched and ducked down. He'd heard a noise on the other side of the fence. He prayed it was an animal. He stayed crouched for a while and listened. His heart hammered against his ribs. His bladder started to ache again.

He set his weapon stock against his shoulder.

One, two, three—

Alex reared, ready to shoot.

The old woman jumped in fright. Then she glared. "Put that down!"

She'd been gathering laundry from a clothesline. He lowered his gun and blew the air out his cheeks in a loud sigh.

"Sorry, ma'am," he mumbled.

"Pointing guns at people," she said. "This used to be a good place to live."

"You betcha." He couldn't help but laugh.

The old lady had obviously missed the announcement there was a war on. Still, he liked how she just declared the whole thing stupid and went on with her life.

She glowered at something past his shoulder. "And you. What are you? You're useless."

Who was she talking to? The woman was crazy—

He jumped as cold metal poked his spine.

"Okay, chief," a voice behind him said.

A second voice: "Easy there. Put the weapon down."

"My husband fought in Vietnam," the old lady lectured them.

"He fought to keep you safe from communism. This is how you repay him."

Face reddening with shame, Alex laid his gun on the ground and raised his hands. They'd nabbed him so easily. Worst soldier ever. He sucked at this. He'd checked the yard. It wasn't fair.

Still, the whole thing came as a relief. He wanted to give up. His war was over.

"You people," the old lady fumed at the men. "What are you good for?"

"Police business, ma'am," one of the pair said. "Go back inside."

"I give up," Alex said. "Don't shoot."

He glanced over his shoulder at the angry, stubbled face of a cop wearing black tactical gear.

Then a black cloth hood slammed over his head, and he saw nothing.

SEVEN

A man lived near the front line. A man of means, he sent his wife and two daughters to live in Canada early in the crisis. He stayed behind to work and protect his home from looters. Many of his neighbors gave up hope and left, but he'd been a dedicated prepper for years. He had a generator and lasting fuel and provisions. He had weapons and knew how to shoot them. While others starved, migrated, and suffered, he'd lived alone for eleven months in relative comfort.

This morning, a mortar shell ripped into his home and killed him.

Standing on the sidewalk before the smoking ruin, Aubrey scribbled in her notebook and closed it. She had everything she needed to write up this tragedy for the *Indy Chronicle*.

After putting out the blaze, the fire department had looted the house. She'd watched tired firefighters with blackened faces haul out weapons and canned food. That made her curious enough to talk to the neighbors still living on the street. One went on the record with details about the owner's life.

She took out her phone to call her editor. By unspoken treaty, the warring sides hadn't destroyed the cell towers. With a growing lack of parts and ongoing electricity shortages, however, service had degraded.

The call went through.

He answered, "Eckert."

"It's Aubrey."

"What have you got for me?"

"Mortar attack. One man confirmed dead."

"Give me two inches and I'll roll it into the war update."

"I think there's a human interest story here."

She heard him take a drag on one of the lousy homemade ciga-rettes he made from tea bags reused until drained of all flavor. He said, "I'm listening."

"The owner was a prepper," Aubrey explained. "Living high on the hog. Then a random mortar round blows him up."

"Self-sufficient man takes every precaution but dies by errant bomb. Make that your lede, and it's got legs."

"I think this story has currency."

Another drag. "Currency, huh?"

"The impermanence of all things. No matter how prepared you are, when it's your time, it's your time."

Since she'd started reporting the war, she always searched for lit-tle stories that told bigger ones. Small details that revealed a larger truth.

"The unreliability of self-sufficiency in these times," he said. "The irony makes it work. Live for the day." Already making it his idea. "It's got *gestalt*. I'll take five hundred words."

Not as big a piece as she wanted, but far better than an obituary and an inch or two in the war update. "I'm heading back to the office. I'll file it by end of day."

"Not so fast," he said. "I need you to do something for me first. Congress and the president agreed to allow UNICEF in the coun-try. Operatives are flying into the major combat zones. I said we'd lend a hand—"

She kicked a charred shingle into the street. "No way."

"—showing her around."

"It's the city's job."

"She needs a fixer. Somebody who knows the streets and people and isn't government. That's why they reached out to us."

"Give it to an intern. I'm not a babysitter, Eckert."

"No, you're a staff reporter, and I'm offering you a goddamn story. I need you to run over to the Castle on West Washington right now."

"The Castle?"

"Meet and greet at the bar. Her name's Gabrielle Justine."

"Okay, I'll do it," she said. "You're an asshole. Bye."

She smiled as she terminated the call. It was turning out to be a great day.

An old luxury hotel now catering to visiting press and dignitaries, the Castle Inn & Suites had electricity, central heating, and excellent food. While Aubrey played tour guide, she could also play tourist. Take a short break from the war.

She mounted her bike and rode down Stringtown's forlorn streets, passing houses, a skateboard shop, and a bar doing a lively trade in rotgut. A crowd of people clutched empty bottles at a city water tanker. Neighborhood militia eyed her with suspicion until they spotted her bike's placard reading, PRESS. Then they waved.

The media had never been more popular, at least on this side of the line.

She pedaled past the zoo with her face set in a grimace, trying not to think about the heartbreaking piece she'd written on the zookeepers' never-ending struggle to keep the animals alive. The bridge over the White was empty, the war and its shortages having solved Indy's traffic problems. In the early days of the conflict, rebel militias had raced across this bridge on the way to city hall to arrest the mayor and overthrow the government. After a gun battle with police, they'd fled along the same route while antifa threw Molotov cocktails at them.

The Castle's baroque architecture loomed between the Indiana

Repertory Theatre and Rhythm! Discovery Center. Bellhops with red jackets and guns on their hips subjected her to an intense security ritual. After it was over, they checked her name off a list and handed her a claim ticket for her bike.

Then Aubrey was inside the opulent lobby. Another world.

The heat. God, the heat was wonderful.

Grinning, she went to the restroom and scrubbed her face with cold, soapy water. She took off her hat, washed her short hair in the same sink, and blew it dry under the hand drier. Then she stuffed every roll of toilet paper she could find into her backpack.

This done, she inspected her reflection in the mirror over the sinks. Her chocolate brown complexion struck her as plain without her customary makeup, but she had only a little left and was hoarding it for trade. The UN field operative would have to take Aubrey as she was.

She returned to the lobby and paused at the bar's entrance, blinking in the gloom. A man in a tuxedo played a grand piano, background music for the patrons but soothing and even a little magical to her. Clean white tablecloths, wine poured from bottles, clinking glasses, calm chatter: She'd stepped into a time machine and went back to a mythical era when people obsessed over the trivial and took the essential for granted.

Two men appraised her from a nearby table. One was a heavyset older man wearing a jacket over an open-collared shirt, the other a younger, roguish sort in black jacket and turtleneck. Glasses half-full of what she guessed was scotch on the rocks rested on the tablecloth. They eyed her with amusement, as if she were some homeless woman who'd walked off the street to invade their private club.

She glared at them. "Can I help you gentlemen?"

"Actually, we were wondering if we might help you," the heavyset one said. "You appear to be either lost or searching for someone."

"The latter. A woman named Gabrielle. She just got into town."

"Ah. The UN bird. I believe she's hiding under her bed at the moment. You're with...?"

"The *Indy Chronicle*."

"Terry Allen, war correspondent for *The Guardian*."

"Rafael Petit," the other man said with a heavy French accent. "Freelance photojournalist on assignment for *L'Opinion*."

"Join us for a drink, *Chronicle*," said Terry.

From covering a mortar attack to drinks with *The Guardian*. Some days, the war delivered wonders. She took a seat.

The server arrived to ask what she wanted. Aubrey blushed. Even before the war, she'd have to stretch her wallet to buy a drink here.

Comprehension crossed Terry's face. He beamed a magnanimous smile. "It's on me, or rather, *The Guardian*."

"I'll have a glass of your best pinot," she told the server.

Terry's eyebrows lilted, but he said nothing about it. "So what's your interest in the UN?"

He wanted to know if she had a story. She'd seen foreign press following each other around the city in their cars, chasing a lead one of them had sniffed out.

Aubrey had nothing juicy to give him. "I'm just her fixer."

"Maybe something will turn up from it for you," Terry offered.

"I've read your stories. You did some amazing work in Syria." This was what passed for small talk among war journalists.

He beamed with pleasure. "Ah. Well. You should read my stories on this war."

"It is difficult for you, reporting the war?" Rafael said.

"I love it," she said.

Terry laughed. Rafael said, "But reporting a war while living it. Making a newspaper in these conditions. Surely, it is difficult."

"We bang out copy on manual typewriters we found in a storage room. In the evening, when there's power, we do our typesetting and printing. We distribute by hand. Finding paper's the hardest part. But we get it done. We sell out in a few hours. Copies get passed around from person to person until used for kindling."

Before the war, her beats included guns and gang violence. Every few years, the newspaper cut staff in an information market still shifting to digital. She'd watched the paper become bloated with opinion and thin on real local reporting.

The war had given her the chance to do serious journalism.

"What's your formula?" Terry said.

"We get national war and political news from the AP," she said. "We do our own local war news and interest pieces on gardening, schooling, war recipes, life hacks, that sort of thing."

"Life hacks?" said Rafael. "I do not know this term."

"Did you know if you stand a crayon upright and light its tip, it will burn for thirty minutes as a candle?"

"I understand."

"We still put out a sports section; even a civil war can't keep us Hoosiers from our basketball. The most popular section these days is the obituaries."

"Ah," Terry said. "Right."

Her wine arrived. She took a sip and sighed through her smile. "God, that's good. Thanks for the drink. What's your interest here?"

"Taking your pulse," the reporter answered. "The war can only have a political solution, but the politicians are waiting for positive news from the battlefield so they get a better deal."

Terry was touring America's killing fields to get a sense of who was winning. Whoever was had more leverage at the Ottawa peace talks. California had nearly cleared the state of rebels, which was why the president had suspended the talks.

Aubrey took another sip of her wine. A nice buzz hummed in her brain. "You know the saying: 'All politics is local.' The same goes for civil war. The big picture isn't relevant anymore to the people here. They're living day to day."

"You had a wonderful country before you drove it off a cliff. Maybe you all should have paid a little more heed to the big picture before you did it."

She bristled. "What do you know about the people here? Have you talked to them? Have you seen what's going on while you take a pulse?"

"I was in Dallas. I've seen horrific things you couldn't imagine."

"And it's clearly made you feel something. Starving kids weighed and measured as leverage. It's a big photo safari for you guys, isn't it? War porn."

Rafael glanced at Terry, who smiled. The men burst into laughter.

"An American journalist saying this," Rafael said.

The wine had gone to her head, and Terry's condescension had made her angry enough to do more than order an expensive glass of wine. "When this sort of thing happened, we did something about it."

This made them laugh even harder.

Aubrey blushed with embarrassment. "You can't bullshit the bullshitters, I guess."

They were right to laugh. They were being objective like good journalists, even if their objectivity was tinged with a mocking cynicism. She was being sentimental, which for a reporter was the greater sin.

"I admire your passion," said Rafael. "If it were Paris burning, well..."

"Actually, we care very much about this war," Terry said. "We have our own fractures and divisions. We're studying this war to avoid one of our own."

"Do you think that's possible?"

"Things were getting dodgy for us even before you Yanks triggered a global crash. Right now, the backlash is directed at refugees, immigrants, other countries. If my countrymen decide to direct it at one another, we might end up with a war of our own." His eyes flickered to the bar's entrance. "And now I suppose you'll be leaving us. Your UN bird has arrived."

Aubrey turned and spotted the attractive young woman gazing wide-eyed around the restaurant as if she'd stepped into a combat zone.

At first glance, she knew Gabrielle Justine wouldn't last a month.

EIGHT

The world went black. His hands were cuffed behind his back.

"I don't want to do this out in the open," a cop said. "In case he has backup."

"The garage," the other cop said.

They hauled Alex to his feet and dragged him along.

Meanwhile, his life flashed before his eyes.

Skateboarding with his friends in the parking lot of a 7-Eleven, talking about the crazy president vowing to stay in office even though the Senate was about to convict. They'd never cared about politics before, but this was big. The news people called it a Constitutional crisis.

How he'd loved the sound of that. A crack in the foundation holding up the lifeless adult world.

A part of him wished it would all get worse. A part of him longed for a revolution, though he didn't know what it should accomplish. Anything, he hoped, as long as he didn't end up like his dad, working his ass off so nothing ever changed.

Cities like San Francisco passed resolutions supporting Congress, cities like Mesa the president. YouTube videos showed bloody street clashes between antifa and alt-right gangs. The media covered the massive Occupy protest at the National Mall in DC. Armed groups seized town halls and federal buildings. *Nothing changed in Sterling until a militia arrived in pickup trucks waving automatic rifles and American flags embroidered with crosses.*

"I got a good look at him," one of the cops said. "He's just a kid."

"He stopped being a kid when he picked up a gun."

"It's just pathetic, is all. Now they got kids shooting at us."

MARSH FOR PRESIDENT *signs cropped up on lawns again. Neighbors turned on one another. Alex skateboarded at the park in violation of curfew, running laughing from militia in the dark. A Venus symbol tagged the garage door, bringing it all home.*

Then everything changed.

Midnight flight in the SUV. His entire life dwindling in the rearview. His room, all his stuff, left behind. His friends, without whom he would have suffocated in boredom years ago. Janice Brewer, the girl of his dreams he'd never had the balls to ask out. All his memories, everything that made him who he was, disappeared in the night.

He shouted at Dad: "I'm not going. You can't make me. They're not going to do anything. They're just trying to scare us."

He couldn't have been more wrong.

They stopped to get gas. Men punched each other by the pumps. He ran away among the cars. Dad roared his name.

A man extended his hand from a pickup. "Climb aboard the freedom express, kid. We'll give you a ride."

It was only later he understood that Dad wasn't working so hard all that time to sustain the same reliable, boring lifestyle. He was sacrificing for his family. And he was no coward. By leaving Sterling, he'd been fighting to keep them all safe.

Alex, meanwhile, had made the biggest mistake of his life. It now appeared he'd pay the ultimate price for it.

The garage door opened. Their footsteps echoed. The faded smell of motor oil reminded him of summers back home.

The guiding hand pushed against his shoulder. "Down."

Trucks roared across the bridge over the White River at sunrise, weaving in and out of Indy's early traffic. American and militia and DON'T TREAD

ON ME *flags snapped in the wind. Alex stared at it all bug-eyed. The men grinned at the prospect of winning a war without firing a shot. A new America dawning.*

Tall buildings loomed ahead. Pale faces flashed by in cars they passed. The city held its breath. Drivers leaned on their horns as the convoy flowed into Mile Square.

A bearded fighter said: "You're lucky, kid. You're about to see history get made. You're about to watch real Americans take their country back."

Bristling with rifles, the column coiled in front of the twenty-eight-story Indianapolis City-County Building. The building housed the city and Marion County government and the Metropolitan Police Department.

The colonel stood up in one of the trucks and made a bullhorn announcement that the mayor was under arrest. A handful of cops gazed out, terrified but defiant.

Then rolling gunfire. Glass crashing to the pavement. Alex cowered in the truck bed and missed most of it. The police returned fire, bullets thudding into the truck's skin. More cops arrived and opened up on the column from all sides. The air filled with hot metal and screams. Figures lay writhing in puddles of blood. Patriots raised their hands in surrender.

The rest took off on screeching tires through gun smoke. Antifa fighters wearing skinny jeans and bandanas over their faces appeared out of nowhere to throw Molotov cocktails. The truck ahead burst into flame, spilling flailing men onto the road.

Alex had gotten what he'd craved. The mundane world crashing down. Excitement and risk and uncertainty and madness. Now all he wanted was to see his boring family again and tell them he was sorry.

He fell to his knees cringing.

"Aren't you going to beg for your life?" one of the cops said. "They usually do."

A glimmer of hope. Alex licked dry lips. "Will you let me go if I do?"

The cop laughed. "The kid's got a mouth on him."

"I'm trying to surrender—"

The hood whipped from his face. He blinked into the cop's gray eyes. The man's face appeared carved of wood, his body fused with his black tactical gear after fighting so long in it.

In the old days, Alex and his friends played a never-ending game with the police. They'd loiter, the cops would roust them, they'd go loiter somewhere else. They'd yell, *Five-oh, five-oh,* when they saw a cruiser on the street.

"What's your name?"

"Alex," he said.

"We have a message for your people, Alex. Are you listening?"

"I'm listening to you." He nodded and squinted his eyes to make a show of it. He was terrified. They were in charge. Whatever they wanted, he'd do it.

"Tell them our front line is reorganizing to feed fresh troops to the Brickyard Crossing offensive. In eight days, there will be a gap in the line. Haughville between Tenth and Michigan will be lightly defended. If you strike hard, you can push through to the bridges."

"You want me to tell them to attack you?"

"That's right."

"I don't understand."

The other cop pierced Alex with his stare. "We can find another messenger."

"Wait! Eight days, Haughville, Tenth and Michigan. We should attack."

Gray eyes said, "I think we found the right man for the job."

Alex ignored the voice in his head telling him to shut up. He just wanted to get the message right. "Why do you want us to attack you where you'll be weak?"

"Don't think. Just do it. Tell your bosses that there are men on this side of the line who support the president."

"Okay."

"Okay, what?"

Alex had served in the militia long enough to make an educated guess. "Okay, sir?"

Gray eyes reached out and gave his face a light slap. "Good boy."

The police officers uncuffed him and let him go. He emerged from the garage and gazed up at the pale sun. He was alive.

Still on his own, still stuck in this shit war. But alive.

He walked back to the front line with his head down, tears stinging his eyes the whole way, barely paying attention to what he was doing. He made an easy target for a sniper now, but he didn't care. Back in Sterling, the cops had always been an adversary, but it was all a game. If they caught you, you'd have to endure a patronizing lecture. They didn't put a gun to your head.

As he neared the front line, he stopped to think about the message he had to deliver. If he told Mitch what the cops told him, the militias might get their chance to crack the Blue line. Or it might be a setup, and Alex might end up getting blamed for the bad intel, assuming he survived the ambush.

The best move was to go back to the camp and tell Mitch nothing. He'd lied to Mom and Dad plenty of times about where he was going, what he was doing, and who with. He knew how to lie and get away with it.

He'd never lied to Mitch, though. Lying to him risked far more than lost phone privileges. The man could spot a lie from a mile away.

His squad waited for him at the trenches. They cheered his arrival. Alex jogged across North Tibbs, rifle ready, making it look good. They clapped him on the back. As much as these men terrified him, as crazy as they were, no matter what they'd done, he found himself glowing at their approval. He was safe again.

"The conquering hero," Mitch said. "What did you see?"

"Cops. I talked to them."

"What did they say to you?"

"In eight days, there's going to be a gap in the lib line between Tenth and Michigan. They said they support the president."

"I thought they might have solid intel."

Alex's eyes began to sting again. "You knew they were there?"

"Somebody sent a message he wanted to meet. I told him you were coming."

If he'd lied, the sergeant would have known it, and his squad would have shoved him against a wall and shot him. And if it was a lib trick, well, Mitch hadn't risked much.

The man grabbed him by the nape of his neck and gave him a paternal shake. "You did good, kid. You're one of us now."

Alex should have been mad but wasn't. He'd proven himself in Mitch's eyes. He was surprised that it meant something to him. He didn't want these men to win, but he wasn't sure he wanted them to lose either.

NINE

One by one, heads turned to take in Gabrielle's arrival. Aubrey scanned the faces. Aside from the servers, almost every single person in the bar was a man.

Indy had no shortage of eager, available women. Soccer moms were selling themselves for food out there. She had no doubt some of these men had arrangements if they were lonely.

But Gabrielle was beautiful and wasn't a needy local, one of few such women in the war zone. That made her a rare species.

Aubrey rose and extended her hand. "Gabrielle Justine?"

The UN worker shook it. "Are you with the paper?"

"I'm Aubrey Fox."

Relief. "Oh, good. It's really great to meet you."

"You are welcome to join us," Rafael said.

Gabrielle regarded Terry Allen with distaste.

"Sorry, boys," Aubrey said. "Girl talk. Thanks for the drink, *Guardian*."

"Anytime, *Chronicle*," the reporter said. "I do hope you'll keep in touch."

Aubrey scooped her wineglass and ushered Gabrielle to another table. She returned a few lingering stares with a little shake of her head. The UN worker ordered a cosmopolitan and sighed, oblivious to the attention.

"Welcome to Indy," Aubrey said.

"Thank you for agreeing to show me the ropes."

The kind of gratitude that came from deep in the heart. It was a bit jarring.

"I should probably be thanking you," Aubrey said. "I understand you're here to help the city's children."

The woman's tension broke. "Yes. That's why I'm here."

Aubrey sipped her wine, alarmed she was getting near the bottom of the glass. In her view, allowing the UN to operate in the country had taken far too long. But overcoming one's pride took time. America saw itself as a nation that helped others, not accepted it from them, even when it was broken.

That and the president's side considered the UN a stock villain in its conspiracy theories.

"I've been here from the beginning," she said. "I've learned to accommodate it in degrees. It must be rough walking into the middle of it."

"I've never been in the field. The war's so big, UNICEF reached out and offered a contract. I love this country and took the job because I thought I could do some good. Now that I'm here, I'm scared out of my mind and not sure if I'll be able to accomplish anything."

Aubrey sat back in surprise. War was like a truth serum. You lied to survive but otherwise sought out confessors. Gabrielle needed a friend.

She raised her hands. "Let's back up a bit. I'll be your fixer, but while I do it I'll be writing a story about what you're doing here."

The woman blushed. "Oh. Right."

"The best way to avoid future heartbreak is if we lay the ground rules upfront. Whatever your arrangement with the paper is, it doesn't obligate me. Anything you say about your mission here is fair game. If you say something is off the record, I may interpret that statement in a different way than you. If you tell me a certain topic is off limits, I may report in the story that you requested it be off limits. If you say you have no comment, I may report you said that. Okay?"

"The UN gave me a little media training. You should know I can speak about what I'm doing here but not about UN policy. Otherwise, I was hoping we could have one meeting where we aren't adversaries."

"We're not adversaries. I'm a reporter, and you're a source."

Gabrielle sipped her drink. "I understand. I'm just feeling raw."

"How about we talk logistics? Where do you want to go?"

"City hall, straight off. The Peace Office."

"The Quakers?"

"They said I could use their space to work. After that, the pediatric clinics and hospitals. Finally, the statehouse to meet with the governor's people."

Aubrey said, "Do you want to talk to the militias? I can get you in."

"At some point, but I need to do my homework first."

As much as Gabrielle appeared a damsel in distress, she seemed to understand her purpose and her job. Aubrey inspected her glass, now empty. She tilted it to drain the last drop, savoring its bitterness.

"I should be going," she said. "I owe my editor some copy. How about I meet you right outside the hotel at ten tomorrow morning? It'll save me the hassle of getting through security."

"That's perfect."

"You'll have to arrange some transportation. Four-wheel drive and good snow tires. A full tank of gas, which will cost you a pretty penny."

"I'll get right on it. This is going to be a good partnership."

Now that she was leaving, Gabrielle appeared tense again.

Aubrey said, "Listen, the best advice I can give you is to take all this one day at a time."

"I'll do that," said Gabrielle. "What I need right now is a long, hot bath."

Aubrey's face tightened into a grimace as she stood to go. She hadn't had a real bath in months. She surveyed the bar and saw powerful men drinking and dealing. None of it was real. She'd craved the Castle's oasis and found a mirage.

Outside, an entire city lived hand to mouth on aid packages and a few hours of electricity per day. When she left, she'd have to bike back to the Chronicle's freezing offices and bang out her story before dashing out to Indy's battlefields for more.

And after that, pedal home to stand in line to fill her water bottles. Ask around to see if anybody was selling firewood. Boil a little water and eat her bland, meager meal of rice and canned tuna fish.

A long, hot bath belonged in another lifetime.

Nothing here could change that. In fact, the contrast made it worse.

She envied Gabrielle Justine, and it stung. Her youth and beauty and even her naivete. Her bath. Her choices. Especially her choices.

Most of all, her potential.

Gabrielle had an opportunity to make a real impact on the lives of the people here. The work Aubrey did for the Chronicle was important, but she often wondered if it made a difference. Did bearing witness to the horror actually help in any way, or was she really just helping herself?

"I'll help you," she said, as if it were only now being decided. Gabrielle tilted her head in an unspoken question, and Aubrey said it again.

The UNICEF worker smiled and nodded. "Thank you."

Again that deep gratitude, straight from the heart.

Aubrey hurried out of the bar before it ruined whatever it was she was feeling.

TEN

High on the acceptance he received after his solo recon, Alex strutted around the campsite with his new rifle until Tom told him to clean his boots.

While many militiamen were smack talkers and braggers, the veteran was the quiet type and a hard read. He wore a checkered keffiyeh scarf around his throat, a souvenir from Afghanistan, where he and Mitch had fought the Taliban.

As with Mitch, when he told you to do something, you did it.

Alex sulked off toward the nearest fire.

"Take good care of those boots," Tom called after him. "They're more valuable than you are."

Alex sat in a lawn chair, took off his boots, and rubbed at one of them with a wet cotton rag.

Jack sat next to him. "How'd it go?"

At sixteen, he was a little older than Alex, one of a bunch of kids Alex had seen serving in the militia. He was in Mitch's squad. Alex envied his confidence. The adults didn't ride his ass much. They called him Combat Jack, which the guys thought was funny for some reason but Alex considered an excellent nickname.

He set down the boot to dry and picked up the other. "I'll tell you later."

Too many guys around listening. He wasn't even sure if he trusted Jack.

"I just think it's cool we're squad mates now," the kid said.

"How do you know we're in the same squad?" Alex hadn't thought about who he reported to now that he was a fighter in the militia. He was used to following orders from everybody.

"Mitch gave you the assignment. That means he wants you in his squad."

"That's good, I guess."

"Damn right it's good," Jack said. "You could have gotten Shook or one of the other sergeants. Mitch is tough, but he's fair."

"What was the point of it? Sending me out there?"

Jack picked up Alex's dried boot, dabbed some olive oil on a rag, and started to rub it against the warm leather. "You have to show you're manned up. The test is you have to face danger all by yourself knowing nobody is going to help you."

Alex poured some olive oil onto his own rag. "I figured it was something like that. It's just too harsh to believe when you're actually doing it."

"Oh yeah, it's all puppies and rainbows in the militia, bro." He said *bro* in a nasal voice that made it sound like *brah*.

"So everybody here went through the same initiation, then?"

Jack smiled. "Hell no."

"How many did it?"

"In our platoon? Six, including me and you. All the kids around our age."

Alex laughed. More *do as I say, not as I do.* "Well, that figures too."

Jack shrugged. "These guys have all seen combat. I guess they already proved themselves, or they wouldn't be here."

"Yeah, maybe." He still didn't like it.

Mitch whistled and pointed at the ground. "You two. Front and center."

Jack jumped to his feet and started moving. Alex pulled on his boots and hobbled after him with his laces undone. The sergeant glowered at something past his shoulder, which made him turn around.

Christ, I'm a screwup, he thought. He'd left his rifle at the firepit.

He ran back to get it then hurried over to Mitch. "Reporting as ordered."

"Fix your boots," Mitch growled.

Alex bent to lace them. Hands shaking, he tied the knots. Then he stood at attention, face burning with embarrassment. "My bad, Sergeant."

"You're lucky you remembered your weapon before you made it over here." He scowled at the two boys and spat in the snow. "Follow me."

"Yes, Sergeant," they said.

He led them to a stack of gear. After rooting around in it, he held up two sledgehammers. "Firewood detail."

Alex grabbed one, Jack the other.

Mitch pointed. "See that white house there? It is no longer occupied. Break it down."

"Yes, Sergeant!"

The boys shouldered their tools and tramped off to the house.

Once inside, Alex surveyed the living room and sagged. Whoever lived here had left in a hurry, taking only essentials. The rest lay strewn around the floor among ramshackle furniture.

"It'll take us forever to break this up," he complained.

Jack smiled. "It isn't so bad. Watch this."

The kid swung his sledgehammer over his head and brought it down in an alarming arc to smash against a cheap dining chair. The chair cracked into two pieces that flopped to the floor.

"Blow off some steam, bro."

Alex grinned and went into the kitchen. The cabinet doors stood open, revealing empty shelves. He swung the sledgehammer and snapped a door off its hinges to ricochet off the refrigerator.

"Anger therapy," he yelled to Jack, who was busy smashing up the living room. "I like it."

He whacked all the cabinet doors and tossed them one by one toward the front of the house. Then he pulled out the drawers and threw them on the pile too.

Jack came down the stairs. "Jackpot. I found some jewelry for trade."

"What'd you get?"

The kid showed him a few trinkets in his palm. "Probably junk. This wedding band, though, is gold."

Alex stared at it. "It's kind of creepy. When you think about what might have happened to whoever wore it last."

"Well, they left it, so it's mine now. Finders, keepers."

"So what was it like for you?"

The kid pocketed his loot. "What do you mean?"

"When you went out on your solo?"

Jack chuckled. "It took me hours just to get there, I was so damn careful." He held his hammer like a rifle and mimed walking real slow. "This was me, doing three-sixties every five seconds. I didn't see the enemy the whole time. Maybe they were all laughing too hard to take a shot at me."

Alex laughed with him. "I thought you were some kind of Rambo kid."

"You got to have an image, bro." *Brah.*

"You act the part well, I'll give you that."

"Hey, you should see me when I'm out with the guys on patrol. I'm a badass."

"What's it like?"

"It's a real adrenaline rush. Our guns are better than theirs. We move to contact, throw a lot of lead, and then hurry back. You'll see when you go out your first time. We haven't had a casualty in over a month. You'll be fine."

Alex said, "Let's put this lib table out of its misery."

They raised their sledgehammers.

"One, two, three—"

The hammers crashed against the table and broke its back.

"Nice," Jack said. "What about you? What happened out there?"

"I found an old lady."

"That sounds scary."

"I couldn't believe she was still living in No Man's Land. While I was talking to her, some cops snuck up behind me and captured me."

"What? Seriously?"

"I know I suck at this, but the Liberty Tree only gave me like a week of real training. I barely remembered how my rifle worked."

It was good to talk to somebody he could admit this to. The adults all wanted one another to know how tough they were.

"But how did you make it back if you got captured?"

"It turned out they were on our side and had a message for the Tree. The Indy 300 is moving out. There's going to be a big gap in the line for a few days."

Jack chuckled. "The libs are idiots. The one hand never knows what the other is up to. One thing I can say for the patriots, they know what they're doing."

"I guess." Alex shrugged. Both sides seemed pretty dumb to him.

"I take it back, though."

"Take what back?"

"About things being easy," Jack said. "If there's a gap in the line, we'll be attacking, you can count on that. This could be the big one, bro. We might end up seeing some real fighting."

Alex sat on the floor fuming. "Just my luck."

"On the plus side, it might be the only battle you ever fight."

"What do you mean?" He frowned. "Because I might die."

"No." Jack grinned. "Because the patriots might win it all."

ELEVEN

Long ago in Afghanistan, humping weapons and gear over mountains in breathtaking desolation, Mitch wrenched his ankle. The ligaments were like plastic holding a six-pack of beer. Once stretched, they stayed that way, and the ankle became unstable, making it prone to twist again or, just as bad, suffer a bout of chronic stiffness. That stiffness was now giving him lower back pain.

He should take it easy, but he soldiered through it. That's how he was raised.

He surveyed his squad while he stretched out his back. The men went about their evening routines in the front yard of the house they'd been assigned. Some played cards by the fire.

Rubbing his bearded face, Mitch took note of everything. He required an orderly camp. Good hygiene, dry socks, and clean weaponry won wars. Regimen and discipline.

Alex Miller was putting supper together. He'd passed his test today and earned his place. The militia needed good fighters.

He said, "What are we having, kid?"

"Beef stew."

"Take one of the beers tonight. You earned it."

Mitch turned toward the western horizon. The sun was setting over a derelict public school. Smoke and particulates in the atmosphere produced lurid, beautiful sunsets rich with reds and purples.

"And keep my supper warm," he added. "I'll be back in an hour."

"You got it, Sergeant."

"I want everybody to turn in early and get a solid eight hours tonight. We're on the front line again tomorrow."

"Where are you headed?" Grady called from the fire.

Mitch gathered up his gear and limped off into the twilight. "Going to see if the colonel wants to win this war."

Yellow light flared in the north at the Brickyard Crossing golf course, followed by booms and crackle. The libs were making one last push toward the Indianapolis Motor Speedway.

The battle had been raging for days. If the libs captured the Speedway, the patriots would be in trouble. They'd have to stretch to hold a longer line using manpower they did not have.

With a brief smile, Mitch recalled the last Indy 500 he'd come to see. Sweltering Memorial Day. Drinking beers at a tailgate party. He'd loved watching the cars scream around the track, engines so loud his ears rang when it was over.

One day, he'd go again, in a free country.

He found the colonel's command trailer, a ridiculous contraption up-armored against IEDs. Before the war, Ralph Lewis made a living as a tractor salesman in Columbus. He knew how to lead but had little practical experience. Mitch knew three ways he could knock the colonel's vehicle off the road using a few simple materials.

Fighting the Taliban for two years had taught him well how to be an insurgent. In the US Army and Afghanistan, he'd learned everything he needed to overthrow the federal government.

He knocked on the door. "Friendly coming in, Colonel."

Ralph tapped keys on the laptop on his desk. "Just updating our recruiting page."

Important work. Alex Miller wasn't the only kid in the company. They had lots of kids, a real children's crusade. Men went home to their families and jobs, or they got shot on the front line. To remain combat effective, the Liberty Tree needed grown men willing to fight for their country. Men with military experience most of all. Women too. If not, Mitch would be upgrading even more kids to combat status. Kids stuck around and didn't ask for pay.

"I got some solid intel today," he said.

The fingers stopped typing. "What's up?"

Mitch passed on the information Alex Miller brought back. Ralph swiveled his chair and rested his forearms on his knees, thinking.

"It's either a major break or a big, fat trap," the colonel said.

"It's a break. We should take it. More than that, we should throw everything we got at it. Blitzkrieg."

Indy was a Blue city in a sea of Red. At the start of the war, the militias had gained control of the countryside easy enough. They'd roll into a town, find out who was friendly and who wasn't in the local government, and make some changes. None of it had been planned. It just happened, a nationwide armed protest that snow-balled into a revolution. So sudden, so widespread across the country, the military hesitated to respond, and by the time the generals figured out what they wanted to do, it was too late.

Gary, Bloomington, Hammond, South Bend, and other liberal-leaning cities fell under siege. The main prize was Indy, the state capital. There was talk of making Fort Wayne the new capital, but that wouldn't do. The patriots wanted it all.

Emboldened, the Liberty Tree militia convened a secret court and convicted Mayor Charles Kingdon of treason. If they took the city, the governor might declare the whole state Red and throw the National Guard into the fight on the patriot side. The fighters mounted their trucks and raced into Indy to seize city hall.

And got their asses kicked, plain and simple.

Swollen with fresh recruits, the patriot groups poured in. Thou-sands fled the city in all directions while thousands more struggled to get in. The militias encircled it, shut off all traffic, and started squeezing.

In no time at all, the liberal elite learned who was feeding them all these years.

But it wasn't working. After nine months, Indy held, the governor remained on the fence, and the libs showed no signs of surrendering. If anything, they were getting stronger. The patriots needed a new strategy.

"Blitzkrieg," Ralph echoed. "What do you have in mind?"

"As long as the Guard holds the airport, we can't starve the libs out. The siege is a sham, a war of attrition we can't win. We need a knockout blow."

"We're a single company. We're good, but we aren't that good."

"I'm saying we pull other militia off the line and concentrate here in Fairfax," Mitch explained. "Send in the shock troops and have plenty more mounted up and ready to race ahead through the breach. Go all the way to city hall."

Ralph fished around the papers on his desk until he found his pack of Camels. He lit one with a puff of silver smoke. "We tried that once."

"Then we do it right this time."

The colonel took another drag and tapped his ashtray. "Won't work."

"Goddamnit. Are we trying to win this thing or not?"

"The other militias won't submit to a single command. And they won't take orders from us, even for an opportunity like this. Christ, you know it would take eight days just to get everybody talking in the same room."

Mitch growled but said nothing. Ralph had spoken the plain truth.

The militias stood united behind a similar narrative, the same general principles and goals. America had virtually become a socialist dictatorship, and President Marsh was trying to fix the broken nation. This had resulted in a soft coup by the Deep State. The Right had taken up arms to defend the president and restore the republic as it was intended by its founding fathers.

Their successes on the battlefield inspired them to demand broad-reaching reforms based on a purer reading of the Constitution. As the Second Amendment guaranteed all other freedoms, zero restrictions on gun ownership topped the list. After that, a balanced budget amendment. Centralization of power to the local level, including control of schools. Dismantling the welfare state. Sell-off of public lands. A national ID card. English as the official language.

Government small enough to fit in a toilet, where it could be properly flushed.

Nonetheless, the factions differed in ideology enough that on a bad day, they went at one another as much as they did at the libs. Mitch himself sometimes fantasized about taking a shot at the First Angels, who fired their mortars into civilian neighborhoods.

"We'll have to do it on our own," Ralph said.

"What do you mean?"

"I mean in eight days, we push hard into that gap. It'll throw the libs into disarray. They'll give up their offensive for sure. They might even pull back, maybe as far as the river. We hit them hard, then tell everybody we're doing it."

Mitch grinned. "That'll get the other militias moving."

"It won't win the siege or end the war in our state, but it'll improve our strategic position. It could even play a part in the peace talks."

His expression soured. "Yeah."

"It's been a year, Mitch. We need to start thinking about the end of this thing. Our position appears strong, but it's weak. Less than thirty percent of the public supports the president now."

"Because of the liberal media spreading lies."

Ralph ground out his cigarette in his ashtray. "We've got a lot of people in this state sympathetic to our cause and supporting us. A solid support system of opinion makers, safe houses, transporters, and the like. What we don't have enough of is fighters."

"So this is how it is. We're going to go for a negotiated settlement."

"That's the real world," Ralph told him. "Getting half of what we want is better than nothing. We score some touchdowns, maybe we get more than half."

"It's how we got into this shit in the first place. Compromising our principles."

"Hey. Big guy. I'm on your side. I'll plan an attack, all right?"

"Yeah."

"We sent a clear message tyranny will not be tolerated. We'll defend our liberty to our last breath, so help me God. If the new America fails its promises, we'll be here, and we'll be ready to do this all over again."

"All right, okay, stop selling me."

"Assuming the intel is solid, we'll push far enough to get the libs on the run. But stay out of the core. We don't need a Stalingrad. We need a big win, and we need every lib in Indy to know we won."

"Yes, sir," Mitch said and left the trailer.

He stood outside fuming. Here they were, giving their blood on the battlefield, while the politicians were getting set to carve up the turkey and sell them out.

Stalingrad. Now there was an idea. He was thinking more of a Tet Offensive.

Ralph had founded the Indiana Chapter of the Liberty Tree out of his own pocket, which explained his lofty rank, one he'd given himself. He'd built the website and did all the administrative work. The members had elected him chair. Now he gave the orders, and Mitch had always followed them.

Some orders required disobedience, however. For him, America always came first. When he pushed through the gap, Mitch would run his boys into Indy and take city hall. The boldness of the attack would inspire the other patriots to make a concerted push. The governor and National Guard might finally pick a side and step in to recognize a new constitution and declare the state Red.

Or the patriots wouldn't follow his lead. The Guard might continue to sit on its ass and let the militias keep fighting. The libs might organize and blow them all to hell.

Mitch knew it was a gamble, but it was one worth taking. He'd sworn he'd fight to the death for the America he wanted. The country every real American deserved.

And that's exactly what he'd do.

TWELVE

Blue UN flag flying from the aerial, the SUV hurtled down the street. It came to a skidding stop in a spray of snow in front of the Peace Office.

Gabrielle slapped at her seat belt until it released. She jumped out, glad to feel solid ground under her feet again. Everywhere they went, Aubrey drove like a maniac while bad news droned on the radio and heat blasted from the vents.

It was the safest way to drive these days. With the gas shortage, few vehicles traveled the roads. Snipers targeted those that did. Another generalized worry, whether a bullet would punch through the windshield at any given moment. And Gabrielle was a worrier. Once she thought about it, she couldn't stop picturing it.

No sane person would ever come here, she thought again. No sane person would choose to live here. No sane people would do this to themselves.

The reporter joined her on the sidewalk. "When this is all over, I'm going to write a book. The working title is, *It Happened Here*."

"When do you think it will end?"

"When the inmates decide to let the doctors run the asylum again."

Gabrielle surprised herself by saying, "Did they ever?"

She wondered how future historians would describe what happened to America. Most likely, they'd agree with Aubrey and call it a period of temporary derangement. But for Gabrielle, who'd followed American news for years, the trouble started long before President Marsh. Derangement, yes, but the country had been slowly losing its mind as long as she could remember.

Aubrey flashed her a look that turned into an approving smile.

She didn't smile back. She was here to help not judge. It wasn't that long ago her own people in Quebec flirted with the idea of insurgency to pursue their dreams of separation. She directed her gaze at the Peace Office, where she hoped she could do some good.

Like other Quaker meeting places, the Vermont Street Friends Meeting House was spare and simple. No steeple or crosses.

Missing posters covered the doors. They showed pictures of family members stranded when the fighting began. Loved ones arrested by various authorities. Disappeared children. Names and birthdates, social security numbers, locations they'd gone missing.

Gabrielle only knew what she'd heard about Quakers. To them, a church was a community, not a building. They believed people were innately good, every human being a recipient of the divine spark. And they were devout pacifists. She wanted to believe they were people who used their faith to make things better rather than reinforce the prejudices they were raised with.

A young man with blond dreadlocks greeted her in the foyer. "Can you bring those in with you?"

"Bring what?"

He pointed at the missing posters on the door. "Would you mind?"

"Sure." Gabrielle collected them.

He accepted the papers. "Thanks."

Aubrey walked in stomping snow from her boots. "What do you do with them?"

"One of our goals is to reunite families separated by the war," he said. "We try to arrange cease-fires for this purpose. People leave them on the door for us."

"Any successes?"

"Some. But, you know, never enough."

"What about you? Is that your job here?"

"Me? No, I'm the bean counter. But we all chip in on what needs doing."

The reporter nodded, mentally filing it for future reference. Gabrielle could tell she smelled a story. Aubrey was one of those type A people who didn't know how to be still and were always working.

She extended her hand. "I'm Gabrielle Justine with UNICEF. This is Aubrey Fox with the *Indy Chronicle*."

"Very glad to meet you. I'm Paul." He shook their hands with enthusiasm and threw Aubrey a sly look. "Fox, huh? The same last name as our founder."

"No relation, I'm sure," Aubrey said.

He laughed, revealing dimples. "Come on, I'll give you the nickel tour."

They followed him into the meeting area. Rows of plain wood benches dominated the main floor, with more seating in a perimeter gallery. Daylight streamed through windows that were set high on the wall so the outside world couldn't distract the worshippers during meetings.

The rest of the building was a series of offices and classrooms along with a kitchen and toilets. Quakers worked in these rooms among desks and stacks of office supplies and files.

"Where will I be working?" Gabrielle said.

"Wherever you like," Paul told her. "You won't have an assigned space. On the days you're here, we'll set you up somewhere."

She'd spent days navigating city hall with its bureaucracy both frantic and glacial. Hours waiting for this official or that to give her the runaround. Aubrey had stewed the entire time, restless and bored, making everybody uncomfortable by writing down every word they said. At last, Gabrielle had made contact with the right officials and received all the authorizations and assurances she needed.

Now she could get some work done.

"Would it be possible to call your people together?" she said. "It'd probably be best if I said hello to everybody at once."

"Sure. Can I get you some coffee?"

Gabrielle knew how expensive coffee was here. She didn't want to burden these people by taking even a cup. "Just some water, thank you."

"I'll take some," Aubrey said. "Cream and sugar, if you have any."

Wearing bulky sweaters, the Quakers gathered in the children's classroom. Despite the lack of heating, the atmosphere was warm and stuffy. Gabrielle exchanged smiles with the newcomers as she shed her flak jacket, helmet, and coat. Her pulse pounded in her ears. After running a sniper-infested gauntlet in a speeding car, the prospect of public speaking still made her sweat. She accepted a cup of water from Paul and downed it.

Then she scanned the crowd, about twenty people. They appeared tired and thin like everybody else she'd seen in Indianapolis, but far more hopeful. Aubrey sipped her coffee while Paul cast furtive looks in her direction.

"I'm Gabrielle Justine, United Nations Children's Fund." She blushed, hating how shaky her voice sounded in her ears. "This is Aubrey Fox with the *Indy Chronicle*. Thank you for the warm welcome. The US government has allowed UNICEF into the States to help children affected by the war. This war is in direct violation of their human rights."

She blinked at their applause and continued in a stronger voice, "I'm here to conduct a needs analysis. There's a huge need in America, and resources are thin. I will do everything I can to justify a fair share for Indianapolis. Once I'm given a budget, I can pull together a staff and NGOs to help distribute supplies."

UNICEF pulled serious weight, and when it wanted something done, it got done. But she wasn't sure that was true anymore. The American war was too big.

"We're with you," somebody called out, and they applauded again.

Gabrielle smiled back at them, enjoying a nice buzz from their welcome. She'd felt like she was in over her head since she'd arrived in Indianapolis, like she was drowning. The entire city seemed to be fighting her. But not these people.

Paul approached smiling as the meeting broke up. "That was great. We may need to reach you when you're not here. Can I get your cell number?"

Gabrielle gave it to him. "Thanks again for such a warm welcome."

"We need all the help we can get."

Paul considered Gabrielle part of his story, not the other way around. After all, the UN had just shown up. He'd been here since the beginning.

He finished thumbing the numbers into his phone. "Where are you staying?"

"The Castle."

His eyes narrowed. "Oh. Okay."

"The UN set it up," she offered.

"That's great," Paul said. "It's really nice there. You're lucky."

"Yeah."

She wanted to say more, but it wouldn't change the fact that, unlike these people, she lived in comfort and could walk away from the war anytime she wanted.

Her buzz evaporated. She'd come to the Vermont Street Friends Meeting House thinking of herself as a savior. She'd leave feeling more than a little like a tourist.

THIRTEEN

Hannah hauled an armful of salvaged wood into the kitchen and stacked it by the blazing oven. She lingered to enjoy the heat and the tangy smells of the eternal stew.

Every day, the cooks put anything they could find into the pot, which the militia ate from but never emptied. It was breakfast, lunch, and dinner. Always rich but never monotonous as its flavors mingled and shifted.

"It's how they did it in the Middle Ages," said Vivian, who ran the kitchen.

She was a big-boned woman wearing an apron over a khaki shirt and camouflage pants tucked into combat boots. Her tawny eyes gleamed on her wide face, which offered Hannah a bright, comforting smile.

Hannah switched her gaze from this smile to the bubbling stew. "I like it."

"I'm glad you do, sweetie."

"Why does it always taste a little different each time?"

"A chef doesn't give away her secrets, but in your case I'll make an exception." Vivian dropped a handful of powder in the cauldron and stirred. "Spices. It's all about the spices. It's how you make a lot out of a little."

"What kind of spices?"

The woman offered her palm for Hannah. "Smell this."

Hannah's eyes went wide. "Cinnamon."

Her mind flashed across a series of memories. Her mother standing by the electric mixer. Scent of vanilla and chocolate chips. The mixer's whir. Mom smiling as she handed over the batter-covered beaters to lick.

Even the memory was delicious.

"While everybody else was panic-buying breakfast cereal, I cleaned out the spice aisles," Vivian said. "Now these spices are worth their weight in gold."

"How would you make a cake without flour or butter?" Hannah asked.

A crushing pressure filled her chest, making her wince. She wished she could touch her memories without them hurting her. This wasn't as hard during the day, when there was plenty of work to do, but at night, she gave in to her tears.

"War cake," Vivian said. "Powdered milk, sugar, cocoa powder, water, some cooking oil, and sliced sandwich bread. It's a wet mess, but it works. Why?"

"My mom was going to make me one..."

A woman entered the kitchen and stripped off her uniform. Nude, she slipped under a white sheet on the massage table set up by the fire. A woman Hannah knew as Sally began to knead her muscles with an oil that smelled like peppermint. This was Sally's job, rubbing away the aches and stress of fighting.

Vivian smiled. "From each according to her ability. Speaking of which, we've got some potatoes that need peeling, please and thank you."

The cause required hard work from everybody, from the frontline fighters to the massage therapist. Right now, it needed Hannah Miller to peel a sack of potatoes resting on the cutting board.

She washed the potatoes one by one in a bucket of melted snow and laid them out on the board. Taking her peeler, she stroked away the thick skin, which she set aside for mulching. Whatever the greenhouse didn't need would go into the pot. The militia wasted nothing.

Her mind went blank as she worked. The babble of women washed over her. It felt like peace. She'd discovered a place she could become both lost and found.

"Hey, birthday kid," Vivian said.

Hannah jumped. How did she know?

Vivian hadn't been talking to her, however, but another girl who'd arrived bouncing in the kitchen. Like Hannah, the girl kept her hair cut short against lice. She wore a bulky pink sweater with a waving Santa on the front. Baggy army surplus pants flared from her boots.

Hannah had seen her helping to clean the rooms, scrubbing at the grime left every night by the oil lamps. She didn't know the girl's name. For three days, Hannah had lived with the Free Women, long enough to run across other kids, though she wasn't ready to make friends. She stayed close to the fire and slept on a cot.

"Hi, Vivian," the girl said. "You wanted to see me?"

"I have something special for you. I know you'll like it."

They went to another part of the kitchen. Hannah put her head down and went on with her scraping. Exposing her potato one peel at a time.

"Thank you," the girl said. "Mm, it's so good."

She traced aimless circles through the hubbub, humming as she slurped from a bowl. Hannah kept one eye on her while running her peeler up and down the same spot.

The girl popped into view. "What's your name?"

Hannah frowned at her potato and said nothing.

"I'm Maria. Look what Vivian gave me."

Wary, she looked up. The girl held a bowl of what appeared to be plain pasta.

"It's really good," Maria said. "You want a bite?"

Hannah nodded and accepted the bowl and plastic fork. She twirled spaghetti onto it and bit down. Cold but amazing, flavored with a little sesame oil.

She prepared another bite but caught Maria's expression. She handed the bowl back. "Sorry, I get carried away with food."

Maria laughed. "Don't we all?"

"It was so good. Thank you."

"It's my birthday today. I'm eleven now."

"Happy birthday."

"How old are you?"

"I'll be eleven just after Christmas."

"We have the same birthday! Well, almost."

"Yeah, that's—"

"Vivian said she's going to make me a cake. They're gonna sing to me tonight and everything. If you tell her about your birthday, she'll make you one too."

Hannah pictured a roomful of grown-ups in makeshift uniforms looking at her while they sang happy birthday. "That's okay. It's no big deal."

"Wait right here. Don't move a muscle."

Hannah went back to peeling. She wasn't going anywhere.

Maria returned with a second bowl. "Look what I got. I asked Vivian if it was okay if I shared mine, and instead she made an extra one for you. Isn't that great?"

Hannah went to grab the bowl but checked herself. She waited until the girl handed it to her. "Thank you. I'm Hannah."

"Nice to meet you, Hannah Banana. We're both Christmas babies. My mom used to have my birthday party in June."

Hannah wolfed down her spaghetti. "That's a good idea."

"It made my birthdays more special."

"Do you live here with your mom?"

"She died on the front line. Where are your parents?"

"The rebels killed them."

Maria gazed upon her as a kindred spirit. "We're both orphans."

Hannah inspected her bowl. It was empty.

Maria said, "Do you want to play?"

She gestured to the potatoes. "Maybe later."

Vivian walked over. "How did you like your pasta?"

"It was amazing," Maria said.

"Thank you," Hannah said.

"I was hoping you two would become friends," Vivian said. "Christmas will be over soon and then it's back to school. Are you girls ready for that?"

Maria nodded with enthusiasm. Hannah shrugged. She hadn't been to school in a long time. She didn't know if she was ready. It seemed kind of strange to learn social studies and spelling when these things had nothing to do with survival.

Vivian gave her a searching look. "Hannah, why don't you go play with Maria for a while?"

Her body went rigid. She was enjoying being around people but still wasn't ready to talk or have fun. "I'm not done peeling these potatoes."

"They can wait. To each according to her need. Go play."

Maria rattled off their options. They settled on hide-and-seek.

An hour later, Hannah ran breathless through the facility, looking for a place to hide while Maria counted down from thirty. It was colder here, away from the kitchen, but she didn't mind. It was good to run.

She entered the stairwell and banged up the stairs to find doors along a stretch of dark hallway. The building was like a cross between a hotel and a house. No place to hide, though. She had to keep moving. They'd played on the main floor until they'd exhausted the best hiding places. This time, Hannah had decided to roam.

She paused in front of an open doorway. A woman lay in bed surrounded by uniformed comrades with rifles slung on their backs. One turned and frowned. As she moved to close the door, the woman in bed offered a weak smile. Hannah gave her a little wave as the door shut.

Back to finding a hiding place.

At the end of the corridor, she stopped at an open maintenance closet. Mops stood in a yellow bucket on wheels. Bottles of colorful liquids filled the shelves. The room smelled like dust and cleaner.

Hannah stepped inside and closed the door.

For a while, she waited. The seconds turned to minutes, but she didn't mind. She liked it here. Dark and enclosed.

"Now where could she be?" Maria said in a loud voice as she walked down the hall. "Ready or not, here I come!"

Hannah got down on her hands and knees and leaned to peer under the crack in the door, a sliver of gray in the black. Maria's footsteps grew louder.

Then receded.

Hannah covered her mouth with her hand so she didn't giggle. Maria had completely missed her hiding spot.

The door flew open.

Maria cried, "Found you!"

Hannah flinched in terror. Then she laughed.

A woman's voice: "Maria, is Hannah with you?"

"Yeah, she's right here. We're playing hide-and-seek."

Sabrina appeared in the doorway and smiled down at Hannah. "And you found her."

"Do you want to play with us?" Maria said.

"I have something different in mind for you."

Hannah stood and dusted her knees. "Where are we going?"

Sabrina said, "Today, I'm going to teach you how to shoot a gun."

FOURTEEN

After leaving the Peace Office, Gabrielle visited the Riley Hospital for Children, where she watched the staff treat kids for bullet wounds, horrible burns, and broken bones.

The doctors said it was worse on the front line. If she wanted to help Indy's most vulnerable children, she had to go there.

Back in the car, she stared out the window, still shaken by what she'd seen. Already, the strength she'd drawn from the Peace Office had drained out of her.

"I think the Quaker has the hots for you," Aubrey said behind the wheel. Despite the banter, she sounded distant and irritable. Something was eating her too.

Gabrielle shoved aside the memory of the hospital. "Which one?"

"Paul. They don't have a leader, but I think he's the brains behind their peace operation."

"Actually, he was into you. He was checking you out the whole time I was giving my speech."

"Then he's in trouble," said Aubrey. "I was a commitment-phobe even before the war. He's too young for me, in any case."

"If love ever finds me, I'll run with it."

"Then again, a roll in the hay would be fun. I'm trying to decide whether those dreadlocks were a turn-on or not."

"I'm not talking about a roll in the hay. I'm talking about love."

"I can't do love and survive at the same time," the reporter said.

"Love is supposed to be one of the things you survive for."

"Don't underestimate the benefit of a good—oh, shit!"

Aubrey slammed on the brakes. Gabrielle gasped during the slide.

They'd turned a corner and come close to plowing into a river of people flowing along East Washington. Protesters marched to pounding drums.

A man called out, "Tell me what democracy looks like!"

The crowd chanted, "THIS IS WHAT DEMOCRACY LOOKS LIKE."

Spontaneous cheering broke out as the vanguard filled the treed lawn of the Indiana Statehouse. Signs and American flags waved amid wool hats and winter coats. Armed with batons and plastic shields, a phalanx of riot police had marshaled on the steps.

Gabrielle gazed across the bobbing fists and signs. SAVE THE UNION, she read. STOP THE CON. DRAIN THE MARSH. Then more protesters streamed past the car and blocked her view.

She'd seen demonstrations in Montreal, students protesting tuition increases and social injustice, but nothing like this. It reminded her of the Occupy the Mall protests on TV during President Marsh's trial in the Senate. Tens of thousands of people braving the cold to camp in front of the Capitol and demand his resignation.

"Look at them," Aubrey said. "A year ago, most of them didn't even vote."

"What's going on? Why are they protesting?"

The reporter leaned on the horn as she tried to clear a path. "It's complicated."

The demonstrators thinned to let them through. Several stayed and locked arms to block their passage. One yelled, "Whose streets?"

"Our streets!"

"*Whose* streets?"

"OUR STREETS."

A woman banged on her window. "Help us! We're starving!"

Protesters swarmed the car as word spread it had a UN flag on it. A woman asked her to get a message to her father, who was being held in Greensburg. A man wanted her help to get to Canada. The rest came through only in fragments, lost in the roar.

Gabrielle cowered. *"C'est pas bon ça, j'aime pas ça."*

The reporter rolled down the window and shouted, *"Indy Chronicle!"*

She honked again. The men blocking the road shot each other looks. One by one, they nodded. They broke ranks to allow the car through.

"Stay safe," a man yelled as Aubrey raised the window.

"It's not up to me," she muttered.

"They let us pass," Gabrielle said in wonder.

"My paper gives them something they never knew they needed."

The black SUV shed the crowds and roared south, passing small groups of protesters streaming toward the statehouse. A mob of children chased the car and threw snowballs at it until giving up, laughing.

Gabrielle fingered her maple leaf pendant and let go of the breath she'd been holding. Those people believed she was powerful and could help them. She had far less power than they thought.

She said, "Maybe we should call it a day and go back to the hotel."

The reporter yanked the wheel to the right and kept driving. "You wanted to see the front line. That's where we're going."

Gabrielle gripped the door in alarm. "We're going the wrong way on a one-way."

"Traffic laws don't matter anymore." Aubrey floored the accelerator. "Hang on to your hat."

The SUV went into an alarming slide as it swerved around a bullet-riddled wreck.

Gabrielle cringed in her seat. *"Calvaire."*

"The Constitutional Convention," Aubrey said. "That's what's got them riled up. There are enough states now to have one. Our entire system of laws may end up being rewritten in Columbus."

Gabrielle tried to focus on what she was hearing. "Okay."

The reporter went on in quiet rage. "If the president and Congress can't come to terms, the states may work things out themselves. Some of the governors are talking partition."

Gabrielle remembered one of the signs, STOP THE CON. "They were protesting the idea of having a convention, then?"

"They were protesting because Indy is a Blue city in a very Red state," Aubrey said. "The governor is a die-hard Republican. If the Union breaks up and we end up in a new right-wing utopia, what happens to us?"

If a new far-right country absorbed Indianapolis, the peace might be even more violent than the war. The live-free-or-die rebels who'd dedicated their lives to fighting a police state would become its police. The government might have lists of "terrorists" to arrest or execute. As a journalist, Aubrey's name could end up on it.

"The protests are getting bigger and more violent," the reporter said. "One of these days, they're going to storm the statehouse and string up the governor. Left-wing militias might join in and stage a coup. If that happens, we could end up with another civil war inside the city. I hate to think what the Guard would do."

"Another civil war? How?"

"The Centrists run Indy. Liberals, moderates, most of the trade unions. They own the IMPD. They want things to go back to the way they were. The Leftists include socialists and anarchists, mostly young people. They want a revolution, and their numbers are getting bigger every day. The Left and Center hate each other almost as much as they do the rebels."

Gabrielle listened, hoping to learn, but hardly understood any of it. "What a mess. I can see why you're upset."

"I'm upset because I'm babysitting when I should be covering the march!"

Unused to being yelled at, Gabrielle blinked in surprise. "I'm so sorry."

Then anger boiled in her chest. How was this her fault? She was tired of everybody here treating her like the enemy.

"Wait a minute," she snapped. "I didn't ask you to do anything."

"Three days doing nothing at city hall. The one good thing I have in my shitty life is my job, and I can't do it!"

"I'm here to help the children," Gabrielle shot back. "I don't want to be in this horrible place. I'm trying to help your children and nobody seems to care!"

Everywhere she went, people demanded her help but then got in her way. She turned away to hide frustrated tears.

Aubrey gripped the wheel. After a while, she said, "Hey, UN."

Gabrielle raised her hand, not trusting herself to speak.

"I'm sorry," the reporter said.

"Okay."

"I want to help. I'm not mad at you, all right?"

"Thank you," Gabrielle said in a dull voice.

"Think about the Peace Office. You have friends here."

"They think I'm a tourist."

"You have to be patient."

The reporter slowed down as she approached the bridge with its deadly patches of ice. Light flashed on the horizon. Distant booms.

"Now pay attention to everything you see," Aubrey added while they crossed the river. "I won't be able to help you forever. You have to learn your way around."

Graffitied houses. Burned-out cars, homes scarred with bullet holes or smashed by mortars. Masking tape x-ing windows that were still intact. Smoke in the air.

Pay attention. Right. Gabrielle had already seen far more than she wanted. The more she saw of this powder keg of hunger and lawlessness, the more she hated it.

And in the middle of this devastation, clothes dried on lines. A woman bicycled down the street. A group of men broke down a yard fence for firewood. A young couple stapled a giant plastic sheet over a broken window. Kids raced around a playground under the protective gaze of soccer moms with handguns.

She said, "How can people still live here right in the middle of the fighting?"

Aubrey shrugged. "They have nowhere else to go."

Haughville was a largely African American working-class neighborhood. About seven thousand people lived here before the war. Most left to escape the war. The ones who stayed were the poorest of the poor.

Less than a mile away to the west, rebel forces occupied Fairfax.

It was a war without warriors, fought by people who a year ago worked in offices and stores and factories. The real warriors had barricaded themselves at the airport.

"Maybe the National Guard *should* do something," Gabrielle said.

"They are doing something," Aubrey said. "They're staying out of the way and making sure foreign aid gets into the city."

"I mean they should stop the fighting."

"Whose side should they take? Our governor hopes the Reds win and end the war in Indiana. But he won't order the Guard to shoot Americans. Not because he's a nice guy, no. He knows the rank and file might refuse the order. They might split apart and start shooting each other. Somebody might even shoot him."

"So that's why the US Army hasn't done anything either."

The reporter parked the SUV on the street outside a clinic. She killed the engine and turned in her seat.

"Last spring, they invaded a piece of Maryland as an experiment," she said. "The majority welcomed martial law. Things quieted down. Then both the Reds and the Blues started fighting them. The military fought insurgencies overseas for the past twenty years and didn't win. They can't here either, and they know it."

"I get it," said Gabrielle.

As a Canadian, she had always found the vast power of the US military comforting if a little alarming. It had seemed so simple to her that it could stop the fighting. Understanding this conflict was like peeling a giant onion. Aubrey had called the war complicated, but that was turning out to be an understatement.

"The military's options are to stage a coup and fight both sides, pick a side and shoot the other, or do exactly what they're doing, which is wait for a political solution." Aubrey took a deep breath. "Okay, are you ready for this?"

Gabrielle took in the sight of the clinic and steeled herself for the horrors she knew awaited her inside. "I just want to know. How did it come to this?"

"I have a simple theory."

"What's that?"

The reporter said, "Too many people believed their own bullshit."

Gabrielle absorbed this and nodded. "Maybe you should make that the title of your book."

Aubrey shot her another look that turned into an approving smile. "Nice." She left the car and started walking toward the clinic.

Gabrielle glanced at her phone, heavy with texts from her parents asking her to come home. She returned it to her pocket. Then she got out.

FIFTEEN

Hannah and Maria followed Sabrina downstairs, where they put on jackets and layers to go outside. Red braids swinging, the soldier led them down the street to a garage, where militia-women practiced shooting at a range they'd set up.

A deafening bang made Hannah flinch at the entrance. Her eyes began to tear up. "Vivian said I have to peel potatoes."

"You have to know how to handle a gun safely and shoot," Sabrina said. "If you don't, you can't be in Free Women."

Hannah looked down the street. Just cold and emptiness and garbage.

"I hate guns too," Sabrina added. "I used to want them banned. Come on."

Hannah followed her and Maria into the garage. Fighters stood around talking and aiming rifles at distant cardboard targets.

Sabrina handed the girls a pair of cotton balls. "Put these in your ears."

When the soldier offered her a rifle, Hannah shrank away from it. She pictured her mother slammed against the asphalt. She wiped at her watery eyes. "I don't want to kill people."

She hated the war and wanted to escape somewhere safe, but there was no way out. The war was everywhere, and even kids had to learn to kill. It would go on forever, and she would grow up fighting it.

"You're too young to fight," Sabrina assured her. "You won't be in combat. But you need to be able to defend yourself. This isn't about killing, it's about empowerment. After we win this war, we can put away the guns for good."

Hannah braced herself and took the rifle. It had a wood stock and wasn't as heavy as it appeared. The barrel shined with oil.

Too much power. The power over life and death. Her stomach went queasy.

She thought, *I could kill somebody with this.*

Sabrina said, "Do you know who Jay Gould was?"

Hannah stared bug-eyed at the militiawoman and wagged her head.

"He was a railroad baron. Richer than God and didn't like to share. You know what he once said? 'I can hire one half of the working class to kill the other half.'"

"Okay."

"This war isn't about impeachment," Sabrina told her. "It's about whether government is allowed to tell us what we can worship, what we can say, what we can do with our bodies. About whether a handful of billionaires and corporations get the whole pie. About whether the mercenaries they hired to fight their war can turn America into a dictatorship. Understand?"

Hannah didn't follow any of it. "Okay."

"When you pull the trigger, always think about why you're shooting. And shoot to kill, because the main reason you're shooting is to stay alive. Are you ready?"

She looked down at the weapon in her hands. *I can't believe I'm doing this.*

"Pull the bolt handle back," the soldier instructed. "Hold it there while you push down on that button. Set the safety. Now the gun won't shoot."

Sabrina taught her how to remove the magazine and load a fresh one. The magazine clicked as it locked in place. Hannah gripped the bolt handle and pushed the lock button again, allowing the bolt to slide forward.

She had a little more control over it, but still the weapon seemed to be a living thing with a mind of its own. *It wants to shoot something.*

"Finger off the trigger," Sabrina said. "Now let's go shoot."

The militia fighters stepped to the side. Hannah eyed the target, a tall sheet of cardboard onto which somebody had painted a crude caricature of President Marsh.

"You can do it, girl," a fighter said.

Sabrina laid gentle hold of Hannah's shoulders and steered her into position. "We're aiming at that target right in front of us. Is it safe to shoot?"

Hannah didn't see any living person in the target area. "I think so."

"It either is or isn't."

"I don't see anybody. It's safe."

"Line up the front sight with the back sight. Breathe in as you do it. Flick the safety off. Yes. Now breathe out nice and slow and squeeze the—"

The gun bucked against her shoulder with a loud bang. Eyes clenched shut, she staggered back, barrel aimed at the ceiling. The rifle fired again before Sabrina grabbed the barrel.

A puff of dust wafted at the sandbags stacked behind the targets. She'd missed.

Sabrina took the rifle from her. "Eyes open next time. And brace yourself against the recoil. For every action, there is an equal, opposite reaction."

"I told you I can't do this."

"You can if you practice." Sabrina pulled the bolt, locked it, and set the safety. "Watch how Maria does it. Show her, Maria."

The girl readied her own rifle, a big, ugly gun with a curved magazine. She breathed out. Her body rocked as the rifle cracked in her hand. She steadied herself and fired again.

"Good shooting," one of the fighters said.

Maria beamed as she secured her rifle. Hannah burned with embarrassment. She wished she weren't so afraid. She wanted the empowerment Sabrina promised.

"The gun she was shooting is called an AK-47," the soldier said. "It's what you'll be using after you master the basics with the..."

The women froze as another fighter entered the garage. They watched her cross the room and dump her gear in a corner. Then they waited as if expecting her to offer some advice or words of encouragement. Instead, the woman drank deep from a water bottle. Her dirty camouflage uniform fit her like a second skin.

"Who's that?" Hannah whispered.

"Grace Kim," said Sabrina. "She's been gone awhile."

"Why is everybody looking at her?"

"She won the bronze in shooting at three hundred meters at the Olympics. Now she's our best sniper. Thirteen kills. A couple thousand to go, and the siege will be over."

The beautiful athlete struck Hannah as the embodiment of cool. Though petite, she had a big presence, tough and poised like the policewoman at Victory Field, graceful as a cat.

Being a sniper meant being strong, alone, and safe.

Grace held up two fingers. The fighters grinned.

"Make that fifteen kills," Sabrina said.

The sniper noticed Hannah staring. She smiled back, though her eyes seemed sad.

"Can I try again?" Hannah said.

Sabrina handed her the rifle and began to repeat the instructions, but Hannah remembered. She readied the .22, braced her legs, and leaned into the stock. Breathed in as she lined up her sights, breathed out just before she fired.

The bullet snapped through the target over President Marsh's shoulder and struck the sandbags.

She frowned.

"Very good," Sabrina said.

"But I missed!"

"You missed the man, but you hit the target. Much better."

"Again?"

"Again."

Hannah lined up the sights again and fired. "I don't see the hole."

The soldier gave her an approving nod. "You hit him in the shoulder."

Maria bounced on her feet. "I knew you could do it."

Hannah shot the Marsh caricature four out of the next six times. Then her arms grew tired and she began to miss. She secured the rifle.

She couldn't imagine herself hurting a living person. Still, the shooting gave her a feeling of power she'd never had. *Empowerment*, Sabrina promised. Yes.

She beamed at Grace Kim. *How did I do?*

The sniper smiled again, though there was still no real happiness in it.

SIXTEEN

Outside the clinic, trash cans overflowed with bloody bandages. A row of bodies lay on the frozen ground. Militia rushed a limping comrade into the building. Heart-stopping booms pounded in the north, thuds Gabrielle felt in her feet.

Screams poured out as she went inside.

The wounded filled the lobby. A soldier with a mangled arm. A woman blinded by flying glass. A trembling teenager lying on her side, leg transfixed by a long sliver of metal.

Gabrielle had steeled herself for the worst but crumpled under the visual onslaught. She stopped just a few steps inside and hugged her ribs. She wanted to help but didn't know what to do, where she might even begin.

Aubrey produced her notepad and moved forward to question one of the nurses. Gabrielle knew the reporter thought she was bearing witness, but she was wrong. Bearing witness required horror. It required nothing short of rage.

How could anybody see this without screaming?

The reporter threaded her way back. "You okay?"

Gabrielle stared at her with wide eyes. "Are you?"

"The doctor who runs this place is operating but says we can go see him now." Again, those bright black eyes bored into hers, probing for cracks. "You know, it doesn't get any prettier in the operating room."

The only way Gabrielle could help was to keep going. "Let's see him."

Even the corridors were filled with people. Aubrey said they were Indy 300, Black Bloc, civilians, even a few rebels, all casualties from the Brickyard Crossing offensive in the north. It was hard to look at them and not picture what they were before. The militia-woman groaning from a gunshot wound, was she a housewife, a bank teller, a CEO? The twentysomething with his hand blown off, did he have big dreams, a girlfriend, savings for his first home? The war had erased everything and reset it to zero. It had reduced everyone to perpetrator, victim, or both.

They found Dr. Walker in his office, where he could operate by daylight flooding the room through a large window behind his desk. With his gleaming round eyeglasses, the slim African American had a stern, professorial air about him.

A soldier lay groaning on the desk while his comrade whispered encouragement and fed him liquor from an old Pepsi bottle. The room stank of rot.

"You aren't losing a limb," Walker told him. "You're gaining your life."

Gangrene had blackened the mangled foot. A nurse shaved the man's shin and calf, prepping for amputation.

The soldier returned a weak nod. "Do it now."

His comrade pressed down on his shoulders. "Don't look."

The doctor injected anesthetic into the wound. "Ready?"

His sweating assistant nodded.

"Scalpel."

The nurse pulled the instrument from a glass of hydrogen peroxide and handed it over. She gave another to the assistant.

They cut into the bulging flesh, straight through nerves to the bone. The soldier's body clenched, his face turning a pale green from blood loss, fever, and sheer terror.

Gabrielle stood transfixed by the scene, determined not to look away, to bear witness herself to the horror.

The nurse tied off the calf with a rubber tourniquet and swabbed the area with disinfectant.

"That's the anterior tibial artery," the assistant intoned.

"Suture it."

Walker started cutting with a backsaw, working fast. The soldier screamed. The anesthetic worked on the wound but not the bone.

Gabrielle fought a surge of bile and turned away. She heard the foot slide along the bloody desk and flop to the floor.

She wasn't as tough as Aubrey and didn't want to be. She didn't want to normalize emotional distance from everything. The more horrors she encountered, the more she valued her innocence. It wasn't enough for her to survive her stay here. Gabrielle wanted to go home with her humanity intact.

When she turned back, the doctor's eyes locked onto hers. "Close for me," he said. "I'll be back after I talk to the United Nations."

He'd wanted her to see this. Observing this simple operation told her everything she needed to know about what conditions were like here.

The doctor yanked off his gloves, gown, and face shield. Stooped with exhaustion, he staggered outside to light a cigarette by an overflowing dumpster.

"We need..." The doctor took a drag as he thought. "Everything. Antibiotics, blood bags, plasma, aspirin. Ketamine for general anesthesia. It can produce hallucinations, but it's the best we can use, seeing as we don't have electricity."

Walker worked hard every day without pay to save lives doing medicine that was just one step ahead of the last American civil war. Like all wars, this one brought out the best and worst among those it touched, though the best always seemed far too little to balance out.

She asked, "How many children do you treat per week?"

"Too many." Walker sighed. "You want to help the children, help me treat their community. Not just battlefield supplies but everything. Insulin, blood pressure pills, you name it. We could use another surgeon. I wrote to Doctors Without Borders, but they're stretched to the limit. Beyond that, a lot of disease is happening because of poor basic hygiene. We need soap and toothpaste."

"I understand. Do you keep records?"

"We'll give you everything you want." He added with sudden force, "Right now, I just want you to listen to me."

Gabrielle said nothing.

"We need food," he said. "Most people here are getting by on a subsistence diet, maybe nine hundred calories a day. In this cold, they need at least twice that. The whole city is slowly starving. And clean water. Barring that, purification tablets."

Walker took a final puff on his cigarette, drawing smoke until there was nothing but filter. He dropped the butt into the blackened snow. "And while you're at it, an end to the war and a million bucks would be nice."

Aubrey smiled as she scribbled everything he said in her notebook.

The doctor sighed. "I don't even know why I'm bothering. Even if you send us everything we need, half of it will fall off a truck before it gets here and wind up on the black market. Because people are damn fools. Come on, let's go back inside and I'll introduce you to Jayla. She'll get you all the info you want."

Walker opened the door and trudged back into the clinic. Gabrielle froze at the threshold.

A girl in an ill-fitting uniform lay in the corridor hugging her stomach, an AK-47 propped against the wall next to her. A boy stood over her, the same weapon slung across his back, side pockets bulging with spare magazines.

Aubrey had told her that Russia smuggled AK-47 rifles into the country in humanitarian aid shipments. The same rifles some of the rebels used. The European Union was helping Congress; Saudi Arabia and Brazil the president. Russia was helping both.

America had taken a flying leap off the global stage and was now on the brink of becoming a failed state. Russia had a simple strategy. As long as the war kept going, America eliminated itself as a world power.

The guns didn't interest her, though. The kids did.

Gabrielle crouched in front of them. "What's your name?"

The Latino boy wiped tears from his eyes. "Are you the doctor?"

"He just came in ahead of me. I can get him for you."

"Yes." He returned his fierce gaze to the girl on the floor.

She said, "First, I just wanted to ask you—"

"*Vete a la verga*," he snarled. "Get the fucking doctor."

Gabrielle recoiled. Not only from his words but from a flashback arriving like a slap, which this suffering girl had triggered. For an instant, she was six years old again, driving across Canada with a man who was going to kill her.

A hand rested on her shoulder. "You okay?"

She flinched from Aubrey's touch. "Don't do that."

Walker returned and shot a glance at the reporter. "Is she all right?"

"It's her first time in the war zone."

Gabrielle glared at him. "You didn't tell me the militias are using child soldiers."

SEVENTEEN

In the late afternoon, the Free Women wolfed down their communal feast in the shelter's dining hall, now warm with body heat and the smells of stew and sweat. Dozens of fighters laughed and talked at the tables. They wore shabby uniforms on their bodies and kept their hair cut short or shaped into dreadlocks, braids, and mohawks.

Hannah sat with Maria and twelve other girls around rickety picnic tables jammed into tight rows. This was her first time attending a meeting in the communal hall, the one day each month the entire militia came together to eat and talk. After days taking her meals alone in the kitchen, she found it overwhelming.

"And then Hannah put one right in Marsh's big mouth," Maria said.

The kids laughed, their bright eyes on Hannah.

"With a .22," Kristy said. She was fourteen, the oldest of the girls in the militia, and the unspoken leader of their gang. "Anybody could do that."

"It was her first time, for crying out loud."

"We'll see how she does with an AK."

"I was told I didn't have to shoot anybody," Hannah said.

"You don't have to," Kristy said. "But you might *want* to."

Hannah didn't think she'd want to either.

Alice, who was seven, nudged Hannah from her other side. "I'm a good shot."

Kristy yanked up her sleeve to show off tattoos running down the length of her arm. Hannah leaned in to inspect them. An anime face, an emoticon sticking out its tongue, a four-leaf clover, and a Venus symbol with a clenched fist instead of a cross.

The girl pulled her sleeve back down. "You learn to shoot, you're in the gang."

"They're really good," Hannah said. "Who drew them?"

Maria beamed, kicking the empty space under the table. "I did. It was Kristy's idea. Every time you do something good for the gang, you get a tattoo."

"It's like being awarded a medal," Kristy said. "It shows status."

"It's not permanent or anything," Maria added. "Pretty cool, huh?"

"Aren't you afraid of getting ink poisoning through your skin?" Hannah asked.

"That's just an urban legend."

She thought the tattoos looked cool. "Are they always the same?"

"It's whatever you want." Maria shot Kristy a look. "She's in?"

"If she wants to be in."

She turned to Hannah. "Venus sign with a fist okay with you? That's our gang mark."

"Sure. I'd like that."

"You'll get the hang of things," Kristy said. "Unless you're needing tampons. Then you just have to make do."

The girl was showing off her age, but Hannah blushed anyway. "Right."

Maria patted her shoulder. "You're in! I'll give you your mark after dinner."

"What does it mean to be in?"

Kristy said, "We watch each other's backs. No matter what."

Hannah liked the sound of that. "Do you guys know Grace Kim?"

"Everybody knows Grace. She doesn't talk to us much. She looks young, but she's, like, twenty-five. She hangs out with the grown-ups."

Maria said, "She doesn't hang out with anybody. She goes out a lot on her own."

Still struck by the sniper's cool at the shooting range, Hannah nodded. "Sabrina said she was an Olympic shooter."

Kristy scowled. "Yeah, well, she only took home the bronze."

"I'm just curious—"

The girls shushed her. Alice nudged her again and stuck out her tongue.

The commander had stood at her table. "Good afternoon, sisters."

"Good afternoon, Abigail," the Free Women chanted, which ended in a laugh.

"We're grateful to be alive and free!"

The fighters roared their approval.

Abigail raised her hands. "New business. The bulletin went out today. The central committee voted on the call for volunteers for the Haughville front. We're going."

Hannah stiffened in alarm as the room erupted in groans.

"We're going," Abigail went on at a higher volume. "We'll be relieving the Indy 300 so they can join the Black Bloc in the Brickyard Crossing offensive."

"Always a militia," a woman growled at her table. "It's about time the IMPD did its share of the fighting."

"The cause needs us there, so that's where we're going. The Library Collective and Fire Station 3 will watch over our building."

Another voice: "For how long?"

"We don't know. I do know if the offensive breaks the Red line, we can end the siege. Start retaking the state. On foot if that's how we have to do it."

"I haven't shot a fascist in two months," Sabrina called out. "I say we go tonight."

More cheering. Hannah didn't join in.

Abigail smiled. "That's the spirit. Now before we get the hootenanny started, we've got some new members. Trish, Lisa, and Hannah, please stand up."

Maria nudged Hannah. "That's you!"

Two gaunt women stood. Hannah did too.

"Trish, you go first," Abigail said. "Tell us why you're here."

"I was antifa back when Nazis were marching in Atlanta," Trish said with pride. "We believed the best way to fight these terrorists wasn't to rely on the cops but only on ourselves. Direct confrontation. Fire with fire. We knew you can't talk to them. You can't ignore them either. And you can't give them an inch. In Atlanta, they showed up with machine guns. The rest attacked us with clubs and shields. The cops were too scared to do anything." She offered a grim smile. "We stood our ground. I've been fighting back ever since. We held out in Tipton as long as we could. You think this is bad? This is nothing compared to what went on there. When the city fell, I made it here. I intend to go on resisting, and I'll never stop. Free Indy!"

The women pounded their tables and roared.

"Congress forever!" somebody called out.

"Wow," Maria said.

"Thank you, Trish," Abigail said. "How about you, Lisa?"

"My story isn't as exciting," the woman said with a shy smile. "I was a middle-class Democrat with an office job. I believed in the New Deal, Social Security, and Medicare. If everybody did better, I would do better. Otherwise, I cared about a woman's right to choose." She frowned and continued in a stronger voice, "Now I'm fighting for this. A safe place for women, where we answer to nobody and live in harmony with one another. I used to want things to go back to the way they were, but not anymore. I want a revolution."

Hannah's heart pounded as the crowd broke into wild cheering again.

Abigail smiled in her direction. "Hannah?"

She wilted under their stares. "I'm Hannah."

"Say it loud and proud, sister," Abigail said. "This is a safe place."

"I'm Hannah," she repeated. "I came here to find a home."

The women cheered even louder as she sat back down. She covered her face to hide her tears. Maria patted her back and told her she'd said just the right thing.

The shelter had begun to feel like home. Now they were leaving. Every time she thought she stood on solid ground, it dropped out from under her.

"We're thankful to have you with us, sisters," Abigail said. "Now let's get this hootenanny started. Enjoy a little of what we're fighting for. Meeting adjourned."

The women cleared the tables from the center of the room while others took out musical instruments, guitars and horns and a mix of bongo and conga drums. They launched into a salsa beat that had a rich, carefree flavor. The floor quickly filled with swaying bodies and acrid smoke. At the tables, women laughed and passed bottles and cigarettes.

Hannah stood and crossed the room to Abigail's table.

The commander smiled. "So you decided to stay after all."

"I was waiting for you to ask like you said."

"It was up to you," Abigail said. "You had a few days to see what we're about. When you came to today's meeting, you told me you wanted to be a part of it."

"But why do we have to leave?"

"We go where the cause needs us. The central committee voted on it. We're all volunteers, but while you're here, we expect total commitment."

"I wanted this to be my home."

The commander smiled. "You're Free Women now, sister. Whenever you're with us, you're home."

Maria appeared at her side and pulled on her arm. "Come on!"

Hannah followed her into the dance area. The other girls were already dancing, faces flushed and grinning. The music flowed through her, then picked her up and carried her along. She closed her eyes and swayed until she became lost in the rhythm.

While she danced, she allowed herself to remember everything she'd lost. Mom babying her while she stayed home from school with the flu. Dad explaining how the tomato plants in their garden grew. Alex messing up her hair to distract her from crying after she crashed her bike. Talking to friends at lunch, comparing likes and dislikes, subjecting one another to merciless teasing about their crushes.

She missed all these things and said goodbye to them one by one, tears streaming down her face while she danced surrounded by women who would fight to protect her, women she'd help to win their war, because from each according to her ability, to each according to her need.

She opened her eyes. The dance area thinned then crowded again as the song changed but never ended. Hannah bounced on the changes and flowed with each new direction. *The music keeps changing, but I'm still here.* Her heart swelled to bursting as she sensed a profound truth she couldn't put into words.

At last, sweaty and tired, Hannah left the girls on the floor to get some space and air. Pulling on her coat, she mounted the stairs and walked up to the roof access door.

The late afternoon sun glared across the buildings, producing startling contrasts of light and dark. The tip of a burning cigarette flared at the other side of the roof.

"Hi," Hannah said.

A militiawoman was sitting on the ground with her back against the parapet. "You should probably stay low."

"Oh. Right." She crouched and scurried over to sit next to her. "I saw you at the shooting range. You're a sniper."

"I'm Grace," the woman said with clarity, as if correcting her.

"I'm Hannah. Don't you want to join the party?"

The cigarette tip flared again. "Maybe I will, one of these days. What about you? Taking a break?"

Hannah didn't know how to put it into words. "I was feeling something and wanted to think about it. Something really big. It's good."

"It's love," the sniper said.

"I don't know. Maybe."

"I used to shoot for sport. Now I kill men I don't even know."

"They're bad men," Hannah offered.

"I don't hate them. I hate killing. Do you know why I do it anyway?"

Hannah had heard the rebel snipers killed for money. Grace Kim didn't strike her as somebody who'd kill for a paycheck.

"You kill them so they stop killing us."

"That's what I do, not why I do it."

Hannah tried to remember all the rhetoric she'd been told. "The billionaires want all the money. The fascists want to make laws that are mean. That's the cause."

Grace smiled. "Close but no cigar."

"What then?"

"Love."

The idea sent a shiver through her. "Love?"

"I do what I hate for what I love," Grace told her. "These women, this city. People I don't even know. So they can live in a safe, just world. That's the cause."

"Wow," Hannah said.

"That's the cause for me. You have to decide for yourself what it means to you. Do you fight for others out of love, do you fight against the rebels out of hate, or do you fight for yourself just to survive?"

"I was fighting for me, I guess," Hannah said. "Now I don't know."

" 'You are what your deep, driving desire is.' That's a quote from one of the oldest books in the world. 'As your desire is, so is your will. As your will is, so is your deed. As your deed is, so is your destiny.' "

"I like it. What's it mean?"

"What you want most will make you the woman you will become."

"I want to be like you," Hannah blurted. "A sniper."

"Please don't say that."

"But you're..." She was embarrassed to say it. *Cool.*

"I've killed more than a dozen men looking them right in the eye through my scope. What I am keeps me up at night. You want to do your part for the cause?"

"Yes." Hannah was light-headed now, her mind swirling with big ideas.

"Grow up in a sane world when this is all over. Keep fighting for yourself. Survive long enough for everything to be normal again."

Do whatever it takes. Her mother's words. Hannah wondered what a normal life would even look like after all this. Another change, maybe the biggest yet.

The sniper ground out her cigarette and gazed at the door at the other side of the roof, which led to warmth, community, connection.

"Some of us will have the chance to live a normal life again," she said. "The rest of us I'm not sure will be able to go back."

EIGHTEEN

Aubrey pedaled past weary protesters on her way to the office. Her head buzzed. *Child soldiers. In America.*

She'd seen kids pitching in here and there, helping with chores and the like. Never, though, carrying weapons. Gabrielle had explained it was the same thing. Either way, children were directly participating in the war.

It was a hell of a story.

Besides that, she had UNICEF's meeting with the Quakers. That and maybe one or more tearful stories about the Peace Office reuniting families across the contact line. In Indy, nobody said, "It's going to be all right," like they did in the first days of the war. The city had run out of platitudes along with everything else. But they craved good news, which still offered hope.

Eckert would eat it up. Babysitting Gabrielle Justine had turned out to deliver more than the chance to drive a car with heat and a radio. She still regretted her outburst. Garcia had covered the demonstration. He was a sharp reporter. She couldn't do everything. And it appeared she'd have plenty to show for her time.

Still buzzing, Aubrey braked her bicycle and called to a young woman walking past. The protest had ended; they were all going home. Maybe she could pull a few quotes for Garcia.

"*Indy Chronicle*," she said. "Can I ask you a few questions about the rally?"

The woman trudged over with a sign reading, ALL OR NOTHING. Her name was Zoey Tapper, she was an anarchist, and she was protesting partition.

"The governor is as much our enemy as the fascists," Zoey said. Aside from a swollen belly suggesting pregnancy, she was thin and had delicate features. "You can't separate the war from the revolution."

Aubrey started writing on her pad. "What revolution are we talking about?"

"People like you look at anarchists as people who want to smash stuff. That's a form of direct action, but that's not what we're about."

"People like me, huh?" Aubrey found the woman's assumption presumptuous but not far off the mark. A lot of young people struck her as all fight and no substance. "What are you about then?"

"We want everything owned by the people, with no central government."

Now that sounded like millennial bullshit. Aubrey found their ability to be both naive and judgmental grating. "No government? Do you think that would work here in America?"

Zoey laughed. "Seriously? Look at the militias. The trade unions taking over the factories. The communes. It's already happening, and it works. The city and the police and the bourgeois want everything to go back to normal. That's not what I'm fighting for." She patted her swollen belly. "I want my baby to grow up in a world that's just."

Aubrey wondered how anybody could be happy about bringing a life into the world right now. "How far along are you?"

"Six months!"

"Congratulations." Aubrey might be able to turn that into a story on its own: Protester fighting for change brings new life into dangerous world. "What about democracy?"

"We believe in real democracy. People making decisions together at the grassroots level. In the workplace, where we've never had it before. Liberty—"

Her head exploded across Aubrey's notepad.

Aubrey fell backward and hit the road hard, her legs tangled in her bike. Screams and pounding footsteps filled the air. Then another rolling shot.

She kicked at the bike and scrambled on all fours to the sidewalk. There, she sat huddled against a wall hugging her knees and shivering with adrenaline.

Gloved hands reached for her. She batted them away.

"Let me help you," a voice said. "You're hit."

She pawed at her bloody coat. No bullet hole. "It's not mine. I'm okay!"

"You're lucky," the man said. "Jesus. Who was she?"

Zoey lay crumpled on the road, eyes turned toward Aubrey even in death, as if waiting for her to come back so she could finish her answer. Something about liberty.

"I didn't really know her," Aubrey said.

Just another girl. Just some poor, idealistic girl who wanted to bring another life into the world in the midst of so much madness.

Aubrey still clutched her notepad. She wiped blood off it with the sleeve of her coat. As it all sunk in, she realized how close she'd come to dying. She cursed her own stupidity. In Indy, you never stopped moving as fast as possible until you reached cover. She'd taken chances and shortcuts without harm for so long, she'd begun to think it could never happen to her.

When a bomb went off, she was one of the few who ran toward the blast. As press, she was supposed to be Switzerland with eyes, but bullets didn't care about one's neutrality. More than one reporter had already died in the fighting.

In her mind's eye, Zoey's brains splashed across her pad.

"Oh, God." She hugged her ribs. "Oh, shit."

Another few inches, and the bullet would have punched through her face. She tried to remember what Zoey had been doing while she'd been scribbling her notes. Had the woman moved at the last second, blocking the sniper's shot? Had Aubrey been the intended target?

Bad enough, knowing a hostile army surrounded the city. It became truly horrifying when you realized one of them was trying to kill *you*.

Seeing Zoey Tapper lying dead on the street reminded her that no matter how experienced she got at surviving, no matter how much hutzpah she showed toward danger, one day her luck would run out.

NINETEEN

After breakfast, Alex crawled into his tent and sat on his sleeping bag to clean his rifle. He removed the magazine, locked the bolt to the rear, and eyed the chamber to make sure a round wasn't stuck in it. Then he released the bolt and set the rifle to safe.

The first thing the Liberty Tree had taught him was the chain of command. The second was how to shoot and take care of a firearm. God forbid he fail to respect either one. A part of the job was keeping his AR-15 clean and lubed.

Like everything about this war, rifle cleaning was cool the first time but then became just another mind-numbing ritual. Between the cold, hunger, stink, sickness, and endless hours spent with the same guys, war had turned out to suck even harder than high school. Never enough sleep, always some bullshit thing to do.

He pulled his backpack toward him and opened a pocket. Inside, he kept his brushes, rods, solvent, and cleaning patches. Wind rippled along the tent's forest-green nylon walls like a reflection of his wavering nerves. The squad was going on patrol into No Man's Land today, and he was going with them.

Jack poked his head in and sniffed. "Jeez. Did you cut one in here?"

"Wait." Alex angled his rear and let out a loud grunt. "Nope, I got nothing."

The kid laughed. "Your first time out today, huh."

"Yeah. Well, second, if you count my solo recon."

"You scared?"

He'd been terrified during the recon but didn't think it would be as bad going out with the squad around him. He wondered if that was part of the reason for the initiation test. "No. Maybe. I don't know. More nervous than scared. Really nervous, actually."

"You don't have to be either one, bro."

"I guess." Before Alex could clean the gun, he had to take it apart. He took a punch from the box and used it to push the take-down pin, which separated the rifle's upper and lower receivers. "Are you just going to sit there and watch me do this?"

Oh yeah, privacy. War meant kissing that goodbye too.

Jack disappeared for a moment before poking his head back inside. He said in a stage whisper, "What I'm trying to ask is if you ever get high."

Alex stopped what he was doing. "Does the Pope crap in the woods?"

The kid laughed again. "What?"

"You could have asked before I took the pin out. Wait for me."

"I'll be right out here."

Alex put his AR-15 back together and returned the magazine to the well. He'd clean it later. He crawled outside.

He wondered where Jack had found a place one could actually be alone. "Who's your supplier?"

The kid threw him a look that warned him to zip it. "Come on, let's bounce."

Jack led him through the encampment, which bustled with uniformed men and women fetching water, brewing coffee, and hanging clothes to dry. They walked behind a house that had been hit by an Angel mortar strike. The blast had sheared off the western wall and revealed its insides like a giant dollhouse. A broken-down, rusting horse trailer sat on bricks in the backyard.

Jack opened the trailer's door and went in.

Alex shook his head. "Are you kidding? Gross."

The creaking door slammed shut behind him. Jack was already rolling a reefer on the floor amid dried bits of straw. The trailer smelled faintly of horse dung. Weak winter light leaked in through the slatted windows.

"You like it, bro?" the kid said.

"You know, they use this trailer as a morgue. They put bodies in here."

Jack licked his cigarette and sealed it. "Which is why it's a perfect spot to fire up a fatty, dumbass. Nobody comes out here unless somebody croaks."

He lit the joint and sucked on it before passing it over. Alex toked and held the smoke in his lungs before blowing it out with a smile. It smelled like skunk piss, but he didn't mind.

He passed it back. "Where'd you get it?"

"You won't believe this. Sergeant Shook."

"Oh." Alex hated that guy. Shook was every bully he'd ever known in school rolled into one.

"All I have to do is find him something when we're out on patrol. Any kind of jewelry. The wedding ring I found in that house bought me this whole bag of weed."

"You need a partner in crime?"

Jack coughed out a cloud of smoke. "I was hoping you'd want in. Two's better than one."

The front line hadn't moved in six months. Neither side had much in the way of artillery or an air force. The libs had more fighters, while the patriots had more firepower and supplies. Stalemate.

The patriots rotated on and off the line, sent out patrols, and skirmished in the ruined neighborhoods. Otherwise, they sat around and talked about how stupid liberals were and what America would be like after the final victory.

Alex welcomed anything that would take the edge off the constant boredom and anxiety. "Cool. Count me in."

"Patrols are so much easier when you're stoned."

Alex closed his eyes, feeling good now. "You have it all figured out, Jack."

"Oh yeah, bro. I'm woke."

They laughed.

Alex said, "You ever do online gaming?"

"Yeah, but I'm more a role-player—"

The door creaked open. Alex blinked at the rush of light.

Tom shook his head. "You kids are a special kind of dumb. Put that shit away."

Alex's heart settled to a lesser gallop. If Mitch had caught him lighting up, there'd be an ass kicking. Tom was a wild card but okay for the most part.

Jack pinched off the end of the joint and pocketed it for later. "It's creepy the way you always seem to know what I'm doing."

"Because I pay attention, Combat Jack. Now get your ass in gear. We're moving out."

The boys grabbed their weapons and followed him into the back of a tattoo parlor, where the rest of the squad had congregated around Mitch.

"Listen up," the sergeant said. "For this patrol, we're going to proceed along the alley next to the liquor store until we make contact. Then we egress in stages. This is a practice run, a chance to gather intel before the big push in three days."

The eight fighters in his squad nodded and checked their weapons.

"Three things to remember at all times," Mitch added. "First is we're fighting in somebody's house. We call it No Man's Land, but people still live in this area. You see somebody armed, you shoot.

Otherwise, this ain't a free-fire zone. We're here to change things and win hearts and minds, not massacre the locals."

The men nodded as they continued their last-minute equipment checks. They acted like they'd heard this speech before at the start of many patrols.

"Second, IEDs are always a worry, so I want good dispersion out there. And lastly, we probably still have the Indy 300 ahead of us. I don't need to remind you they're good. Say what you want when you're off the field, but respect them while you're on it. Ready?"

"Hooah," the men shouted, locked and loaded.

"Donnie, you take point." Mitch set his eyes on Alex. "Kid, you'll provide security in the rear on this run."

"But not mine, homo," Grady said.

Alex reddened as the men laughed at him. Always this bullshit.

"Let's go," Mitch ordered.

The squad filed outside in an atmosphere of excitement. Even after a year, they never tired of this. They loved it.

Wearing Ray-Bans, Sergeant Shook grinned at them. "Get some." He blocked Alex's path. "First combat patrol, huh, Mary?"

"Yeah." Alex added a nervous chuckle because he never knew what the guy was going to do next.

"Just because Mitch gave you a gun don't make you one of us. Think fast."

He faked a punch at Alex's groin, making him double over.

"Sergeant Shook," growled Mitch. "You are stepping on my op."

"Just kidding around with my buddy here."

"Go kid around somewhere else."

"Oh yeah?" Again the psycho grin. "And if I don't?"

Mitch's face darkened as he strode up to the giant and leaned in.

"I'll fuck you up," he said in a quiet voice, though Alex heard it. "Like I did on the road to Indy."

Shook smiled down at the soldier while his eyes took on a murderous gleam. He shot a look at Alex, who turned away to mind his own business. His squad slowly rose to their feet and fingered their weapons.

"Hello, men," a voice said.

Alex stiffened and saluted.

"At ease, soldiers," Lieutenant Taylor said. "What's the word?"

Shook smiled into Mitch's glare. "Alpha was just getting set to show us how to do a combat patrol."

Taylor was a rich donor's son. He commanded the platoon but spent most of his time in a heated RV behind the lines, which he called his headquarters.

"That's right, sir," Mitch said.

"Outstanding," Taylor said. "Good hunting, gentlemen."

Mitch gave the lieutenant a look that was difficult to read. Then he gave Shook one that wasn't. "Let's go, Alpha. Move your asses."

The squad filed into a house that would serve as the patrol's staging point. Mitch went upstairs to take a final look at No Man's Land. The militiamen milled around exploring, though there wasn't much to see. The place had been cleaned out. Bits and pieces of somebody's life littered the warped and filthy carpet, broken plates and a bowling shoe and a few dusty photographs.

Jack sat with his back to the wall. "That guy is nuts."

Alex parked next to him. He wished they could get blazed again. His buzz from the poor-quality pot was already fading. "You mean Sergeant Shook?"

"Yeah."

Tom said, "You can't choose your family. You can't choose your army either."

Alex thought the militia was more like high school than a family. While they revered the official chain of command, the men mostly followed a few alpha dogs. Mitch and Shook's hatred went deeper than basic rivalry, though. There was history there that had caused bad blood between them, though Alex couldn't guess what had happened on the way to Indy.

Grady nudged Alex with his boot. Middle-aged and overweight, he was already wheezing from the exercise. "Watch and learn, kid. You do this right, we'll see about getting you a scope for that rifle."

"I'd be happy if you guys let me have a beer." The squad always partied after a successful combat patrol.

The men laughed.

"Kid's smarter than he looks. You ever been laid, kid?"

Alex reddened. He'd never passed second base but brazened it out with a white lie. "Came close once."

Another laugh.

"I'm fifteen years old," he reminded them.

"Well, first time you shoot a lib, we'll get you squared away," Grady said.

Alex scanned their grinning faces. What were they talking about?

"There's a big house behind the line," Jack explained. "Girls."

"Tiffany will get him manned up," Tom said.

The militiamen hooted.

Mitch stomped downstairs. "We're heading into a combat zone. That means shut up, get in line, and watch your sectors."

"Yes, Sergeant." The men jostled into formation.

"Now move out," he growled. "Let's do this."

Then he surprised Alex by tossing him a wink.

TWENTY

Eckert's office was a chaotic mess of file cabinets, stacks of paper, and multiple In and Out boxes. Sitting at his cluttered desk, he gaped at Aubrey with his good eye. "What the hell happened to you? Is that blood on your face?"

She handed over her copy. "It's not mine."

He rubbed his hands for warmth before accepting it. Her editor had been a handsome man before the war thinned him out and ground him down. He wore an eye patch, the result of taking a club to the face during the street fighting in the early days of the troubles.

"So what happened?" he said.

Aubrey sat in one of his visitor chairs and gestured to the papers. "It's all there. UNICEF, and another story about a sniper shooting."

He started reading. "You've been a busy beaver."

Days of running, two hours of typing. A reporter devoted very little time to writing. She spent most of her time finding the story and sticking with it. Being at the right place at the right time, as close as possible to the action.

That's how Eckert ended up with fuzzy vision in one eye and she almost ate a bullet on Meridian. Journalism was now a hazardous profession in the USA.

"Oh, I have something else for you." She reached into her backpack and tossed a carton of Marlboros onto his desk. "Courtesy of our friends at the UN. A thank-you gift for forcing one of your peons to act as their fixer."

Eckert blinked and snatched it up, her copy forgotten. He ran it under his nose as if he could smell the sweet tobacco through the packaging. "See this, my friend? This is how you butter up an editor. Watch and learn."

"I'm happy I won't have to smell those lousy roll-ups you've been smoking."

Eckert tore the carton open like a Christmas present. The packs spilled out. He picked one up and unwrapped it with glee.

"Look at you," she said. "Why don't you quit while you're alive?"

"Because then I'd start drinking again."

The editor lit up in violation of a building regulation nobody cared about anymore. Like the medical professions, Indy's psychologists worked nonstop to serve Indy's population of walking wounded. Everybody was a bag of nervous tics, suppressed memories, and raw need. For Eckert, smoking got him through the day. He made it look good. Aubrey knew better than to try one, though. She'd get hooked in an instant, and it was a habit she couldn't afford.

"After you're done reading, I've got two more ideas in the pipeline," she said.

"You're going to have one hell of a resume when this is all over."

That wasn't why she worked so hard. The job was her bad habit. Her fix.

"Not that I—"

She stopped. Eckert was reading. He produced his dreaded red pen and started marking up her copy, shaking his head.

"And the word *its* doesn't always have an apostrophe," he said. "Overall, this UNICEF story is pretty solid. What's she like? This Gabrielle Justine?"

Aubrey flashed to the UNICEF worker at the clinic, quaking

with rage as she demanded information about the use of children in the war. "Competent. Fragile. Totally hot. You'd fall in love with her."

"It's a war. I fall in love with everybody."

Eckert started in on her next story about the sniper shooting. His smile, left over from his witty remark, evaporated as he read.

He finished his cigarette and ground it out in his ashtray. "I can't run this."

She'd written eight hundred words on what it was like to see the bullet strike the person next to you instead of you. "I know it's not my usual—"

" 'The main thing that held America together so long was common ideals,' " he read aloud. " 'Equality and opportunity. Democratic government. The Constitution. Without them, America is just another multiethnic empire. A bunch of tribes. In the past decade, environmental depletion and income inequality created scarcity and hardship. For many, America stopped delivering on its ideals. Instead of solving these problems, we retreated into tribalism. Fed by alternate news sources, we ended up living in divergent realities and different stories. Competing ideas of what America is about. Marsh's election was a symptom, not the disease. Two Americas, but if Zoey was right, maybe more. Maybe many more. The war awakened something primal in us. The war may end, but we may never come together again unless we rediscover that unifying idea of what America is.' "

He set it down. "It's compelling, but it ain't news."

"We run tons of opinion and analysis."

"Yeah, from experts. People who spent their whole life studying politics. I have expert analysis coming out my ass. What people need are facts, and what I'm lacking is trained reporters. I need you to deliver facts."

"Sometimes, it works best to tell people's stories," Aubrey said.

"That's how you make the reader care. One person's story can tell the story of an entire war."

"You can do that while remaining objective," he told her. "We're called the fourth estate because we're the fly on the wall. You made yourself the story in this piece. You went through a horrific experience and needed to purge it. I've got reporters who want to turn my newspaper into their diary."

He handed back the story. "Give me facts I can print. You said you have two other stories on the go. What else have you got?"

"For one, newsflash: You're an asshole."

He shrugged. "Noted."

Aubrey told him about the Peace Office's work and her visit to the clinic in Haughville, where she saw child soldiers.

"Child soldiers," Eckert said. "In America. Sweet baby Jesus. Give that one everything you've got."

"I'm not sure how much I can give it. I'm on UNICEF's agenda."

"And the hot UNICEF lady has a car and gas, right? Put two and two together. Run over two birds. Just make sure you get both sides."

"Both sides?"

"Yeah," he grated. "That's what reporters do. They cover both sides. See if you can get any rebels to talk to you. Work your contacts."

Aubrey sat back. Eckert's request was like asking her to seek out the sniper who'd almost killed her and question him about his attempt on her life. "You know how they feel about the press. And African Americans. Anybody who doesn't look and think exactly like them."

The rebel factions broke down into White supremacist blood-and-soil types, religious zealots, Ayn Randians, and patriots. None of them liked her.

"If we run a story on child soldiers in Indy, the president's media will make hay out of it," the editor explained. "We need to show this is an American problem. Figure out a way to get somebody on the other side to talk. Make it work. We do this thing right, it could change things. As for the story, it could get syndicated. It might even get Pulitzer interest."

The Pulitzer Prize, the reporter's holy grail.

Aubrey tried to suppress a wide smile but was only partly successful. "I'll see what I can do. In the meantime, you keep this to yourself."

"Scout's honor."

She pursed her lips to show him what she thought of his honor.

He lit another Marlboro and smiled. "The reporter isn't the story, but the story is always the reporter. What the reporter wants, and how far she'll go to get it."

TWENTY-ONE

Across the street, a line of derelict houses terminated at a looted store called Global Liquors. Automatic weapons fire had shattered its windows and pockmarked its walls. The squad dashed across the grimy snow and found cover behind the building. Alex followed, his head swirling.

For months, he'd eaten Second Platoon's crap. All the hazing had a point, which was to force him to man up. *Pain is your friend*, the militiamen liked to tell him. Mitch would have called Mom and Dad's loving parenting part of the pussification of America, where everybody won a participation trophy without having earned anything.

Mostly, however, Alex found the hazing pointless and mean. To survive, he'd learned to read everybody's mood, especially the sergeants, and in particular Shook, who was like hanging around a violent and alcoholic cousin.

He'd thought Mitch sticking up for him before the patrol had more to do with bad blood between him and Shook more than anything else, but now he was starting to think it was because Mitch looked after his own. The way the guys talked to Alex back at the staging point clinched it. They'd never talked to him like that before.

He'd graduated to the bottom of a much smaller totem pole.

The soldiers ahead of him leapfrogged up the alley. Whatever they'd been before, they'd found a higher purpose here, fighting their civil war with a mix of conviction and cosplay. Alex suddenly regarded them with something like kinship. He still didn't buy into everything they talked about—the globalist Marxist cabal, Agenda 21, the global warming hoax, the New World Order, and the rest of it. He didn't even understand half of it. But he'd try to believe, if only to belong.

He certainly looked the part now. He wore a six-point light assault rig over his camouflage jacket. His rifle attached to it using a tactical sling, which helped ensure steady and accurate shooting. The webbed harness held five magazines, a canteen, and a radio.

In short, he looked pretty badass, though the only people around to admire him were guys dressed just like him. Janice Brewer, his old crush back in Sterling, might as well have been on the moon.

The militiamen raised fists as a halt order passed down the line. Alex turned to see if anybody was sneaking up on him. Nobody there. By the time he turned back, the squad was moving again, fire team A bounding while B provided security.

No contacts so far. Mitch said today's patrol was a practice run to probe the Indy 300's line. In three days, they'd be doing it for real. A big offensive, maybe the last—

Gunfire rent the air.

Alex dove behind a dumpster. His bowels liquefying, he peered out. His squad had melted into the scenery. The firing built to a steady roar. Bullets ripped past him. He gawked at it all, mesmerized.

Holy crap, it was so cool. Like being in a movie.

Men shouted over his radio. Mitch gave orders. Jack darted across the alley and disappeared. The squad was spreading out to probe the enemy line.

Rounds pinged off Alex's dumpster. He ducked back behind it laughing, amped up and breathing hard. That's why these guys did it. Now he understood. It was all a big game. Every sense tingled, fully alive. A whole different kind of high.

He wished the libs would come test him. He went prone and peered out again at the empty alley. Muzzle flashes winked in the distance. The air had gone hazy with smoke. Alex aimed down his barrel using iron sights and squeezed off a few bursts, whooping.

He barely had any idea what he was firing at. In the movies, the hero always saw who he was shooting, but this was real. Mitch called it fire superiority. Throw enough bullets at the enemy so they can't shoot back.

Voices on the radio. Any moment, the squad would break contact and call it a day. All Alex had to do was keep his eyes peeled so they didn't get flanked.

He sat up with a jolt. He was supposed to be watching their six.

When he turned, he spotted a Black man carrying a big hunting rifle. Indy 300.

The man was sprinting right at him.

Alex watched dumbly as his brain struggled to process it. Then alarm shot through him like electric current.

The man was *coming to kill him.*

Fight or flight. Nowhere to run. They raised their weapons at the same time.

The guy was shouting at him in a strong, loud voice. Alex yelled back at him to surrender, but the words caught in his throat and came out in a weak, high-pitched whine. He was shaking now, unsure he could even shoot.

Time stretched into eternity.

He started to raise his hands in surrender. The man stepped back at the sudden movement, his rifle discharging with a heart-stopping bang. Alex flinched. The bullet cracked against the dumpster and whirred away.

He was already firing back as if his gun had a mind of its own. The rifle snarled and jolted in his grip. He found his voice in a scream as he held down the trigger and drained the magazine in seconds.

The man turned to run. Red mist puffed from his back. He spun like a top as the bullets tore into him. The rifle flew from his hands. He hit the snow hard.

Eternity collapsed into a single instant.

Alex frantically patted his body looking for a wound. He was okay. The Indy 300 fighter lay spread-eagled. With an anguished moan, Alex staggered toward his victim, oblivious to the firefight still going on in the alley.

He fell to his knees. The man gaped back at him, face twisted in a wide-eyed grimace of pain and terror. His jacket had smoking holes in it. The force of the shots had knocked his hat off. Blood spray colored the snow.

"I'm sorry," Alex said. "I'm really sorry."

The enemy fighter gasped for air. Rapid, shallow breaths.

Footsteps pounded behind him.

Jack yanked his tube mask down, breathing clouds of vapor. "Holy crap, Alex."

"I didn't mean it! He shot at me."

"Yeah." The kid stared at the dying man. "I hear you."

More footsteps behind. Tom shouldered Alex out of the way. He pulled out his med kit and pressed wads of gauze against the wounds.

Mitch approached. "We got hostiles on our six. Keep it moving."

"This man needs our help," Alex said.

"His people will take care of him."

Tom stood. "He's gone."

Alex stepped back. The world swam in his eyes. He couldn't stop shaking. "I didn't mean to. I didn't. I'm really sorry."

Mitch gripped his shoulder. "You did good."

"He shot at me first!"

"Whatever you're feeling, save it for later. We have to move out."

Whatever he was feeling.

Relief. Accomplishment. Sadness.

A terrifying sense that it had been way too easy to shoot a human being.

That this wasn't a game after all.

Grady smiled. "We tell the kid we'll get him laid if he shoots a lib, and look what he does."

"Shut up, Grady," Tom said.

"I was just saying—"

"Say another word and I'll knock you flat." Mitch's eyes bored into Alex's. "You're all right, kid. We're moving out now. Got it?"

Alex shuddered. "Okay. Yeah. I'm good."

The men nodded at him before running off one by one. Jack lingered a moment to pat his back in sympathy or approval or both.

Alex was one of them now. He'd earned their respect.

He wondered if gaining it was worth losing his own.

TWENTY-TWO

Streetlights across Mile Square winked on to emit a weak glow. Aubrey pedaled faster, not wanting to miss out on the daily ration of electricity. Most of the city's juice went to keep essential services going. In the evening, however, everybody got to use it for a short time.

Along the way home, she thought about the impossible task Eckert had given her. The impossible question he wanted her to ask Gabrielle Justine. She was sitting on a big story, a story that could have a real impact. She had it all to herself. But first she had to confirm whether the rebels were also using child soldiers.

Which might get her killed.

The Reds regularly targeted the mainstream press, which they regarded as part of their pantheon of liberal evils. To many of them, anything to the left of Fox News was Marxist propaganda. In their minds, people like her had started the war by turning the public against President Marsh.

In the early days of the troubles, every network covered the massive Occupy protest at the National Mall in Washington. Just before masked gunmen began shooting into the crowd, they targeted the journalists first. One by one, the camera feeds covering the protest died. They'd been shooting at the press ever since.

It was hard to be objective when one of the sides in the conflict you were covering considered you a combatant and wanted you dead. People who would put you in prison or against a wall if they won the war.

The usual armed guard stood watch in the building lobby. He let Aubrey pass and went back to stomping his feet to keep warm. She hauled her bike up the stairs. The third-floor hallway was smoky and smelled like boiled food and waste.

Back in her apartment, she turned on a single table lamp and plugged in her cell phone and laptop to charge. She opened her music app and started a classical playlist. There was something about war that made her yearn for traditional forms, which she now found soothing, almost spiritual.

The *Spartacus* overture washed over her. It sounded like civilization. A reminder of humanity's incredible capacity for beauty amid so much savagery.

Aubrey went through the day in professional denial of the horrors surrounding her. Earlier, she'd watched a doctor saw off a man's foot in a clinic filled with misery. A pregnant girl's head exploded right in front of her. It was only now, in the privacy of her apartment with her music, she allowed herself to strip away her armor and process it all.

She stood weeping with her back to the wall. *That poor girl*, she thought. *That poor stupid girl who thought she could change the world.* Murdered in broad daylight on a busy street.

Once, that would have been big news, but the war had reduced individual tragedy to the mundane. *Dog bites man* wasn't news while *man bites dog* was, but everybody was biting dogs these days. Now if fifty Zoey Tappers had been killed in a single attack, maybe a hundred...

She caught herself with a start and checked her watch. She barely had enough time to prepare and eat her dinner. She forced her feelings aside like Pandora in reverse, putting all the world's evils back in their box.

Aubrey lived in her kitchen now, which was away from the front windows, their fragile panes crisscrossed with electrical tape. She'd seen what flying glass did to the human face. The rebels didn't have artillery, but the First Angels had two mortars they liked to fire randomly at the city and airport. They were evangelicals who believed if there wasn't a God, humans would go on a rampage of murder and rape. It turned out it wasn't God holding them back but the police and laws everybody once agreed to obey, laws the war was busy rewriting.

She had a bug-out bag in easy reach in case she needed to leave in a hurry. Two-liter 7UP bottles and milk jugs filled with water. Bathtub down the hall acting as a reserve water supply, which she refilled during random times water service was available. Coleman stove and half-full propane bottle. Mattress standing on one end against the nearest window.

Through careful rationing, Aubrey had stretched her last aid package. She measured out some rice and hoped to never have to eat it or beans again after the war ended. She'd grown to hate it along with the garbage building up in the streets, the lack of electricity and water, the snipers and general hopelessness.

While the rice boiled, she finished a can of tuna and saved the oil for her homemade lamps. Another life hack. Drench some cotton with oil in a coffee mug and light it, and you produced a sputtering yellow light, along with grime that coated everything. Add a little salt to the oil, and it burned longer.

She finished her meager meal and dragged her mattress into the kitchen. She'd sleep fully clothed, covered in blankets, her breath fogging the cold air. Alone again. Maybe she'd swing by the Peace Office sooner than later and bat her eyelashes at Paul. Aubrey couldn't afford love—not real love, not during this war—but she often missed the touch of a man. Touch and body heat. Body heat and blissful forgetting.

There was a time before the shooting started when she was a

normal thirty-something reporter who worked and played hard. She'd regarded her job with gratitude and idealism, though it was just that, a job. When the troubles came, one by one her friends disappeared. Her more conservative friends left first, heading for the small towns and farms where they said the real America still existed. Her more liberal friends became increasingly distant when she didn't mirror their growing radicalism. Others died along the way from fighting or sickness.

Aubrey had found herself the way she was now, alone with her job, which for her had become a far greater cause than the opposite sides of this conflict. That cause was digging into the war's open wounds to yank out the truth like bits of shrapnel.

The power went out and plunged the room into darkness. She heard groaning from other apartments, somebody cursing. Only an hour of electricity today. She struck a match and lit one of her oil lamps to produce a struggling yellow light. She stared at its glow and thought again about Zoey Tapper patting her belly just before the sniper round tore through her skull.

The girl had wanted to change the world and raise a new life in it. So much hope among so many horrors, struck down by being in the wrong place at the wrong time. Her hope had died along with her, and her baby too, the hope of the future.

Aubrey was done crying. She felt a stirring in her chest again, that unsettling feeling of wanting to *do* something, something important like Gabrielle was trying to do. She'd thought that writing about Zoey's death would somehow accomplish that. She'd wanted to reach beyond the facts and connect with the reader's emotions. Put their collective scream into words printed in black and white. Express an even bigger truth about the war.

But Eckert was right. That wasn't what the *Indy Chronicle* was about. And screaming wouldn't change anything.

She *could* do something. She could write her story about the child soldiers. Put a harsh spotlight on it. Stir an international outcry.

At one time, America didn't give a crap what the world thought. Now the world gave aid that kept a huge number of Americans alive another day. Important countries would pressure the warring sides to stop using children as weapons. It would change things. Fewer children would die. Even better, if the militias stopped using children, it might shorten the war.

All she had to do was convince Gabrielle to let her drive out to the rebel lines. Which might get the UNICEF worker killed too.

Aubrey winced as she remembered Eckert's words. *What the reporter wants, and how far she'll go to get it.* She hated that she might be rationalizing putting Gabrielle in danger to get a story.

She inspected her gloomy, cold, grime-coated apartment. So many had lost everything, including their lives. What was her life worth? Why was she alive when so many died?

In the end, the job was all that Aubrey had. Helping the children, however, might make it all actually mean something. After seeing Zoey Tapper die from a random gunshot, the job wasn't enough for her. It wasn't enough for anybody unless it changed things for the better.

Maybe Gabrielle would let her use the car while staying behind. She decided to ask. Explain what she wanted and the risks in the harshest terms possible. But she'd ask.

Aubrey now had an even bigger cause than the one for which she'd already risked everything.

TWENTY-THREE

Wearing his customary cowboy hat, Ralph popped his head up from the trench to track a drone buzzing across the gray sky. Theirs or the enemy's, Mitch didn't know. If it stuck around too long, they'd shoot it down.

"Stay low, Colonel," he said. "You're offering a target."

Liberty Tree had drawn blood today. Sooner or later, the Indy 300 would come around looking for payback. Gunfire would shatter the silence before the libs disappeared like ghosts back into the ruins, the way they always did.

The drone flitted away and was gone.

"No more patrols until the offensive," Ralph said. "We kicked the hornet's nest. I want things nice and quiet for a while."

"I can live with that."

"Though I like hearing you bagged one today."

"The kid did all right," Mitch told him. "Popped his cherry."

Ralph risked another look at the houses across the street before returning with a wistful sigh. "Maybe I should go out with you sometime. Do my part."

"You're right where the fight needs you, sir."

"How's the kid doing with it?"

"Don't worry about him."

Tough love and training had molded Alex into a fighter. And something new in the militia, a man who fought for neither God nor country but instead merely to belong. Mitch hoped Ralph moved more of the teens like Alex and Jack up to combat status.

If things kept going as they were, he might have to. People in the rear were sick of the war, fighter enrollment was at a standstill, and what the Liberty Tree could pay was hardly worth the paper it was printed on thanks to inflation.

And the militia's wealthy donors, who wanted the war to end with the Constitutional Convention, had made it clear funding would be limited from here on out. If the Liberty Tree wanted more money, it had to produce results. Mitch knew these donors, not the president and certainly not the American people, were pulling the strings. They were bankrolling the entire militia network now. They'd been involved from the beginning, starting with the first bold moves that led to the war.

Teenagers, on the other hand, didn't expect payment. Mitch wished he had an army of Alex Millers. When the crony capitalist billionaires finally sold them out and cut a deal with their old pals in the Deep State, he'd be able to tell them to go to hell and keep fighting. They'd find out they weren't using him, he was using them and for a far nobler cause.

And he'd win. The Three Percenters had it right: Only a tiny fraction of Americans had fought in the revolution to kick out the British and start a new country. Victory didn't require a huge army, not when they had right on their side.

Mitch and Ralph squeezed through a break in the foundation wall of a church with a Mexican name. They clicked on flashlights. Upstairs, the worship area stood bare and empty, the pews and altar burned long ago for heat. Three militiamen played cards on the grimy carpet while a fourth—another teenager, barely fourteen and already a hard-ass—manned a machine gun at a window.

Ralph unfolded a gas station map. He motioned to a street.

"That's the main strategic route. West Walnut." He pointed out the window. "Right over there."

The offensive would step off in stages. First and Third Platoons would push east into Tibbs Court and neighboring alleys while Second Platoon would be mechanized and lying in wait. At 1000, they'd mount up and race down Walnut all the way to Belmont. There, they'd spread out toward the river and its vital bridges.

"We need more vehicles," Mitch said.

"They'll be here, and on time."

"Including a bulldozer."

"You'll have that too."

"We'd better, or we ain't going anywhere."

A wall of rubble barricaded Walnut. Without the bulldozer, the whole plan was useless. They'd be attacking on foot, which hardly made for a blitzkrieg.

What Mitch really wanted was one of the Army surplus vehicles the Feds used to sell local governments for policing. A big, fat MRAP armored vehicle, SHERIFF painted on the side, would be perfect. But the counties and towns had their hands full maintaining order and wouldn't give up anything so valuable.

He'd go to war with the army he had, not the one he wanted.

"If we succeed, we'll be in position to threaten both the city core and the libs' flank at Brickyard Crossing," the colonel added. "We do this right, we could change the strategic situation in Indy dramatically."

While Mitch had grown cynical about the war, he hadn't about its ideals, and now he couldn't help but be swept up in the boldness of the assault and reflect on the life that had prepared him for this great event.

After fighting for his country in Afghanistan, he'd come home numb to his family, easily provoked to rage, and unable to sleep. He'd treated his PTSD with alcohol, resulting in episodes where he'd get blackout drunk. It was a time of darkness and seething anger. Americans worshipped celebrities while real heroes died in faraway wars most people no longer cared about. Veterans lived under bridges while the government rolled out a red carpet for Muslim refugees. Mitch hardly recognized America anymore. At some point along the way, it had stopped being the great nation where his father had raised him. Snowflakes needing safe spaces, the liberal war on free speech, lazy welfare bums, no jobs with good wages.

Somewhere in that blur, his daughter, Jill, died from a heart defect, and after that, Abigail left him. He hit rock bottom. The Liberty Tree offered him a lifeline. It explained everything in black and white. He wasn't going crazy, the world was. The Tree told him he had a part to play in a righteous battle between good and evil. He quit drinking, found counseling for the PTSD, and readied his hands for war.

For years, he sat in living rooms with other men discussing the coming collapse and dictatorship. The Liberty Tree's policy was to never start a fight but make sure they could finish it. Still, the government would never act boldly; it would take away their freedoms one at a time. The monster had to be provoked. Some of the guys talked about knocking over banks and assassinating officials and blowing up buildings. They drank beer and trained in the woods. They debated actions and the timing of actions. Otherwise, they did a whole lot of nothing.

Then President Marsh said he would break the system. Stick it to the fat cats on Wall Street and liberals whose answer to everything was to blame America. Bring the boys home from overseas, tear up trading deals that were bleeding American industry, seal the borders against immigrants stealing American jobs, get rid of government intrusion in people's lives.

Mitch knew he didn't have long to wait anymore. When the Deep State launched its soft coup, he was ready.

"Hey," Ralph said. "You still with me?"

"This is the big one," Mitch said. "It's going to change everything."

Finally, the decisive battle he'd prayed for. The chance to achieve his purpose and make everything right again. Everything in his life had led up to this.

The colonel eyed him. "You're not to go into the core."

"I know," Mitch growled.

"Guerillas are in our rear wreaking havoc on our supply lines," the colonel said. "We think we control most of the state, but we don't. We have to be careful with what assets we have left. We can't just gamble everything on a roll of the dice. I need to know you understand that."

Mitch glimpsed the ghosts haunting the colonel. The man had gone into Indy with a hundred men and barely made it out with sixty. It wasn't just the war or the cause or even his goddamn donors he worried about. It was his honor and his drive to go on playing a leading part in something that gave him meaning.

"I understand completely," he said.

Held up by a fight at a gas station and then Sergeant Shook's idiocy on the road, Mitch had missed the final pell-mell drive into Indy and attack on city hall. Which in his mind was part of the problem. Ralph had gone for broke with only half his strength. The colonel hadn't been bold, he'd been rash, and they'd all paid for it. Now he was overcompensating.

When Mitch went into the core, he wouldn't make the same mistake.

Ralph eyed him. "Any questions? Ideas? You know I trust your judgment."

"The plan is solid. Getting through the street barricades is the hardest part. Make sure that damn dozer shows up."

"You'll have it."

"When we launch our attack, tell the other militias what we're doing. Keep it under your hat until then. Don't even tell the donors."

Ralph extended his hand. "You're the bedrock of this company, Mitch. We can't do it without you. I mean it."

They shook. Mitch returned to his squad. The boys were laughing around a Coleman stove set up in a dugout.

"Where's the kid?" he said.

Donnie grinned. "He's throwing up. One too many Old Styles."

"I didn't ask how he's doing. I asked you where he is."

The soldier pointed. "Over there, Sar'."

Mitch walked along the trench and found the kid retching into a bucket. "How you feeling, boy?"

"I'm not feeling anything at the moment, Sergeant."

"You did good today. You should be proud."

Alex spat. "Thanks."

"I know how you feel."

"I've never seen you drink," the kid slurred.

"I mean I shot four people while I was in the 'Stan."

"Oh."

"My first was during an ambush near Bazbek. As we neared the village, its lights went out. We knew we were in for some shit. The Taliban fired at us from concealed positions. I turned around, and there was this kid flanking us with an RPG. He was about your age."

Alex pushed the bucket away and sat panting with his back against the trench's frozen earth wall. "What did you do?"

"I shot him without even thinking about it. At the time, he was just a target."

"Jeez. Yeah. It was the same for me."

"I didn't feel a damn thing until it was over," Mitch said. "Then I felt like Superman. Then I felt like shit. After that, nothing again. You know why?"

Alex shook his head.

"Because I got a good look at what him and his Islamoterrorist buddies had done to my company. Men who were the best friends I ever had. What I did to that kid wasn't on me. It was on him. And he had it coming for what they did."

The kid nodded. "Thanks, Sarge."

"Take some time with it. Then man up. We need you on the line tomorrow. Whatever is happening here is bigger than you. Remember that."

"I'll be good to go."

"I know you will. You'll find your way. All you young ones will." Mitch gazed into the twilight. "You know, I had a little girl once."

"I didn't know that."

"No sons, though."

He'd like to have a family again. Maybe someday, after the war.

He left the kid with his bucket and walked back to where the rest of the squad huddled around their Coleman stove.

"How's he doing?" Donnie asked him.

Mitch handed him two packs of Camels from his side pocket for use as trade. "When he sobers up a little, get him cleaned up and some food in him. Then take him to the hooker shack. If he's old enough to kill, he's old enough to get laid."

The kid had earned it. Let him have some fun.

In three days, there was a good chance they'd all be dead.

TWENTY-FOUR

Sunlight gleamed on the icy road. The Free Women marched in a straggling column, hauling their weapons and supplies.

Hannah trudged at Maria's side at the rear of the pack of girls. Backpacks bulging with linens, they leaned against the wind blowing across the White River.

The move had made Hannah so nervous she hadn't been able to eat her breakfast. A *bugout.* The word conjured a vision of people scrambling for their lives. She didn't know anything about Haughville other than there might be fighting.

As for bugging out, she knew it all too well.

The militia rolled through the neighborhood in a rumbling parade. Dad called them evangelical paramilitaries. He stayed home from work. Each night at dinner, he told Mom about new city council laws. Gays and abortions outlawed, doctors arrested. Pharmacies no longer allowed to sell female birth control. A massive bonfire at the public library.

Hannah didn't understand what was going on and why, though bullying she understood. The newcomers were picking on people just for being who they were. They were telling everybody how to live.

At school, Ms. Sykes refused to teach religion and got fired. The new teacher told his class they were going to learn the Bible so they could gain a stronger relationship with Jesus Christ. He slapped a student who said she didn't believe in God and told her to either start believing or find a new place to live. Hannah had always enjoyed school, but she went home shaking that day and didn't want to go back.

Somebody tagged Husani Farouk's parents' house with MUSLIMS OUT *and* FUCK ISLAM. *The next morning, his family moved away. Later, people Hannah had never seen before looted what was left.*

Dad grew even more worried. He paced the house checking the door locks, watching the news, sometimes staring into space. Hannah often caught him studying her with a heartbreaking look in his eyes, as if he wanted to protect her but didn't know how or from what.

Then somebody painted a Venus symbol on their garage.

The women started to sing. Hannah didn't know the song's name, though she recognized it. Maria, Kristy, and the other girls joined in and raised their fists in what Hannah had learned was a salute, one that cried, *Power to the people!*

Hannah trotted until she caught up with Abigail. "Hi."

"*Namaste*, sister," the commander grunted.

"Are you okay?"

"My knees ain't what they once were."

"I can carry your pack if you want."

"Everybody has to pull her weight. That's how it works." She chuckled. " 'I Am Woman.' "

"What?"

"The name of this song. I used to think it was a bit much, but hearing the girls sing it, it's powerful. I have to admit, it makes a good revolutionary song."

Hannah listened to the women sing and glanced at her forearm. Under the thick jacket sleeve, her Venus clenched its fist, now a symbol of power, not fear. It reminded her she was militia, Free Women for life.

She said, "Do you really think the fighting will end the war? Where we're going?"

"If we break their line, I think it might end the siege."

"What if the rebels surrender? What would happen to them?"

"No matter what, they're still Americans," Abigail said. "I'd like to think they'd just go home and let us live in peace. That we could work together to solve our problems."

"Sabrina said they should be punished. She said there's no going back after this, no living with them again. Not after what they've done."

"I can see her point of view. They declared war on reality. They elected a maniac who almost broke the country. When he failed, they rose up and broke it themselves. You can't reason with them, and they hate our guts."

Hannah thought about it. "What if you knew one of them?"

"My ex-husband is fighting for them. Him I know all too well."

"Why can't both sides just talk to each other and work it out?"

"From the mouths of babes."

"I don't want to kill people. I don't think I could."

Abigail winced at the pain in her knees. "You've obviously never been through a divorce. The truth is I don't want you to kill anybody either, sister."

Hannah looked around for Grace Kim but didn't see her in the marching throng. The sniper was off on her own again.

The women ended their song with a throaty cheer. The militia marched across the West Washington Bridge in an uplifted atmosphere. The White below had partly frozen over. Hannah heard banging in the distance, like somebody pounding a car with a hammer.

"That's where we're going," Abigail said before Hannah could ask. "If the rebels try to hit us, you'll work with HQ. You and the other kids will act as runners."

"What's that?"

"Do you know how to run?"

"Yes."

"That's the job. I write messages. You take them to the units. If they write a message for me, you run it back."

"Like a postman," Hannah said.

"A postal worker. That's right."

"That doesn't sound hard."

Abigail winked. "You have to run real fast. Think you can?"

Yeah, she knew how to run.

After the Venus symbol showed up on the garage door, they packed whatever they could fit in the car. Hannah whined and stalled until Dad yelled. Alex said he wasn't going. It wasn't fair, his life was here. He and Dad shouted at each other all the way to a truck stop crowded with honking cars stacked up in long lines to get gas. Police car lights strobed in the night.

Alex left to use the bathroom and didn't come back. Dad stomped off in a dark fury. Two men traded punches at the pumps while their families struggled to pull them apart.

Cheering men in pickup trucks rode up to the station. They hopped down and pushed people out of the way so they could fill their tanks.

Hannah whimpered in the back seat. Mom tried to talk to her, but she didn't hear it. She just wanted Dad and Alex back. She'd never been so scared in her life. They should keep running. This was a bad place.

The men in the pickups had guns.

"Dad," she said with growing alarm.

"Don't worry," Mom said. "Your father—"

"Daddy," she screamed. "I want my daddy! Where is Daddy?"

Gunshots, terrifying and loud. She jumped as if shocked by electric current. People were screaming and running.

"DADDY!"

Dad appeared next to the car and wrenched the door open. He flinched at another deafening burst of gunfire and threw himself into the seat. He sat pale and sweating.

"Where is Alex?" Mom said.

Dad didn't answer.

"Harry! Where's our son?"

He pounded the wheel with his fists. "Fuck!"

"Don't be mad," Hannah cried. "He's okay. He's okay, right?"

Dad stared back at her with wild eyes. He blinked as if just recognizing her. Then he turned back and twisted the key in the ignition. The car roared to life.

Mom opened her door. "I'm not leaving him—"

The car lurched, flinging her back in her seat. It careened around a fleeing couple before peeling out onto the road.

"They killed a deputy right in front of me," Dad gasped. "It's not safe."

"Stop the fucking car, Harry!"

"Listen to me, Linda. SHUT UP. Please. I'm taking you and Hannah somewhere safe. There's got to be a hotel or something up ahead. Once I get you there, I'll go back for him."

Mom was crying. "He's our son."

"I don't like this," Hannah bawled. "I want to go home."

She turned in her seat. The truck stop and its flashing police lights dwindled into the darkness. Then she heard something she never had before.

Dad was sobbing.

"Let me get Hannah somewhere safe," he said. "Please let me do that. Then I'll find him. I'll do whatever it takes. I swear—"

BOOM.

Flash of light and roar. Metal ripped through the car and cobwebbed the glass. Dad slumped against his seat belt as the car spun off the road.

"Hannah?" Abigail said. "You okay?"

"Dad tried."

"Who? Your father?"

The car stopped spinning. The headlights illuminated a wall of dust. Dad turned smoking in his seat to paw the air in front of Hannah's face, still trying to protect her.

"Are you okay, honey? You okay?"

"He really tried. It wasn't fair!"

The woman touched her shoulder, which she accepted with a shudder. Then Abigail put her arm around her and pulled her close.

"You're okay," she said. "Whatever you're reliving, it's in the past. You're safe now."

They walked like that for a while, Hannah leaning against the woman's warmth. Face half buried in her wool coat, she pretended this soldier was her mother. "I know how to run."

Abigail gave her another squeeze. "That's good."

"I can run real fast."

That's all she'd been doing since she left her home in Sterling. One day, she'd stop, and she'd find enough strength to fight back.

"That's the spirit," Abigail said. "Remember, sweetie, they can hurt us, but if they don't kill us, they only make us stronger."

TWENTY-FIVE

Gabrielle called Wolfgang Gruber from her hotel room using her satellite phone. As UNICEF deputy executive director for North America, the German reported to Carol Lake, who ran the show in New York City.

"I do not know why you are calling when it is obvious I have no answers for you," he said in his usual brusque manner, as if talking to her was a painful chore. "We have only just received your analysis."

"I'm calling about something else. May I have a minute of your time?" He answered with a noncommittal grunt, which she took for a yes. "Have there been any violent incidents between UNICEF personnel and the rebels?"

"You must be more specific. Both sides claim to be fighting for the legal authority and consider the other to be rebels."

"The forces that support the executive branch," she clarified.

"Why are you asking this?"

"My understanding of my mission is to help all the people here, not just one side. I'd like to go out and talk to them today."

"This is a bad idea," Gruber said.

"Why?"

"It is not safe. Obviously."

"A reporter is acting as my local guide," Gabrielle said. "She has contacts. We were promised safe conduct."

"You still have to drive across the contact line," he said. "Not safe. If the executive faction wants our help, it will be done through proper channels. We would make the arrangements for you."

"Have there been any incidents?"

"Yes. Is there anything else you wished to discuss?"

She didn't. She ended the call, pulled on her coat, and went downstairs, where Aubrey waited in the car.

The reporter started the engine. "What did he say?"

"We're good to go."

Her mission was clear. Observe, evaluate. Then focus UN resources on helping as many children as possible. She'd begun to wonder how much UNICEF would be able to accomplish. If what Terry Allen and Dr. Walker had told her was true, a fraction of the supplies would end up reaching children in need. The militias and profiteers would take the rest. By feeding the militias, UN assistance might even prolong the conflict.

She believed what she'd heard. In Somalia, the UN hired local militias as bodyguards and distributors. The fighters drove around in Toyota pickups with .50-caliber machine guns welded onto the back. These trucks became known as *technicals* because the UN couldn't put *contract thugs* on its books and instead called them *technical assistance*. The militias stole as much of the supplies as they could. She'd thought the Americans might be different, but they weren't.

Gabrielle reminded herself that if even one child who might have died instead survived, then it was all worth it. In the final tally, UNICEF would do a lot of good here. But she saw an opportunity to make a more immediate impact.

The reporter wanted to write a story about the child soldiers but needed to confirm the rebels were also using them. Driving the car to the rebel lines was the best way to accomplish that. Aubrey had sounded guilty when she'd asked to use the car. Gabrielle agreed on the condition she come along too.

Gruber said there'd been incidents. The risks terrified her, but she couldn't allow Aubrey to face them alone. She couldn't live with herself if the reporter went out on her own and something terrible happened. Because Aubrey wasn't using her to get a story. She was using Aubrey to get the word out about the use of child soldiers.

Gabrielle had prominently mentioned them in the needs analysis she'd sent to Gruber. This information would eventually be published in a UNICEF report on the conflict. Important officials would read the report and begin to act. But that would take a long time. Getting articles in the press would make a stronger and quicker impact. The public outcry would stimulate a stronger, more immediate response than UN officials skimming field reports. This phenomenon was well-known among relief workers, who called it the CNN Factor.

The car raced toward the West Washington Bridge. First, they'd touch base with the local Blue militia, which Aubrey's contacts said was the Free Women, arriving to replace the Indy 300. Then they'd move on to the rebel line.

"I once knew a guy who'd do anything to avoid conflict," Aubrey said. "He hated it. But if you messed with his kids, he'd tear your head off."

"Oh?" said Gabrielle, wondering.

"You remind me of him."

"What happened to him?"

"One of his kids died in a mortar strike. He fights for a militia now."

"Are you still friends?"

"After Ian died, John turned into this guy whose whole life became conflict. If you disagreed with him about anything political, he saw you as the enemy. I felt for him and tried my best, but we parted ways. I'm a reporter. I don't do propaganda."

Gabrielle thought for a while and made a decision. "Can I tell you something that's personal? Just between you and me? Can we do that?"

Aubrey considered. "Okay. Whatever you tell me, I won't print."

"I was in the news once. Twenty-one years ago."

The reporter threw her a look. "What, when you were a toddler?"

"I was six." Gabrielle took a deep breath. "I was abducted at a park. We drove out of the city with me in a booster in the back too scared to do anything."

"Jesus," Aubrey said.

The man drove west, every kilometer taking her farther from safety and everything she loved. She obeyed his instructions in mute terror, believing if she did, he wouldn't hurt her.

At night, the man checked them into a motel. In bed, he lay next to her but otherwise didn't molest her. She could hear him breathing in the dark, his large frame hot against her back and his alien smell in her nostrils.

For hours, she thought about slipping out from under his arm and running for help. She lay rigid, too terrified to move. He hadn't hurt her yet, not physically. If he caught her trying to escape, he would.

"I was at an age where my biggest fear was a monster in the closet," Gabrielle went on. "I would ask my mother to make sure the door was closed, or they'd get out. I had no idea the world was filled with monsters, and they wore human faces."

Aubrey winced. "How did you escape? If you don't mind sharing."

"We stopped at a gas station in Ontario. The man went to the bathroom and told me to stay put. He had me pretty well trained by this point. He knew I'd stay. A man at the pumps smiled at me through the window. *Help me*, I told him. Not out loud. Just mouthing the words. His smile died on his face. I did it again, still too scared to say it out loud. *Help me, please.* I kept doing it."

Men were shouting outside the car. Her abductor bolted toward the driver's side. He'd take her far from here and then he'd hurt her for what she did. The other man cranked the door handle and banged on the window.

Get out, he yelled. *If you need help, come out of there now.*

"I jumped out as the man got in and drove away," she said.

Strange how that was the one part she couldn't remember. One moment, she was in the car giving up hope. The next she was outside and shaking like a leaf. It had almost made her believe in divine intervention, but it had been the work of a single man doing the right thing.

Either way, she'd come to believe she'd been saved for a reason. When the UN began staffing for the American war, it had been like another door opening. She'd considered it her calling. Her chance to pay it back.

"Did they catch him?"

"No. They never did."

"Fuck," Aubrey said. "I'm so sorry that happened to you."

"Ravi Patel. That's the man who saved me. I kept in touch with him my whole life. He was a dentist. He died two years ago."

"I don't know what else to say, Gabrielle. Holy shit."

"Anyway, now you have your answer. It's not hard to figure out why I am the way I am. I've been to more therapy than you can imagine. One traumatic thing that can happen to you as a child can change your life. Change who you are and the person you were meant to be."

"I'm really sorry, I mean it. If you ever want to talk…"

"I'm done talking." Talking about it always soothed her, but Gabrielle had been talking as long as she could remember. "Now I want to do something."

TWENTY-SIX

The Free Women arrived at the Living Spirit Child Care Center with a cheer. The column dissolved as soldiers dropped supplies and milled about looking for orders.

Hannah looked up at her new home. Constructed of red brick, the daycare building stood massive and tall. A concrete and wrought-iron fence protected the courtyard.

Kristy admired it. "It's a great spot for our headquarters."

Hannah narrowed her eyes, trying to see it as the older girl did. "How do you know?"

"It's set back from the street, see? And it's got a fence. That makes it safer if any rebel shows up with a car bomb."

Maria threw her pack to the ground next to Hannah's. "But how do you know?"

"Sabrina told me."

Alice nudged Hannah. "Kristy says you think you're too good for us."

"Why?"

"Because you don't sleep in our room."

Maria grabbed Hannah's hand. "Don't listen to her. Come on, let's bounce."

The girls threaded the excited mob, darting around coats and rifles. They arrived panting at the building's doors and went inside.

Hannah expected a real daycare filled with toys, paper and paints, and drawings left behind by the kids. Instead, they found a dark, cavernous space cluttered with garbage and shell casings. WELCOME TO HELL was graffitied on the wall.

"Yuck," Maria said.

Sabrina walked in behind them. "They had it far worse than us."

"Can we take a walk and look around the neighborhood?"

The fighter scanned the chaos. Soldiers milled around chatting and dropping boxes everywhere. The Indy 300 was supposed to be here so there'd be a smooth transition, but they'd apparently bugged out for the fighting in the north.

"Sure," she said. "But don't go too far."

Maria grabbed Hannah's hand again and yanked her back outside.

Abigail was talking to Grace Kim, who'd ranged ahead of the militia to make contact with the Indy 300. The other central committee members read from clipboards and called out instructions to a crowd of shouting women. As if imitating them, Kristy held court with the other girls.

"Shouldn't we stay and help?" Hannah said.

"Do you really want Kristy bossing you around?"

She'd had her fill of that. "Okay, let's go."

The militia's babble faded as they walked down the street. It was so empty here. Downtown Indy had its hazards, but you could always gauge them by watching what others were doing. People moved in herds. As soon as one person sensed danger, everybody reacted to it.

"So why don't you sleep in our room?" Maria asked her.

"I don't know."

The girl frowned. "Fine."

Hannah was in the gang now. She'd gotten her first mark. More important, she'd made a new friend in Maria. She didn't want to mess it up.

"I'm scared, okay? I'm not as tough as you guys with your tattoos."

"Talking tough doesn't make us tough," Maria said. "You take all the time you need. I just wanted you to tell me the truth. We're friends."

They crossed several blocks. Hannah gazed at the derelict houses lining the street ahead and imagined them filled with rebel snipers. In the distance, a blue slab blocked the road. Behind her, the militia seemed very far away now. The air was cold, but she was too amped up to notice.

"Don't worry, Hannah Banana," Maria said. "They won't shoot kids."

Hannah hesitated at the muffled reports of gunfire. The fighting in the north was still raging. Maybe the rebels didn't shoot kids on purpose, but stray bullets killed just as well.

Maria turned. "Come on."

Hannah gave the daycare another longing look. "Sabrina said don't go too far."

"I've been cooped up in the same place for a year. I want to explore. Please. We'll go as far as that big blue thing down there. That's it, I promise."

"What is it?"

"I don't know." The girl marched off. "That's why I want to go see it!"

The blue slab turned out to be a shipping container. Before the war, Hannah had seen them hauled by tractor trailers on the highway.

She marveled at the strangeness of it. "What's it doing here?"

"Blocking the road, silly. So enemy trucks can't drive through and kill us."

They walked around to the other side. The container's face was spray-painted with a black skull and crossbones and the words, INDY 300. Some terrific force had ripped gaping holes in the metal. Scraps of it littered the asphalt.

Maria started climbing it using the holes as handholds.

Hannah watched her in alarm. "What are you doing?"

Her friend peeked over the edge. "Nothing on top."

"Get down!"

"Okay, okay. Hold your horses. Doesn't anybody want to be a kid anymore?"

"The alive kind," Hannah said.

Maria reached the bottom. Her eyes flashed with excitement. "Come on, let's keep going."

This was the girl's first taste of freedom in months, sweetened with risk. As for Hannah, she'd had her fill of risk. Right now, she wanted a sense of security.

"Can we go back, please?"

"I've been scared of them for a year. I have nightmares about them."

"Maria, no. No way."

"I've never actually seen one."

Hannah had, during her family's flight to Indy, after the IED killed Dad. An experience she'd never forget and had no wish to relive.

"They..." *No, I'm not sharing this now.* "I'm not going with you."

Maria frowned at this betrayal until she caught the look on Hannah's face. "Hey, it's okay. You stay here. I'll be right back, I promise."

Soon, Hannah would be alone without knowing when her friend was coming back.

"Wait!" She ran to catch up. "You're a lunatic, you know that?"

"I know." Maria grinned.

"If we're going to do this, let's stick close to the houses."

"Yeah! Good idea."

"Shhh," Hannah scolded.

"Okayyyy. This is supposed to be fun, you know."

"I'm really scared."

Maria took her hand. "Just a little farther."

They crept across the yard behind a house facing the rebel line. The back door was gone. Snowdrift reached into the kitchen, where dead leaves littered the floor. Drawers, cabinet doors, and anything else that burned had been removed for firewood.

Nobody home. It was exciting, being in somebody's house. And sad too. People lived here once, laughing and loving and working hard to get by. The war had killed them or driven them out just as it had Hannah's family. She mounted stairs decorated with framed pictures of a smiling Black man and woman and their teenage daughter. Hannah hoped they'd made it somewhere safe.

Like downstairs, people had ransacked the second floor for valuables and removed anything that burned.

"Hannah!" Maria hissed from the master bedroom. "Come here!"

"What?"

Her friend crouched grinning in front of the gaping hole where a window used to be. "Check it out."

Across the street stood a church surrounded by trenches and dugouts excavated from the earth. Heads bobbed along the trench.

Hannah was looking at the rebels.

A soldier turned the corner behind the church, zipping up his pants. He froze and looked directly back at them.

She flinched from the hole, her heart slamming so hard she thought it would punch through her ribs.

Maria waved at him.

Hannah grabbed her arm. "What are you doing?"

Her friend laughed. "He's waving back."

"He's the enemy!"

"He doesn't know that. To him, I'm just a kid."

The rebels killed Dad during the flight from Sterling, Mom in the middle of Mile Square. They'd hurt Mom first on the road to Indy. Not this man, but men like him.

Did she hate him?

Abigail had told her the rebels were people like her but different. They saw the same problems, wanted the same things for their kids. But where the liberals wanted the government to make things better, these men saw it as only capable of making things worse. Even though they were the enemy, the commander said, they deserved compassion.

Sabrina hated the rebels. The way she'd explained it, what they'd done, nobody could forgive. And if she had her way, she'd kill them all to make room for the world she wanted. Hannah found the woman's hatred kind of scary but also thrilling, even righteous.

You were your deep, driving desire.

She peered past the jagged edge of the hole at the soldier in his camouflage outfit. He was grinning and waving at Maria.

He seemed happy to see them. It was hard to hate him.

"You really are a maniac," Hannah said.

Another soldier left the building and shoved his comrade inside. Hannah and Maria waved at him too. He smiled and aimed his rifle up at the window.

"Pow," he yelled.

They bolted down the stairs.

Fueled by blank terror, Hannah ran until the shipping container came into sight. Maria huffed next to her, running for all she was worth.

They stopped gasping at the container, still bouncing with tension.

Maria smiled at Hannah, who giggled.

They hugged each other and couldn't stop laughing.

TWENTY-SEVEN

G abrielle's stomach flipped when the militia fighters stepped into the road. "That must be them. The Free Women."

The fighters signaled to park in front of a daycare, where a crowd of militia waited.

"Yeah, that's them." Aubrey stopped the car and killed the ignition. "You're about to kick a beehive. You sure you want to do this?"

Gabrielle stared out the grimy windshield at the uniformed women cradling rifles. Plenty threatening, though they didn't seem hostile. "They're Blue, right?"

"That's not the point," the reporter said. "Actually, that is the point—"

"If they have child soldiers, I need to know it. I don't care if that upsets people. They want the UN's help, they can stop using children as weapons."

Aubrey shook her head. "I'm talking about the political situation. You might end up hiring militias for security, right?"

If Gruber awarded Gabrielle a budget, she'd stay on as monitoring officer. She'd hire an accountant, PR firm, administrators, and drivers, and reach out to nongovernmental organizations such as the Red Cross to help distribute supplies. She'd also need to rely on the IMPD and in some cases militias to safeguard the flow of aid throughout the city.

"A UN contract is money and prestige," Aubrey went on. "You're about to talk to the Free Women, a Leftist militia. The Left Bloc will use your visit in their propaganda, and the Centrists won't be happy about it. The government, the IMPD. Little things like this can upset the balance of power."

Gabrielle spotted two girls standing by the daycare's gate. About ten years old. Black winter jackets and hats, army surplus pants bloused into boots. Big bright eyes. Cheeks glowing a healthy pink in the cold.

They stared at her with open curiosity. She stared back.

Then she got out.

"Well, okay then," the reporter said as Gabrielle closed the door.

One of the fighters said, "I'm Sabrina."

"Gabrielle Justine, UNICEF."

The woman raised her arms. "Can you go like this for me?"

She did. Sabrina frisked her, then Aubrey.

"Where's the Indy 300?" the reporter said.

"They went to arrest President Marsh and end the war," the woman said. "We're holding the line until they get back."

Aubrey smiled at this clever way of saying, "No comment."

A stout, middle-aged woman cut through the throng of fighters. They parted for her, showing respect. *The commander*, Gabrielle surmised.

The woman shook their hands. "I'm Abigail Fulham. Welcome to the Free Women."

Gabrielle gave her the usual speech about the UNICEF mission. "We're passing through. I'm on my way to the rebel lines to talk to them."

Abigail raised her eyebrows. "Are you now?"

"I have evidence they are using child soldiers in violation of the Geneva Conventions and international law."

The woman glanced at the two girls still standing by the gate. "I see."

"It doesn't matter whether they participate in the fighting or not. If they are children and serve in a militia in any way, they will witness violence and may be injured or killed. They're soldiers."

It came out harsher than she'd intended. While the United States had agreed to these international laws, the major combatants were police and civilian militias. Most of these women probably weren't even aware of the prohibitions.

Even so, it was common sense. You didn't use kids in war. Full stop.

Abigail said, "Maria, Hannah, come over here."

The girls gave Gabrielle a wary look as they approached. She crouched to talk to them. "Hi, I'm Gabrielle. I live in Canada. I'm with the United Nations. A special part of it that helps children like you."

"Hannah, tell her what happened to your parents," Abigail said.

The girl's gaze dropped. "They were killed by the rebels."

"And where would you be if you weren't with us?"

Her eyes widened in alarm. "Orphanage."

Abigail shot Gabrielle a questioning look. "Have you been to the orphanages?"

"A few."

They were filthy places run by a struggling hodgepodge of churches and other organizations. Kids growing up way too fast but still half-wild. Scarce food. Rumors of abuse. Little real schooling. The city streets were their primary teacher.

"Then you understand why we haven't sent these girls there."

"Part of my mission here is to make the orphanages better," Gabrielle said. She'd already put in a request for aid packages, school kits, and funding for counseling.

But all this wouldn't come until later. It didn't help these kids now.

"We have fourteen girls," the commander said. "We took them in because they had nowhere else to go. No place safe. We care for them like they're our own."

"Using them as soldiers is a war crime."

"Fair enough," Abigail replied. "When are you taking them to Canada?"

"As much as I'd like to see that happen, Canada can't take all the children."

"Okay. How about you personally? Take Hannah here with you."

The girl burst into tears. "No!"

Gabrielle winced. "I wish I could, but I can't."

"Then you came here to lecture us without having any solutions."

"This is my home!" the girl screamed.

The shouting drew more fighters, a crowd bristling with weapons.

"Hannah," Abigail snapped. "Nobody's taking you anywhere, sister."

On the verge of hysteria, the girl stepped back panting and bolted to the gated building.

Gabrielle glared at Abigail. "You're wrong."

"They're victims of violence," the commander said. "They've endured what no child ever should. But they're safe here. They're fed and warm and schooled. They're *loved*. Every one of us is their mother. Guarantee me a place they can get what they need that's away from the fighting, and I'll let them go. I'll be happy to do it. Until then, I won't let you hurt them. They've suffered enough."

Abigail then shot Aubrey a look. "You getting all this down?"

The reporter nodded over her notepad. "I sure am."

"Good. Feel free to quote me. Now you should leave. We've only just arrived, and we're still settling in. If we don't hold the line here, far more than the children will suffer."

Gabrielle started to respond, but the commander had already turned away to talk to one of her people. She stood in awkward suspension until she gave up and returned fuming to the car.

Aubrey got in and put her notebook away. "That was interesting."

"You could have helped me out there."

"Why? I got everything I need for the article. Great stuff."

Gabrielle scowled and yanked at her seat belt. "I'm glad you're so happy."

The reporter laughed as she started the car. "I was wrong about you dividing the militias. You may have just united them. Against you."

"Because I can't bring a child back to my tiny apartment in Montreal," Gabrielle complained. "Because I don't want these girls to kill or be killed or watch others die. I didn't write the Geneva Conventions. Yet somehow I'm the bad guy."

Aubrey glanced at the rearview as they left the Free Women. "When we get to the rebel line, let me do the legwork, okay? I'd rather not get shot today."

"What do you have in mind?"

"Repeat after me: 'I'm here to offer aid to children in the Red combat zones.'"

"And then what?"

"Leave the child soldiers to me," the reporter said.

TWENTY-EIGHT

Hannah paced the dirty snow in the courtyard. "I don't want to leave."

Maria hung upside down with her legs draped over the courtyard's iron fence. "It's safe in Canada. What if we could go together? I could have my old life back."

"It's a lie."

Her old life was gone and would never come back, even if the UN lady drove her to her old house and all her things were right where she left them.

"I'm sick of being a grown-up," Maria said. "I want to be a kid."

"It's not about that. This is my home now."

"This crappy place? A big, cold, stinky—"

"I meant the Free Women."

Kristy and the other girls marched through the gate and surrounded them. "Get down, Maria. This is militia business."

"Okay." She fell in a tumble.

"We're not letting that UN person take you anywhere, are we, girls?"

They shouted their agreement.

"She might do it anyway," Hannah said. "All of us. She said kids can't be soldiers."

Maria dusted snow from her sleeves. "We aren't kids anymore. And we aren't even real soldiers anyway. What does she know?"

"That lady's just stupid," Alice chimed in.

Stupid, maybe. But she was a grown-up. More than that, a grown-up with authority. She wanted to decide what was best for Hannah, thinking it was for her own good when it was the worst thing imaginable.

Hannah said, "She'll end up sending us to an orphanage."

"Won't happen," Kristy said. "We watch each other's backs, remember?"

"Yeah," Maria said.

"I heard you went out to the front line. That was pretty gutsy." She raised her voice. "They should get a mark. What do you say, sisters?"

The girls cheered.

Maria said to Hannah, "What do you want me to draw this time?"

"Wait." Hannah spotted Sabrina heading into the building. "Hey, Sabrina?"

"Hey yourself." She paused. "You okay?"

"Can that lady make us leave?"

"That's up to the central committee." The fighter chuckled. "I think the commander made it pretty clear what she thought of it."

Hannah seethed. *It isn't up to Abigail either.*

The grown-ups had torn her from her childhood and dropped her in their world to suffer. She'd earned the right to choose. To each according to her need, but nobody was asking what she needed.

"Teach me more shooting," she said. "Can you do that?"

Sabrina gestured at the chaos around them. "Everything is still a mess. If the fascists attack now, they'll find us unpacking pots and pans."

"Can I come with you and help then?"

The fighter started again for the front doors. "Just ask around."

Grown-up code, telling her to go bug somebody else.

"You girls should go play," Kristy said. "There'll be plenty to do later."

Hannah turned on her heel and started walking. Kristy was showing off her age again by imitating the grown-ups, but she had the right idea. Act like them, and they respected you.

She remembered Alex getting sucked into watching YouTube videos during the troubles, shaky footage of antifa and alt-right street gangs brawling in the streets. She'd sneaked a look over his shoulder at people clubbing and pepper-spraying one another.

That's disgusting, she said.

No, he said. *It's cool. It's real.*

Mom and Dad say they're stupid, and everything is going to be okay.

You believe anything, he said. *Grow up.*

She'd burst into tears. He'd pushed her buttons again. It was so easy for him. The only button she could push back was telling on him, which she did.

Why grow up? Mom said. *You're only a kid once. Enjoy every minute of it. When you're my age, you'll miss it. Watching you grow up, I get to be a kid again myself.*

But is everything going to be okay, Mom?

Of course it is.

Now Mom was dead, and Alex was right. About the war, about her. After everything that had happened, she felt grown up. She needed to act like it.

"Where are you going?" Maria called after her.

Hannah walked over to a bunch of boxes stacked on a tarp. She hugged one but couldn't get her arms around it. She heaved anyway. It didn't budge.

Vivian appeared at her side and scribbled something on her clipboard. "It'll be a while before I need you. Go have some fun."

Hannah turned and started walking again, this time heading west.

"Be back in time for lunch," the woman called after her.

Maria caught up. "Where are you going?"

"I'm gonna go play."

"By yourself?"

"I'm playing war."

Maria set her jaw. "Count me in."

They returned to the shipping container and crossed back into No Man's Land.

"We need to pick a different house this time," Hannah said.

She'd learned that trick from living among snipers. They fired a few shots and then changed location before the local militias honed in on them. That was how a handful of bad men terrorized an entire city.

"What's the plan, *chica*?"

"We're gonna count enemy soldiers and then tell Sabrina."

Maria's lips curled in a deadly grin. "Recon mission."

"Maybe we'll get another mark," Hannah said, though she didn't care about marks anymore or even what Kristy thought of her. She wanted to be useful to the militia. While she still hadn't figured out what the cause meant to her, the important thing was she had a cause, which was staying with the Free Women.

"You should draw mine this time," Maria said. "Are you any good at drawing?"

Hannah raised her finger to her lips. "Quiet as a mouse from here on out. And the answer to your question is, 'Yes, I like to draw.' "

"Roger," her friend whispered. "And yay, because I want a good drawing."

She crept down an alley to another house, more resolute than scared this time. The back door had been removed here too. Behind her, Maria giggled through her nose.

Hannah wheeled. "Will you please shush?"

"I can't help it. I was remembering that guy yelling 'Pow' at us." The girl clamped her hands over her mouth to stop giggling.

They entered a kitchen, which was stripped down and trashed like the other house. The living room was similarly empty except for loose junk nobody wanted. Hannah pointed up the dark stairs, her shoulders clenching with the first pangs of fear. She used to be afraid of ghosts she'd never seen, but now her terror had a very real face. Maria nodded, her own face pale with fright.

They mounted the stairs. Hannah gritted her teeth as their footsteps produced loud creaks. At the top, they found an empty bedroom. Clothes hangers, busted lamps, and a dirty toothbrush lay scattered around a bare box spring.

Maria was already peering bug-eyed out the window. Hannah crawled until she could look out from the other side.

The rebel entrenchments around the church were right where they'd left them. She counted the heads she glimpsed among the earthworks and scratched marks in the wall with a shard from a broken table lamp.

When they were done, they found another observation post a few houses down. They worked their way up the block this way to Tenth Street, where they called it a day and headed back to base.

Maria walked beside her with her chin held high. "Only eleven men in the whole block. That's not a lot."

"We didn't see everybody," Hannah said. Her stomach growled with hunger.

"We have a lot more than that on our side is all I'm saying." The girl grinned. "Okay, that's it. I'm gonna say it if you won't."

"Say what?"

"They didn't see us once! We kick butt! Wait until we tell Sabrina!"

Hannah was having second thoughts. They were probably already in trouble for missing lunch and making Vivian worry. "Maybe we should just tell Kristy."

"Why should she get the credit? She's not the boss of me."

"We'll get in trouble." That was how grown-ups thought.

Hannah was picturing her grand plan backfiring on her. *Oh dear,* Sabrina would say. *I should have never let you put yourself in that position. I'm sending you to the orphanage.*

"Don't tell me we did all that so Kristy Rockford could be a hero."

"It'll be easier all the way around if we do." Kristy liked being top dog.

"No way. Trust me."

"Fine." Hannah sighed. "We'll do it your way."

The crowd at the daycare had thinned as units moved off to their billets. Most of the mess had been put away. The deployment was really shaping up.

They found Sabrina talking to Vivian inside.

She shook her head as the girls walked up. "And look who it is. What did I tell you about going too far? I was just about to go out looking for you."

Vivian was also frowning. "You two had me worried half to death."

"We were scouting the rebels," Hannah said.

"What possessed you—?"

Sabrina raised her hand to silence her. "What did you see?"

Hannah told her the number they'd counted. The fighter asked more questions. What weapons did they have, did they seem happy, did they have vehicles, was there smoke behind the line suggesting more men were back there, and more. Hannah answered as best she could.

"Good work," Sabrina told them. "But don't do it again. We're pushing out patrols. I don't want to see you carried back on a stretcher after getting shot by one of your comrades."

"Okay, sister," the girls said.

"Stick around," Vivian said. "I'll whip you up something for lunch." She jabbed her finger at the corner. "Right there. I don't want you two out of my sight."

Hannah and Maria trooped where they were told while Sabrina went to share her information with Abigail.

"Didn't I tell you we'd be heroes?" Maria beamed.

"Sabrina is going to tell the commander. We could still be in trouble."

Or maybe, like Sabrina, Abigail would get the message Hannah wasn't a dumb kid who could be ignored when an important decision about her welfare was being made.

Her friend rolled her eyes. "You're such a worrywart. Roll up your sleeve for me. What do you want me to draw?"

Hannah had already planned out her next tattoo, a grinning cat or a spell from *Harry Potter*, maybe *expecto patronum*, which banished Dementors. Then she thought about the shipping container, how the Indy 300 marked their territory.

"Skull and crossbones," she said.

"Yeah. You got it, sister."

While Maria inked her arm, Alice walked over, her kewpie doll face contorted in a barely suppressed smile. "Kristy says you're too good to hang out with us."

Maria gave her the stink-eye. "Beat it, half pint. We're busy."

The smile disappeared. "But we're playing capture the flag."

"We were out for a walk and missed lunch," Hannah said. "We'll come out and play after we eat. Okay?"

Alice's face shined with a gap-toothed grin. "Okay."

Hannah would play capture the flag, but she was far more interested now in playing war. Though she was done thinking of it as playing.

TWENTY-NINE

Aubrey drove in circles looking for a way through the road-blocks, which consisted of piles of rubble and in one case a shipping container. It was slow going as the car blazed a trail through unplowed streets. A white pillowcase swung from the aerial.

"What about the railroad tracks?" Gabrielle said.

Aubrey stopped the car and took the roadmap from her. "We'd get stuck in the snow for sure." She studied the map and tapped it. "There."

Running along the north side of the green space surrounding the tracks, North Centennial and West St. Clair were cul-de-sacs. The dead ends appeared near enough to attempt a crossing.

When they reached the end of Centennial, Aubrey smiled. Thirty yards of open ground separated it from St. Clair. "That's how we'll do it."

"Are you sure we can get across?"

She grinned and revved the engine. "Hang on to your hat."

The UNICEF worker blanched. "I hate when you say that."

Aubrey whooped and stepped on the gas. The car fishtailed before lurching across the snow. It thumped over the curb with a jolt. Engine howling, the tires spun. Then they bit into the ground and brought the car onto St. Clair.

"Just like Thelma and Louise," she said. "Thank God for four-wheel drive."

"*Osti d'tabarnak,*" Gabrielle swore.

Aubrey slowed the car to a crawl. "We're about a block from the rebel line."

So close now to getting her story. Their encounter with the Free Women had been wonderful. The commander challenging UNICEF to guarantee a safe, caring, livable environment for children. The kid screaming she didn't want to go.

The whole thing made her wonder. Were Hannah and Maria better off in the militia? Aubrey supposed it depended on the militia. The girls didn't seem to be doing any fighting. The Indy 300 kids she'd seen at the clinic, however, had.

Slippery slope, she surmised. A child served as a cook until one day the militia needed fighters. The Indy 300 had suffered more than most. At some point, they must have become desperate enough to throw kids into combat.

Surely, Gabrielle was right, and it was best for the children to be as far as possible from the war zones. But where could they go?

Her readers could wrestle with that question. It was her job to tell them uncomfortable truths, regardless of whether there were easy answers.

Beside her, Gabrielle took a deep breath and released it. "I hope they know it's us coming."

"What do you mean?"

"Your contacts assured us safe passage."

"Oh. I lied about that. Sorry. My contacts came up dry. We're taking a chance. You want out? I can leave you here and come back for you."

"I lied too," Gabrielle said. "When I told you there'd been no incidents."

"I'll be damned. I think I'm a bad influence on you."

Aubrey braked as men rose from the nearest trench. The rebels crossed the street pointing their rifles.

Gabrielle flinched. She'd probably never had a gun pointed at her before.

"Don't freak out," Aubrey said. "Keep your hands on the dash."

"Don't tell me you're not scared too."

"Are you kidding? I'm terrified."

The rebels flashed one another hand signals that displayed a bravado bordering on playacting.

The guns were real enough.

An overweight rebel in a digital camouflage uniform appeared in Gabrielle's window. He pointed his rifle at them. "Get out of the car! Get out now!"

"Chill out," another fighter said. His bearded face filled the window as he peered in at the women. He tapped the glass.

Aubrey rolled down the window and held up her press badge. "*Indy Chronicle.*" The man just stared at her in disbelief. "Take me to your leader."

He smiled. "We'll see about that, ma'am. Open the door nice and slow."

She did as she was told. The man frisked her while the other groped Gabrielle. The men bound their wrists with plastic cord. The rest covered them or aimed their rifles at nearby buildings.

Aubrey thought that it was over, but it was only beginning. They tore apart the trunk and squinted under the hood. A rebel appeared with a mirror and circled the vehicle, checking for bombs attached to the chassis.

The big man held up Gabrielle's blue UN flag. "Look at this!"

"Care to explain that?" his calmer comrade said.

"She's with UNICEF," Aubrey said.

"You mean the United Nations?"

"Yeah."

"Seriously?"

"That's right," Gabrielle said.

"Your accent. You French or something?"

"French Canadian."

"Even better." The soldier keyed his throat mike. "Branch One-Six, this is Branch One Eyes, over... Uh, we got two females at the wire, sir. They arrived in a vehicle... Yeah, we checked it out, it's clean..." He grinned at Aubrey. "Well, uh, one's a Black liberal-media reporter, and the other's a French-Canadian UN relief worker. They want to talk to the colonel." He laughed. "No, I am not shitting you... Winning our hearts and minds... Roger that."

"What's next?" Aubrey said.

"I have been instructed to give you the red carpet treatment."

He nodded to a rebel behind Aubrey. The world went black as a hood dropped over her head. She bit her lip and fought down a surge of bile. She'd never been more scared.

A strong hand clasped her arm. She let out a strangled sob.

"Aubrey!" Gabrielle cried.

"I'm okay. Don't worry."

The hand guided her to sit in the back seat of the car. She slid across as Gabrielle landed next to her. The UN worker was breathing hard.

The car started and drove for a while.

"Where are we going?" Aubrey said.

No answer. From the number of turns they were taking, the rebels seemed to be driving in circles to disorient their captives.

Aubrey had made a big mistake coming here.

The car stopped. The men got out and helped her back onto her feet. They removed the restraints and yanked the hood from her face. An alley lined with houses appeared. Rebels walked around on their martial errands or sat by wood fires in a backyard.

"I'm Colonel Lewis," the smiling man in front of her said.

The commander wore a clean camouflage uniform under a

wide-brimmed cowboy hat. Mirrored sunglasses hung from his webbed harness, a pistol in a leather holster on his hip. He'd spent money to look the part. Otherwise, he was average in height and paunchy, hardly Aubrey's idea of a militia warlord.

She took a moment to collect herself. "I'm Aubrey Fox, *Indy Chronicle*. This is Gabrielle Justine. She's with UNICEF."

"The UN and a newspaper, all in one day," he mused. "What are you writing, Ms. Fox? Doing a big story on America's heroes?"

"I just write obituaries. Gabrielle's the one who wanted to come here. UNICEF is new in town, so I've been showing her around. She wanted to see you."

The colonel's eyes flickered to Gabrielle. "And why did you want to do that?"

"To help the children suffering because of the war."

Lewis looked around at his leering troops. "Miss Justine, you're welcome here, but your organization isn't."

"Look, I don't care about the politics," Gabrielle said. "I just want to help the children."

While they talked, Aubrey checked out the area, which she hoped appeared as idle curiosity to these soldiers. Her gaze settled on a boy cleaning his rifle by the fire. Next to him, a giant in camouflage and ballistic armor stared back at her. Their eyes met across the distance.

Framed by a neatly trimmed goatee, his lips curled in a slight smile. He didn't leer so much as consume the sight of her.

Beyond them, she spotted women in militia uniforms hanging laundry on a clothesline. They were likely as dangerous as these men, though seeing them gave her a little comfort.

She turned to one of the rebels. "Mind if I sit by the fire and keep warm?"

He grinned. "Sure thing, ma'am. No pictures, though."

"Okay." She huddled on a crate set in front of the flames. Across the fire, the boy went on breaking down his rifle and cleaning each part.

"It looks like you're pretty good at that," she said.

"Thanks."

"How old are you?"

The boy turned to the giant sitting next to him.

The man took a pull from his beer can. "Go ahead, Mary. Tell the nice reporter."

"I'll be sixteen in March."

"What's your real name?"

"Alex."

"Have you ever shot anybody with that thing?"

The boy's face darkened. "It was that or get shot myself. I did what I had to."

"Did you see the Indy 300 on your way here?" the giant said.

"We passed straight through," she lied. "We didn't stop."

"What do you write for the paper?"

"Obituaries," she lied again. "What's your name?"

"Sergeant Damon Franklin Shook," he said, as if this were a formal interview.

"Is Alex your son, Sergeant Shook?"

The man grinned. "Take a good look at this broad, kid. This is what we're fighting against. The lying liberal media."

"You don't believe in a free press?" Aubrey said.

"You think you're free to tell the truth, but you aren't. It's a slave press. It's all rigged to turn Americans into slaves."

This rebel believed in a free press, but only if it told him what he wanted to hear. She wondered if he was even aware of the contradiction. She wondered if he knew how he sounded lecturing her about slavery.

"I write obituaries. Is that a lie? I make it all up that you kill people?"

"How many aborted babies make your obituaries?"

Was he seriously going to pretend he was pro-life? "Plenty of babies make the obituaries these days."

"More lies. Like the libs always bitching about the snipers. The truth is they kill their own and blame it on us. False-flag ops to justify dictatorship. That's what the real media is saying."

Even when they brutalized people, they never stopped playing the victim. Anger flooded her chest, displacing her fear. "You can believe whatever you want, but it isn't true."

The rebel leaned forward, eyes blazing. "You murdered the truth."

"Tell her, Sarge!" a fighter called out.

"You and your schools and Hollywood celebrities and comedy shows all comparing President Marsh to Hitler," the giant went on. "Stirring up the bums to turn against their country and terrorize law-abiding citizens, until we stepped in. As far as I'm concerned, you and your hot Miss UN are the real enemy."

Aubrey clenched her teeth and stared at the fire. Being a journalist meant neutrality. You didn't act, you observed. You observed and reported.

But sometimes, she really wanted to pick up a rifle and start shooting.

"Like I said," she told him. "You can believe whatever you want."

"You might think you're this tough broad, but that don't mean shit out here," the rebel said. "In fact, it's a liability. Here's a fact. We could take you into that house over there and do whatever we wanted for as long as we wanted it. If we were so inclined."

"Grab her by the titties, Sarge!"

Aubrey's body clenched with terror as the rebels laughed. This man didn't care about the contradictions in everything he said. All the lunacy wrapped in the flag. The truth didn't matter, only feelings. Feelings of being right. Of winning. Of power and control.

"After we're done with you, we'll shoot you in the head and leave you in a ditch, and nobody will care. It won't even make your obituaries."

She steeled herself for a fight. "Is that what you're going to do then?"

The boy looked at Sergeant Shook in alarm. The giant reached out to stoke the embers, making Alex and Aubrey both flinch.

"Not today," he said. "The colonel wouldn't like it."

More laughter.

"Then I'm free to walk away," she said.

He swept his arm in a mocking gesture. "It's a free country."

Aubrey stood and crossed her arms. She wanted to say something to show she wasn't afraid of him. *Nice to meet you, Alex. Good luck!* She didn't trust herself to speak, though. Her legs shook so badly that she could barely trust herself to walk.

She waited by the car counting the seconds until Gabrielle left the nearby house, escorted by Colonel Lewis and two soldiers.

"I hope you'll come out and visit us again sometime," he said.

"Thank you for your time and hospitality," Gabrielle said.

The colonel touched the brim of his hat. "Like I said, young lady. Anytime."

The women got in their car and waited while a pair of rebels removed the roadblock.

"Please get us out of here," Gabrielle said.

"I'm on it."

Aubrey stepped on the gas. Grinning rebels filled her rearview. She took a final look at the sergeant and the boy. The giant went on drinking his beer without giving her so much as a parting glance. He'd already gotten what he wanted from her, which was her fear. Fear he confused with respect.

They drove along St. Clair and jumped the green space onto Centennial. After a few blocks, they were back in Blue territory.

Only then did she notice how badly she was shaking.

"Did you get it?" Gabrielle said.

"They're using child soldiers."

"Stop the car."

Aubrey tapped the brakes until the car slid to a halt. Gabrielle opened the door and leaned out to vomit. It rushed out of her into the snow. She spat and spat again. She reached under her scarf and gripped a pendant she wore around her neck.

"You okay?"

Gabrielle wiped her mouth and closed the door. "I'll be fine."

"Did they do anything to you?"

"It wasn't what they did. It was what I thought they were going to do. It was everything they might do. The way they talked and acted. It was like being back with *him*."

Aubrey nodded and resumed their drive back to the core. Neither of them spoke the rest of the way. It took that long for her trembling to finally stop.

Outside the hotel, she killed the engine and handed over the keys. They sat for a while in silence.

"Do you have enough to write a story?" Gabrielle said.

Aubrey nodded.

The UNICEF worker sighed. "Then maybe it was worth it."

No, Aubrey thought. *It wasn't.*

Her ambition didn't justify putting this woman at risk. What she'd done today horrified her. The risks she'd imposed on Gabrielle to get a story. The danger she'd put them both in because she'd wanted to use her job to do something real, something meaningful.

"I can't be your fixer anymore," she blurted.

"What's wrong?"

"I'm going to get you killed, for starters."

"I wanted to go today."

"Because you still don't know any better."

Gabrielle winced. "Are you mad at me?"

"No," Aubrey said. "I'm mad at me. You need a better teacher. Take care of yourself, Gabrielle."

The woman steeled herself with a visible effort. "Okay. If this is what you want."

Aubrey opened the door. "You'll be all right. You'll do just fine. You're way stronger than you think you are."

Maybe stronger than me, she thought as she got out.

"Wait."

"What?"

Gabrielle leaned across the seat to gaze up at her. "Thank you again for everything. And you take care of yourself too."

Aubrey responded with a lopsided smile. Half-happy, half-sad. "I always do."

THIRTY

Colonel Lewis waved the women out of sight while he chuckled at some private thought. "Anytime, ladies. Anytime."

Then he and Mitch and Shook went into the house to talk.

Alex finished cleaning his reassembled AR-15 with drops of lubricant on the mag release and bolt catch buttons. He didn't understand why they'd had to hustle out of their trenches and set up here like they were camping.

He asked Grady what was going on.

"Do what you're told and shut it," the soldier said. "That's what."

"We staged a big photo-op," Tom explained.

Alex still didn't get it.

The man shook his head. "Never mind. Stop asking questions."

Alex pointed the rifle at the fire, pulled the bolt to the rear, and released it. He placed the weapon on safe and squeezed the trigger. The hammer didn't drop. He released the safety and squeezed again. The gun dry fired with an empty *click*.

He set the rifle down and reached for a beer.

"No beer for you until you help Jack mend the socks," Tom said.

"Seriously?"

The veteran stared at him for a few seconds before answering. "Yup."

Alex had shot a man. He'd earned his place. And still they didn't show him any respect. He got up and walked away from the fire.

"And no beer for you after, either," Tom said. "You're drinking too much."

He went to another fire, where Jack sat on a lawn chair darning one of a mound of socks. "That was surreal, wasn't it?"

A Canadian UN worker and a Black newspaper reporter showing up like something out of one of Liberty Tree's myths.

Jack stuck a tennis ball inside a sock to stretch out the hole. "This stink is surreal. They could wash these goddamn things before making us fix them."

"Did you hear the way Shook talked to that reporter?"

"The guy's sick in the head."

"I know. But the matter-of-fact way he did it. Like he was ordering something off a menu. No fear."

The kid frowned as he worked his needle back and forth over the hole. "That's what trolls do, bro. You don't feed them, and you don't admire them. He gets us our stuff, and we pay him for it. I don't want to be friends with him."

Jack didn't understand what he was getting at. Alex didn't admire what Shook had said, which was horrible. He'd never talk to another human being that way.

What impressed him was Shook said it at all. No self-doubt, no drama. Total self-control. The rules didn't apply to him. He made his own rules.

"He does whatever he wants. They made him sergeant for it."

"While you darn socks." Jack reached to the pile and tossed an olive-green wool sock into Alex's lap. It stank like cheese. "Starting with this one."

He regarded the mound bleakly. "All these have to be done?"

Jack smiled. "War is hell."

His friend was right about one thing. Nobody would ask Shook to darn socks. Alex didn't want to be like Shook, but he wanted that kind of power.

"I may have to do it again," Alex said.

Jack stopped smiling. "Yeah, I know."

"You too."

"You think I don't know that?"

"I want to not care. I want to just do it and not feel so crappy about it. Know what I mean? Boom. Like scratching an itch."

At night, alone in his crummy sleeping bag, Alex saw the man running at him with his big hunting rifle. He experienced the shooting all over again, elation and despair.

He wanted the guilt to go away. The rage. He wanted to finally feel like he belonged here. He wanted to be free, like Shook.

"It's us or them," Jack told him. "They're the enemy. That's the bottom line."

"But why?" Alex demanded. "What's it all for?"

"We're taking the country back." Jack sighed. "I don't know. You should ask Tom. He knows about this stuff."

"I'm talking to you."

"Well, let's talk about something else," Jack said. "How was Tiffany?"

Alex remembered the tired blonde greeting him at the door in a nightie. She was old enough to be his mother. He didn't want to do it but didn't think he had a choice.

In the end, he didn't have to do anything. Instead, Tiffany hugged him and stroked his hair for an hour while he cried.

"She was awesome," he said, meaning it. "She'd been kind to him.

"You lucky dog."

Alex held up his smelly sock. "So lucky."

Jack laughed, then turned toward the house as its screened front door banged open. Colonel Lewis and Mitch stepped outside.

"Report to me when you get back," the colonel said.

Mitch sketched a salute. "Will do, sir."

The sergeant marched with purpose toward the encampment. Something was up.

"Back to the trenches, Sergeant?" Jack called to him.

"Nope," said Mitch. "Drop what you're doing and man up."

Alex and Jack exchanged a grin. "Yes, Sergeant!"

The squad got busy getting ready for whatever Mitch wanted them to do. Alex stood and pulled his assault rig over his camouflage jacket. Like his gun, all the gear had been cool at first but was now just another ball and chain.

Patrol, however. That never got old.

The rush of combat. There was nothing like it. The tension that broke as a quiet street erupted into pure chaos. That sense of being in his own skin, detached yet aware, fully present.

He didn't want to kill people, but oh, man.

All or nothing. That's what he wanted to feel until this war was over. That was his new motto.

"Get over here," Mitch said to his squad. "Take a knee."

The men gathered around.

"We're going out on patrol. But we ain't going to the lib line. We're gonna follow tire tracks." The sergeant fixed his stare on Alex. "Kid, you'll take point."

"Roger that, Sergeant."

Leading the squad was a big responsibility. The men's safety would be in his hands. The other guys bitched about taking point, but he thought it was cool. Mitch was showing trust.

"You fuck this up, I'll shoot you myself, kid," Grady said.

"Shut up, fat man," Alex said.

The squad froze. Somebody whistled. Jack grinned. Grady started to bluster, but Alex ignored him, waiting for the order to start moving.

Mitch eyed Alex. "Lead us out. Everybody, stay sharp."

Alex got to his feet and started walking to the road. He couldn't go head-to-head against the entire squad, but he'd decided he didn't have to take Grady's crap anymore. He'd work his way up the totem pole until he could dish it out and only take it from a select few.

He found the tire tracks and followed them north. The church stood on his left, near the auto repair shop. It was occupied by friendlies. A big industrial building loomed on his right. Telephone poles slanted over the road. He studied every detail before moving on.

The tracks turned right onto St. Clair, a narrow street flanked by houses and trees. He scanned the houses as he passed them, focusing on windows and doors. He skirted a pile of rubble, which might hide a roadside bomb.

He itched to shoot something. He wanted more chaos. Violence seemed to be the key to unlocking everything in this new world. Hate, meanwhile, was the key to violence. Tonight, when he lay in the dark and relived the shooting again, he wouldn't wonder if the Indy 300 fighter was a good man or about who mourned his death. He'd think about all the ways the guy had it coming. He'd make up a story in his head and repeat it until he believed it. Then he'd fight for that. That would become his cause.

As he neared the end of St. Clair, Mitch whistled. Alex went prone and waited as the squad scurried into the nearest cover.

Boots crunched snow behind him. The sergeant crouched next to him and studied the scenery with his rifle's close combat optic.

Alex strained to see what the sergeant did. He checked out the dark windows again but saw no threats, no movement at all. He'd screwed up somehow. What had he missed?

Mitch's gaze settled on the tire tracks that ran up and over the curb, across an empty patch of white, and continued on Centennial beyond.

"What do you see, Sergeant?" Alex said.

Mitch grinned. "I see a door, kid. And they left it wide open."

THIRTY-ONE

Aubrey went to the bellhop desk to retrieve her bike and decided instead to go inside for a drink. The usual security protocols confronted her at the door, more degrading than boarding an international flight. She had a terrible feeling that no matter who won the war, this was America's future. A paranoid police state.

At the end of this, they still might not allow her inside. She had no reason to be here. She thought about waiting for Gabrielle to help her get in but decided against it. Aubrey had knowingly led the UNICEF worker into the lion's den so she could get a story. She never wanted to see the woman again.

And to make her shame even worse, Gabrielle had thanked her and told her to take care of herself. Aubrey had felt something again, a stirring in her heart. The idea that meaning could be found in trauma, that they'd done something good today.

The bellhop inspected her press badge. "Which guest are you visiting?"

"Terry Allen or Rafael Petit."

"They're expecting you?"

"The last time I was here, they gave me an open invitation to visit."

The bellhop thumbed the names into his tablet and waited for a response. He was a thug but a professional one. He didn't care if she got in or not.

He said, "Mr. Petit will meet you, Ms. Fox. Welcome to the Castle."

"Thank you," Aubrey said, exhausted.

She trudged inside and went to the lavatory, where she repeated her ritual of washing up and stealing every roll of toilet paper in sight. She'd brought water bottles this time, which she filled at the sink. When she emerged, Rafael Petit was nowhere to be seen in the opulent lobby.

Aubrey found him in the bar, sitting with glasses of red wine set on the table in front of him. She smiled and sat.

"Hello, Aubrey," he said. He was better looking than she remembered.

She pointed at the two glasses of wine. "Is that for me?"

"Yes, of course."

She scooped one and swirled its contents. "But what are you going to drink?"

He smiled. "What brings you back to our oasis? More UN work?"

Aubrey took a hefty sip and sighed, more out of relief than satisfaction. "Honestly? I needed a friend." He raised his eyebrows, so she added, "Sometimes you need to talk to somebody who, you know…"

"Understands?"

"Yes," she said.

"Another reporter. No, a war correspondent."

She set her glass down. "Bingo."

"Terry will be jealous of our meeting. He thinks you have access to good stories. The other day, I saw him reading one of your articles."

"He was?" She took another sip to hide her smile. "As a matter of fact, I'm sitting on a huge one."

"Are you interested in sharing it?"

"Not yet. Once I get it written up for the *Chronicle*, I'll let you in."

"So what did you want to talk about?"

After we're done with you, we'll shoot you in the head, the rebel sergeant said.

She knew the man wasn't thinking about her right now, but he'd be living in her brain for quite some time.

She said, "Do you ever find yourself having to choose between doing your job and living with yourself?"

Rafael reached down and pulled a leather satchel onto his lap. He removed a photo album and leafed through it. Then he placed the open book on the white tablecloth between them, revealing a large color photograph.

Bodies in a mass grave. So many tangled together they appeared snarled into a single entity. Yellow bulldozer next to the pit. Men and women in shabby uniforms and surgical masks exhumed the corpses. Impossible to read their faces, though their eyes broadcast pain. More bodies were laid out in a neat row in the mud.

It was like something from a World War II concentration camp, though she knew it wasn't. It was America, and it was now. "Where was this taken?"

"Dallas. These people were Muslims."

Aubrey spotted children among the corpses. "Oh, God."

"I remember very clearly when I took this. The Blues had found this mass grave and dug it up. They wanted the world to know. A horrible atrocity."

"Horrible," she agreed.

He tapped the photo with his finger. "See this body? A man wearing a shirt that is red, white, and blue like your flag. He was trying to show he loved this country up to the very moment they murdered him."

Aubrey winced.

He continued, "I thought at the time, how wonderful, the shirt really adds a nice touch of color to the image."

Rafael closed the book. "A child is shot by a sniper. A terrible thing. She is lying bleeding in the street. What do you do?"

"I would help her, then write a story about it."

"And if you were a photojournalist like me, for whom moments count?"

She didn't even think about it. "I'd take the photo first."

Rafael shrugged. "Then that is who you are. We are the same. Someone has to tell the story. Anything else is just something you must live with."

Aubrey said, "Show me more."

He gestured to the book and sat back in his chair. Aubrey turned the stiff pages and took her time inspecting each photo. Militiamen flashing victory signs. A terrified woman surrounded by grinning men decked out in hunting gear. A skyscraper burning in black and white. Children scavenging in piles of garbage built up on the sidewalks, playing among bomb craters.

Each told a story. Who, what, where, when, and how. But never why, which was up to the viewer. Where she strived to tell a big story from a small event or a single person's experience, he accomplished this using a simple image. What she felt when she listened to her classical music, these photographs pulled to the surface.

"They're beautiful," she said. "Beautiful and horrible."

Rage, despair, hope, dignity, horror. The human pageant of beauty and savagery. She not only saw their stories in the images, she read the story of humanity. History repeating itself forever despite its brutal lessons.

She'd been exploring the book back to front, going backward

in time as she neared the beginning. Police fighting rebels, prone shooters and blurred runners, a barricade of burning tires in the background. A demonstration, people of all ages and races and creeds filling a square. Rafael Petit had been in America documenting its civil war since the beginning.

Aubrey remembered the massive demonstrations in Indianapolis in the early days. Gunmen in ski masks had put up barricades around the city. People poured into the streets demanding peace and unity. The country was falling apart, but not Indy. Not us. Not here. Our city would not be divided. The barricades came down. The crowds returned every morning to march for peace until a bomb went off in Mile Square.

After that came days of police officers exchanging fire with rogue cops and right-wing gunmen in house-to-house fighting. A militia drove into Indy and tried to take city hall. People beat and shot one another to settle old scores. Others organized militias to defend their neighborhoods. And the fighting, once a separate thing and unthinkable here, became everything.

She said, "Does it ever get to you?"

"Of course. I am just a man."

Aubrey waited for him to say more.

He added, "I would say, 'As much as I allow it to,' but the images I capture affect me whether I let them or not. I will not know how much until I return to Paris and one day they are not just in my book but within me."

"It's not the sadness," she said. "It's the deeper wounds."

"Yes."

"It doesn't make us as special as we think, though."

"No," he admitted. "This war affects everyone it touches. Bearing witness to suffering is not the same as suffering. Still, it eventually has its effect, and with that come feelings of responsibility. A desire to do something about it, not just tell its story."

Aubrey finished her wine. She was starting to feel human again.

The bar's dim lighting, hushed voices, and piano washed over her and filled her with a sense of peace.

Rafael raised his hand to get the server's attention, and she thought, *If I have another drink, he might just get me into bed.*

He ordered two more glasses of pinot.

THIRTY-TWO

The squad returned to the trenches. Mitch asked them again to take a knee.

"You all did real good," he said. "We're still attacking tomorrow, but now we'll be taking a different route. The UN was kind enough to show us the way."

Alex was barely listening, too amped up from the short patrol.

Grady asked, "How fast are we going to be able to go in this snow?"

"We'll have a top speed of forty to fifty miles an hour."

The men looked at one another in disbelief.

Mitch smiled at the growl of approaching vehicles. "Right on cue."

The entire platoon whooped as the steel column zoomed into the alley. A rusting orange rig led the way. Shaped like a dump truck, it was specially designed for heavy snowplowing. Somebody had painted impressive rows of shark's teeth on its curved blade.

Mitch said, "Courtesy of the Department of Transportation."

The next drew louder whoops. Fluorescent green, it was shaped like a camper but massive, riding on eight giant wheels. A rooftop crane terminated in a thick metal spear. Below the sloped glass windshield, a nozzle protruded.

Jack laughed. "It's like something out of a Mad Max movie."

"Striker 8x8," Mitch said. "Big and heavy, but it can reach a speed of fifty miles an hour. It's used for airport runway firefighting. Five thousand gallons of water and foam."

Great for dousing a burning plane, Alex guessed. Just as effective at suppressing enemy fire. He'd hate to be on its receiving end, especially in this weather. If the platoon ran into trouble, the Striker would pound it with a continuous, high-pressure blast of water.

The rest of the trucks were basic Chevy and Ford pickups outfitted with small angular snowplows graffitied with obscene messages for the libs. The first and last of them had an M240 machine gun mounted on a swivel welded to the bed.

Tom chuckled. "Like the technicals the skinnies had in Somalia."

A bulldozer rumbled along next, which would be used to move rubble and wrecks. And finally a cherry-red fire truck, whose ladder would help the militia assault tall buildings and rooftops. A modern-day siege engine.

Sergeant Shook sprang from the trenches with his fists raised in the air. He ran toward the approaching steel column. "Get some! Get some!"

Alpha squad laughed at him. Thudding over potholes, the big vehicles slowed to park in the alley. One by one, their engines cut out. The drivers got out and lit cigarettes.

"The colonel spared no expense," Mitch said. "Go on and take a look."

Alex joined the other fighters gathering around the machines. They admired the retrofits and speculated on the enormous amount of lib ass they'd kick once they unleashed these monsters.

Jack nudged him. "Pretty cool, huh?"

"No doubt."

"I can't believe you stuck it to Grady like that. I was laughing my head off."

"Do you think he'll do anything about it?"

"Probably not. Guy talks way tougher than he is."

"Too bad," Alex said. "I want to fight."

"Just wait until tomorrow. You'll see plenty of it."

He had nothing against Jack. He liked Jack. Jack was one of the few in the militia who was kind to him.

Alex punched him in the eye.

The kid reared in surprise. "What the hell, bro?"

He swung again, but Jack flinched away from it.

Then the kid laid into him.

Alex didn't feel the first punch. The world spun. The second smashed into his nose and shot a bolt of pain up through his brain.

A hand pressed against his chest and shoved. The stars cleared. His squad mates were dragging Jack away from him.

The kid shrugged them off. "All right! I'm done!"

Mitch said, "You don't pull that shit before combat."

"I didn't do anything," Jack protested. "He just started hitting me like a wild animal."

Alex spat in the snow. It was red. Blood was pouring into his mouth. He held up his arm to press the sleeve against his swelling nose.

"Hold still." The sergeant inspected his face. "He messed you up good, kid. Maybe you should sit out the attack. We'll do okay without you."

Alex spat again. "No way, Sergeant. I'm good to go."

"Damn right, you're good to go." Another test, this time to see if he was shirking. "Now shake hands before I pound both your asses."

Jack held out his hand. "Why are you smiling like that?"

Alex shook it. "No reason."

The kid laughed. "You're crazy, you know that?" He rubbed his jaw. "You landed a pretty good one on me."

"Next time you boys want to fight, I'll give you one you won't forget," Mitch growled. "Now go get your supper before I knock your lights out."

Alex walked back to camp with his arm draped over his friend's shoulder. "I really needed that." Punching. Getting punched. Both.

"Yeah, we should do that again sometime."

The sock darning awaited them after chow. Jack had a better idea. They returned to the horse trailer and sat on the floor to get blazed.

Jack produced a joint and lit it with his Zippo. "How's the nose?"

Alex probed it with his fingers and grimaced. "Hurts."

"Your voice sounds funny." Jack handed over the joint.

"It wasn't as bad as I thought it was going to be. Getting punched."

"Why'd you do it?"

Alex drew a lungful of smoke. "I don't know."

"You're not mad at me, though."

"No, you were there, that's all. I don't know why I did it. I just needed to do it. I'm sorry, man. My eyes just went red."

"You don't have to say sorry to me. You got the worst of it."

"You're good at fighting."

"Am I?" The kid's face morphed into a pleased half smile. "It was my first."

"Mine too."

The boy laughed. "I had no idea what I was doing. I just reacted. I wasn't raised like that."

"Where are your parents?" Alex immediately wanted to take back the question but couldn't.

Jack's eyes glazed at some memory. "Work camp in Fort Wayne. The militia sent me down here with some other kids to help with the siege."

A man laughed outside the trailer. "Christ, you're breaking my heart out here." The door creaked open to reveal Sergeant Shook, who dropped a baggie of pot on Jack's lap. Then he laughed again, this time at the sight of blood on Alex's face. "That's a good look on you, Mary."

Alex's buzz soured. Everybody seemed to know about their private place.

The sergeant said, "Combat Jack told me you want to work with him. That's fine. I'm looking for jewelry, good watches. Don't bring me anything else unless it's gold or something I can trade for gold. Yeah?"

"Got it," said Alex.

"Tomorrow, we'll be in new territory to salvage. Keep your eyes peeled. I got something special for you two for the occasion. You're going to love it."

He extended his fist and opened it to reveal a vial of dull white powder.

Jack squinted at it. "What's that?"

"Psycho fuel." Cocaine.

Alex said, "What's it like in combat?"

"Turns you into Superman. You don't feel a thing."

"It's really addictive, though," Jack said.

"Only if you let it. I can take it or leave it. But I always snort before a fight."

Perfect. Alex reached for it, but Shook's hand clenched into a fist again.

"Jewelry and watches. Gold most of all. And porn, if you find any. Yeah?"

"Roger, Sarge."

The sergeant swung his arm toward Jack and opened his hand. The kid caught the vial out of the air.

"Say one word to Mitch about our arrangement, and your face will look a whole lot worse, Bloody Mary. Happy trails."

The door banged shut. Alex reached for it again. "Come on, let's try it."

All or nothing. The drug promised both.

"Tomorrow," Jack said. "We've got to use it sparingly. Shook isn't selling it cheap. He wants payment."

"Then let's go eat. I've got the munchies already."

Back in the camp, they ate an early supper of franks and beans cooked in bacon grease. The fire's heat blasted Alex's face. The air smelled like smoke. A militiaman wearing a floppy bush hat played guitar. After the meal, the men policed their plates and opened cans of beer.

Tom handed one to Alex. "Put it on your nose first before it turns into a balloon."

Alex grinned. "Thanks."

The veteran shook his head and muttered, "Dumb kid."

The men quieted as the light waned and the long day wound toward sunset. This was normally a time for them to tell stories about home or share their theories and complaints about tyranny and cultural Marxism. Today, however, they stayed quiet as they considered the coming battle, the only sound the crackle of the firepit.

Tomorrow morning, they wouldn't be playing soldier anymore. This wasn't a routine patrol, in which they'd throw a couple of hundred rounds downrange and jog home giving one another high fives. This was a major assault against an entrenched enemy that knew the ground. The militia would suffer casualties.

Alex shared their fears about combat. Nonetheless, he longed for it.

Mitch stood and said, "Tomorrow is the big one. The fight that could end the war. Blitzkrieg."

Around the fire, the men cracked wolfish grins.

"We know we're better than the libs," Mitch went on. "We've got superior training, firepower, equipment, and right on our side. And if our intel is correct, resistance should be light. Still, we know they can fight. Tomorrow, I want you to stay frosty, give your all, and hold nothing back. God willing, your victory will restore the republic in this proud corner of the dying United States."

The men belted out a cheer and raised their beer cans in salute.

"I'm proud of you boys," he finished. "Make sure you get a good sleep tonight."

Alex left the fire and crawled into his tent to be alone, his imagination buzzing about the upcoming battle. It didn't last long. Lying on his sleeping bag, he again saw the Indy 300 fighter wheel and try to run, only to topple spinning in a bloody mist.

He still didn't hate the man, but he would keep trying.

THIRTY-THREE

Aubrey opened her eyes and laughed. "God, I needed that."

"Now Terry will be very jealous, I think," Rafael said.

He lay panting next to her on his hotel bed. His pale body was slick with sweat. Tousled hair fell over his forehead. He had quite a bit of black hair on his arms and legs. He was a little paunchy, the result of middle age and a travel diet.

She snorted. "Everything's a competition with you guys."

He studied her face. "I was going to say it is because you are amazing."

Aubrey looked down at her breasts rising and falling with each breath. Living on subsistence rations had done wonders for trimming her excess fat. But she smelled bad. A musky funk. And she'd stopped shaving her armpits long ago, razors being scarce.

"Oh, please," she said. "You can stop selling. You already closed the deal."

"Not only this." He traced a lazy line from her throat to her navel with his finger. "I am talking about who you are."

"If you're going to touch me like that, I'd like to wash up first. I stink."

"You can take a shower, but please keep it under five minutes," he said. "Water is expensive."

"Seriously? God, this place is amazing. Now *my* friends will be jealous."

Rafael watched her get out of bed. She smiled at the attention and pictured burrowing back into the sheets with him. She hadn't known how much she'd missed a man's touch. And she found his extra pounds sexy. In a city filled with starving people, it was even more exotic than his accent.

He gazed at her with longing. She suspected Rafael was lonely just as she was. He'd been in America too long.

"Hey," she said. "Don't fall in love with me, okay? Rule number one."

"Even if I do, it is war."

"It's war," she agreed. "Right now is all that matters."

"Give me something of yours to read while you shower."

Aubrey knew what to give him. She crouched in front of her backpack and pulled out the story she'd written about Zoey Tapper's murder.

The first page had a light, bloody thumbprint on it.

"Read it and weep," she said. "It's unpublished. The *Chronicle* won't run it."

In the bathroom, she turned on the shower and stepped under the water. It was freezing, but she was used to that. Then it grew steadily warmer until it was piping hot.

"Oh my God."

Pure bliss. The last real bath she'd enjoyed had been back in September. It had been cold whore's baths ever since, wiping herself down with a damp sponge.

It made her laugh. All that soul searching, while life boiled down to such simple pleasures. A couple of glasses of wine, good sex, and a hot shower.

She soaped up and rinsed. Brown water pooled at her feet and went down the drain. She washed her hair next. After that, she shaved her armpits with Rafael's razor. This was turning into one hell of a date.

Aubrey stepped dripping from the tub and wrapped a towel around her body. She wiped the foggy mirror and inspected herself.

"This is very good," Rafael said from the main room.

She peered past the doorframe to see him sitting up in bed, reading glasses perched on his angular nose. "And you're post-coital."

"Where did this happen and when?"

Aubrey told him.

"I would like to photograph the place. Would you show me exactly where?"

"Sure, I can take you there."

He moved to the edge of the bed and pulled on his boxers.

"Me and my big mouth," she said.

He smiled at her. "There is time for everything."

"If it's one thing the war's taught me, it's that ain't true." She sighed and began to dress. "You know, it's just a bloodstain. And probably gone by now. People walk along there all the time."

"Faded is fine," Rafael said. "Gone is not. I know the street. You are right, it is a busy thoroughfare. There will be people about. They will be walking past the spot where a sniper killed a woman who was at the wrong place at the wrong time."

"Okay," she said, trying to picture it.

"Her blood is there. It marks the exact spot where she last lived. It is as much her grave as the lime pits at the American Legion Mall. The city has many unmarked graves such as this. The streets are filled with them."

Aubrey imagined the scene. The blurred legs of hurrying people surrounding a black stain in center view. The one who didn't make it. She found herself again appreciating Rafael's eye for using a simple visual to tell a story.

At the same time, it seemed too realized. Too artistic. Maybe they were in the war porn business after all.

"I need that image," he told her. "I intend to submit it with your story to *L'Opinion*. An American perspective. They may publish it."

She stared at him. "Really."

"Would that interest you?"

"Are you kidding?"

"First, we must get the image. The two work hand in hand." He checked his watch before putting it on. "We must go now before I lose the light."

They went outside into the cold gray afternoon. After a long hike, they arrived at the stretch of street where Zoey Tapper died. Aubrey pointed out the black stain on the snow. Rafael adjusted his camera and started shooting. This was important, documenting the violent end of a life. The document would have meaning, and the act of capturing it had meaning to her.

She spotted another stain beyond the first. Older, more faded. It alarmed Aubrey on some primitive level but fascinated Rafael, whose camera clicked in search of the perfect shot. She wanted him to stop. They'd been stationary and out in the open far too long for her liking.

Her memory flashed an image of blood splashing across her notepad. The stains reminded her they were all standing on thin ice and at any time might fall through into the eternal darkness. She didn't want to become a stain, a stain that time and feet would gradually erase.

"We should keep moving," Aubrey said.

Rafael stopped shooting and looked around. He trusted her instincts. "Okay."

They started to walk back to the hotel, where she'd left her bicycle. She bounced with nervous energy. She wanted to stay up all night.

She thought: *If he invites me in* . . .

No. They were past that now.

She said, "I'm staying over tonight."

He smiled and said he would like that.

Maybe he was falling in love with her. Let him. It was war.

Right now was all that mattered.

THIRTY-FOUR

D ressed in full battle rattle, the militiamen breakfasted on jerky while gunfire crackled in No Man's Land. Alex drank some coffee and forced down an energy bar he'd been saving. Then he packed up his kit and waited for the order to unleash Armageddon.

In the distance, a roof blew into the air. Shingles and wood splinters rained down from a mushroom cloud. Alex stared in fascination.

"Get some!" Sergeant Shook howled at the sky.

Nobody laughed this time.

The convoy of idling vehicles snorted like steel beasts, spewing exhaust into the frigid air. The men policed their trash in silence, put out fires, made last-minute equipment checks. They wrote final notes to loved ones and kissed their talismans and gun barrels.

Small arms fire popped. The atmosphere was charged with potential energy. Even now, Alex couldn't believe this was really happening.

The first two stages of the assault had already begun south of them. The other platoons were engaged. Soon, the sergeants would give the order for Second Platoon to mount up.

The bearded chaplain approached brandishing a rifle in one hand and a Bible in the other, an impressive sight. He wore a camouflage stole sewn with cross patches. The platoon crowded around and took a knee.

The chaplain cried: " 'Blessed be Yahweh, my rock, who teaches my hands to war, and my fingers to battle.' "

The men bowed their heads to recite the Lord's Prayer. Guns crashed in the south. Alex spared a glance over his shoulder. Ruined homes stood dark and empty. Clouds of dust and smoke drifted across the gray sky.

Jack bowed his head even lower and sniffed. He came up smiling and opened his palm to show Alex the vial filled with white powder.

"My turn," Alex hissed.

Jack tapped a little on the rim of his hand. "Quick."

Alex snorted and wiped his nose, which went numb. He sniffed. His mouth flooded with a bitter taste.

At first, nothing happened. Then his eyelid began to twitch. His heart galloped in his chest. The cold air's bite faded.

Then euphoria.

The drummer started pounding out a martial cadence, the sound crisp in his ear. Whistles blew. It was time to load up and get rolling.

The chaplain lowered his Bible and held up his rifle. "God is with us!"

The men stood as one with a wild cheer. Alex howled along. The cheer turned into a long rebel yell as they streamed toward the vehicles. He climbed aboard his designated truck and sat in the back between Grady and Jack, his leg bouncing.

"Let's go kill some motherfuckers," Jack said.

Alex grinned. "Let's go, let's go!"

He was breathing hard, face flushed, skin crawling. The top of his head was achieving liftoff.

Suddenly, he could do anything.

"Here we go," Grady yelled. "This is it, boys. This is it!"

Flags waving from the aerials, the column began to roll. The giant plow cleared the road for the rest, which followed at a steadily increasing speed. Pops and booms punched the air. Another thunderous explosion sprayed clods of frozen earth.

"That's the Bible thumpers," Grady shouted over the noise. "Helping us out with the mortars they got."

Jack nudged Alex. "How you doing there, bro?"

"I'm invincible."

Some of the guys in the truck ahead of them tried to strike up a patriotic song but got no takers. The men were too keyed up. Instead, they launched into another strident rebel yell as the trucks humped the green space between St. Clair and Centennial. Alex joined in, screaming his head off. They were officially in lib territory now, ready to stomp ass.

A woman holding a rifle appeared between two houses.

Alex wrestled with his AR-15. "Contact!"

The truck zipped past. The woman disappeared from view. Small arms fire erupted in the rear.

"Light her up!" Jack whooped next to him.

Alex itched to shoot something, anything. He had a magazine in the rifle well and five spares in his assault rig. He wanted to burn one off into these houses just to see the bullets fly, but he knew Mitch was watching.

A terrific explosion rocked the earth. Trucks slammed their brakes all down the column. The sudden stop hurled him against Jack, who laughed and shoved him back.

"IED, I'll bet," Grady said.

Jack pounded the side of the truck. "Come on, keep it moving!"

Mitch roared from the next vehicle in line: "What the hell are you doing? Get out and check for secondary IEDs! Set up a security perimeter! And keep your eyes peeled for the triggerman!"

Grateful for some action, Alex hopped off the side of the truck. His boots struck the ground. The squad fanned into a circle around the pickup, weapons aimed outward. He brought up his rifle the way they taught him.

He crouched and waited, knee bobbing with adrenaline and cocaine.

The vehicles honked in sequence down the line. The sergeants roared into the din. Time to move again. Alex climbed back into the truck as it started to drive away. Two militiamen grabbed his arms and hauled him up.

"Gonna miss the party, dumbass," Grady said.

"Shut up, fat man," Jack said, which sent him and Alex into hysterics.

The column was rolling again, though at a slower pace now. No more rebel yells. The militia hunkered down and scanned their sectors for targets.

Alex passed the flaming wreckage of the snowplow. Blood streaked the cab's windows. Two trucks had parked nearby, one discharging fighters.

"Wow," he breathed.

They were near the front of the line now. Sergeant Gore's squad led the way in trucks with mounted machine guns, followed by the big Striker with its firefighting cannons. The column started to pass a big redbrick building on the left.

"We caught the libs napping," Grady said. "The intel was solid. Another minute or two, we'll be through Haughville and into Stringtown."

"How do you know that?" Alex said.

"Because I studied the goddamn map—"

Red spray. Crashing gunshots. Grady slouched, coughing blood, his back shredded. The air filled with the rattle of automatic rifles.

Alex stared at the dying man.

"Contact!" militia screamed down the line.

The truck ahead of them somersaulted with an electrifying roar, tossing men like dolls before crashing back to the earth.

The Striker screeched to a halt on its massive wheels. The turret swiveled and pounded the windows with a moving jet of water.

"Come on!" Jack shoved Alex, then threw himself out of the truck.

Pure chaos arrived in all its fury.

Alex rose to his feet and watched the scene transform into bedlam. Tracers flashed between the halted column and the redbrick building in a constant, rolling roar. Bullets punched through the truck's thin metal skin.

Nothing could hurt him. He had a special role to play in this movie.

A round snapping past his ear jarred him back to reality. This wasn't a movie. Grady lay dead at his feet, blood and bits of him everywhere.

Alex dove and landed in a hard roll. Behind him, glass sprayed from the truck's windshield as heavy weapons fire stitched across it. Muzzle flashes blazed in the windows. A man screamed for a medic. Thick black smoke poured from the overturned vehicle ahead. The brick facade shed a screen of dust as hundreds of rounds raked it.

A hot wave of oily smoke rolled over him and filled his lungs with an acrid burn. On all fours, he coughed it out of him. His bile was tangy and foul. He spat a black mess. A round cracked off the asphalt near his hand.

"Lightly defended, my ass," Jack shouted.

Alex stayed put as his euphoric high fought its own losing battle against the horror surrounding him. His feelings of invincibility dissipated like more smoke. Threads of fear wrapped around his guts and yanked them into a tiny clenched fist.

Flying metal filled the air around him. His every instinct now screamed at him to curl up in a fetal ball. His limbs became dead weight and refused to obey him.

Shaking, he forced his body to rise. He aimed his AR-15 into the dust and burned through a mag. The rifle's stock hummed against his shoulder. Empty shell cases flickered in his peripheral vision. He had no idea if he was shooting at the enemy or putting the hammer to the building's facade. It was good just to shoot back. With each burst sent downrange, he gained a little more control over his trembling limbs until they became light again.

A car snarled out of the intersection and smashed into the column.

His vision distorted into fragments as time seemed to slow to a crawl. The militia hosing the vehicle with automatic fire. Bodies twitching on the ground. Fighters turning to engage new hostile forces approaching from the south.

He saw it all clearly now, the entire situation. They were about to be surrounded.

"I don't see Sergeant Thornton," Jack cried. "What do we do?"

A Molotov cocktail burst on the road behind them. An intense fireball bloomed into the air.

"If we run, we're dead," Alex said. "We stay here, we're dead."

That left only one option.

"Hell no," Jack said. "No way."

Alex rose to his feet and charged.

THIRTY-FIVE

Reporters filled the desks next to the windows, taking advantage of the morning light. They chattered about deadlines and column inches and sources. Manual typewriters clacked. Aubrey finished her story and yanked the sheet.

Then she went to see Eckert.

She waved her hand to clear smoke from the air as she grabbed a chair. "You should pace yourself with those."

"I wish I could," he said. "Listen, I'm glad you're here. I need to talk to you."

Aubrey held out her copy with a smile. "Wait until you read this."

He paled as he accepted it. "That's what I wanted to talk to you about. Is it what I think it is?"

"I got the story, Eckert. Yesterday, I visited two militias, one on our side and one on theirs. They were both using child soldiers."

"You went to the rebel lines?"

Her smiled turned to a grimace. "Yes."

"What was it like?"

Aubrey wanted to brush it off, show how tough she was. Even now, she romanticized the idea of the crusty, hard-bitten reporter.

After we're done with you, we'll shoot you in the—

"It was terrifying," she admitted.

"I'm sorry I sent you out there."

She gestured to the copy in his hand. "I got the story. It's all here."

He tried to give it back. "I mean I'm sorry because I can't publish it."

"You didn't even read it!"

"Listen, Aubrey—"

She stabbed her finger at his face. "No, *you* listen. I risked my neck. A rebel suggested he might rape me like he was talking about the weather. This is a big story, and I don't want any of your bullshit. It's factual. Print it."

"That's exactly why I *can't* print it."

"Argh! What's going on?"

"If you settle down a minute, I'll tell you," he yelled.

"Tell me then," Aubrey seethed. "Or I'm going to reach across that desk and stuff those cigarettes down your throat."

"The owners don't want this to see the light of day."

The Webb family, one of the richest in America, owned the newspaper. George Webb, Sr., its patriarch, was an old golfing buddy of the president's.

"Now hang on a minute," Eckert added. "Before you hatch a conspiracy theory, what you think is going on isn't."

She crossed her arms and waited, thinking, *This ought to be good.*

"You know the city's government and military is factionalized around the Centrist and Leftist blocs," Eckert explained. "Right? Yes? You with me?"

"Yes, Eckert. Of course I know that."

"Well, here's something else you should know. We run this story, it could bring the whole house of cards down."

"Whatever happens, happens," she said.

"Are you out of your mind?"

"We print the truth. That's our job. What comes from it is up to our readers. If using children as weapons upsets them, they can stop doing it."

"Christ, you still don't get it."

"Enlighten me."

"If we run this story, the *Chronicle* will rock the boat and upset a lot of people. And yeah, maybe it'll get the militias to stop using child soldiers, which would be one for the win column. The problem is," he held up his thumb and index finger, "we are *this* close to government censorship. Some commissar telling us what we can and can't print. Once they start that, it's only a matter of time before they take over the newspaper and write it themselves."

"Now look who's the conspiracy theorist," she said.

"They won't need reporters anymore. They'll just make up propaganda. As for you, they'll arrest you on some BS charge."

"You're full of it. You're just worried about your job."

"They'll put you in a deep, dark hole," he said. "You know I'm right."

The jails were already filled with people arrested for treason.

"They don't have to censor us," she spat. "We'll just do it ourselves."

Eckert stuck a fresh Marlboro in his mouth and lit up. "The only reason the government hasn't taken us over before now is because the Leftist militias won't allow it. But if we upset enough people by running this story, the government might see an opportunity to act. If the Leftists react, there'd be a bloodbath. I'm talking civil war inside the city."

She knew how much the Leftists and Centrists hated each other. Eckert was right, though that didn't make it any easier to swallow.

As a reporter, Aubrey had always been shocked by the right wing's war on facts. They regularly vilified anybody in fact-based professions, from scientists to doctors. They generated and consumed propaganda and called anything else fake. For them, reality wasn't as interesting as a good simple narrative that had them righteously and perpetually enraged.

President Marsh had polarized the country so much that in the year leading up to the war, she began to see the same alarming phenomenon on the Left. And if Eckert was right, it was getting even worse. If things kept going as they were, even newspapers like the *Chronicle* might be forced to print propaganda. They'd become generators of news that incensed rather than informed—that created enemies and then dehumanized and demonized them for an insatiable market. And not just to serve an ideological end, but as an end in itself. For raw power.

America was fast becoming a nation where nothing was real. Among the greatest casualties of its war was truth.

"Webb won't be able to keep it suppressed," Aubrey said. "The UN already knows about it. They'll publish a report, and it'll get out."

Eckert leaned back in his chair and crossed his feet on his desk. He blew a plume of smoke and regarded her with his one good eye. "Awesome."

"Awesome?"

"You think I like kids shooting guns at each other? I *want* the story to get out."

But the *Chronicle* couldn't publish it.

Deep booms pounded like thunder in the distance. The building vibrated for an alarming second. The windowpanes shivered.

Past Eckert's shoulder, a smoke cloud mushroomed across the river.

The editor turned in his chair. "What was that?"

Another explosion hurled debris sky-high. The crackle of small arms fire thickened until it became a constant muted thunder.

"That's not Brickyard Crossing," Aubrey said.

Eckert jumped to his feet. "Come on!"

He shoved her out the door and led her to the stairwell, where they joined a stream of colleagues heading up to the roof for a better view of what was happening.

Excited staffers crowded the parapet, talking and pointing.

"Garcia, what are you doing?" the editor roared. "The rebels are launching a counteroffensive. Get your ass out there and bring back the story!"

The reporter rushed off with a grimace. "I'm on it, boss."

Aubrey and Eckert found a spot facing west. From where they stood, it was impossible to see anything other than a pall of smoke and dust hanging over the skyline.

"That's Haughville," she said.

The rebels were hitting the Free Women hard.

Another explosion rocketed into the dusty air. The First Angels militia in the south wanted in on the action and were firing their mortars into the district.

"This new development might solve our ethical problem," Eckert said. "If they break through, they'll kill every one of us."

The rebels had their chance to do her in yesterday but hadn't taken it. "I don't think—"

Then it hit her.

They hadn't harmed her and Gabrielle because they were preparing an offensive. Killing or taking them hostage might have drawn attention. Instead, the rebels had put on a show. *Look at us doing nothing. We're not about to attack.*

If this offensive weren't occurring, she might be dead or wish she was.

She shuddered. "I have to go."

"Where are you going?"

"I'm taking the day off," she called over her shoulder. "And you're an asshole."

"Shooting the messenger. Now you see how it works."

Aubrey returned to the stairwell. A long way down. She unlocked her bike, brought it to the street, and started riding.

An air-raid siren revved up at city hall, its wail building in volume until it drowned out the distant roar of guns. The streets were already clearing. The few people still out hurried to get home. Red and blue lights flashing, a column of BearCat armored police vehicles roared past.

She and Eckert were too much alike, except for one critical difference. He put the newspaper above everything else. She put the truth first. These priorities were supposed to go hand in hand, but they didn't always.

He was right about one thing, though. Every so often, a story became the reporter. What the reporter wanted, and how far she'd go to get it.

Aubrey had one last card to play. She pedaled as hard as she could toward the Castle.

THIRTY-SIX

Clusterfuck, Mitch thought.

The intel had been solid. The chatter on the company net told him the Indy 300 had bugged out. But an army of Amazons had taken its place. They were disorganized, but there were a lot of them, and they were fighting like maniacs for this building.

He scanned the street with his close combat optic. The platoon had an open road out of here, but a jam of burning vehicles blocked it. His men were stuck until they cleared the wrecks, losing precious minutes while the enemy rallied and probed from the south.

Frantic voices filled the platoon frequency.

"This is Root One-Six," he said. "Clear the net, over."

Nobody was able to raise the lieutenant. He was either dead or cowering.

"I said, clear the fucking net." Mitch was now in command of the op.

One by one, the voices dropped off.

"Move the vehicles to make a path so the dozer can get the wrecks off the road," he ordered. "Establish security until it's done. This is a speed bump, nothing more. One-Six, out."

He spotted Alex Miller running toward the daycare's iron fence. Jack and Donnie bolted from cover to join him. The kid was thinking like a soldier. You find the enemy, you attack. The enemy finds you first, you attack.

A bullet whined past Mitch's ear and cracked into the road behind him.

"Now we're having fun," Tom said.

Somehow, the platoon had stumbled onto what appeared to be the enemy's base. If they captured it, they'd disrupt the resistance and hopefully free themselves from contact so they could continue their advance.

Mitch visualized the operation. Take the building, clear the wrecks, leave a screen facing south, and then remount and keep driving east toward Indy's heart. If they stayed too long, the libs would come in from the north as well and snag their collective balls in a vise. If that happened, it'd be the aborted assault on city hall all over again.

Forget Stalingrad. It'd be Custer's Last Stand.

"Follow me," Mitch shouted to his squad.

They ran through a hail of fire. A militiaman yelped as his legs gave out. Two other fighters tossed his arms over their shoulders and hauled him wincing and hopping to the fence.

Jack fired at a window. "You want some freedom fries with that?"

Alex's eyes were wild. "We didn't know what to do, so we moved up."

"We're taking that building," Mitch said. "Move out."

The squad threw covering fire. One by one, the men scaled the iron railing and raced across the courtyard to the wall. Enemy fire slackened as the airport firefighting vehicle pounded the windows with water.

Then it was his turn. He went over the fence and landed hard on his bad ankle. He grunted and kept going.

Tom planted C-4 on the doors. The men plugged their ears.

"Fire in the hole!"

The doors disappeared with a crash. The fighters charged in and swept the area with their rifles.

Crack, crack. A scream.

"Got one," one of his men yelled.

"Make sure she's down," Tom said.

Mitch entered a large open space filled with cardboard boxes, gear, and trash. An old woman lay bleeding on the floor. Somebody had graffitied WELCOME TO HELL on the wall.

"Clear!" the men called out.

Shook burst through the doorway with his SAW, followed by panting fighters. "This is *my* building."

Bravo squad jogged to the stairwell and started up.

Mitch exchanged a glance with Tom. Shook would either sweep the building with his machine gun or get killed before he reached the top.

Knowing Shook, he'd probably make it. In Mitch's view, the man was the worst kind of soldier, a psycho with a lucky charm up his ass.

Alex headed up the stairs after them. The kid had a little psycho in him too but wasn't as lucky as Shook. Mitch and Tom followed while the rest of the squad finished clearing the first floor.

Mitch heard a woman crying in a room down the hall. Her voice turned into a terrified howl. Shook's SAW spat a burst. Somebody laughed.

Tom shot another look at Mitch, who knew what the soldier was thinking: *We should put him down like a rabid dog.* Mitch wagged his head. Shook had been a liability from the beginning, but there was no use starting a fight within the platoon right now. He may have been a psycho, but he was their psycho.

They split up at an intersection. Mitch cleared the rooms one at a time but found nothing living. Broken glass and shell casings covered the waterlogged carpet. A dead militiawoman sat propped against the wall surrounded by bloody bandages.

No sign of Alex Miller. Mitch was starting to worry a little and not just because Alex was one of his own. He'd taken a liking to the kid.

He was limping now, wincing with each step.

One more room to go. Then he'd radio the platoon to start mounting up. Leave one squad here to hold this building while the rest continued their eastward advance.

The room was an open office area filled with grimy office furniture and computers. Bullet holes scarred the walls. Bits of drywall floated in the air.

A child was crying.

Mitch crept forward until he spotted her across the room.

The little girl knelt by a dead militiawoman. She looked up at him and wiped tears from her cheeks, leaving behind a dirty smudge.

With shock, Mitch realized he'd seen her somewhere before but couldn't place it. By the look in her eyes, she recognized him too.

Then it came to him. A moonlit wreck by the side of the road.

He smiled and relaxed a little. "Hey, little one. I see you made it to Indy all right."

The girl grabbed the militiawoman's AK-47 and raised it.

"Put it down," he said. "I'm not shooting a kid today."

Click.

He jumped. *Son of a bitch.* "You try that again and I'll—"

She ejected the empty magazine with practiced ease. She reached for a fresh one from the dead woman's pouch.

Mitch aimed his rifle. "Stop!"

She slammed the magazine into the well and loaded a round in the firing chamber.

"Don't do it! I'll shoot!"

She was going to make him kill her.

The girl heaved the rifle to her shoulder.

"Shit," he said and dove for the doorway.

The AK-47 cracked behind him on full auto. The rounds destroyed the doorframe. Mitch crawled through freezing water and filth as the gun chewed through the wall and filled the air with dust and splinters.

Christ, I'm getting lit up by a ten-year-old girl—

The firing stopped. A hand reached under his armpit and pulled. It was Tom.

"A kid in there with an AK," he said as he got back to his feet.

Tom's eyebrows shot up.

Mitch growled, "I gave her every chance to give up. I don't shoot little girls."

"Then she's going to shoot us. You know how this works."

"I don't shoot little girls," he repeated.

"What do you want to do?"

"I'll distract her, then you grab her."

Tom shrugged. "It's your neck."

Mitch moved to the edge of the doorway while Tom roamed deeper down the hall to take her from the far entrance.

"This is it, kid," he called out. "Last chance to put down your weapon."

He wished he had a flash bang grenade. The girl was crazier than Shook.

Hannah, he remembered. That was her name.

Mitch shot his head around the corner for a quick look inside.

To his relief, the room was empty save for the dead.

THIRTY-SEVEN

The church was filled with writhing forms barely visible in the weak light of oil lamps. Smoke drifted along the ceiling from cigarettes lit by wounded fighters who were still awake.

Hannah stood guard with her AK-47, cocking her ear at the odd splash of gunfire that interrupted the night's quiet. The commander sat with her back against the altar, her blood seeping into the carpet.

"Today, it's income inequality," Abigail said to nobody in particular. "Tomorrow, climate change. So stupid. We're so, so stupid."

She'd started raving an hour ago. Curled up like cats on the floor, the girls stirred in their sleep. Any minute, the rebels would burst through the doors.

"We didn't have enough sense to solve any of it."

Hannah was barely listening, not that she understood much of it anyway. She was far more worried that Abigail's wound was still bleeding. She eyed the nuns ministering to the wounded and wondered if she should say something.

"Soon, it'll solve us," the commander said.

The doors banged open. The church inhaled a breath of freezing night air. The oil lamps sputtered where they were hung.

Electrified, Hannah raised her rifle.

Then lowered it. Sabrina had come.

Abigail's eyes were bright and feverish. "The world's coming to an end so slow that nobody cares. Do you think we're giving our blood for capitalism? So the few can take it all? The only answer…" Her words dissolved into a pained growl.

Sabrina fixed her gaze on the commander and marched up the aisle to crouch next to her. "How bad is it?"

"They had to fix her arm," Hannah said.

The soldier unslung her medical bag. "Take your finger off the trigger before you shoot yourself. Why are you smiling like that?"

"I'm really happy to see you." Everything was going to be okay now.

Sabrina removed the dressing around Abigail's arm to reveal a jagged red line seamed with crude stitches. The flesh was swollen, bloody, and bruised.

"Revolution," the commander gasped.

"This is going to hurt." Sabrina poured alcohol onto the wound. Abigail growled again. "Goddamn, yes, it does."

"Will she be okay?" Hannah said.

"The bleeding is slowing down," Sabrina said. "She's strong. She'll survive the wound. Infection's another matter. If gangrene sets in…"

She didn't finish the sentence. Hannah didn't want to know. Outside, a short machine-gun burst broke the night's stillness.

"That woke me up," Abigail said. "I need a drink." She accepted Sabrina's canteen, drank thirstily, and gave it back. "Now give me a real drink."

Sabrina handed her a silver flask. "Here."

Another long pull. "Talk to me."

"We stopped them at Tremont, but tomorrow, who knows. The front line's a mess. We might have to bug out in the morning." Sabrina looked around the casualty collection station as if trying to figure out how she was going to move all these people.

"How many did we lose?"

Sabrina redressed the wound. "So far, nine dead, twenty-six wounded, seventeen missing."

The commander gritted her teeth. "Nearly a third..."

"We weren't ready. It's like they knew. One big setup."

Hannah stared at her with growing alarm. This she understood.

"Central committee?" Abigail asked.

"Among the missing," Sabrina said. "They were at HQ. You're it now."

"No," Abigail said. "You. Take command."

"We're in a bad spot. We lost most of our supplies at HQ. The IMPD won't come. They're fortifying the bridges behind us."

"The Centrists don't care about winning. Just holding on to what's theirs."

"I was thinking, yeah, we might be on our own for now. We should send people to the Indy 300 and Rainbow Warriors on our flanks, see if they'll help."

"I'll go," Hannah said.

Sabrina shot her a look. "We'll talk later." Code for *zip it*.

Abigail gripped the soldier's arm with her good hand. "No matter what happens, hold the line. You hear? If you don't, the whole front will collapse."

Sabrina prepared a hypodermic needle. "We'll hold."

Abigail sighed as the drug flooded her system. "The government is selling us out. We can't rely on them."

"You need to rest now."

"We speak truth to power," she said dreamily. "This is them speaking power to truth."

Her eyes drifted closed. She was finally asleep.

Sabrina stood and surveyed the room. A small crowd of women had gathered, walking wounded with bandaged limbs and slung rifles.

They raised clenched fists in a power salute. Wanting back in the fight.

"It's on us now, sisters," Sabrina said.

Hannah said, "Me too."

The militiawoman held out her hand. "Give it here."

Hannah tightened her grip on the rifle. "If you don't want me to come, I'll stay here and protect Abigail."

"She doesn't need protecting. She's not the commander anymore."

"That's not fair!"

"She knew what giving up command meant. Now give me your AK."

Sabrina wasn't asking. Fuming, Hannah handed it over. The Free Women's new commander checked the magazine and passed it to another fighter.

"I fought today," Hannah said. "I was at HQ."

"I know."

"I can help. You won't let me."

"Tomorrow, sister," Sabrina said. "I'll be relying on you to help me forge the new line. Get some sleep. It's going to be a tough day."

The band of fighters left the church.

Hannah bent over Abigail to make sure the woman was breathing. Whether Abigail was in command or not didn't matter. She'd given Hannah a home. The woman would always be Hannah's commander.

The cause didn't work like that, however. It wasn't any one person.

Now the Free Women had a new leader, and everything would change again. Abigail was tough but maternal. Sabrina was just tough, more a big sister. Maybe that was okay. Maybe that was what the militia needed to survive this.

A massive yawn overtook her. There was no point in standing watch anymore. She curled up next to Maria and pulled the blanket over both of them. The girl flinched and whimpered in her sleep.

Hannah wrapped her arm around her shivering friend and closed her eyes. It was calming, sleeping next to a human being.

In her mind's eye, Vivian poured automatic fire out the window while she and Maria huddled shaking against the wall. Bullets rattled off the building like the loudest hailstorm she'd ever heard. The cook was screaming over the noise: *Get out, girls! Run!* Then her shoulders jerked and she crashed to the floor like a bloodied sack of meat.

Maria ran howling while Hannah cried for the woman who'd been so kind to her, who made a lot of a little merely by adding spices, who knew the secret of war cake, who'd told her to play because to each according to her need.

Vivian was gone now. Tomorrow, maybe all of them.

Hannah didn't think she'd ever sleep again, but she did.

She dreamed of *him*.

The rebels stood silhouetted in the glare of truck headlights. Dad still sat behind the wheel of the wreck smoking on the side of the road.

A rebel returned from the car wearing a grin. He was a giant of a man whose armor and helmet made him look even bigger. "That your husband back there?"

"Yes," Mom said in a tight voice.

"What's left of him, anyway. What did he do for a living?"

"He's a lawyer."

"ACLU," the giant said. "Got to make sure the moochers and flag burners get their rights."

"He practiced corporate law."

The man spat. "ACLU, I says." He smiled at Hannah. "Your daughter is really pretty."

Mom growled. "She's ten years old."

"So we understand each other then. Somebody here has to make a choice."

"We need help." She stared at the rebels with wild eyes. "Will nobody help us?"

The rebels stirred. They didn't like this. Still, she had no takers.

Mom knelt and hugged Hannah. "You'll be okay, honey." She was crying. "I'll be gone just for a little while. Don't worry about me."

"No," Hannah cried. "Don't leave me here."

"Come on, lady," the giant said. "I ain't got all night."

Mom gave Hannah a final reassuring smile that came out a grimace. The giant took her hand and pulled her weeping toward the wreck.

Alex was gone. Dad was dead. Mom had left her.

Hannah stood alone in the dark, crying.

Headlights flashed on the road. The men around her raised their rifles as a truck pulled off. More armed men spilled out.

One of them strode over and sized up Hannah with a glance. "What's this?"

"Refugees, Sergeant."

The man bent to look her in the eye. "I'm Mitch. What's your name, little one?"

"H-Hannah."

"War's no place for little girls, Hannah. Where's your mommy?"

Still blubbering, she pointed at the wreck.

Mitch sighed. "Come on. We'll drop you somewhere safe along the way."

"No! He's in there with my mom."

Understanding crossed the man's face, leaving behind a mean scowl. "I'll take care of it."

"Sergeant, we don't have time for this," another soldier said.

Mitch hesitated. He gazed down the road, where his war waited for him.

Then he said, "Yeah, Tom, we do."

He walked off into the dark. The car door opened. The giant roared in anger, which cut to the sound of a hand slapping meat.

Mitch reappeared, shoving the giant ahead of him. "Keep walking, asshole."

The giant spat blood. "I don't report to you."

"All you boys, get back on the road. The colonel's waiting. We're taking Indy tomorrow."

"You're letting him go?" Hannah said.

"I'm fighting a war, kid. I can't fight him too."

The giant and his soldiers returned to their truck and sped away, the giant giving Mitch the finger until he disappeared in the darkness.

Hannah ran to the wreck. Her mother lay curled up in the back seat, clutching her stomach and moaning.

"She's hurt!" she cried. "Help!"

"Mount up," Mitch said.

She ran after him. "You can't leave us. Please help my mom, she's hurt!"

The soldier looked down at her. "You're going to be okay, kid, but you have to be tough for a little while."

"No. No." She grabbed hold of his leg and clung. "Don't go. He hurt her bad."

He pried free of her grip. "We're fighting a war."

The truck roared away into the night, leaving her alone with the muffled sound of her mother wailing.

She awoke gasping and struggled against the arms that held her.

"It's okay," Maria said. "You're okay."

Her clenched body relaxed.

"It's just a bad dream." Her friend hugged her tight. "I got you."

Hannah took a deep breath that forced air into her lungs. "I'm okay now."

"You sure?"

"Yeah."

"You want to talk about it?"

"No. No, I'm okay."

Maria yawned. "Okay. Good night."

Hannah lay awake in the dark and listened to her friend breathe. The gunfire had stopped. The oil lamps had gone out. The entire world slumbered around her.

Love or hate. For days, she'd wondered what the cause meant to her.

She now realized it was both.

Love for the Free Women, hate for the men who'd destroyed her family and her childhood. Love for her sisters, hate for the man who'd hurt her mother on the way to Indy and for the other man who'd ignored her pleas for help.

If she ever got her hands on a rifle again, she'd never give it back. She'd fight for what she loved against those she hated. The men who'd destroyed her world.

Next time, she'd shoot straight, and she wouldn't miss.

THIRTY-EIGHT

Gabrielle's alarm clock startled her awake with its grating buzz. She turned it off and went back to sleep.

When she woke again, bright daylight streamed through a gap in the curtains. The room was cold, though it was nothing she wasn't already used to, growing up in Montreal. She checked the clock. Late morning, and still she had no interest in getting out of her warm bed.

Gabrielle had heard stories about humanitarian workers too long in the field. Chronic fatigue, post-traumatic stress. She put her own malaise down to simple exhaustion and a little homesickness. Her whirlwind tour of the city and harrowing visit to the rebels was catching up to her. She needed a break.

There were still things to do, always some report to satisfy the UN's insatiable hunger for documentation, but nothing that prevented taking a day off. Gruber had her needs analysis, and he'd respond when it suited him. Aubrey had gotten her story about the child soldiers.

Aubrey's decision to dissolve their partnership had hurt, but

Gabrielle understood. They were a bad influence on each other. Aubrey made her reckless. She made Aubrey care.

She reached for her cell phone on the dresser. The hotel Wi-Fi was slow but working. Another batch of text messages from anxious family and friends had come through. She was tired of sending stock replies that she was okay, mostly because she wasn't sure she was.

In her first eight days in Indy, she'd seen things that couldn't be unseen. Things she'd take home with her. Her parents and friends watched the daily stream of horrific news. They knew America was devouring itself. But how could she ever explain to them what she'd already experienced in such a short time?

Percussive thuds outside. Snarl of rifle fire. A fierce battle raged less than two miles away from the warmth of her bed. The rebels wanted in.

She thumbed her stock reply to her parents, thinking, *Forgive me, Mom, Dad.* For her entire life, she'd been content to nestle under their protective wings. When she told them she was going to America to help the children, they were horrified. They'd tried to talk her out of it, but going was something she had to do. Now she thought of them with a deep sympathy.

Part of becoming an adult was realizing your parents were flawed human beings on their own journey. As she grew older, she appreciated their suffering. The terror of losing their only child, the miracle of finding her again, the constant worry it wasn't real and fate would snatch her away. What had happened to her had also happened to them, and it had shaped them just as it had her.

Before she'd boarded her flight to Trenton, Dad hugged her one last time. Gabrielle told him not to worry. He said he wouldn't. Then he'd laughed, because they both knew he would.

It was happening again now. Her texting she was okay. Them

believing her and worrying anyway. Her not sure she was okay and feeling caught in a lie.

She missed them. She missed home. She couldn't go back until she'd accomplished her mission, though. Something she had to do.

Her satellite phone rang. She snatched it up. "Justine."

Gruber barked, "I am reading your e-mail. Your account of crossing the contact line. Which was a very foolish thing to do."

"I wanted to help the reporter source her story about the use of child soldiers," Gabrielle explained. "Get public opinion going our way."

"You are young and idealistic. You have yet to learn the world is not on your shoulders. In fact, you do not matter."

Anger burned in her chest. "It'll matter when the newspaper—"

"You are not understanding," he grated. "You do not matter. I do not matter. Systems matter. Your mission will be to put systems in place to address the problems you identify. Not try to solve them by yourself."

"I saw a kid shot in the hip. I had to do something—"

"Stop talking. You are not helping by risking your life with reckless stunts. You can only help by doing what I tell you."

She said nothing.

He let out a loud sigh. "Are you there?"

"If I say anything, you'll just yell at me more."

Gruber snorted. "Then you are capable of learning. I reviewed your needs analysis based on your contacts with your local NGOs and IDP centers."

UN speak: NGOs were *nongovernmental organizations* such as the Red Cross, Amnesty International, and the Peace Office. IDPs were *internally displaced people*—people forced to flee their homes but still residing in their country. Refugees, though not in the legal sense.

"Things are bad here," Gabrielle said.

"Obviously," Gruber agreed. "I am approving a budget for you, drawing from CERF." The Central Emergency Response Fund. "You are to build a team, develop a humanitarian action plan, and coordinate a network of NGOs to address the issues in your assessment."

She grinned at this news. "Including the child soldiers."

"Set up your network and let it do its work. Bring in additional NGOs such as Geneva Call as needed. If they have capacity, they can contact all armed groups and negotiate a Deed of Commitment to get them to stop using children."

Gabrielle said, "That will be my top priority."

"There are three hundred thousand children fighting around the world at any given time. Now there are more. Address it through the system. Do not go on a personal crusade."

"Okay," she lied. "And thank you. For the resource allocation."

Gruber sighed again. "Gabrielle. If you take on the war's problems as your own, it will grind you down. The process is slow and complex and tedious, but it is far more resilient than any one person. If you trust in it, it will produce results."

"Okay," she said again and meant it this time, though she took his advice with a grain of salt. The system hadn't saved her all those years ago—a single man had. If a middle-aged dentist hadn't taken a risk while filling up his gas tank on his way home from work, she'd be dead.

Instead, that one man had saved a child's life.

A splash of gunfire. Gabrielle couldn't tell if it was coming from outside her window or Gruber's end. New York had its own share of fighting.

She added, "I really appreciate you giving me the green—"

"Right," he grunted. "You are doing good work. Merry Christmas. Goodbye."

Gruber terminated the call. Abrasive to the last, but she didn't care. She bounded out of bed into the chilly room. Still exhausted and more than a little homesick, but eager to get to work.

Then she stopped and snatched up her phone.

Smiling, she texted her parents again. She didn't tell them she was okay this time. This time, Gabrielle was able to tell them she was doing great, and for once, she really meant it.

THIRTY-NINE

The Free Women's headquarters grew increasingly frantic as the rebels advanced behind a wall of devastating firepower. In a daze, Hannah gazed at it all from a great distance, as if reality had become a TV on in the background. She'd made five runs through smoke and gunfire this morning to deliver messages and supplies, and she was exhausted.

Kristy staggered into the house and handed over her message to Sabrina's staff. Then she collapsed against the wall next to Hannah.

Hannah nestled against her friend's arm. "You okay?"

Kristy hugged her knees and shivered. "I don't like this anymore."

"It can't go on forever, right?" *God, I hope it can't.*

"I want my mom. I really miss my mom."

"I know. Me too."

"The last time I saw her, I was really mean." The girl bent her forehead until it touched her knees. "I'm so stupid."

Hannah put her arm over Kristy's shoulders. "No, you're not."

"Runner!" a fighter called out.

Hannah gave her a squeeze. "Everybody looks up to you, you know. Because you're strong. I won't let you down."

Kristy straightened her shoulders and wiped her eyes. "I know you won't."

"I need a runner!"

Hannah hauled herself to her feet. "Volunteer."

Sabrina studied a road map thumbtacked to the wall. The map revealed the front line, *X*'s and *O*'s countering each other like a runaway tic-tac-toe game. She erased and redrew an *X*. The warped front line had bent a little more, fluid but still unbroken. Beyond her, militia worked feverishly to prepare meals and make bombs in the kitchen.

"Give her the backpack," the commander said.

A fighter helped Hannah get her arms through the loops. Bottles clinked inside. The pack's weight settled against her back. It was heavy.

Sabrina pulled a grimy notepad from her hip pocket and scribbled. "Run this message and give them the pack."

"Here, Hannah." Another fighter was pointing at a spot on the map.

Hannah rubbed her eyes and committed the location to memory. *Go out, turn right, then right again at the intersection . . .* "I can do it."

Sabrina tore out the sheet and handed it over. "I know you can, sister."

Hannah threaded the shouting women and went outside. The sun was a pale disk behind a cloud of smoke. Several hours of daylight left.

She spotted Maria coming the other way and dashed ahead to wrap her friend in a hug.

"Hannah Banana!"

"Maria Macaroni."

The girl fought to catch her breath. "We're flanking them on Walnut."

It was good news, though Hannah had no idea what it meant. She'd seen the big picture on the map back at HQ but hadn't understood much of it.

Right now, she had to tell a unit to fall back across Pershing, and every second counted. "I have to go. I'm glad you're my friend!"

Hannah raced down the street and paused to crouch as a mortar round whistled through the air and struck somebody's backyard far behind the line. A rifle cracked nearby. She got up and kept going.

She reached the house and peered through the living room window to make sure the Free Women still held it. The militiawoman standing guard jumped at the sight of her. Hannah waved.

The fighter opened the door. "You runners are the unsung heroes. I'll get the sergeant." She turned and bawled, "Sheila!"

Still gasping from her run, Hannah went inside and shucked her pack. From where she stood, she had a clear view of the kitchen. Bullets had shattered the cabinetry, the wreckage covered in powdery white dust. A fighter knelt on the counter to shoot a few bursts through a small window over the sink. Shell casings clattered across the linoleum.

The woman ducked away as rounds thudded into the house. She caught sight of Hannah and smiled, her face blackened by soot.

Another fighter strode into the room. "What's the word, sister?"

Hannah handed over the note.

Sheila crumpled it in her fist. "We're bugging out."

The sergeant pulled a Molotov cocktail from the backpack and thrust it in her ammo belt. It was a wine bottle filled with turpentine and a little dish soap. Once lit, the cloth wick turned the bottle into a bomb.

She removed a handful of energy bars next. A large plastic freezer bag bulging with bullets. Jars of gasoline worth a small fortune.

"Gather up anything that will burn," Sheila said.

Hannah had seen them do this before. *Scorched earth policy*, Sabrina had called it. They were going to torch the house to cover their withdrawal. She reminded herself this scarred shell wasn't a real home, not anymore.

A rifle banged upstairs.

The sergeant splashed the gasoline across kindling stacked against the baseboards. "That's Grace. Go get her, Hannah. Tell her we're bugging out."

Hannah hustled up the stairs and found Grace Kim in a bedroom overlooking the house's backyard. The sniper knelt with her rifle perched in a small hole blasted through the outer wall.

Grace recoiled. "Get down!"

Hannah threw herself to the floor as a machine gun pounded outside. The rounds tore into the room. Paint chips filled the air like confetti.

The gun shifted to a new target. The sniper pulled her up. "Are you okay?"

Hannah's legs were shaking. "You're bugging out."

Grace helped her navigate the stairs. "I remember you. I hope you figured out what your cause is. Whatever it is, you'll need it today."

Sheila waited for them at the bottom. "There's a squad in the house behind us. Leapfrog into the one behind that."

Defense in depth, Sabrina had called it. The strategy was to make the enemy pay a heavy price for every house until the offensive wore itself out. The new commander seemed to have a real knack for fighting.

Hannah lingered to watch the sergeant light a handful of newspaper and toss it. The gasoline ignited. Fire whooshed along the baseboards.

Grace pulled her out the door. "Time to go."

They crossed Pershing as thick black smoke began to pour out of the house. The air filled with the rebel yell.

Sheila waved them into her squad's new base. "Rest up for the next game."

Hannah staggered to the nearest wall and slumped against it. "I'm so bushed."

Grace tore the wrapper off a granola bar and gave it to her. "You shouldn't be here at all."

"I'll go back in a minute," Hannah panted. "Just need to catch my breath."

"I meant the war."

She bit into the stale bar and chewed without tasting it. "You asked what my cause is. I'm right where I'm needed."

"You also need to think about what comes after. Having a normal life again. Everything you do here will stay with you the rest of your life."

There it was again, that embarrassment the grown-ups shared. Shame at their destruction of the old world. Pride in all the little ways they survived the new one.

They didn't understand. The old world wasn't coming back. Hannah's childhood had ended when a sniper shot her mother dead in the street.

Hannah said, "This is normal."

She pulled on her empty pack and went out the back, where she'd retrace her steps to HQ.

You are your deep, driving desire.

She was a soldier.

FORTY

G abrielle drove like a maniac through Mile Square.
Eyes darting across her field of view, she performed rapid
life and death calculations. How fast she could go, where a sniper
might shoot from, what she'd do if a bullet pinged against the car. It
was exhausting.

But also a source of pride. She was starting to think like a local.
Gabrielle had learned a lot from Aubrey. She missed the reporter's
reassuring presence, if not her predilection for blasting heat, droning radio news, and smooth jazz.

A police cruiser sat in front of the Peace Office. Alarmed, she
parked behind it and hurried up the walk. She collected the new
missing posters and went in.

An officer in black tactical gear stood inside, his automatic rifle
pointed at the floor.

"Is everything okay here?" she said.

The cop eyed her as if she might be a threat. "Why wouldn't
it be?"

"I'm looking for Paul."

"Dreadlocks guy?"

"Yeah."

"Conference room."

She hurried down the corridor to find Paul sitting with another police officer wearing a dress uniform. He looked up at her with an anxious expression.

She shucked her coat and scarf. "What's going on?"

"Officer Jennings here just informed me the IMPD is shutting us down."

The man raised his hands. "Nobody's saying that."

"You said we can't try to locate family members on the other side of the contact line," Paul said. "That's what we do."

"No, it isn't. You're a religious community. You may continue to conduct your worship services without interference."

"But we can't do our religious work."

"Political work. The rebels have launched a major offensive in Haughville. Until the front stabilizes, we need to eliminate any contacts outside the city."

Paul said nothing. He seemed tired, hungry, broken. The war had taken so much from him. For a while, it had also given him something valuable—a sense of purpose, a chance to do good works amid so much misery. Gabrielle understood the power of purpose. It had drawn her here, into a war that wasn't hers.

The government had just robbed him of his. The front would never stabilize. The IMPD was shutting them down permanently.

Jennings stood to leave. "Thank you for your cooperation."

She held up the sheaf of missing people in her hand. "The Peace Office's work is for UNICEF."

Thankfully, Paul didn't contradict her lie, which she hoped in the end would become only a white lie.

The police officer smiled. "You must be Gabrielle Justine."

"Yes."

"I've been hoping to talk to you. I understand you're in need of help moving aid to the combat zones. You've been having some meetings. You should have checked in with the IMPD first about providing security."

As Aubrey warned her, word had gotten around about her meeting the Free Women, which was a Leftist militia.

"I was planning to talk to the government for security." It was UN policy.

"Excellent." He produced a card and handed it over. "When you're ready, give Public Affairs a call."

"In the meantime, we want to continue our work here reuniting families across the contact line."

Still smiling, he said, "No."

"But—"

"You call us when you're ready to get the aid flowing. We'll make it worth your while." He squared his hat. "You have a great day."

The man's hint at a bribe confirmed her worst fears that a big part of the aid would end up on the black market. "Wait."

He turned. "Yeah?"

She took a sharp breath. "I'm talking to militias about security too."

Jennings's grating smile disappeared as if switched off. He removed his hat and set it on the table. Then he resumed his seat while keeping his eyes fixed on her. "That's not a very friendly position for the UN to take with its host."

Paul looked between them with alarm but wisely kept his mouth shut.

"Maybe we could be friendly to each other," Gabrielle said.

"I already told you we're more than willing to make things worth your while."

"I'd like to tell you how you can. First off, you don't impede any of our operations."

"I said it's not up to—"

"Whatever the city may decide, you decide whether to enforce it, right? So don't enforce it in this case. In return, UNICEF will grant you a security contract."

Jennings's expression became thoughtful. "A contract."

"You section off some of your officers and form a private security corporation, which we'll hire on a retainer basis." She had that latitude.

"An exclusive contract, you mean."

"With a bonus if all shipments reach where they're supposed to go, subject to audit. If our audit shows anything fell off the truck, there's no bonus, and I take my business elsewhere."

"Such a bonus would have to be substantial."

"Substantial enough," Gabrielle said.

A more genuine smile crossed the police officer's face as he stood again and offered his hand. "I'll take it to my superiors. We'll be in touch."

She rose and shook it. "Good. In the meantime, we'll continue our work."

Once he'd gone, she let go the breath she'd been holding and collapsed back in her seat. Despite the chill in the room, sweat trickled down her back.

After a few moments, Paul said, "I'm not sure what just happened there, but I think you saved our ass. Are we still in business?"

"New York reviewed my assessment," Gabrielle told him. "I'm funded to produce a humanitarian action plan and get aid flowing."

"That's great." He still seemed bewildered.

"I need staff. In fact, I'd like to hire everybody in your operation."

She needed accounting, media relations, administrators, drivers. With unemployment so high in the city, she could have her pick of the best talent Indy offered.

But she didn't want a choice. She wanted these people. Like her, they were committed. For them, it wasn't a job, it was a calling.

Paul smiled. "You'll need an accountant, I take it."

"I do."

"Then I guess I'm your man."

"Good. Because I have to find room in the budget to pay off the IMPD so they don't rob us blind. And make it look right on the books."

Paul studied her. "You know, you're tougher than I thought you were."

Gabrielle had learned from the best. It was sink or swim in Indy. Nobody would protect her here. She had to fight for what she wanted.

Even so, she wasn't that tough. "The jury's still out on that, Paul."

"I'm liking what I'm seeing so far."

"Since I'll be staying, it's about time I moved out of the Castle and found an apartment. Maybe you could help me find a place?"

"I can do that." He rubbed his hands. "I'll call the staff together. We can tell them the good news."

"Sounds good." Gabrielle's phone trilled. "I'll be right back."

She left the room as Paul went to round up his staff, who filled the hallway with excited conversation as they filed into the conference room.

She answered the call. "Justine."

"It's Aubrey."

"I was just thinking about you. How are you? Are you okay?"

"The *Chronicle* refused the story about the child soldiers. They think it would blow up in their faces. The government could step in. They could lose the newspaper."

Gabrielle frowned as she processed this news. "So it was all for nothing."

"Not yet," Aubrey said. "I have a card to play at my end. I was wondering how committed you still are at yours."

"You know the answer to that."

"Good. Get yourself on the radio or TV. Get the story out."

"You're okay with not breaking the story?"

"I can't break anything if the *Chronicle* won't print it," Aubrey told her. "If you get the story out, the paper may feel safe to cover it. Meanwhile, like I said, I have another card to play."

Gabrielle liked the idea of teaming up with Aubrey again. She'd do it.

The reporter said, "And try to find out how many child soldiers are being used in the city militias. Even if it's a ballpark estimate."

Gabrielle was already on that. They said their goodbyes. She returned to the conference room, now filled with the Peace Office's staff. The conversation died as she entered.

"So," she said. "Anybody here have experience with media relations?"

Gabrielle gazed across the hopeful faces, grateful she was no longer alone in trying to make a difference. She felt a whole lot tougher with friends like these.

This war's sides believed in their cause enough to kill and die for it, but she had a nobler cause, and would give it no less of a commitment.

FORTY-ONE

Alex searched the basement for something he could give Sergeant Shook. The floorboards over his head creaked as the rest of the militia rifled the house for their own souvenirs and goodies. So far, he'd found nothing but plastic junk. The Indy 300 had held this territory for months, and they'd picked it clean.

Goddamn Sergeant Shook. Alex was exhausted from the fighting. The coke's short-lived euphoria and two days of constant combat had drained him to the last drop. But this was how he had to spend the few hours he had before it was his turn for sentry duty.

So far, he'd come up with nothing. Unless Shook wanted some leftover house paint or a power washer, he was getting zilch.

Boots thudded on the stairs. Jack shambled into the basement nursing his forehead. "Find anything good?"

Alex gestured at a NordicTrack treadmill standing by a washer and dryer.

His friend nodded, still rubbing his head. "Keep looking."

"I looked everywhere."

"Hey, check it out," Jack said.

Alex wheeled. "What? What'd you find?"

Jack was inspecting a box containing a board game. "Monopoly. I used to play this." He smiled. "What do you think?"

"Bring it upstairs," Alex said. "We can use it for fuel."

His friend frowned and put it aside. "Right."

"My skin feels like it's crawling. I need another hit."

"No way, bro. Only when we're fighting. That's the rule."

"Please? Pretty please? It's Christmas Eve, dude."

"Nope, and stop asking. We only have a little left."

Alex had morphine in his medical kit. One shot, and he'd float to his happy place. Bravo did it all the time, but not Alpha. He couldn't risk Mitch finding out.

"Let's go see if there's any beer then."

They tramped upstairs. The squad sat on metal chairs set around the kitchen island, playing poker for a small pile of cigarettes while supper warmed up in a tin on the Coleman.

Alex dropped the Monopoly game on the countertop. "Some play money for your poker game. Or you can pretend you're Democrats and burn it."

The men laughed. Smirking, Tom reached into the cooler and set a beer in front of him.

Alex cracked it open and took a deep swallow. He looked around for Jack. The kid was lying curled up in a fetal ball in his sleeping bag, already sound asleep.

The veteran raised his can. "To Grady. Rest in peace, brother."

They drank again to Casey, who'd caught a ricochet in the leg and had been taken to a nearby clinic. Alex chugged what was left in his can.

Tom eyed him. "Pace yourself."

Alex had watched Grady cough blood, his lungs shredded. A flipped truck crush men while they were dismounting. Screaming militiamen, set alight by a rain of Molotov cocktails, duck and roll in the snow. That was how the libs had finally stopped them at Tremont. One by one, the trucks burst into flames.

Pace yourself. Right.

The men frowned and tilted their heads toward the windows, where Donnie stood watch.

Voices. Women's voices. The women they'd been fighting these past two days.

They were *singing*.

"'Silent Night,'" Tom said, sounding wistful.

Donnie yelled out the window, "On the first day of Christmas, my true love said to me, let's hang a liberal from a tree!"

Nobody laughed. Jack moaned and turned over in his sleep. The women went on with their ghostly and angelic singing. The men began to hum along in a deep baritone.

Alex smiled as the music seeped into his soul. It didn't make him nostalgic for Christmas. Instead, he thought about Janice Brewer. When he closed his eyes, he remembered the tumult of feelings he had for her but couldn't quite picture her face. Her laugh, he could recall clear as day. An easy laugh suggesting she and the world were on good terms and that maybe she was a little wild. It used to fill him with a strange longing, something like hunger.

He didn't know if it had been real love. He hoped to survive this war so he could see what it was like. He'd fought and killed, but until he experienced love, he wasn't yet a man but a boy playing grown-up games.

Janice's mom and dad had planted a MARSH FOR PRESIDENT sign on their front lawn, so maybe the evangelicals had left them alone. He imagined coming home a hero after the great war for liberty, a quiet and moody veteran weighted by the things he'd done. Her laugh would remind him of happier times, and her love would save him. He'd rolled this fantasy often while lying in his sleeping bag at night. The women's singing brought it back full force.

Then the song ended, leaving him in a drab ruin that stood like some forgotten castoff of creation.

The men sighed with their own longings.

One of the militiamen laid down his hand, showing three tens. He took the meager pot.

Tom dealt a new hand. "Ante up, gentlemen. We were talking about Grady. Phil, you knew him better than anybody."

"I guess I did," the militiaman said. "He didn't talk much about his life before. He had it rough. Two divorces. His ex-wives took everything from him. The second got a judge to say he couldn't see his own kids. Can you believe that?"

The men bristled. One said, "That shit is ice cold."

"The Tree was all he had. I know he would have wanted to go out the way he did, in combat."

"I'll miss his stories about being a bounty hunter," Donnie said from the other side of the room. "He saw some crazy stuff in his time."

"Did you ever hear him talk about the times he went out on patrol down at the border?"

"Hell, yeah. He told me once how these Mexicans—"

There was a commotion at the back door. The sentry called out a challenge. Another man answered.

"Friendly coming in," the sentry said.

Sergeant Shook stomped into the house. "Where's the boss?"

Tom put his cards facedown on the table. "He's with the colonel."

"I ain't looking for him anyway." The sergeant scanned their faces and zeroed in on Alex. "You're the one I want."

Shook had come to find out what Alex had gotten him for Christmas. Mitch wasn't here to protect him this time, and he wasn't sure his squad mates would step up on his behalf, not when a debt was being settled.

The sergeant was going to drag him outside and turn him into hamburger.

The man walked up to him and thrust out his massive paw. "You were shit hot the other day, soldier."

Alex let go the breath he was holding and shook it. "Thanks."

"You charged that building like John Wayne."

Alex had only a vague notion of who John Wayne was, but he got the idea. He wasn't sure what to say and settled on the default response. "Hooah, Sergeant."

"I told my squad they could learn from you. Once I got those pussies moving, we took that building in no time."

"We'll kick their ass again tomorrow, Sergeant."

"You want to share some war stories, come find me. Bravo's in the next house over. We got a lot of beer." He sneered at Alex's squad. "Carry on, ladies."

After he left, the men cracked grins. They saw Shook as just another thing they had to put up with along with the weather and camp food.

Alex said nothing, surprised the sergeant's approval meant something. When a man like Shook complimented you on your behavior, it probably wasn't something you should be proud of.

Nonetheless, there was a strange kinship in that handshake.

Tom shook his head. "Stay away from that guy, kid."

"I think he gets it," Alex said, just as he believed he understood Shook.

Shook gave lip service to the cause. He railed against government goons and taxation as theft and handouts for the lazy and the slow death of free speech. But the guy didn't really care. He simply liked getting coked up and shooting people.

He was crazy, plain and simple. To him, the whole war was a big joke, a chance to go wild with impunity, an excuse to fight for its own sake.

Tom narrowed his eyes. "What do you mean?"

"Nothing. Forget it."

Donnie laughed. "Yeah, well, you're a psycho, just like him."

In Alex's book, Shook was more real than any of them. He

crumpled his beer can, tossed it into the kitchen sink with the other empties, and headed to the door.

"Where are you going?" Tom called after him.

"I'll be back in time for my watch."

Over with Shook's squad, nobody would tell him to pace himself.

FORTY-TWO

Hannah's meager meal consisted of cold ramen noodles and a little beef jerky washed down with swallows from her canteen. Wiped out by the day's fierce fighting, the other kids chewed with shocked, blank expressions.

The headquarters staff sat and ate in their own daze. Only Sabrina was on her feet, studying the strategic map with its *X*'s and *O*'s. The line had held another day.

Outside, snow fell steadily from the graying sky.

Maria eyed the pacing commander. "What's she thinking?"

"We're counterattacking tomorrow," Kristy whispered. "Mark my words."

Hannah doubted it. Who would want to fight in this weather?

"I can't believe we're still alive," Maria said. A moment later, she was snoring.

Hannah watched her sleep with envy. Every time she sat still for too long, a vague panic settled in her shoulders and made her neck clench.

"Hey," Kristy hissed. "Hannah."

"What?"

The girl extended her hand with her palm facing outward. "Thank you. For cheering me up before."

Hannah smiled and interlaced her fingers with Kristy's. "I'm glad we're on the same team."

"Girls rule."

"Girls rule," Hannah echoed, as if this were a simple fact.

She squinted at the big gray squares of plastic sheeting stapled over the windows and judged the light. "I'm going to go see how Abigail is doing."

"You're not tired?"

Hannah wanted to leap out of her skin. After the last two days, her feelings seemed too big for her body. So much love and hate, it hurt.

She stood and dusted her pants. "I'll be back."

Sabrina had been listening. "Take your bedroll. It'll be dark soon."

"I will."

Maria started awake. "Where are you going? Do you want me to come?"

"You go ahead and sleep."

"Okay." Maria nodded off again.

Hannah hoisted her pack. "See you tomorrow. Good night."

The guard opened the door to let her out. "Merry Christmas, Hannah."

She went outside into the biting cold. The world paled as the blizzard gathered force, the driving snow covering up the war's scars. She tilted her head to catch snowflakes on her tongue. Aside from the hum in her ears left over from the day's gunfire, the neighborhood was quiet, even peaceful.

A wisp of music wafted through the ruins.

Men's voices, singing, "O come, let us adore Him…"

Tonight was Christmas Eve.

She flashed to Dad putting up the tree last year, a real tree she'd decorated with him and Mom while Alex sat on the couch sighing with practiced boredom. They'd enjoyed their family tradition of opening one present on Christmas Eve. Hannah got the new sweater she'd been dropping blatant hints about. She stayed up late and went to bed flush with anticipation.

Christmas was once a magical time.

"O come, let us adore Him…"

One by one, the houses around her joined in as the Free Women added their voices to the song: "O come, let us adore Him, Christ the Lord."

She clenched her teeth and kept walking. These men had no right to sing. They'd destroyed Christmas for her. They had no right to make her remember. She wanted the Free Women to sing "I Am Woman" again. Shout it right in their fascist faces.

Driven by her anger, Hannah trudged through the heavy snow-pack and blinding snowfall. The white world darkened to gray as the sun went down. She reached the church as night fell and paused at the threshold to stomp the snow off her boots.

"Who goes there?" a familiar voice trembled behind the holy water font.

"Hey, Alice," she said. "It's just me, Hannah."

Holding a broom like a weapon, the girl emerged from the shadows, trailed by the other younger girls who'd been left behind. "How's Kristy and everybody?"

"They're all fine," Hannah said. "How are things here?"

The girl shot a terrified look at the far side of the church, where a row of bodies lay with their jackets draped over their faces. "Can we go with you?"

"I'm staying the night here."

"Okay. I've been protecting these girls. I'll protect you too."

"I'll bet you could," said Hannah, eyeing Alice's useless broom.

Alice put on her war face. "You can count on me. Sister."

Behind her, the girls raised their fists in a plucky power salute. Hannah continued into the church and found Abigail where she'd left her, sitting with her back against the altar.

Hannah knelt next to her old commander. "Hi."

Abigail stared at the dead and wounded lying on the floor. Her face was worn and pale. She seemed to have aged ten years in the past few days.

She offered Hannah a faint smile. "*Namaste*. What brings you here?"

"I came to see how you're doing."

"My arm hurts like hell, but that's a luxury of still having one, I guess." She sighed. "Otherwise, there's nothing worse than having too much time and nothing to do but think about everything you did wrong."

"You didn't do anything wrong," Hannah said.

Abigail returned her bleak gaze to the wounded. "This war isn't worth even one of them dying."

"You didn't start it."

Another weak smile crossed the woman's face. "From the mouths of babes."

"Sabrina's doing a good job. The line is holding."

"I have no doubts about Sabrina McCann. I don't know if she's an artist forced to become a general, or a general forced to live the wrong life until somebody gave her a chance to fight."

Hannah tried to reconcile Sabrina as an artist and antigun activist with the militia chief she knew. "I didn't know she was an artist."

"She owned an art gallery down the street from the Collective. She spent most of her time curating, but her own paintings are amazing."

"I'd like to see them sometime," Hannah said.

"She insisted we use them for kindling."

Hannah wanted Abigail to see her the way she saw Sabrina. "I ran messages a whole bunch of times today."

"Something else I regret. Don't take this the wrong way, but that UNICEF woman was right. I never should have let you and the other girls into the Free Women."

Hannah recoiled as if slapped. "I want to help. I'm not a kid anymore."

"You remind me of my Jill. She saw injustice, she'd attack it with everything she had."

"Where is she?"

"She died when she was about your age. Heart defect. In insurance terms, a preexisting condition."

Hannah winced. "That's awful."

"My ex-husband fought for this country and came back changed," Abigail said. "He couldn't get enough help from the VA hospital because of budget cuts. When Jill died, I left him to start a new life counseling women who were going through what I'd gotten out of. When the Democrats retook Congress, I was hoping they'd fix healthcare once and for all, but they did nothing. I got mad. I wanted justice. I wanted justice not just for Jill but for all the little girls being hurt by the system."

Hannah had heard the Free Women talk about social and economic justice. She'd always thought it was about punishing criminals. They'd told her it meant treatment that was right and fair.

"I want justice too," she said. Both kinds.

"Now the little girls I wanted to help are fighting. We took away your childhood. When I look at you, sometimes I hate myself."

Hannah lay and put her head on Abigail's lap. "You saved me."

She fell asleep in an instant.

FORTY-THREE

Gabrielle inspected the furnished apartment while Paul explained its features.

"It's the fifth floor," he said. "The best I could do. A long walk up."

With all the displaced people, housing was at a premium in Indy.

"That's fine. I need the exercise."

"The furnishings are nice. Granite countertops, high ceilings, stainless steel appliances when you have electricity. You'll be right by the open-air market at Monument Circle. The doorman has a shotgun."

Large picture windows flooded the living room with daylight. A balcony overlooked East Washington below. Gabrielle drifted to the bedroom, which had a redbrick south-facing wall. The whole apartment had an urban loft feel. Compared to her cramped little unit in Montreal, it was luxurious.

These niceties didn't mean as much as they once did, however. The larger windows allowed in more cold, not to mention more flying glass if a bomb shattered them. The higher floor not only meant more running up and down but greater danger if there was a fire.

Already, she was thinking about how she'd fortify it.

"So that's the tour," Paul said. "What do you think?"

The place was cold. The framed art on the walls was bland, almost corporate. The red blotches on one painting looked like blood splatter. It would have to go.

"I'll take it."

She began making a list in her head of the things she'd need. More blankets, portable stove, matches, candles, water bottles, duct tape, propane.

When she moved into this place, she'd be a Hoosier.

"Cool," said Paul. "I'll make the arrangements."

Gabrielle checked her watch. "I have to get to the radio station for an interview."

"Can I come with?"

"I don't see why not. It'll save me time driving you back to the office."

Paul smiled. "Yeah, about that. Do you mind if I drive?"

They went downstairs and got into the car. Paul grinned and bounced behind the wheel. Expecting him to burn rubber like Aubrey, Gabrielle gripped the handhold on the door.

The car accelerated to a fast but far less terrifying speed than the reporter favored. She blew out a sigh.

"I never knew how much I enjoyed driving until I ran out of gas," Paul said.

"I may be getting the Peace Office its own car."

"What's stopping you?"

"My accountant has to tell me if we can fit it in our budget."

"Hell, yeah, we can. I'll make it work. Getting a car is easy. Gas, not so much."

Gabrielle gazed out the window with a smile. In just a few days, they'd already made a lot of progress. In about a week, the first of the aid shipments was scheduled to land at the airport. A few boxes of biscuits and school supplies, mostly, but it was just the beginning.

Paul cleared his throat. "You, uh, still talk to that reporter? Aubrey?"

"Now and then."

He shot her a sidelong glance. "I was just wondering if she was seeing anybody."

Gabrielle smiled. "You should call—"

Something cracked against the rear passenger door. An object rattled around the back seat with a series of alarming thumps.

She wheeled in alarm. "What was that?"

The back window exploded in a shower of glass.

Paul blanched and stomped the accelerator.

The car fishtailed in the snow. Gabrielle reached over and grabbed the wheel to help steady it. Paul took the next corner in a terrifying slide. Then they were out of danger.

Paul blew out a sigh and said, "You can let go now."

Trembling from excess adrenaline, she released her grip. *Aubrey was right. Never slow down. Never stop moving until you reach cover.* "Just get us there."

"Shooting at a car flying the UN flag. These people want to fight the whole world."

They found a parking space near the radio station and dashed to the doors. Minutes later, they arrived gasping in the third-floor lobby. The lights were on here. The station had its own power generator.

Paul caught his breath and grinned. "You're one of us now."

"You say that like it's a good thing."

A man emerged from a nearby office to grab their hands for a pronounced shake. "You're here! I'm Jimmy, the show's producer. Kevin's really looking forward to this."

Kevin Olson was one of the most popular voices in Indianapolis. Before the war, he had a political AM talk program with a small but loyal liberal fan base. For years, he'd predicted civil war would come to America. Now he was the city's voice of the Left, broadcasting a nightly show called *The Resistance with Kevin Olson*.

Jimmy ushered them into the studio. Two bearded men sat around a circular counter on which a collection of computer screens and scissor-arm suspension boom microphones rested. The jittery one wearing a leather jacket and blue armband was Kevin. The other, the technical producer introduced as "The Maestro," brooded in headphones worn over a floppy hat.

"Welcome to *The Resistance*," Kevin said and pointed at a chair. "You can sit there."

Gabrielle did, still a little out of breath. "Thanks for having me on your show."

"I'm glad you reached out. Most of our show will be spent talking about what's going on in Haughville. This is our chance to give the Hoosiers some good news before the New Year. Pull that microphone toward you and say something."

"Hello," she said. "My name is Gabrielle—"

"She's mugging the mike," the Maestro said.

"Back up from the microphone just a bit," Kevin told her. "Try to talk across the mike. It reduces pops and hisses."

"Like this?"

"Good, but not so loud. Keep going."

"Testing, testing…"

The Maestro gave a thumbs-up.

"Airtime is six p.m.," Kevin said. "So obviously this is prerecorded. I can see you're nervous, but don't worry. If you freeze up, we'll edit it out."

"Got it." Knowing they'd edit gave her a little more confidence.

"You ready?"

From picking an apartment to getting shot at by a sniper to being interviewed at a radio station. Another surreal day. "Yes."

The Maestro gave another thumbs-up. "We're recording."

"Well, Hoosiers, we've got a special guest in the studio right now, none other than Gabrielle Justine from the United Nations," Kevin said. "UNICEF, to be exact. That stands for the United Nations

Children's Fund. UNICEF is now working hard in American cities to help children affected by the war. Welcome to Indy, Gabrielle."

"I'm very happy to be here," Gabrielle said, making sure she talked sideways across the microphone.

He asked her about Montreal, what Canadians thought about the war, how she got involved with UNICEF. He was warming her up, helping her get over her stage fright. Recalling her media training, she kept her answers short and personable, avoiding both monologues and one-word responses. Remembering to breathe.

"So what exactly is UNICEF doing for Indy's children?"

Gabrielle explained the types of aid that would soon be flowing into the city. Vaccines and immunization, school supplies, nutritional supplements, safe drinking water, hygiene kits, psychological support.

"One very important aspect of our work is stopping the use of child soldiers," she said.

Kevin's smile faded. "Child soldiers?"

"Militias on both sides of the contact line are using children as porters, cooks, runners, spies, and even fighters. Our goal is to get all parties to agree to stop using children as weapons. We are developing resources to rehabilitate and reintegrate them back into society. Offer them a place that supports their health and dignity."

"Wait. You're saying our militias are using child soldiers too?"

"I've seen it. Children carrying machine guns, lying bleeding on hospital floors from gunshot wounds. We can't allow it to continue. We're better than this."

Kevin steered the conversation back to the first UNICEF shipment coming early in the New Year, and how parents could access this aid to benefit their kids.

Nailed it, she thought.

"Thank you for taking time to visit with us, Gabrielle," Kevin said. "You're doing great work, and we're all rooting for you."

"Thank you, Kevin."

Kevin eyed the Maestro, who gave him a thumbs-up. "And that's it. You did good, Gabrielle. That was about fifteen minutes. We'll edit it down to somewhere around five."

"As long as you keep the part in about the child soldiers," she said.

"Right, right," Kevin said. "No."

"No? I don't understand."

"It's not airable."

She stared at him, but he didn't offer to explain. "Why?"

"We're the voice of the resistance. Our goal is to strengthen the resistance. We air this, we'd be hurting our own side."

"Both sides are doing it, and both sides are wrong."

"Maybe later, we could run it. Maybe."

"How many kids have to die before it's the right time?"

"We live here," Kevin said. "Our kids live here. The Free Women are hanging on by a thread in Haughville. If the rebels break through, everybody you see in this room will be killed."

"What I'm hearing is you think war crimes are okay," she shot back, "as long as they help your side win."

Kevin tossed his hands. "Jimmy, help me out here."

"It's the politics," Jimmy said. "It's a very delicate—"

"If we air that part of the interview, the militias will shut us down," the Maestro cut in. "End of story. If you don't like it, start your own radio station."

Gabrielle looked at the men's faces one by one hoping for an opening, a compromise, some way to get the word out. They stared back at her offering nothing. She wanted to say more but knew it would do no good. In fact, it might burn her relationship with them. She needed them on her side.

But she wasn't on their side.

"*Vous êtes trou d'cul*," Gabrielle spat. "*C'est d'la marde.*"

The men bristled further. Whatever she was saying, they didn't like it. Which was appropriate, as she'd called them assholes and the situation a pile of shit.

"And you know what?" she went on. "Any side of this war that uses children as weapons doesn't deserve to win."

The men's faces hardened. It was time for her to go.

And there, she thought, *goes my CNN Factor.*

FORTY-FOUR

The Castle bar had a name, the Keep. Appropriate for a city under siege, Aubrey thought, though nowhere in Indy was exactly safe. To her, the bar was instead an oasis, a place to escape for a while, not hold fast. So that's what she called it.

Right now, she found its opulence stifling and the helpful service irritating. Even the piano grated on her nerves. She fidgeted, eyes glued on the entrance, oblivious to the murmur of the lunch crowd surrounding her.

Rafael rested his hand on hers. "He will come."

She pulled her hand away and sipped her wine without tasting it.

He was right, nobody showed up anywhere on time these days. Protests, strikes, snipers, shelling, not to mention the terrific amount of snow blanketing the roads. Commuting had gone from hassle to hazardous.

"You're a wonderful man and I like you a lot," Aubrey said. "But don't pet an alley cat waiting for her mouse."

The photojournalist sat back and crossed his arms.

She said, "I told you not to fall in love with me."

"Your mouse is here."

Terry Allen huffed to the table and sat. He eyed the drink in front of him. "I hope that's what I think it is and that it's for me."

Before they could answer, he scooped up the scotch and water that Rafael had ordered in anticipation of his arrival. He took a hefty sip and sighed.

"How bad is it out there?" Aubrey said.

Terry had come from city hall, where he'd mined his contacts for an update on the strategic situation.

"Nothing much is happening this morning, from what I could tell," he grunted. "The foul weather."

"Do you think the Free Women can hold?" Aubrey asked next.

"The situation is precarious. The real story is the government response, or should I say lack thereof. They're sending supplies but no reinforcements, while they wank on about how they're all united behind defending Haughville."

For now, the IMPD was staying on the east side of the White.

"The government doesn't care," she blurted, the insight surprising her. "Territory doesn't matter, only holding out until peace is declared in Ottawa. Meanwhile, the rebels and Leftists tear each other apart."

"I think that's a fairly astute assessment," Terry said. "Now what did you want to talk to me about?"

She leaned forward. "I have a story."

He nodded as if he'd expected this. "I'm all ears."

"The *Chronicle* won't publish it for political reasons." Gabrielle, meanwhile, had tried but failed to get the major radio stations interested in talking about it, more self-censorship in action. "I'm hoping *The Guardian* will take it on."

Terry's big shoulders raised in a shrug. "I'll be happy to consider it."

"I need to be clear on this. It's my story. I'm offering a partnership."

He inspected his drink. "A shared byline?"

"That's right."

"Well, that's bloody unorthodox." Terry shot Rafael a look. "Is it worthwhile?"

The Frenchman nodded. "*L'Opinion* has its own interest. Aubrey does not need to work with you. However, she believes this story is very important to her country and wants it to appear first in a prominent English-language newspaper."

"What about your interest?"

Rafael smiled. "I am freelance."

"So you're available if I'd need photos." Terry finished his drink. "All right, *Chronicle*. If it's as good as you say, I'll get you a shared byline. I give you my word on that. Should I take it on, however, it's *my* story. I'll be making final decisions on content. Understood?"

"Deal," she answered. "But after this, I'm not sure I'll be with the *Chronicle*, so you might as well start calling me Aubrey."

"Now that we understand each other, what's this all about?"

"The militias are using child soldiers," Aubrey said. "Kids working as porters, messengers, even fighters. Kids with guns. Kids who are fighting and dying."

Terry turned to Rafael. "Were you aware of this?"

"Yes. In New Orleans. I believed what I had seen was isolated occurrences, but I was wrong. From what Aubrey says, it seems to be systematic and growing, at least in this city."

The journalist reddened. Aubrey guessed he hadn't known. Though a war correspondent, he stayed away from the fighting. He preferred to work behind the lines to get his stories. In his view, the front lines were always the same everywhere and offered little in terms of hard facts.

Instead, Terry focused his attention on the top. His gift was seeing through the government's bullshit while cultivating contacts who gave him pieces of the real story. He wasn't interested in exploring larger issues in singular stories. His Grail was finding truth in the big picture, a needle in a smoke cloud.

Aubrey didn't care how he did his job. Whatever he was doing, it worked well for him and his readers. He produced timely and accurate stories. But men were men. Terry thought he was losing macho points being the last to know something.

He growled, "Let me see what you've got."

She handed over her story and notes. He started reading and paused to push his empty glass across the table.

"Order me another of these," he said. "If it's not too much trouble."

Rafael raised his hand for service and ordered another drink. Aubrey squeezed his leg under the table while she watched Terry read.

The reporter set the papers down. "This is a good start."

She bristled. She'd read him wrong as a mouse. He was an alley cat, like her.

"What do you mean, a *start*?"

"Look, there's no depth. It's a fair piece, but this is a much bigger story than you're letting on. For example, we don't really know why this is happening."

Aubrey had supposed child soldiers were being used because the militias lacked manpower and money to pay fighters. She'd guessed the children came to the militias on their own, just as Hannah had, or were brought along by their parents.

But Terry was right, she hadn't asked Hannah, Maria, or Alex to explain it in their own words.

"What do you propose?" she said.

"Two items," the reporter answered. "We take a more comprehensive look at how many child soldiers are actually being used in the city. Then we get some of them to tell their story."

He was proposing a lot of legwork, but he was right. She'd fast-tracked in the rush to get to print first. This was journalism. Time and energy to build a story piece by piece. Biting down on its leg and never letting go.

His big picture that told the truth on the ground, her human stories that revealed a single bigger truth. They would make a good team.

His drink arrived. Barely two o'clock in the afternoon. Aubrey guessed it wouldn't put a dent in him. In her experience, war correspondents drank like fish.

"We can start with Hannah and Maria." She stood and took out her phone. "I'll call my UNICEF contact while you finish your drink. They're working on a ballpark estimate of the number of child soldiers in the militias."

"Just a moment," he said. "First, I'd like to know what's in this for you."

Aubrey resumed her seat. "I'm not following."

"You just informed me your newspaper won't publish the story for political reasons. I take that to mean these facts are upsetting to very powerful people."

"That's right."

"But you feel the story is important," he said. "Children being used as weapons. Dreadful stuff. You're hoping that getting the story out will put a stop to it. That's why you reached out to me."

"That's also right."

"You do realize you're still going to upset very powerful people?"

"I could be fired." Seeing Terry raise an eyebrow, Aubrey added, "Or worse."

"Then why ask for a shared byline? I can run with this on my own. I'm a foreigner. The worst they'll do, I think, is send me home."

She hesitated. There was no simple answer. Plenty of justifications had already crossed her mind. The First Amendment, the America she believed in, the need for her countrymen to see a fellow American had broken the story.

"I assure you," he added, "I'll give this my all. It's despicable, involving kids in this war. I'm a father myself, with two little ones back home."

"I appreciate that, but I still want in."

"Why?"

Aubrey said, "Because the truth matters, and it's my job to tell it."

Terry eyed her for a few moments, seemingly torn between accepting her answer and trying again to talk her out of risking her life.

In the end, he nodded and tossed back his drink. "No need to waste daylight, Aubrey. We have a story to write."

FORTY-FIVE

In the ruins behind the front line, Alex trudged through drifts dropped by yesterday's snowfall. The wind blew tiny bits of ice against his face. He dipped his head, mesmerized by sunlight glittering on the fresh snow.

Mitch and Tom followed in his tracks.

Alex was hungover and bone tired. Last night, Bravo had gotten him good and lit. He'd stayed up late hearing their war stories. After that, he'd stood guard duty and caught a few hours of fitful sleep until dawn.

He was glad there'd be no fighting today. Getting shot in the cold would be the worst—

Alex flinched at a sharp shock to the head.

"You want to get killed?" Mitch growled. "Pay attention."

They were supposed to be behind the front line, but that wasn't a sure thing. The line now snaked all over the neighborhood.

He clenched his teeth. "Roger that, Sergeant."

Something had put the sergeant in a black mood.

It probably had something to do with whatever he'd found out at last night's meeting with the colonel. The Christmas offensive had bogged down under the women's ferocious resistance and the blizzard. They seemed to be winning, but maybe their position was more precarious than Alex was being told.

As long as he isn't mad at me, he thought.

The clinic was a simple, boxy white building. Garbage bins over-flowing with bloody linens stood out front in a ragged line. A few starving dogs rooted through piles of rags on the ground. They fled as the militiamen neared.

Alex walked up to the doors and entered bedlam.

A few exhausted nurses worked the crowded reception. The wounded lay in their own filth. The air stank of blood and piss and death. The nurses triaged the wounded, shouting for IV drips, resuscitation gear, immediate prep for surgery.

Alex stepped aside as two Liberty Tree fighters carried a comrade out on a stretcher. The worst off were being moved to a militia hospital behind the lines.

A hand clutched his ankle. Alex recoiled from the blanching brown face and kicked until the hand released him.

"Water," the man groaned.

Militia, but not Liberty Tree. Alex scanned the room again. The place was filled with a mix of Liberty Tree, libs, civilians.

"You with the Indy 300?" he said.

"Water." The man licked his lips. "Please..."

Alex shot Mitch a questioning look. The sergeant nodded.

The lib took a few gulps from his canteen. "Thank you."

Alex said nothing. Rejoinders flitted through his mind. *You did good out there. You guys are tough. Hey, in the end, we're all Americans.* Each more trite than the last. The man groaned and clutched a bloody rag against his guts.

You're going to die for nothing.

Mitch whistled to get his attention. He'd found Casey, one of his militiamen, sitting in a nearby corridor, bandaged leg stretched out in front of him. Alex knew little about the man other than he'd left his family farm to fight.

"How are you?" Mitch asked him.

The man grimaced. "I'm hanging in, Sergeant."

"We'll give you something for the pain," Tom offered.

Mitch crouched to inspect the swollen leg. "Let me take a look at it first."

The sergeant unwrapped the bandage. Alex glimpsed a jagged, bloody hole in the muscle around the soldier's shinbone. He shifted his gaze to study the wall.

"You'll be all right," Mitch said.

His arm shot out to block the path of a nurse rushing down the hall hugging a pile of linens. She froze and stared at his rifle.

"This man needs his leg fixed up," he said.

The nurse gaped at him.

"Do you speak English? Go get a doctor. Now."

She ran off, ignoring the cries of the wounded sitting or lying on the sides of the corridor. A man emerged fuming from a nearby room.

"I'm Dr. Walker. Can I help you, sir?"

"This man is under my command. I need you to patch up his leg."

The doctor wore a surgeon's smock peppered with lines of blood spray like grisly modern art. "He was triaged. He'll receive treatment in order of priority."

Mitch put his hand on the grip of his rifle. "I ain't asking you again."

The doctor's laughter surprised them.

"I don't care if you're asking or telling," he said. "We have a small staff, our supplies are down to almost nothing, and we have a lot of people here who will die if they don't get treated first."

"I see plenty Indy 300 here," Tom said. "You treating them over our guys?"

"You think it matters to me what uniform they wear? Whoever needs life-saving treatment gets it first. Just as I treated your men first if they needed it when the 300 controlled the neighborhood.

The 300 went along with that, and I expect you to accept it too."
He eyed Mitch's rifle. "Are you going to shoot me?"

Mitch released the grip. "No."

"Then kindly get out of here so we can do our work."

"Wait up, Doc. You need anything?"

"Cigarettes," said Walker. "So I don't have to operate while
going through withdrawal."

Mitch nodded. "We can get you some."

"And anything else you can spare. Gas for the generator, or if you
don't have that, some car batteries. Antibiotics, blood bags, aspirin,
ketamine, plasma. It's great you guys show up here with your blood
type written on your sleeve, but it doesn't help if I have no blood.
Help me help you, sir."

"I'll talk to the colonel."

"Good." Walker turned and called back over his shoulder, "Men-
thol, if you don't mind."

"Well, shit," Tom said in wonder.

"We don't need him," Mitch said. "I'll do it myself."

He gave Casey a shot of morphine from his med kit. The man's
sweaty grimace morphed into a dreamy smile. This time, Alex
didn't turn away. Mitch poured alcohol over the jagged hole and
worked the bone with tweezers until he wiggled a squashed chunk
of metal free. He flung it away.

"That ain't the bullet that's going to kill you," the sergeant said.
He thumbed a bullet from a spare magazine and pressed it into
Casey's hand. "This is the one. You keep it. As long as you have it,
it can't do its job."

Casey nodded, his face slick with sweat. "Thanks, Sergeant."

Mitch taped the wound shut. "We'll scrounge up some penicil-
lin. Until then, keep it clean, and hang tight."

The farm boy's eyes closed. "I'm good."

Worry etched Mitch's face. Grady was dead, Casey wounded.

The platoon had taken thirty percent casualties. *Maybe that's what's bugging him,* Alex thought. Tough love was still love. Maybe Mitch had taken it all hard.

Alex wanted one of those lucky bullets for himself.

The sergeant stood and dusted his pants. Time to go. Alex looked forward to putting this place out of sight and mind.

"A lot of ladies here," Tom observed. "They're the ones we've been fighting."

Mitch squatted in front of a woman lying on her back. "We expected nobody, or maybe the Indy 300. Instead, we got you. Who are you?"

"My name is Trish."

"I mean what's your outfit."

She struggled to prop herself up on her elbows. "The Free Women."

"Never heard of you."

"You won't forget us, though, I think." She grinned. "You fucking fascist."

He stood to full height. "You ain't free anymore."

She lay back with a nod and tuned him out. She didn't need to be reminded she was going to a deep, dark hole for the rest of the war.

The squad left the clinic to the rumble of vehicles.

A motley convoy approached, pickups and SUVs and even a yellow school bus and an ancient olive-green army truck. Men and women sat in the back of these vehicles, all wearing black berets.

"What's this?" Alex said. "Who are these people?"

Mitch spat on the ground. "Reinforcements."

Alex expected them to cheer as the patriots always did. *Death to the libs. God bless Marsh. USA, USA, USA!*

Instead, they rolled past in an eerie silence, their sole concession to celebration a succession of satisfied smiles plastered on grim faces.

"They look serious," Tom observed.

Alex understood now why the sergeant was in a foul mood. The colonel had made a deal with another militia to join forces along this stretch of front. And Mitch didn't like it. Alex wondered why.

"The First Angels," Mitch said. "America's very own Taliban."

FORTY-SIX

Aubrey drove them out to the front line, Terry grousing in the passenger seat and Rafael sitting taciturn in the back. The men wore flak jackets and blue helmets.

The SUV slid as she took a corner too fast. Terry blanched. "This isn't the bloody Indy 500. I'd rather not see us go arse over tit before we even get there."

It was his car, but she'd insisted on driving after their first round of trips across the city. "I've seen how slow you drive. I'm surprised you're alive."

"Now that I've seen you do it, I can return the compliment."

As they approached the bridge, she spotted the police positions. The IMPD had begun fortifying in the event the rebels broke through. BearCat armored vehicles flanked the entrance, machine guns aimed at the far end. Police in black armor warmed themselves at burning trash barrels. Construction crews in orange vests poured foundations for concrete pillboxes.

The sentry squad raised their AR-15s and shotguns.

"I think now is a good time to slow down," Terry said.

Aubrey stopped the car. "You know the drill. Hands on the dash."

A stony-faced cop came forward and inspected the press badge she held up. He rapped the glass with his knuckles.

She rolled down the window. "We need to cross the river."

"Sorry, ma'am. Nobody's allowed to cross."

She checked out the men and women manning the checkpoint, who gazed back at her with professional disdain. After working the guns and gang violence beats for years, she'd come to know a lot of people in the department. There were no familiar faces here, however, nobody who could help her out.

Before the war, the IMPD had more than a thousand sworn officers plus special units like SWAT and mounted patrol. Many had been killed or disabled on one side or the other in the early fighting. The IMPD now boasted over twenty-five hundred officers, many of them recruits like these people pointing rifles at her.

Few had the same training as the veteran police. The IMPD now functioned like a militia, and they were the city's largest. More accurately, the government army, designed by the Centrist Bloc to eventually replace the militia system.

She said, "I have authorization to report in the combat zones."

"Ma'am, turn your vehicle around now."

A smiling cop approached the car. "As I live and breathe. I got this, Ford."

The other officer retreated scowling.

Aubrey grinned. "Sergeant McGrath. I see you're still ticking."

He leaned on the doorframe. "Somebody's got to keep the wolves from the door. And it's Lieutenant McGrath now, if you please. I'm moving up in the world."

Same old McGrath with his affectations playing up his image of the veteran Irish cop. She held out her hand to shake, and he clasped it, pocketing the two packs of Marlboros she'd slipped him. The last of her stash of cigarettes Gabrielle had brought from Canada and given her for trading.

"Congratulations on your promotion," she said.

"You're looking good, Aubrey. You still single?"

"You still married?"

The cop laughed and called out, "Let them through."

He offered a jaunty salute as she started the car. She navigated the concrete barriers and sped across the bridge, passing straggling refugees going the other way.

"I'm impressed," Terry said.

"Don't tell me you've never greased the wheels for a story."

"I'm impressed it only cost you two packages of cigarettes. I had no idea the going rate was so cheap."

"I get the local discount."

"A little flirting does not seem to hurt either," Rafael said.

Aubrey glanced in the rearview. "You jealous?"

He smirked. "I thought we were not falling in love."

She slowed the car to a crawl as they approached the border between Stringtown and Haughville. The front line was unnervingly close, but the battle's energy had petered out for the time being, simmering in random flashes of automatic weapons fire. Soon, she was stopped again, this time by a band of fierce women wearing a collection of motley uniforms.

Aubrey repeated the ritual of holding up her press badge. "We're looking for Hannah and Maria. They're kids serving with you."

A militia fighter scowled. "What do you want with them?"

"We'd heard they'd done some heroic stuff during the battle."

"Maria's at HQ. Hannah's probably at the aid station. St. Peter's."

Aubrey knew the church. "Where's your headquarters?"

"I'd tell you, but then I'd have to kill you."

The woman smiled, and Aubrey knew she meant it.

"We'll try St. Peter's. Thank you."

"Peace." The fighter tapped the roof, giving them permission to leave.

St. Peter's was a Catholic church that before the war served as many as three hundred worshippers. Now it was dark, its pews removed, its organ and hymnals burned for warmth. The only reminder it had once been a house of worship was the altar and stained glass windows depicting the Stations of the Cross. That and the nuns tending the groaning wounded, which lent the place the air of a medieval hospital.

Aubrey spotted Hannah right away. The girl sat on the dais next to a middle-aged fighter propped against the altar.

"Commander," she said in greeting.

The woman gestured to her bandaged arm. "Not anymore. It's just Abigail now. You come to cover the battle?"

Aubrey pointed at Hannah. "Actually, we came to talk to her."

"War crimes, right. All these women here fighting and dying for their city, and you drove all the way out here to tell that story."

"Everybody already knows the other one." Aubrey crouched. "Hi, Hannah."

The girl clung to Abigail. "You can't make me go with you."

"I'm not going to make you do anything you don't want to do. Hannah, I write for a local newspaper. This is Terry, who writes for a British newspaper. And this is Rafael, who works for a newspaper in France."

"Okay," Hannah said warily.

"We want to tell a story about the children who are fighting in this war. People all over Europe will read it. We believe if we tell that story, the use of children as soldiers will change, which would be good for all these kids. It might even shorten the war. Will you talk to us?"

The child soldier looked to Abigail, who said, "We're a volunteer army, sister. It's up to you. There's no harm in telling your story. I think the world should hear it."

Hannah nodded. "Okay."

"Would it be all right if I take your picture?" Rafael said.

The girl shrugged. Rafael took out his camera and squinted at his surroundings, judging composition and light.

Terry sat on the floor and took off his helmet. "How old are you, Hannah?"

Gone was the cynical, swaggering journalist. His tone had become gentle. Aubrey remembered he was a father of two back in England.

"I just turned eleven."

"Happy birthday."

"Thanks," she deadpanned.

"I have two little ones of my own. A boy about your age, a girl who's a little older."

Hannah perked up. "I have an older brother. He's fifteen."

"Where is he?"

"He's in rebel country."

"What's his name?"

"Alex."

Aubrey flashed to the gangly kid cleaning his rifle by a firepit. She wondered if it was the same Alex and if she should bring it up. They certainly looked alike.

She decided against it. She wasn't sure, and it'd probably do the girl no good for her to believe her older brother was one of the rebels shooting at her. The kid had enough problems.

Terry finished his questions about her background. "Thank you, Hannah. Now I hope you'll tell us how you ended up making friends with the Free Women. Go as far back as you want to remember."

Abigail took Hannah's hand in hers and held it tight.

The girl told her story. In matter-of-fact language, she described the horrors of her life. Everything she said struck Aubrey as supremely tragic, but for this girl, it was normal. If it had been any other way for her, it was a long time ago in her mind, a life she'd largely forgotten as irrelevant to her survival.

Terry prompted her with a few questions but for the most part just listened. Even Rafael stopped snapping pictures. They were all moved by the girl's story.

As the interview finished, Aubrey asked only one question. "If we could take you away from here to somewhere safe, would you go?"

Terry shot her a surprised look, but it was a legitimate question, one to which Aubrey believed she already knew the answer, even after all the fighting.

The girl said, "No. I don't want to leave."

"I'm talking about a warm place, very safe, with plenty to eat—"

Hannah wagged her head. "No."

"Why not?" Terry said.

The child soldier looked at Abigail. "If we win, no other girls will die. And no other girls' moms." She turned back to Aubrey and set her jaw. "I want to stay and do my part."

Terry scowled at Abigail. "This is no place for a child."

"I'm not forcing her to do anything," the woman said. "I don't like her being here either. But after what she's suffered, she can make her own choices."

"I know you think I'm a kid and that what I think isn't real," Hannah said. "I'm tired of being ignored because I'm a kid. I want this. The Free Women are my family now, and I don't want to leave them."

The reporters trooped back to their car in silence and got in. Aubrey turned the key in the ignition. The SUV roared to life.

"Wow," she said at last.

"Just a kid," Terry said with disgust.

"You see a child," Rafael said. "In some ways, she is as old as you."

He'd lingered on the way out to take one last photo. A wide-view shot of Hannah sitting with Abigail, their backs to the altar, framed in bright stained glass.

"Yet still not old enough to die," Terry said. "She's been brainwashed."

Then he broke into a smile and chuckled.

Aubrey inspected him. "You okay?"

"That, my dear, was a blinding interview. I smell Pulitzer."

Aubrey smiled, though it didn't last. Hannah's story had gotten under her skin.

She and Rafael once talked about how being a journalist often meant having to ignore what was right to be able to tell a story about a wrong.

Every once in a while, however, a war correspondent had the opportunity to get the story and do something good.

FORTY-SEVEN

It took the First Angels two days to roll into camp, about eighty strong. In a strip mall parking lot, the men and women unloaded supplies from their trucks and stacked them on the ground.

Aside from their black berets, they wore no uniforms but instead dressed in threadbare coats. Half were as poorly armed as the libs. They talked little and otherwise ignored Alpha squad, who fingered their high-tech rifles and eyed them with disdain.

"What a bunch of cucks," Donnie said.

"This ain't a big dick contest," Mitch said. "They're on our side."

Alex studied the newcomers. They weren't the same people who'd taken over Sterling, but they had the same ideology, which made them the same tribe. Mitch had said the Angels didn't care about popular support or even governing, their church being all they needed.

From what Alex heard, they believed their cause justified any level of violence. They were like an army of Sergeant Shooks, only they had God on their side. Dad had been smart to make a run for it, though he'd waited too long out of worries about his family.

A teenaged girl caught his eye. Her long blond hair spilled out from under her beret. The webbed canvas belt around her coat accentuated her slim waist.

"Amen," Jack said.

"She's really pretty," Alex agreed.

"Remember, we're the pros," Mitch said. "Be sure to act like it at all times."

"Yes, Sergeant." This response had become a simple reflex for him.

Colonel Lewis stood in a group of their officers discussing some important matter. He threw his head back and roared with laughter. The Angels didn't laugh with him.

Alpha squad bristled at the sight and banded closer together.

"Trigger discipline could be a problem," Tom said. "They don't have any training. We could have friendly fire incidents."

Donnie spat on the ground. "Look at the way they used their mortars during the attack. Some of their shells fell on our heads."

Tom nudged Alex. "They start shooting at us, it's okay to shoot back, kid."

Whoever's side the Angels were on, the Liberty Tree didn't think much of them, and it went way beyond their fighting ability. While there were no atheists in the Tree's foxholes, their liberty had driven them to take up arms against the government, not their religion. The gulf in their ideological differences was nearly as wide as the one separating them from the libs.

"Whatever Mitch says, goes," Alex said, stating a simple truth.

He didn't care about ideology. He watched the pretty teenaged girl unload boxes.

"We need them," Mitch said. "Let's wait and see what the colonel works out. Then we'll know what the play is."

Colonel Lewis left his huddle. His smile melted from his face. He walked over to clap Mitch on the back. "This is going to work out just fine."

"How long do you see the Angels being in our area of operations, sir?"

"You wanted the other militias to join the offensive, well, this is who we got," the colonel said. "Now we really need them. You did good, Mitch. Too good. It's put us in a tight spot."

Like a spear, Alex's platoon had penetrated almost all the way to Stringtown. The men had spread out to create a bulge, but they were overextended for the manpower they had.

Colonel Lewis added, "With their help, we'll push these libs back to the river. We do that, the entire front will collapse. Because of us, the Brickyard Crossing offensive stalled out. We do this right, it'll be a whole new ball game. We'll be right on their doorstep."

Mitch watched some of the First Angels tag houses with crosses and evangelical slogans. "As long as my boys get credit for what they did."

"Are you kidding? We're gonna be heroes, Mitch."

The colonel's eyes lit up like he was picturing kids learning about him in school the way they learned about Paul Revere and the Minutemen.

"Second Platoon is coming off the line as the Angels move up," he went on. "Your platoon will refit and redeploy alongside First. The next offensive will be a coordinated push from the north and east with twice the strength."

The Angels were taking over the Liberty Tree's forward positions, and there'd be hard fighting ahead. Alex had heard everything he needed to know. He watched the girl leave the main group and join her friends, who were spray-painting black crosses on a house.

He didn't see any harm in one of the pros doing a little fraternizing with an ally.

Alex nudged Jack. "Be my wingman."

Using his gloved fingers, the kid rough-combed his hair to make a crude side part. "I think you mean that the other way around, bro."

"Don't make me fight you again."

Jack laughed. "You sure you want to go there?"

Checking to make sure his gear was in order, Alex walked over to the house and cleared his throat. "Hi. I'm Alex."

"I'm Jack," his friend chimed in.

The girl was even prettier close up. Mouth parted in surprise, she turned scarlet. Her girlfriends tilted their heads to get a good look at the Liberty Tree boys.

Flushed at the attention, Alex didn't know what to say next. He glanced at the wall she'd decorated. "I, uh, like your crosses."

Jack burst into laughter. The girl giggled.

Alex ribbed him, hoping he'd say something smart.

"I like them too," his friend said. "They're really awesome."

Then they were all giggling like fools. It could have gone smoother, but Alex didn't mind. He was smiling at this pretty girl, who was smiling back. Her blue eyes flashed. She wasn't looking at Jack; she was looking at *him.*

"We've seen some really hard fighting," he said, showing off. "Nothing we couldn't handle, but we're glad you're here to help."

The girl's smile faded. She nodded. Good, they were communicating now, but he wished she would say something. He was dying here.

"So where are you from?" he asked her.

"She can't talk to you," a voice said.

The First Angel wore a long black dress coat belted at the waist with pouches, canteen, and pistol. Alex barely noticed these details as he focused on the boy's face. More specifically, his pale blue eyes, which seemed to radiate light. Alex guessed his age at about sixteen.

"Are you her boyfriend?" Jack said.

The kid wore a dreamy smile. "I'm Jacob. We have rules."

"We just wanted to say hi," Alex said.

Jacob set his laser eyes on him. "You don't belong here."

The girls moved on to the next house. The blonde glanced over her shoulder to give Alex a parting smile, which he returned. "We didn't mean any harm."

"You aren't one of us. You don't believe."

Alex barked a laugh. The boy's words unsettled him. He wanted to punch that dreamy, smug smile. "Whatever you say, dude."

Gunfire erupted in the distance. Alex tightened his grip on his AR-15, but there was nothing to shoot at.

"Who's shooting?" Jack said. "What is that?"

The firing was happening down the street, behind the front line.

Jacob only smiled and said nothing.

"Come on. Let's get out of here." Alex turned and started walking.

His friend caught up, his face turning pale. "That shooting is happening at the clinic. Should we tell the sergeant?"

"Look at his face. Mitch already knows." Just thinking about it made Alex sick. "These people are maniacs."

"Who would do something like that?"

He turned for one last look at the pretty blonde. To his surprise, she was looking at him. She glanced side to side before giving him a little wave.

Alex didn't wave back.

FORTY-EIGHT

In Terry's room, Aubrey worked on his laptop while he sprawled on the bed reviewing his interview notes. Rafael inspected his photos on his digital camera.

The keyboard buzzed as her fingers raced like hummingbirds across the keys. A world of information was at her fingertips again. With the electricity shortages and almost nonexistent Wi-Fi, she'd learned to live without the Internet, but it was good to be back.

Google was still working. The network backbone was still operational, though many websites it once connected had gone dark or were no longer being updated. The major media was online, a comforting sight, and she caught up on the top headlines. The Mexican Army blew up part of the Texas border wall. California pacified Bakersfield. A bombing in Times Square killed eight people. President Marsh said he might return to the Ottawa peace talks.

Aubrey glanced through it all and then conducted a search for any mention of child soldiers being used in the American war.

"Nothing in the mainstream media," Aubrey announced. "A few bloggers are talking about it." She rattled off a list of states.

Terry peered at her over the rims of his reading glasses. "Now we need to confirm it."

"Confirm?"

"You know the industry proverb. If your own mum tells you she loves you, check it out."

"I already confirmed that child soldiers have been *reported* in these states."

"Call Gabrielle and see what she's got."

She sighed. "Can I use your phone?"

The reporter handed it over. "Mind my minutes."

"Okay, Dad." Aubrey thumbed Gabrielle's number.

The UN worker answered. "I'm in the hotel. I'll be right down."

"She's on her way," Aubrey said after the call disconnected. "I bookmarked the blogs in case you want to make contact with them."

While she waited, she opened Facebook and entered another search. A few people were talking about child soldiers. She followed various social networks, absorbing opinions. The majority of pages she found stopped within a few months of the outbreak of war.

In those that were still active, the civil war was being fought here too, with words, just as it had long before the cultural cold war turned hot. Social media had promised to bring people together but only helped polarize them along new tribes isolated in separate echo chambers.

Aubrey's next search found Gabrielle Justine's page, which was filled with people wishing her well and asking if she was okay. Her albums showed photos of her with university friends skiing at Mont-Tremblant and kayaking in Saguenay. She always stood at the center of the group, fresh-faced, no makeup, smiling shyly at the camera. She had plenty of friends, some of them male, all of them protectors. They were in love with her, Aubrey guessed; Gabrielle was like some rare and beautiful bird that had a broken wing.

Every day, she marked herself as safe in Indianapolis.

The page gave Aubrey an idea. She did another search and swiveled the laptop so Terry could get a better view of the screen. "Check this out."

He leaned for a closer look. "What did you find?"

"Hannah Miller."

Hannah had told them her mother's name and hometown. While Miller was a common surname, there was only one Linda Miller in Sterling.

Terry eyed the images as she scrolled through them. Linda seemed a vibrant woman and caring working mother. She'd posted about the trivialities of life and a few major passions, such as baking. While she was sparing in posting photos of her children, they appeared in a few vacation and holiday series along with her husband, Harry.

He said, "I can't believe it's the same girl."

Aubrey pointed at the screen. "That's her brother, Alex. I met him. He's fighting for the other side on the same stretch of front."

In the most recent shots, Hannah hammed it up while Alex scowled, aching to be somewhere else but without any idea where he wanted to be.

"Brilliant. Perhaps—"

"Don't even think it. They'll shoot me this time."

"Would they shoot me?"

"Right now, I'm pretty sure they would."

"All right, sod it then. Bookmark that page for me, would you? I'm having a brainstorm. What if we print out a few of these photos for Hannah, and tell her about her brother being on the other side?"

Rafael looked up from his camera. It was great journalism.

"No," Aubrey said.

"I let you drive, but don't forget who's running this story."

"Just no. Okay? She's been through enough. I'll let her know once the fighting dies down, but it'll be off the record."

Terry looked to Rafael for support. The Frenchman shrugged.

"All right. We'll do it your way, but only because we're against the clock."

A knock at the door. Aubrey went over and let Gabrielle into the room. The UNICEF worker launched into a hug.

Aubrey stiffened in alarm at the sudden contact. Then she returned it with a smile. "How are you?"

Gabrielle handed her a sheet of paper. "Some numbers for you."

Aubrey scanned the list of Indy militias. The figures with asterisks were considered reliable. The rest were pure estimates, either because the militia wouldn't talk or because they might be hiding something. Plenty of question marks, unknowns.

She handed the sheet to Terry, who scrutinized it.

"Right now, we're estimating about twelve hundred children are serving in militias just on this side," Gabrielle said. "There are many unknowns—"

Terry held up his hand. "UNICEF is estimating twelve hundred child soldiers in Indianapolis, just on the Congressional side. Am I correct?"

"Yes."

"That's all I need."

"We caught wind it's happening in other states," Aubrey said.

Gabrielle blew out a sigh. "This next part will probably get me fired."

Before Aubrey could offer some options, the UNICEF worker handed her another sheet of paper showing a list of American states.

Next to thirty-one of them, a checkmark.

"Jesus." She passed the sheet to Terry, who grinned.

"Jackpot," he said.

"This is based on UNICEF humanitarian assessments submitted in forty-four of the fifty states," Gabrielle explained. "So. Is this enough?"

"This is plenty," Aubrey told her.

"My people are working on more media appearances. I'll do what I can at my end. I only hope it all comes to something."

She left out the sentence hanging in the air, *I hope it's all worth it.* Gabrielle was risking her job. Aubrey her liberty, possibly her life.

Aubrey swiveled Terry's laptop. "A reminder why we're doing this."

The UNICEF worker crouched to study a photo of Hannah and Alex at the Indiana Dunes State Park. They stood on a beach in their swimsuits, Lake Michigan a rich blue behind them. Photographs from another time and place, another world.

A single tear coursed down her cheek.

Rafael's camera clicked. Aubrey threw him a sharp look.

"Sorry." Gabrielle wiped her eyes. "I'm a little emotional right now. I'm moving out of the hotel tomorrow."

"Where are you going?"

"The Peace Office found me an apartment to rent. The CERF budget is limited, and, well…"

"What?"

Gabrielle glanced at Terry. "I didn't want to feel like a tourist anymore."

The journalist didn't deliver the cutting remark Aubrey expected. Instead, he smiled. "You've come a long way in a short time, UN."

Aubrey smiled too. They all had. Her and Terry's words, Rafael's images. They had everything they needed now. It was going to be one hell of a story.

A story that might change everything.

Gabrielle stood to go. "Thank you. For everything." Again, that gratitude that came from deep in the heart.

This time, Aubrey accepted it.

FORTY-NINE

In the record store where he'd set the platoon HQ, Mitch propped his leg on a crate. He wasn't getting any younger, and his body took longer to bounce back from punishment. Nearly a week after the offensive, his ankle and back were still killing him.

Bud, the platoon radio/telephone operator, or RTO, sat on a lawn chair facing a rickety card table, relaying orders to the far-flung units in the bulge. Next to his station, a strategic map hung on the wall with duct tape.

The story it told was promising. Second Platoon didn't end up crossing the river, but Mitch knew ops rarely worked out as planned. You shot for the stars and grabbed the moon. This was how wars were won, moving the ball a few yards at a time.

I should be satisfied, he thought.

The radio operator said, "You mind if I light up, Sergeant?"

"It's a free country, Bud."

"It's slow going out there. At this rate, it'll be tomorrow by the time the Angels deploy and our guys take up their new positions."

"If that's what it takes," he growled, "then that's what it takes."

Bud took the hint and smoked his cigarette in silence.

Mitch wasn't satisfied at all.

Every minute of delay allowed the libs to reinforce and entrench, but that wasn't what bothered him.

The Angels had dragged the libs' wounded out of the clinic and shot them like dogs. It disgusted and enraged him enough he'd made a point of staying clear of them out of fear he'd switch sides and start another war.

Later, he worried maybe they were onto something.

Shock and awe. Maybe the only way to win the war was to inflict a Biblical level of destruction on the enemy. Strike them with sheer terror. Total war. The stakes were high enough to justify almost anything.

Still, even after a year of fighting, the libs never felt quite like the enemy. Even now, he had a hard time hating them. He saw them more as spoiled, ungrateful children than an evil needing to be destroyed.

Mitch stood with a grunt and limped over to inspect the map. Drawn in different-colored grease pencils, squares marked the patriot and lib positions. Red for Liberty Tree, blue for the Free Women, and black for the First Angels. In two days, the Angels would attack and find out if God really was on their side.

The door opened to admit a blast of light and cold. Alex and Jack walked into the store and froze at the sight of their sergeant.

"Sorry," Alex said. "We didn't know this was HQ."

Mitch pinned them with his stink-eye. "What are you boys up to now?" Looking for another secret place to smoke their cigarettes, probably.

"Just exploring."

Aside from Bud, the HQ staff was off getting their supper. He saw no harm in them looking around. "You like records?"

The floor was covered in vinyl. The sleeves had all been salvaged for kindling.

The kids glanced at each other and knelt to inspect the mess.

"I don't know any of these bands," Alex said.

"What's the one you got in your hand?" Mitch asked him.

The kid read the label. *"A Lot About Livin'. And a Little 'bout Love."*

"Alan Jackson. That one takes me back. 'Chattahoochee' is a great song."

"What kind of music is it?"

"Country, son. God's own music."

"Yeah." The kid put the record back on the floor. "No."

Mitch snorted. "You kids don't know what's good. Rap ain't even music."

"How old were you when this came out?"

"Hell, I was about your age. The summer that year, my dad drove me and my brothers into the woods with a truck full of tools. We built our own log cabin."

A simpler time. Together, they'd cleared the land and marked the footprint, then poured out the concrete and set the piers. Every day over that long, hot summer they worked, laying joists and flooring, joining logs, framing the roof. That was how Dad did things, with his own hands and know-how, and screw the permits and codes.

"Wow," Alex said. "You're lucky. I never did anything like that."

"My brothers didn't feel so lucky. After a while they complained they were giving up their entire summer. Dad caught wind of it and disciplined all of us."

"Even you?"

"Yup. Even me."

"But that's not fair," Alex said. "You weren't the one complaining."

"And I didn't complain about getting punished either. Dad was teaching me that life ain't fair. It don't owe me a thing. And something else. If you want something, you work for it. You pull yourself up by your bootstraps. And if you agree to do something, you do it, no excuses. A man is defined by his word."

Years later, Mitch joined the Army to serve his country while his brothers moved away to its far corners, as if trying to put as much distance as possible between themselves and the old man. They didn't even come back for Dad's funeral.

Mitch hadn't hated his father. He'd respected him. He wanted the man to be proud of him. And Dad was. Though he didn't show it, Mitch knew. His father had taught him life was hard, and if you wanted to be a man, you had to be hard too. Mitch had always accepted this severe teaching as a form of love.

He was glad Dad died before America became a place where you weren't even allowed to say, "Merry Christmas."

"My dad isn't as tough as you," Alex said.

"That's the America we live in."

"He's strong, just in a different way. I didn't see that until a little while ago."

It was good to see the kid respect his old man. For Mitch, it was what the war was all about. Respect for the old ways. Self-respect.

The door creaked open. Donnie tramped in looking glum, followed by Tom.

"What now?" Mitch said.

"The cathouse closed down," Donnie complained.

"Which one?"

The soldier lay on the floor and glared at the ceiling. "All of them."

Tom leaned against the wall. "The guys told me the Bible thumpers rousted the girls. They're gone."

"The Angels? How do you know it was them?"

"Who else would paint crosses and *WHORE* all over the walls?"

Mitch didn't visit the cathouses himself, but he allowed it. He knew how important it was to morale. Men loved to fight, and after they fought, they wanted to fuck. The patriots were a volunteer army and needed to blow off steam.

The First Angels had only just arrived. Already, they'd pissed off his entire platoon and impaired their combat effectiveness. Half the neighborhood was covered in crosses.

"Plenty of female flesh just ahead of us," Bud said at the radio. "I've been picking up their chatter."

"That does it, Sarge," Donnie said. "I'm switching sides."

Mitch frowned. During the battle, the Free Women had used kids as runners for communication. If they were using shortwave radios, the police were supplying them. He wondered what else the IMPD was sending over.

"Can I listen in?" Jack said. "Just let me hear them talk."

Bud glanced at Mitch, who nodded. He adjusted the radio until he found the Free Women's frequency on the police band.

A woman's voice: "—runners will be swinging by with food and ammo."

The RTO grinned. "Most of the time, they don't even use a code."

"Or they want us to think they don't," Mitch said. "Either way, we should put a man on listening in on their communications."

Another voice: "I hope they hurry. This war diet is bad enough as it is."

Laughter on the radio.

Jack smiled. "Can we say hello, Sergeant?"

Tom snorted. "Didn't you hear what he said? If we break silence, we'll let them know we're listening in."

"It's all right," Mitch said. "Who wants to go first?"

Donnie scrambled off the floor and snatched the radio from Bud's hand. "Hey, baby, what are you doing tonight? Over."

The radio went quiet. The men laughed. Mitch smiled. If they couldn't get their nut, they could have a little fun. It was worth tipping off the Free Women their communications were being monitored. They weren't going to learn much anyway. Meanwhile, the squad had fought hard. The boys had earned a boost.

A female voice said, "Putting a bullet in your fascist ass. Over."

The men laughed again.

"I do like 'em feisty," Tom said.

"Come on," Donnie said. "Isn't your type supposed to make love not war?"

"You're right about that, lover boy," the woman's voice purred. "Why don't you come on over here? There's a lot of women dying to meet you."

"Oh my God." Donnie grinned at his comrades. "Can you guys leave for a while? This is getting good."

"Hello," another voice appeared on the line. "Any of you boys over there know Mitch Thornton?"

The squad stared at him.

Mitch held out his hand. "Give it here."

Donnie reluctantly parted with the radio.

Heart pounding, he keyed the handset. "Hey, Abigail. Been a long time."

"Hi, Mitch. I just knew I'd find you over there."

She'd never liked him going away on weekends with the Liberty Tree. *Armed hooligans*, she used to call them.

Well, these so-called hooligans were about to change America, just like he always told her they would.

"You know why I'm here," he said. "What are you doing over there?"

"I don't want to fight with you, Mitch."

He smiled. "Then surrender."

"How about you stop this nonsense before more people get killed?"

"Funny how you think standing up for the Constitution is nonsense. You're in open rebellion against the legitimate president."

"You ain't standing up for anything," his ex-wife said. "I know you, Mitch. You haven't changed one bit."

"I'm stronger than I ever was. And I know what's right."

"You ain't doing this to save America. You're doing it to save yourself. You're doing it this way because you're a mean son of a bitch."

If he wanted to hate the enemy, she would do nicely. His face burned with a sudden and massive rage that left him shaking. "I fought for my country in the worst place on Earth. I came back, and you gave me hell every damn day. You took off on me after we buried our little girl. You want to know who changed, it was you. You ran off when I needed you most, you goddamn bitch."

The radio went quiet. The squad looked away, embarrassed.

"Like I told you," Abigail said. "You haven't changed one damn bit."

Mitch exhaled a frustrated sigh. "I'm sorry I said that. I told you a thousand times I was sorry about everything I did. You know I had a hard time after the war. But you don't know me anymore. Don't pretend you do."

"I can understand fighting so a little girl can live. I can't understand why you fight against it. Why you hate other people who have nothing instead of the people who took everything from you. You're the guy who goes postal on his coworkers when he should be taking his gun to the next board meeting."

She had no idea why he was fighting. Mitch had always held to a single maxim: Every time the government tried to make things better, it ended up destroying a little more freedom, so it governed best when it governed least.

A simple principle, but one he'd never been able to make her understand.

He said, "I'm hanging up, Abigail."

"Before you go, somebody here wants to say hello."

"I don't need another crazy woman yelling at me tonight."

The radio bleeped: "Mitch?" A child's voice.

"Who is this?"

"You don't remember me?"

It was the girl he'd met on the road to Indy. The girl who'd tried to commit suicide by soldier back at the daycare serving as the women's HQ.

He chewed his beard for a moment, then keyed the handset. "Yeah."

"Next time, I won't miss. I'm gonna kill you and the giant."

"I got no quarrel with a ten-year-old girl, Hannah. You should go home before you get yourself hurt."

Alex Miller rushed over and held out his hand. "Please, Sergeant."

"Why?"

"I think that's my little sister."

Stunned, Mitch handed over the radio and walked out of the house, feeling strange as hell as all the dots connected. He'd stopped Shook from raping Alex's mother, and the boy later ended up fighting alongside him. He'd left his sister standing on the roadside, and she'd become a child soldier intent on killing him.

What a crazy war. Maybe Abigail was right, and the whole thing was nonsense.

The cold evening air braced him as it always did, but it did little to still his restless mind. Talking to Abigail again had unleashed an even stronger flood of feelings and memories, many of them happy ones, the rest dark and inflamed, love and hate all mixed up. They say time heals all wounds, but the scab was always there, waiting to be picked off.

And boy, did she ever love to pick.

Screw it all, he thought. So what. It changed nothing.

He needed to put all this drama behind him and get back to business. One thing he knew for sure, the day after tomorrow, they'd go after the libs with everything they had. And after it was all over, Abigail would see. They'd all see what the militias were fighting for, and that this war had been worth fighting.

Boots crunched snow. Ralph said, "How's everything, Mitch?"

"It's going all right, Colonel."

"Any news?"

"The Free Women have radios now. We started tapping their communications."

"The IMPD must be helping them. Interesting." Ralph rubbed his hands to keep them warm. "You get any decent intel?"

"They're staying put, and their morale seems good."

"We'll cure them of that shortly."

"I'll have the last of Second Platoon moved by tomorrow. The Angels will be in position to launch their attack the day after that."

"Wednesday," Ralph said. "New Year's Day."

Mitch spat in the snow. "Yup."

The colonel pulled a wrinkled pack of Camels from his side pocket and lit one. "I'll be glad when the offensive gets going. The sooner the First Angels are out of our hair, the better. They don't like us much, and I don't trust them."

"They like the libs even less." The Angels, they knew how to hate.

Ralph's face darkened. "The enemy of my enemy is my friend."

"Yes, sir. With friends like these . . . Still, you got to admire it a little. The will."

"The only thing I admire about them is they have guns and they're willing to use them against the libs. We're not like them, Mitch."

"No, sir. We ain't." Still, he worried about surviving this war with his moral integrity intact.

The colonel dropped his butt in the snow and appraised him. "You did an outstanding job taking over the platoon after Taylor got hit."

"Thank you, sir."

"No, I'm thanking you, Mitch. And I'm going to do something

I should have done from the get-go instead of kissing donor ass and letting Taylor anywhere near combat. I'm promoting you to lieutenant, effective immediately."

Mitch's stomach soured. "Excellent, sir."

"I know what you think of it. In fact, it's why you're perfect for it. The boys look up to you, you have experience, and you keep your head under fire." The colonel stuck out his hand. "Second Platoon is yours, Lieutenant."

He took a deep breath and shook it. "I'll do right by you, Colonel."

"I know you will. You're an officer now."

"Oh, brother."

Ralph gazed into the sunset and grinned. "This is it, Mitch. New Year's Day, the Angels will unleash hell, and then we'll go in and mop up. It'll be the start of a new era. We're going to take Indy back. Then America."

"Yes, sir," Mitch said with more feeling. "We've come a long way."

They were so close to victory now, he could taste it. Still, his ankle was killing him. He needed to rest and sleep off the pain and this feeling of strangeness that wouldn't pass. The war could wait. He saluted and limped off toward his sleeping bag, where he hoped to forget the whole thing for a few hours.

It had to end soon. The Liberty Tree wasn't like the Angels, but in another year, it might be. In another year, he might hate the libs enough to justify anything. As a platoon leader, order it. A year after that, they'd all cross a line where the war was no longer worth fighting but was being fought for its own sake. And after yet another year, it might be impossible to ever live together again in peace.

The war had already reached a brutality that shocked even him. Evangelicals shooting enemy wounded in the head and leaving them on the ground like roadkill. Now there was a little girl out there who was hell-bent on murdering him.

Hannah Miller, he didn't hate. No matter how much she hated him, he couldn't hate her. He felt like he and Shook created her that night.

FIFTY

Alex pressed the talk button. "Hannah?"

His squad mates stared at him, still absorbing the news he'd been shooting at his little sister this whole time.

"It's me," he said. "It's Alex."

He waited. The radio was quiet. He turned up the volume in the hope of hearing something, anything.

A bleep, then crying.

A woman's voice in the background: *Are you okay, sweetie?*

The crying filled the room. Their faces gray, the militiamen looked away. Then the radio went silent again.

Jack said, "Is that really your...?"

Alex covered his eyes with his free hand, face screwed tight to hold back his tears. He didn't want them to see. He wanted to try again in the hope Hannah would answer, but he didn't trust himself to speak.

The radio blatted again. "Alex?"

"Merry Christmas, sis."

He kept his hand over his eyes, which allowed him to imagine they were completely alone. That the militias, the war, and everything else didn't exist.

"You were stupid to run away."

Alex smiled. "I know. Sorry." He'd never been so happy to talk to somebody in his life. "Are you okay?"

"I'm good," she said. "Why are you fighting for those men?"

"What are *you* doing fighting?"

"I'm not a kid anymore, Alex."

"What do Mom and Dad think about it? How are they?"

The radio went silent again. Then: "They're okay. They're worried about you."

Alex sank to his knees with a strangled sob. His sister had always been a terrible liar. He managed, "That's good to hear."

"Why did you run away?"

"I just wanted to go home. I didn't want anything to change."

But it did. And now his parents were dead. The knowledge severed his last hope things could ever go back to normal.

"We should have stayed together," she said.

"Will you tell Mom and Dad I'm sorry?"

Another pause. "I'll be seeing them soon. We're going to have a big dinner to celebrate Christmas."

"Do you think they'll forgive me?"

"Of course they will. It's Mom and Dad."

Alex snorted. Mom and Dad would forgive them anything. It was one of the things that had driven his perverse need to test them.

Still, he was glad to hear it. Glad and heartbroken.

"Hey," he said. "I'm sorry to you too. That I left you alone."

"It's okay. I'm not alone anymore."

It was still hard for him to reconcile the needy little ball of energy he'd grown up with and the voice on the radio. When had she gotten so strong? His dumb little half-nerd sister with her diary and constant nagging and obsessions over this TV show or that. She used to bug him until he said, *Eat my shorts*, and then she'd run off to Mom to tell on him. When his friends spotted him babysitting her on an outing, he'd almost died from shame. They were merciless in their ribbing.

Typical family stuff. His embarrassment seemed ridiculous now. He gazed back at his anxious teenage world and its problems with nostalgia.

Hannah wasn't that annoying little brat anymore. She was a soldier now, just like him. He guessed they'd filled her head with a bunch of propaganda and the gullible kid had swallowed all of it like she always did, but that wasn't the end of it. Whatever she was now, she'd earned it.

While he'd cooked and saluted and carried stuff around for the men who'd started all this, she'd suffered. She'd watched their parents die. She'd buried them. She'd joined her own militia.

And in the process, she'd grown older than him, an unsettling thought.

He wanted to ask what had happened, but he didn't. Maybe it was for the best he believed her lie. Mom and Dad were in Indy right now. They were fine. They were getting ready for a late Christmas dinner.

"I guess I'm not alone anymore either," he said.

Radio silence. He'd made a mistake. He shouldn't have brought up the war that separated them. He didn't want her to leave.

He added, "Do you want to come over here to this side? Whatever you think you know about Mitch, you've got it wrong. He isn't a bad guy. He's taken good care of me."

"Not after what the giant did to Mom."

"What happened to Mom? What did Mitch have to do with it?"

"He was there. He let the giant go. He left us on the road."

Alex wheeled to glare at his comrades. They were all studying their hands, minding their own business. Avoiding his eyes. Only Jack stared back at him. He hadn't been there.

She said, "I'm here because I want to be. I belong here."

"You belong with me, Hannah. I'll look after you."

"Dad got a turkey. They're saving it for my next visit."

He sighed. "Hannah—"

"And brown gravy."

He paused. "Stuffing?"

"Just potatoes."

"Sweet potatoes?" His favorite. His mom used to bake them smothered in bacon, lemon juice, and brown sugar.

"You betcha," she said.

Alex was picturing it. Another holiday meal with his family, no longer boring in his mind but downright exotic and wondrous. Mom yelling at him not to text at the table, Grandpa drinking too much, Dad trying to steer the conversation away from politics. All of it.

"Sounds like a great time," he told her. "Wish I could go."

"You should come."

"I can't. I belong here too."

"I have to go, Alex. The Free Women need the radio."

"When this is all over, I'll see you at our house, okay?"

"Okay."

"You go to Sterling first chance you get and wait for me. I'll be there. I love you, kid. Take care of yourself. Don't do anything stupid in the meantime like get hurt. I'd go out of my mind if anything happened to you."

"You better not shoot at me. I love you too, you big fart-face."

He smiled at this glimpse of the old Hannah. "And one more thing..."

"What?"

"Tell Mom and Dad I love them too."

"I will. Goodbye, big brother."

"See ya, sis."

A woman's voice burst through the ether: "Runners are on the way, ladies. Section three, if you were listening, you know the amazing Hannah will be a little late with your dinner. Hang tight."

Alex handed the radio back to Bud.

The RTO dropped his cigarette and ground it out with his boot. "She's a tough little lady, huh?"

"She's just a kid."

"It was nice you got to talk to her," Jack said.

Alex wheeled on him. "What happened?"

His friend raised his hands. "I have no idea what she was talking about."

He glowered at the rest of the squad. "Who's going to tell me?"

The men looked away again.

"Was it Sergeant Shook?" Alex demanded. "Did he do something?"

"Nothing happened," Tom said.

Donnie winced, confirming it was something and it did happen.

Shook had done something awful to his parents. To his *mom*. The militiamen wouldn't say what, but he could imagine plenty. Shook was capable of anything. The rules of war and peace alike didn't seem to apply to him.

Alex's vision went red. "Son of a bitch."

The militiamen jumped to their feet, unsure whether to allow him to leave or tackle him to the ground. Tom's arm shot out to block the doorway.

"Move," Alex growled.

The veteran calmly lowered it. "How about you and me take a walk?"

He snatched up his rifle and followed Tom outside. "Make it quick."

The man gave him a warning glance. "I'm trying to help you out."

"What happened?"

Tom kept walking. Alex gave chase. He wasn't sure he wanted to know, but he had to know. The darkness closed in around them.

The soldier told him everything.

The IED killing his father, Shook coming along, Mitch stopping it. The squad on the clock, which forced them to leave Hannah and her mother behind.

"That IED wasn't us," the soldier added. "Probably antifa. It was dark. More than likely, they thought your family was militia on its way to Indy. They caught the bomb that was meant for us."

"Did he...?" Alex winced. "Did he kill my mother?"

"No. She was alive when we left them. Your sister might have been telling the truth. About her still being alive."

Alex already knew the truth. If she were alive, she'd never allow Hannah anywhere near a militia, much less join up with one.

His vision blurred as he started to bawl. The militia valued aggression and punished weakness, but he couldn't stop it. He cried for Mom and Dad, and Hannah. He cried for himself. It just poured out of him.

They'd trained him to be a soldier, but he wasn't a soldier. He was a fifteen-year-old boy who wanted his mother.

Tom placed his hand on Alex's shoulder and squeezed. After a while, the tears slowed. He took a few long, jagged breaths. Then the rage returned.

"I'm going to kill him." He started walking.

The world rocked, and he couldn't breathe. The soldier had him gripped in a headlock. Alex struggled against it, but the man's thick arm only tightened until he saw stars.

"Are you smart or are you stupid?" Tom said. "Give me a nod if you're smart."

If Tom tried to stop him, he'd kill him too.

"If you go over there and shoot him, Bravo will cut you up," the soldier said. "Which will hurt morale and ruin Mitch's day. I can't allow that."

Alex didn't give a crap about Mitch's day.

"So if you want to kill him, you have to be smart."

He stopped struggling. Tom had his full attention now. The

soldier released his hold but kept his arm wrapped tight around Alex's shoulders.

"Do you know what friendly fire is?"

Alex nodded.

Tom clarified anyway. "You wait until the shit starts flying, and then you frag his ass."

He took a sharp breath and nodded again.

"You don't tell anybody you're doing it. You don't tell anybody you did it. You just do it. After you do it, I'll have your back."

"Why?"

"Why what?"

"Why would you do that for me?"

"Shook is a stain on our cause," Tom said. "He doesn't follow orders. He shoots prisoners. I'll be happy to see him dead."

FIFTY-ONE

Aubrey raised her glass. "You guys are awesome."

Face flushed with champagne, Terry smiled and held up his own glass. "Here's to a very successful partnership."

Even the moody Rafael was grinning. *"À votre santé."*

They clashed glasses and drank. The champagne went down like silk.

New Year's Eve. The reserved Castle bar had turned boisterous. A cover band played a loud pop tune while the smiling patrons talked and drank.

They were all fiddling while Rome burned, but Aubrey wasn't one of them. She had a big reason to celebrate tonight.

"Let me see it again," she said. "One more time."

Terry held out his phone. She gazed rapt at the image of two hands holding today's issue of *The Guardian*. There was her story, with a large photo of Hannah Miller, on the front page below the fold.

Aubrey still couldn't believe it.

"What will be next for you?" Rafael said.

"The sky's the limit," she said, glowing.

"Maybe the New Year will bring peace. I cannot believe it has lasted this long."

One of the patrons was dancing with a server while his friends cheered him on. The pretty blond girl swayed in her white button-down shirt and black bow tie.

The patrons no longer seemed like fiddlers to her. They were celebrating surviving a year of war.

The girl looked like Zoey Tapper. Aubrey pushed the thought aside. *Not now. Not here.*

"Come and dance with me," she told Rafael.

He inspected his champagne. "Maybe after I finish this drink."

The Frenchman carried his photos inside him, and they haunted him. She found it both attractive and annoying. She wanted him to let go and have some fun.

She said, "What about you, *Guardian*?"

Terry chuckled. "Not for me, thank you. If you dance like you drive, you'd give me a stroke."

"Fine," she pouted. "I wore my best dress tonight for nothing, it seems."

"And you look ravishing. But I have to be at least somewhat fit for my flight tomorrow."

"What flight? You're leaving?"

"I wasn't sure how to broach the subject with you," the journalist said. "I don't think this city will be a safe place for me for the near future."

"Christ, you're both such downers," Aubrey said.

"I've already overstayed my welcome. This is, after all, a tour."

"Where are you going next?"

"New York, for a few days. Then back to London. My American adventure is coming to an end. It's time to return to my family and start working on my book."

"You are not worried?" Rafael asked Aubrey.

"Of course I'm worried," she said. "Or I will be tomorrow. The war doesn't get to have me tonight."

She wanted to hold on to this feeling as long as she could. Drink herself stupid and dance all night. If only Gabrielle were here, she could get this party going. But the UNICEF worker was busy preparing for tomorrow's aid shipment.

"I will worry for you then," Rafael said.

"You want somebody to worry about you." She caught the look of dismay on his face and cupped his chin. "I could be persuaded."

Tomorrow, if past brushes with champagne were any indication, she'd wake up with a crushing hangover. That was the least of her worries. She might be arrested. She might be assassinated. But that was tomorrow.

She took Rafael's hands in hers. "Come on. You've finished your drink."

"Aubrey..."

"Dance with me. Make me think about you. And whatever happens..."

He smiled. "It is war."

Terry laughed and rose from his chair. "My dear boy, I believe this is one of those offers you can't refuse. I shall leave you to it. Goodbye, *Chronicle*, and good luck."

Aubrey hugged him. "Thank you, *Guardian*."

Terry returned it with a surprised grunt. "Human touch. It's the only thing we truly miss when traveling. If you're ever in London, do look me up."

War ground down the spirit, normalized horror, and destroyed permanence. But it also created strong bonds among those who survived it. Terry's invitation was earnest. They were the same tribe now.

He extended his hand to Rafael. "And you. Stay safe. It was a real pleasure working with you. Honestly, you're the best at what you do."

"I am glad we had the chance." The men shook hands.

Aubrey watched the British reporter shamble out of the oasis with foreboding. The night's high was slipping away. Tomorrow's worries crept along the edge of her mind, wanting attention. She pushed them away and focused on Rafael.

"It appears I am all yours now," he said.

"You bet your ass." She led him toward the band, where a few patrons were dancing.

She wrapped her arms around his neck and swished her hips in time with the rhythm. Rafael matched her movements with their own masculine counterpoint. He knew what he was doing, and she quickly lost herself in sound and motion, back on the top of the world.

The next song was "Auld Lang Syne." She buried herself in his warm arms, face resting against his chest.

The song came to a sudden stop.

No, she thought. *Don't let it ever end.*

"Ten!" the bartender called out.

"Nine!" the crowd roared.

"EIGHT...SEVEN...SIX..."

Aubrey raised her head and kissed Rafael for all she was worth.

"HAPPY NEW YEAR."

She flashed to Zoey Tapper's murder on a busy street. A man killed in his house by a random mortar round. Hannah and Alex Miller fighting a war. Dozens more whose lives she'd observed, lives disrupted or abruptly ended in mindless savagery.

The conflict had raged for a year now, and a new year was beginning. How long could it go on?

Aubrey's eyes welled with tears. She returned to Rafael's embrace to hide her weeping. She thought she was tougher than this. Look at her now, blubbering when she should be happy. She was crying for them all the way she did each night while she listened to her music, her one time of the day she allowed herself to feel anything. Music that reminded her of humanity's bright light, made only brighter when contrasted against the overwhelming darkness of war.

Like Rafael, she carried all the people she'd met inside her, both the living and the dead, and she hoped this somehow honored them.

FIFTY-TWO

Hannah awoke to the crash of guns.

Next to her, Maria rolled over and pulled her sleeping bag over her head. "Tell them to shut up."

Hannah shoved her friend's shoulder. "Get up!"

The girl shot upright. "What?"

This wasn't another skirmish. It was an attack across the front. The other women in the house where they'd stayed the night were already on their feet and checking their weapons. The radio buzzed with frantic voices.

The fighters hurried to the windows and the firing holes they'd drilled through the walls. There were six of them in all, four downstairs, two up.

Hannah went to the nearest window and looked out. Nothing to see except the empty yard and street. The crackle of gunfire in the distance built to a single roar.

The women tensed at their firing positions.

"What's going on?" Maria said.

"Something big."

"What should we do?"

"I don't know." With the new radios, the militia had little use for runners. "They'll call us if they need somebody to mule ammo."

"So we stay here."

Again, Hannah didn't know. Their house was third in a defensive line three deep, the safest place to be on the battlefield. "We should be okay here."

One by one, the houses at the front of the line went up in flames. A rolling wall of black smoke blotted out the sun.

Maria gasped. "They're bugging out already?"

The gunfire grew louder. The enemy was closing in fast, hitting the second line of houses.

"Get ready, girls," the sergeant yelled.

The fighters replied with a fierce shout.

"Hannah," Maria said.

"Yeah?"

"I'm really scared."

She gripped her friend's hand. "No matter what, I have your back."

Maria squeezed back. "No matter what."

The house in front of them began to come apart.

Debris sprayed in the air as rounds tore through the structure. A fireball burst from a second-floor window. Smoke poured out of the building.

Maria was shaking. "Oh my God."

The house's back door slammed open. Militia dashed out of the burning building. One slid on the porch steps and went down hard. It was Grace Kim.

Hannah winced as if she'd fallen herself. *Come on, get up, get up.*

A man in a long blue coat marched out of the house wearing a large tank on his back and a white cross stitched over his left breast. He pointed a tube at Grace, who was scrambling for safety.

Run!

Hannah screamed as the tube belched fire across the sniper and engulfed her in flames. She flailed across the yard until she collapsed.

The man eyed Grace's burning remains with a pained expression as if realizing he'd done something no human should do. Then he looked up at Hannah screaming at the window.

He offered her a reassuring smile as if to say: *It's all going to be okay.*

Other coated figures rushed from between the houses, shooting as they moved.

The last of the Free Women bolted into the house and fell sprawling and gasping. A fighter writhed on the carpet, shrieking and pawing at her bloody shoulder. Another rolled to smother the flames devouring her jacket.

Eyes clenched shut, Maria wrapped her arms around Hannah. "Stop! Stop!"

"Let 'em have it!" the sergeant cried.

The fighters let up a banshee howl as they opened fire on the attackers. The man with the flamethrower jumped in the air as the rounds tore into him. The tank burst in a fireball that splashed the deck with orange flame.

Enemy fighters went down, but more appeared, waves of men and women in black berets and long coats.

They weren't Liberty Tree. They were something new, something terrible. They seemed more like robots than people.

What they'd done to Grace Kim. To Hannah, it was the worst way to die.

Maria clung to her, screaming.

Bullets shredded the wall. A fighter jigged and collapsed. The sergeant flew back from her firing position. An explosion rocked the house and hurled the girls to the floor.

Dazed, Hannah rose to all fours. "Maria?"

Another blast knocked her down in a blinding flash of light. A wave of intense heat washed over her. The Free Women were dumping homemade bombs and Molotovs out the windows. The line was about to be broken.

Hannah rose again and staggered through flying glass and debris.

Insulation, dust, and smoke filled the air around her. She spotted a body lying in a pool of blood. The sergeant. She was dead, her chest a smoking hole.

"Hannah?"

She wheeled. "Maria!"

The girl lurched toward her. "Help me!"

Explosions shook the house in rapid succession, *WHAM, WHAM, WHAM.* The front door burst into splinters. Gaping holes appeared in the living room wall. Maria flew into the rolling cloud.

Hannah found herself lying on the floor choking on dust, her ears ringing. The house crackled as fire began to consume it. The sergeant's AK-47 lay within reach. She picked it up.

"Maria, where are you?"

She stumbled over wreckage and bumped into a man in a long coat.

Hannah closed her eyes as she squeezed the trigger. The rifle banged in her hands. Even with her eyes shut, there was no way to miss.

He crumpled and lay twitching. She gaped at his body with horror and relief.

The dust cleared to reveal a giant hole in the wall. Beyond, a dozen figures raced toward the house. One paused to fire a jet of flame at the second floor.

Hannah knelt and sighted down the barrel. The AK's wood stock jolted against her shoulder. A woman shrugged and collapsed. She aimed again through a blur of hot tears and shot the man with the flamethrower.

The enemy wavered, pointing at something to Hannah's right. One of them pitched forward in a spray of blood.

The gunfire was escalating again. Black and Hispanic men and women in a motley collection of uniforms swarmed down the street, firing as they moved.

Hannah watched with numb fascination, too dumbstruck to cheer.

The Indy 300 had come home.

She rose to her feet with a scream and charged.

A man was limping away from her. She raised her AK and sighted him. He toppled with a puff of smoke.

Fighters were coming from the other direction. She shifted her aim.

One of the Indy 300 waved at her. "Don't shoot at them, kid! They're Rainbow Warriors!"

The world tilted. The rifle she'd been carrying suddenly weighed a ton. She staggered under its weight and fell to her knees.

Shaking, she threw up in the snow.

A woman's face materialized. "You okay, sweetie?"

Hannah opened her mouth to talk but could only produce a whimper.

"Let me help you. Where's your people?"

She turned with an anguished cry. The house she'd left was ablaze.

"Hey!" the woman called after her.

Hannah ran across bloody snow and into the inferno. "Maria!"

The heat was incredible. Paint boiled off the walls. The air was filled with smoke and swirling ash. Dust-covered bodies lay scattered around the room.

"Maria?" she croaked.

She started coughing and couldn't stop. Her lungs were on fire. She was choking. Her scream came out a jagged, keening wail.

Then strong hands grabbed her shoulders and yanked her off her feet.

FIFTY-THREE

Alpha squad waited in yet another crappy derelict house for the go order to advance and mop up. Alex paced the living room with his rifle. He had a simple plan. Once the battle started, he'd work his way behind Bravo squad and put two in the back of Sergeant Shook's head.

The radio burst with chatter. Tom listened to his squad's marching orders.

This was it. The order to attack. Alex shot Jack a look.

His friend shook his head. "We're out, bro. We used it all."

"Just a little. That's all I need."

"You want more, go see Shook."

Tom terminated contact with HQ. "We're aborting. We aren't going anywhere."

The squad gathered around growling. They'd been sold out. The Angels wanted it all for themselves.

"The Angels are being wiped out," their new sergeant told them.

He called it a pincer movement that would have made Rommel proud. The Free Women had held their ground against the First Angels' focused human-wave attack just long enough for the Indy 300 to sweep in from the north and the Rainbow Warriors from the south, squeezing the bulge like a vise. The Angels were surrounded and dying in a dozen last stands.

Alex pictured his little sister out there going Rambo on the Bible thumpers.

Tom glared at him. "What's so funny?"

"It's just unbelievable."

The men snarled their agreement.

"The colonel ordered us to be ready to withdraw back to our old positions at Fairfax," Tom said. "We're vulnerable to being flanked."

The squad erupted at this news. After everything, they'd end up right back where they started.

A mortar thumped. The round whistled through the air.

Donnie looked up and said, "At least we still got—"

"Incoming!" Tom roared.

Alex dove to the floor and landed hard. The round smashed into the street outside. The windows burst with spraying glass. Shrapnel and chunks of asphalt battered the house.

"What are they doing?" Donnie raged.

Alex flinched as the next shell struck the ground near the house next door.

Jack lay next to him with his hands covering his head. "I'll bet the libs captured the Angels' mortars."

Alex turned to gaze at the back door, which promised an exit from all this. The war was all a big joke, but it wasn't funny anymore. The endless skirmishing had turned into a real war. The militiamen saw the libs as pussies, but it turned out the pussies could fight. They had a Rommel doing pincer moves. They had mortars. They were smart enough to set up their attack using runners while they kept the Liberty Tree busy listening to bull on the radio.

They'd just wiped out the First Angels, and now they were coming for the Liberty Tree.

Another blast shook the house. Shrapnel crackled along the siding. Clouds of dust and insulation settled on the floor.

"Why are you all looking at me?" Tom growled.

"Are we bugging out?" Alex said.

"We're holding for now. We fought for this ground."

"Hooah!" The squad pulled themselves off the floor and hurried to their firing positions.

Alex took another longing look at the back door and went into a den that doubled as a guest bedroom. The mattress and bedding had been removed, leaving a metal bedframe. He took his assigned position next to Jack at the window.

"We were doing fine before the God squad showed up," Donnie said from the hallway. "The libs come at us, we'll kick their ass like always."

The men cheered. Even now, they refused to believe the libs could fight. But the libs were coming, fractious yet now united, three militias strong with all their captured weapons, which now included flamethrowers.

It was time to start planning how to get out of Dodge. "Hey, Jack."

"I told you I'm out."

"That's not what I—"

A house down the street exploded with a deafening crash.

"Contact!" Donnie yelled and started shooting.

Alex peered out the window in time to see a muzzle flash across the street. He threw a few rounds at it.

"Conserve your ammo," Tom called out. "I want aimed fire."

Judging by the gunfire in the distance, most of the lib militia were mopping up the Angels. Black smoke drifted in the air from battle fires. The enemy in front of them weren't attacking; they were skirmishing.

"What were you going to say?" Jack said.

Alex withdrew his rifle from the window. "We should get out of here."

"What do you mean?"

"I mean go find someplace where nobody tells us what to do or tries to kill us."

"Don't even say that," Jack hissed. "They'll shoot us."

"The Angels used flamethrowers on them. They yanked wounded fighters out of the clinic and murdered them. You know that happened, you were there. The libs just wiped them out, and they're coming for us next. They're out for blood."

Jack aimed and let off a burst. "We can't just walk out the door."

"All we have to do is hang back during the attack and be ready to bolt. When the libs break through, we run and don't look back."

"That's the dumbest plan ever."

"You got a better idea?"

"I don't know, bro. Surrender?"

"Think about what we did to them. They'll shoot us with our hands in the air."

"I don't know! What else can we do?"

Alex had no answer for him. Mortar rounds crashed in the distance.

Jack sighed. "Okay."

"Okay what?"

"If they come at us like you think they will, we'll keep an eye out for our chance to run."

"Good." Alex was glad to have his friend with him on this. "Until then, all we have to do is stay alive."

Jack snorted and went back to shooting out the window. "Is that all?"

The hours rolled by trading potshots with the libs. They might not attack until tomorrow, but when they did, Alex would be ready. When the bullets started flying, he'd shoot Sergeant Shook in the head and get the hell out of here.

Shook had taught him the war was one big joke. Alex would be happy to teach him in return that sometimes, the joke's on you.

FIFTY-FOUR

A woman Hannah didn't know led her by the hand. She was Indy 300. They were on the same side, so Hannah trusted her. She gripped her AK-47 in her other hand just in case.

"I'm Imani," the woman said.

Hannah walked in a daze. She was alive, her friend was dead, and nothing was fair. She flinched at a fresh round of gunfire crackling in the distance.

"You don't have to worry about them," Imani said. "That shooting is us mopping up. After what they did to us and our neighborhood, I doubt there will be any of them left."

"You have a pretty name," Hannah said.

The woman looked down at her and smiled. "It's African. Kiswahili, actually. It means *faith*. What's your name?"

Hannah, she thought. *My name's Hannah. It spells the same forward and backward. Mom told me she'd named me after Hannah Montana.*

She let out a wracking sob. After watching her father die in the wreck and her mother hauled off the road like garbage, she'd thought it would have gotten easier to lose somebody she loved, but it only got harder.

Hannah had to face her helpless grief all over again. She stopped walking, overcome with a need to cry so powerful she doubled over retching.

"Jesus...Are you okay?"

"I've got her!" a familiar voice called out. "I'll take her home. Thank you for bringing her back." Kristy appeared at her side and hugged her. "Oh my God. What did they do to you?"

"I want my mom," Hannah wailed.

Then Kristy was crying too. "I know. I know you do."

Still holding each other, they trudged back to headquarters. Sabrina hurried outside and knelt in front of Hannah. "My good, brave girl. I'm so glad you're okay."

"They're all dead," Hannah said. "They didn't run."

"Come inside and get warm."

The headquarters staff's eyes widened as she entered the house. Her jacket was charred. She was covered in black soot. Her face was raw and aching.

Then she was surrounded by smiling faces as the girls mobbed her.

"Let me through, sisters," the medic said. The woman inspected Hannah's face and wet a cotton ball with alcohol. "This is going to sting."

Hannah winced as the medic dabbed her cuts. "What did I miss?"

The girls all shouted at once. They told her what she already knew. First Angels. Human-wave attack concentrated along a small front, led by flamethrowers. Horrible casualties. The Indy 300 and Rainbow Warriors surrounding and destroying them.

"We didn't fight today," Kristy said. "But we will tonight."

"You're fighting tonight?" Hannah said.

"We're all fighting," Sabrina said. "All of us. One last fight."

Hannah glanced at the strategic map behind the commander. It had been completely redrawn. The X's were where she remembered them, but there were a lot more O's. Three militias, now united.

"What's going on?" she said.

"We're going to break the rebel line and end the siege."

"Boom," Kristy said.

"Boom!" the girls yelled.

The medic applied Band-Aids and gave Hannah a bottle of water and handful of chewable vitamins. "You're good to go, sister."

She pictured the war ending. No more fighting, no more snipers, no more living in terror. "What about me?"

"You've done enough for one day," Sabrina said. "I think you've earned a rest."

Hannah said nothing. Instead, she raised her clenched fist over her head. A simple salute that symbolized support, solidarity, resistance.

The commander nodded. "I guess you've also earned the choice."

"I don't want to be a runner. I want to fight."

"Tonight, you'll do both. But first..." She held out her hand.

Hannah tightened her grip on her AK. "I fought today."

"I'm going to trade you something better."

Hannah followed her into the kitchen, where fourteen green canvas messenger bags rested on the floor. The commander opened one.

Connected by wires, brick-shaped boxes filled the bag.

Hannah stepped back. "Is that a bomb?"

"Five pounds of C-4. A Christmas present from the IMPD. Don't worry, it's safe until it's armed."

"What am I supposed to do with it?"

"Deliver it to the Liberty Tree at midnight. Sergeant Martinez will give you an address on North Holmes. You sneak up on the house, set the timer, and drop the bag in a window."

"Okay."

"Then you run as fast as you can. Got it? You run. Twenty seconds is all you get before one hell of a bang."

"Okay," Hannah repeated, a little less certain.

Sabrina's eyes probed hers. "Did Abigail ever tell you why we're fighting?"

"We fight for justice."

"That's right. A fair shake. But there will never be justice for anybody if we don't win. That's my cause. Kill all fascists. Until we do, everything else is just bullshit. Understand? If we kill the few, we'll save the many."

"I think I understand." She didn't like it, but after what she'd suffered today, maybe Sabrina was right. There was no other way of dealing with them.

"I'd rather not have you anywhere near the fighting, but this is it. The big one. After the houses go up, I need every fighter I've got for the assault."

Hannah pictured dropping her satchel on Mitch and the giant and blowing them sky-high. "I'll do it."

Kristy called: "Hannah, get back here."

"Wait," the commander said. She unbuckled her gun belt with its handgun in a leather holster. She handed it over. "You earned it. I'm proud of you, sister."

Hannah held it in a tight grip. "Thank you."

In the living room, Kristy huddled with the other girls, all twelve wrapping their arms around one another to form a tight circle. Hannah joined them and became part of something bigger than herself, something that was both loving and strong.

"Sisters," Kristy said. "Tonight, the war's going to end, and we're going to end it. We're going to pay them back for what they did to Maria. I love all of you."

The huddle broke up. Hannah sighed at the sudden loss of warmth.

Kristy said, "Hannah, you're with me. Pack up some food and get your bag."

Sergeant Martinez gave them all addresses and a lesson on how to prime the bomb and set the timer. Twenty seconds then boom. The sergeant issued rations and blankets and gave each of them a kiss on the forehead.

The girls trooped out of the house.

A band of Rainbow Warriors marched past. At the sight of the girls, they raised their fists.

Hannah smiled back. Tonight, her war would be over, making all the suffering and loss finally mean something.

"Come on," Kristy said.

They shouldered their heavy packs and canteens and started walking. The front line smoldered. The morning's fighting had razed an entire block to the ground. They skirted this wasteland and ran into an Indy 300 patrol, which guided them to the house where they'd stay until it was time to attack.

Inside, a powerfully built woman wearing a blue head scarf greeted them. "Welcome to the 300. I'm Vicky." She fixed her fierce gaze on Hannah. "You fought this morning. You're the girl who held the Alamo."

"I'm Hannah," she said shyly. "This is Kristy."

"This is my crew."

The fighters smiled and waved from the floor, where they'd set up a Coleman stove. Only one didn't, a man aiming his rifle out the window.

Vicky read the addresses they gave her. "You're in the right place. Can I see it?"

Hannah opened her messenger bag. "Five pounds of C-4."

The fighter whistled and gestured for the girls to follow her to the window. "Hannah, take a quick peek out there. You'll see a gray house right across the street. That one's yours. Kristy, your house is next to it on the right."

Hannah raised her head. The house seemed abandoned and very, very far away. She caught a flicker of movement and ducked as a muzzle flash lit up a window. The round smacked into the siding.

"Pick your own spot, but stay low," Vicky said. "We'll keep them busy until midnight. You rock those houses, and we'll come running. Any questions?"

"Did you get your name because there are three hundred of you?" Hannah said.

"There used to be." The fighter pointed at the floor. "Wait."

Hannah and Kristy sat and unwrapped their meal, which consisted of hunks of hard cheese and stale granola bars.

"Let's see your arm," Kristy said.

Hannah rolled up her sleeve to reveal the gang's Venus symbol, skull and crossbones, and a banana that originally was intended to be a sword, Maria's idea of a joke: Hannah was now forever Hannah Banana.

"Maria just wanted to be a kid," she said.

"We're not kids anymore. Roll up your sleeve as high as you can. This is going to be a big one. Any ideas?"

"I want you to write Maria's name."

"I love that."

"Then I'll do you."

Kristy shook her head. "I haven't earned it. You can give me one tomorrow, and I'll give you another. An angry smiley face with a burning wick."

Hannah slumped against the wall and gnawed her cheese while Kristy inked her arm. "What are you going to do after the war?"

"Find my mom."

"Oh. I thought she was..."

"No, she's in San Francisco. I flew out here to see my dad. During the troubles, he...I ended up stranded here."

"It's nice you have a home you can go back to when it's all over, though."

Kristy finished coloring the R. "Do you really think we can go back to the way it was before?"

"I guess not."

"What about you?"

"I don't think about it."

"But you have a brother, right?"

Hannah gestured outside. "They're making him fight for them."

Kristy stopped drawing. "You don't think he's in one of those houses, do you?"

"He's a kid. They probably have him behind the line." She didn't want to think about that either.

"You always have a home with me, you know. After the war, if you don't have anywhere to go, you can come with me to San Francisco."

Hannah tried to picture it. "We'd be sisters."

"We already are. Okay, I'm done. Check it out."

Hannah inspected her tattoo. *MARIA* in big black letters. "It's good."

The skirmishing tapered off as the sun went down. The Indy 300 stopped talking and extinguished the Coleman.

The world seemed to hold its breath.

Hannah wrapped herself in her blanket. She was so tired that her eyes hurt, but she didn't think she'd ever sleep again. She slid into a deep slumber anyway, wracked by feverish nightmares filled with flamethrowers and Maria crying for help.

A hand was shaking her.

She sat up with a cry. "Stop it!"

The room was dark and cold. She looked around in alarm.

"It's all right," a voice said. "You're all right. Be quiet."

She focused on Vicky's face. "What happened? Where's Kristy?"

"Your friend left already to get in position. It's almost midnight."

Hannah took a deep breath and let it go. "Give me my bag."

This was it. One last night. One last fight.

FIFTY-FIVE

His watch nearly over, Alex dozed at the window. As usual, he couldn't sleep when he had the chance, and now he could barely stay awake.

The libs had fired at the house at random intervals all day. At sundown, the shooting stopped, making for uneventful watch duty. Behind him, the squad snored in their sleeping bags. Outside, the world was quiet.

Too quiet, he thought in an ominous movie voice.

As if. Right now, there was no such thing as too quiet. Very quiet was just how he liked it. Still, it was unnerving, knowing the enemy slept right across the street.

Nothing to see out there. Almost pitch-black.

Tom's sleeping bag rustled. "There he goes! Shoot him!"

Nothing to worry about. Everybody in the squad knew the veteran muttered in his sleep, dreaming of some horror he'd lived during the war. Or maybe it was the other war he and Mitch always talked about, the one in Afghanistan, which had started before Alex was born.

He wondered why Tom and the other guys kept at it, despite the toll it was taking. If Alex commanded the militia, he would have sent everybody home by now. They liked to fight, he got that part. They wanted respect. They fought for liberty. Because they were angry.

Alex wanted to be free to drive a car, stay up as late as he felt like, skateboard, and watch his favorite shows on TV. He wanted the kind of respect where guys weren't always riding each other in a tiring game of dominance. He wasn't angry at the government; he was angry at the man who hurt his family.

He found Jack and kicked his foot.

His friend sat upright, already reaching for his rifle. "What's that?"

"Your turn for watch."

"Aw, man." The kid left his warm sleeping bag and stumbled to the window.

"Have fun."

"Yeah, yeah."

Alex went outside. The air was tangy with the smell of smoke and burnt chemicals. The stars shimmered in the haze. A quick walk brought him to the house next door. Bravo was awake.

A militiaman let him in. "Hey, Rambo. You want a beer?"

"Sure."

"Get your ass in here," Sergeant Shook said from another room. "What's the word?"

Alex passed through the kitchen and down a short hallway. He entered the living room and looked around. It had a similar floor plan as his billet. He noted the windows, where Shook would stand tomorrow facing the enemy.

"No word, Sarge," he said. "It's quiet out there."

The squad sat around an LED lantern with a red bandana draped over it to dim the light. A small portable stove burned wood for heat. The soldier they called Blister stood watch at the window wearing night-vision goggles.

"Well, they're coming tomorrow," Shook said. "Sure as shit."

"Yeah."

"You going to sit with us and have a beer, or just stand there?"

"I'm too wired."

"You won't even look at me is what I'm noticing. Maybe you're nervous about my Christmas present. A certain debt you owe me."

Alex's eyes circled the sergeant before settling on him. He tried to smile, but it came out a grimace. Shook didn't smile back.

"It's all a big joke, right?"

The big sergeant burst out laughing. The rest of the squad joined in.

"Kid," said Shook, "you hit the nail right on the head."

"What I don't get is why."

Alex watched with mounting fear as the big sergeant stood and crossed the dim room. The man smiled like a snake.

Then Shook slapped him.

His head snapped back. His cap flew off his head. Alex cupped his stinging cheek, his eyes watering with surprise and shame.

Shook slapped him again. "You gonna cry?"

Alex tried to laugh it off. "Okay, you made your—"

Another crack. The pain was one thing. The humiliation and panic that surged through him felt worse. The squad watched with interest, eyes burning in the dim red light, like they wanted in on the action.

Alex took a step back and raised his arms to protect himself. He wasn't allowed to run. Fighting back would only get him an even harsher beating.

Shook matched his step and hit him again even harder. "You gonna cry, faggot?"

"No, Sergeant." Trying to sound tough and failing.

Another slap. "What are you gonna do?"

Alex pictured Shook doing this to his mother. He pictured doing this to Shook. He lowered his arms and stepped glaring into Shook's space.

Go ahead and hit me again, he thought. *Hit me as much as you want. Because tomorrow, I'm going to kill you.*

Then he smiled at his own private joke.

Without breaking eye contact, Shook held out his hand. "Beer."

A militiaman handed him one from the cooler. The sergeant cracked it open and gave it to Alex. "Now you know why. Now you know everything." He returned to his seat on the floor. "Take over for Blister. Why? Because I said so."

Alex put his cap back on and went to the window.

Blister passed him his night-vision goggles. "You got to earn your beer in Bravo."

Alex pulled on the goggles and powered them up. He wondered where Bravo had gotten the batteries. While the goggles had a binocular visor, the lens was monocular. Immediately, his field of view shrank to forty-degree tunnel vision on a phosphor screen.

The LED lantern flared in his eyes, and he turned to the window, peering out from the edge so as not to offer a target. He could see outside now. The gen-3 goggles rendered the snow-covered landscape in shades of green.

He pictured the libs hosing the house with gunfire tomorrow. Shook standing here laughing as he blazed away at them with his SAW.

That's when he'd empty his rifle into the man's back.

His face stung in the cold night air. He remembered Tom telling him to be smart. He had to make it look like the libs did it.

Tom had grenades.

Toss one in the room and run. Grab Jack and keep running until he'd gained his own liberty. Keep going until he reached Sterling. There, he'd wait for the war to end and Hannah to come home.

He tilted his head for another swallow of his beer and stopped. Somebody was moving outside.

A figure made a dash toward the house.

He tucked his AR-15 into his shoulder and pointed it out the window.

God, it was a kid.

Gunfire popped in the distance, making his nerves tingle.

The kid wasn't armed. He was carrying a messenger bag. Just some refugee trying to get out of town. Alex hunkered behind his rifle just in case, finger twitching next to the trigger.

Another round of shots broke the stillness. Something was going on.

The kid had crossed the street and paused to reach into his bag before breaking into a mad sprint.

Alex flinched as his vision flared a blinding green and an explosion roared in the night, followed by a clatter of debris raining across the neighborhood. Another blast erupted on the road.

"What's going on?" Shook said. "You see anything?"

The kid was carrying some kind of bomb. Alex aimed at him center mass, finger on the trigger now.

The kid wasn't a boy.

"I don't see anything." His voice sounded far away in his ears.

Bravo squad stirred anyway, gathering up their weapons and gear.

Hannah's face, grim and determined, in crisp shades of green.

"I have to get back to Alpha."

"You stay right there until we're in position, fucknuts," Shook growled.

He couldn't run, couldn't yell at her to stop, couldn't shoot.

Every second brought her closer. Sweat trickled down his ribs. No choice. Just a little pressure on the trigger—

He fired.

Hannah flinched at the warning shot but kept coming.

She was all he had left, and she was going to make him kill her.

Shook and Mitch had taught him that life wasn't fair. Beneath all the noble ideals, this truth was where all the anger and paranoia came from, and guns and limited government would never cure it. Even if the patriots won, they'd never really win, and while the shooting might stop, the war they fought would never end.

They'd taught him another truth. Life was dog-eat-dog, survival of the fittest. You didn't whine or complain. You toughened up so you could do the dishing. You didn't rationalize or make excuses, as there were only two ways to look at everything, right and wrong, and a man deserved the freedom to choose either one.

Kill or not kill, Hannah or him.

She'd made her choice.

He fired again.

She didn't stop.

She'd buried Mom and Dad and wanted to pay back the men who'd killed them, and now she was here, about to die for what she wanted. Vengeance for the parents he'd abandoned because he didn't know how important his family was.

He did now.

Alex wheeled and bolted for the back door. The messenger bag thumped on the floor behind him.

Shook yelled, "Hey! Where are you—?"

FIFTY-SIX

One by one, explosions banged down North Holmes like the Fourth of July.

Walls flashed and burst in a hot wind, belching dust and bodies across front yards. Sections of roof blew into the air. The ground trembled.

The bangs echoed into an eerie silence that rang in Hannah's ears. She regained her feet on the sidewalk as pieces of lumber clattered around her like artificial hail.

Kristy lay in the street, shot dead.

The last bits bounced off the road. A massive pall of dust hung over the shattered hulks of the houses. The silence returned at a deafening volume.

Then a savage cheer went up along Holmes Avenue. The Indy 300 had their revenge.

In reply, muzzle flashes lit up the windows of the houses that escaped destruction. The cheering disappeared in the crash of automatic weapons. The Indy 300 fired back. Bullets snapped through the air.

Hannah drew Sabrina's handgun from her holster and ran toward the house she'd bombed. She wanted her own revenge.

The window where she'd tossed the bag was now a large hole exhaling a settling dust cloud. A man staggered out in a daze.

Hannah raised the gun and fired. He spun and crumpled to the ground.

Her ability to shoot to kill on reflex stunned her. While letting her loved ones go grew harder each time, killing only became easier.

She skirted the body and stepped into the blasted house. Shredded corpses lay scattered around, half buried in rubble.

Today was Hannah's lucky day.

The giant sat slumped against a twisted metal support. Parts of him were missing, the rest charred and smoking, but he was still alive.

She aimed the gun at his face. "Do you remember me?"

"Need a medic," he rasped.

"You hurt my mom. You hurt her on the road to Indianapolis."

The giant didn't answer. His good eye stared off into empty space. His breath whistled in his lungs.

Hannah called upon her rage to help her do what she'd imagined doing for nearly an entire year of her life. While her love had many faces, her hate had only two, and his was one of them.

Instead, she wavered at the brink of justice.

His eye flickered to take her in. "Nope."

"You can't say you didn't do it. I was there."

"Nope," he repeated. "Don't remember."

What he'd done was so trivial to him he didn't remember doing it. Or he'd victimized multiple women, making Hannah's mother impossible to single out for recall. To him, Hannah's mother was just roadkill.

His eye settled on his machine gun. He tried to reach for it. "Let me...die with my—"

Hannah emptied the 9 mm into his body and stood panting in the aftermath.

She'd done it. There was nothing to do now but secure the house and wait for the Indy 300 to show up. She slid a fresh magazine into her gun and crept toward the kitchen. After clearing it, she'd check the upstairs.

Another body lay near the back door.

Hannah knew who it was before she even reached him. Knew this would happen when she picked up the AK-47 at the burning house and then accepted Sabrina's bag of bombs. Knew it would happen the moment she found out he was still alive.

Because everything she loved got destroyed. For everything the war gave, it took away far more. Gaining the ability to kill hadn't protected her like she thought it would. Now she was the one killing what she loved.

Hannah fell to her knees next to him. "Alex?"

He was still breathing. He lay crumpled on the floor, his arm trapped under him at an odd angle, but alive.

"Alex!"

His eyes flickered to her face. He whimpered.

Hannah pulled out her med kit and pushed a handful of gauze against his leg, which was bleeding. She pressed her other hand against a second wound on his hip.

It wasn't enough. He'd been hit everywhere.

"I'm sorry," she sobbed. "Please don't be mad at me."

"Scared," he managed.

"I'm sorry. Don't die."

"Really scared."

"Help!" Hannah screamed. "Somebody help me!"

"Joke," said Alex.

He shuddered. Then the lights in his eyes went out.

Crying, she heaved at him until he sat upright, and hugged him. He'd never liked it when she'd try to hug him. He'd push her away, but his irritation only spurred her laughing to keep trying until he laughed too and called her a maniac.

This time, he didn't protest.

"I'm sorry." She was wailing now. "I'm sorry."

All she'd wanted was to feel safe and serve a cause bigger than herself, a world where nobody shot people from far away or got sliced by shrapnel in the road.

Hannah had killed her brother for it.

A ripping sound in her brain—

Her tenth birthday party, the last time she felt safe before her world ended and her war began. Her friends sat around the dining table and sang to her. Allie, May, and Jenny.

Allie was her best friend, though they had a crush on the same boy at school. She was really smart and funny. May wasn't but was the kindest girl Hannah knew. Jenny was a wild card, super cool but a prankster.

Tonight was going to be great. Alex had locked himself in his room and was playing some violent shooter game. Mom was ordering pizzas. Her friends were staying over for a slumber party. They'd stay up all night giggling and talking about life.

Dad came out of the living room and said to Mom, "The president won't resign. He said the Senate conviction is illegal. He said he's not leaving."

"What?" Mom said. "What does that mean?"

The look on Dad's face told Hannah everything. Helplessness and panic she'd never seen before. His wild eyes roamed across the girls and settled on her with a fierce love.

Then his eyes flashed back to Mom. "The protesters camped at the National Mall . . . Something bad happened."

The phone rang. Minutes later, her friends' moms showed up to take them home. Her birthday ruined, Hannah burst into tears.

Dad hugged her and told her not to worry.

"I'll keep you safe no matter what," he said.

Farther back she went. Dressing up as Hermione for Halloween, waving a plastic wand and yelling, *wingardium leviosa!* Making cookies with Mom in the kitchen, sneaking chocolate chips, the counter a mess of flour, the warm smell of baking in the air. Dad tossing a football to her and Alex at the park. Her parents beaming at her from the audience during a school concert.

Then even farther to settle on a perfect summer day at the beach. Mom and Dad smiling on a blanket, enjoying this rare time off with family. Alex aloof at first but later laughing. Hannah wearing goggles, splashing through the water and going under to see what there was to see down there. She and Alex made castles in the sand and watched the tide wash them away.

Hannah's family and childhood were gone, but they were always there in easy reach for her to remember. Her mind retreated deeper until they came alive again, and this new world, this horrible, cold world, faded away to nothing.

FIFTY-SEVEN

Mitch drove the platoon HQ truck toward the roar of gunfire. The libs had hit one out of three houses along Holmes Avenue and blown it sky-high. The survivors were hitting back with everything they had.

It was time to bug out for Fairfax. They had plenty of prepared firing positions there. They knew the ground, and they'd be less vulnerable to flanking.

With the losses they'd taken, they had no choice. Unless the colonel's recruiting efforts hit pay dirt, the Liberty Tree would be playing defense for the duration.

Mitch wondered if they could even hold Fairfax.

He'd expected the libs to celebrate their victory over the Angels and go back to trading potshots, but the war had suddenly entered a new phase. The Angels had punched a hornet's nest with their shock and awe. The libs were united and out for blood, and they had a commander who knew what she was doing.

The same simple math applied now just as it did then. His side had greater training, weapons, supplies, discipline, and unity. Theirs had more people. The difference now was they were uniting behind this commander who seemed willing to fight hard until one side lost in a brutal war of attrition.

The kind of war his side couldn't win.

He parked the truck and limped into a house, where he found his old squad in the midst of a vicious gunfight. Tom left his firing position at the window and scurried to meet him.

"We're dumping ammo to keep them back," Tom shouted over the rattle of gunfire. "But we got gaps in the line. You really thinking about pulling out?"

"We can't hold this ground."

"If we stretch out, we can."

He shook his head. That kind of thinking had already created a disaster. It was time to cut their losses. "That's a no go. Get ready to move."

Jack stepped aside from the window and put his back to the wall. "They sent a runner at the house with a satchel charge. I killed her. Just a kid."

"Where's Alex Miller?"

"He went next door to talk to Bravo. They got hit."

Mitch limped to the next house over, now just a shattered hulk. When he twisted the doorknob, the door fell out of its frame and flopped to the ground.

"Jesus Christ," he said.

Hannah Miller knelt on the debris-strewn floor amid shredded bodies, staring into space and hugging her brother's body.

Something inside Mitch broke.

The kid had thrown her charge into the house and wiped out Bravo. The fortunes of civil war had ordained she kill her brother in the process.

He raised his rifle and aimed at her head.

Hannah kept on rocking the boy in her arms. Past her, Mitch saw tracers flash in the dark. The libs let up an eerie banshee howl, their version of the rebel yell. A squad of Indy 300 fighters was making its way toward the house. One of them had a flame-thrower.

Out for blood.

"Goddamnit," he said.

He grabbed Hannah Miller by the scruff of her jacket and hauled her to her feet. He dragged her out into the snow.

"All Root units, this is Root Six," he said into the radio. "Clear the net, clear the net. Commence withdrawal immediately. Bud, do you copy?"

"I copy, over," the RTO said.

"Tell Colonel Lewis that Second Platoon is pulling out now." The colonel had to trust his judgment and order the other platoons to withdraw as well.

"Roger," Bud said.

"Root Six, out."

Fire teams were already exiting the houses. Mitch opened the truck's door and tossed Hannah Miller inside. Then he climbed in and started driving toward the rear.

He didn't know what to do with her. This was one of those rare times you owned it if you *didn't* break it. He leaned over to open the door and kick her to the curb. Easiest solution for all concerned. He stopped himself.

If only she didn't remind him of Jill. If only she wasn't Alex's sister. If only he didn't feel partly responsible for what she was. When he looked at her, he couldn't see a soldier. He saw a little girl who shouldn't be at war.

Hannah slowly swiveled her head to gaze at him.

"You," she said dreamily. She had a Band-Aid on her forehead.

"Take it easy. I'm trying to get you somewhere safe."

She reached to her empty gun holster.

"Goddamnit," he said. "Give it a rest."

The clinic was a madhouse. The wounded writhed on the floor, triaged by frantic nurses close to the breaking point.

He contacted Bud by radio. "I'm at the clinic."

"Negative contact, Six. Send again, over."

"I'm at the clinic. Request Colonel Lewis have a vehicle recover our wounded and transport them to our new forward base. Over."

"Roger, Six."

"Six, out."

He scooped Hannah Miller like a football and carried her through the chaos. Dr. Walker was operating in his office by the light of oil lamps.

"Doc, I need your help."

"Clamp that bleeder," the doctor told his assistant. "Sergeant, I thought I told you how I prioritize my patients."

"It's 'lieutenant' now."

Walker kept working. "Uh-huh."

"I captured this little girl. She's hurt."

The doctor glanced at her. "She's in shock."

"She's a lib fighter. I don't want to take her prisoner. That facility is no place for her, and I can't send her back. She's a kid. She needs to be out of the war."

"Then keep her out of it."

"I can't take care of her. We're in the middle of a battle."

"And I have loads of free time, is that it?"

Mitch growled and turned on his heel to leave.

"Take her to the UN," the doctor called after him. "UNICEF. When they're not plotting Marxist tyranny, they're actually doing some good. And, Lieutenant?"

"What?"

"I hope they kill you for what you did to the Indy 300."

Mitch dropped a pack of Camels on the desk on his way out. "It wasn't me."

He returned to the waiting area and found two walking-wounded soldiers from First Platoon. "You two. Find any libs here and load them in my truck. I'm taking them to their lines."

The men glanced at each other. "Are you serious?"

"Move," he said, "before the doc has to tweezer my bootlaces out of your ass."

They snapped to it. "Yes, sir."

The soldiers hauled the wounded libs and set them in the truck bed. When all of them were loaded up, Mitch tied a bloody sheet to the aerial and got in.

"Stupid," he thought aloud.

Hannah Miller said nothing, still feeling around her holster as if her gun might magically appear.

He started the truck. "I'm trying to help you, kid. Don't ask me why."

Sure, she reminded him of Jill, and he felt like he owed her for ditching her and her mother on the road to Indy, but that wasn't enough to justify what he was doing. The entire militia was beating it for Fairfax, the libs hot on their heels, and here he was driving around looking for the UN.

To hell with it. He stepped on the gas and started moving. He was doing this, and that was it. He didn't owe anybody an explanation except maybe himself. If he survived, he could wrestle with it later. All he knew right now was he wanted her out of the war. As long as she was in it, Abigail was right—it wasn't worth fighting.

He said, "You should know I had a soft spot for your brother, don't ask me why on that either. I can tell you he was a good kid. A good soldier too."

Hannah said nothing, which was just as well.

A knot of fighters flagged him down. He pulled over and rolled down his window. "What's your unit?"

"Third Platoon. You're Mitch Thornton, Second's commander."

"That's right."

The soldier eyed the white sheet hanging from the aerial. "Are we surrendering?"

"Keep it moving," he said. "We're going back to Fairfax."

"Yes, sir."

He drove back onto the road. Soon, he'd run into the libs and probably get drilled full of holes for playing the Good Samaritan.

They were going to kill him.

"Stupid, stupid, stupid," he said.

The first libs he found were Free Women. They emerged like wolves from the darkness as he approached honking. He turned off his radio and extended his hands out the window for them to see. He hoped they saw the white flag and that a white flag still meant something.

They didn't shoot. Maybe they were too damn surprised. They surrounded the truck and pointed their guns at his head.

A woman peered inside and settled her eyes on him. "You lost?"

"I'm looking for Abigail."

She scowled as another fighter called out, "He's got our wounded in the back!"

"I'm bringing them to you so you can take care of them. The docs can't handle it." Mitch gestured to Hannah. "I also brought her."

The woman turned to her comrades. "He's got Hannah Miller with him."

"I want to bring her to Abigail. Abigail Thornton."

"Thornton's her married name. She isn't married."

"Abigail Fulham then."

"How do you know her?"

"I'm the guy whose last name is Thornton."

The woman's face stretched in an unfriendly grin. "So you're Mitch."

"That's right."

"You're crazy, is what you are. I should shoot you now and make her day, but she'll probably want to do it herself." Her facade slipped. "You know you just put yourself in deeper shit than you can imagine. What are you trying to do?"

"I didn't want her growing up in a prison camp. I'm taking her to Abigail. She'll know what to do with her. This girl needs to get out of this war."

The woman stepped away and talked on her radio while Mitch sweated in the truck and hoped Hannah stayed quiet.

"Mount up, sisters," the woman said. "We're going to see Abigail."

She went around to the passenger side and hopped in. The women climbed into the back and tapped the roof. They were ready to go.

"You want me to drive?" Mitch said.

"That a problem?"

"I thought you might want to blindfold me."

"Because that's how you think. We want you to see our strength. I will, however, be sitting here with a gun pointed at your head."

"Fair enough."

Mitch drove east. The libs grew thicker until crowds of them marched down the streets. Many of them carried torches and flags. He spotted Free Women, Indy 300, Rainbow Warriors all marching together and chanting, "THE PEOPLE, UNITED, WILL NEVER BE DEFEATED."

"Take a good look around," the woman said.

He already was. They had impressive numbers, he had to give them that. Plenty of weapons, including quality weapons captured from dead patriots. No police, though. The IMPD was still staying on the other side of the White. This was useful intel. The libs weren't as united as they thought they were.

The crowd thinned as he drove on toward Stringtown. The woman told him to park in front of a Catholic church.

Abigail came out glowering. "Mitch Thornton. You've got brass balls, I'll give you that."

He got out of the truck and appraised her. "You look good, Abigail."

Her glare softened a bit. "I see your ankle's still bothering you."

"Nothing I can't handle." His eyes dropped to her arm in a sling. "Looks like we dinged you."

"And we dinged you back. A whole lot of women, Blacks, Latinos, and gays who aren't taking your crap anymore. How about that?"

He shrugged. He didn't care what his enemies looked like or did in the bedroom. He only cared they wanted a different country than he and the founding fathers wanted.

The women started unloading the wounded and bringing them into the church.

She said, "So what is all this, some kind of mission of mercy?"

"Call it whatever you want." He jerked his thumb toward the truck. "Mostly, I'm here because of her."

Abigail ran over and led Hannah out by the hand. "What happened?"

"You know she had a brother named Alex?"

"Oh, no."

"Yup. And she was the one who did it."

She hugged the girl tight. "Oh, baby."

"She doesn't belong here. I'm hoping you can get her out of it."

"This was our war," Abigail said to the girl. "We never should have involved you. I'm so sorry."

"You can get her out," Mitch repeated. "Talk to that UNICEF woman."

"Mitch Thornton." Abigail stood. "After all this..."

"Don't get sappy," Mitch said.

"Don't tell me what to feel. I'm trying to say you did good."

"Just paying a debt."

"I'll let your conscience decide that. And now you'd better get going before somebody shoots you. Patrice, take him back to his people."

The woman who'd accompanied Mitch here glared at him. "Just like that?"

"I came under a flag of truce," he pointed out.

"That used to mean something before you started shooting prisoners."

"That wasn't me."

"Yeah," Patrice said. "You were just following orders, right?"

"I said it wasn't me. My militia doesn't shoot prisoners."

The woman said to Abigail, "Sabrina will know what to do with him."

"No," Abigail said. "It ain't a dictatorship. At least not yet."

"She's the commander."

"Wasn't I your commander for a year? Did I do wrong by you? We all know what his people have done. Sometimes, we can put the war aside for a minute and do what's right. He just did. I figure we can do the same."

Patrice stared at Mitch as if picturing his balls in a vise. "All right, sisters, you heard the lady. Mount up!"

"Thanks, Abigail," he said. "I know you'll take good care of her."

"You take care of yourself, Mitch. Watch yourself out there, because we ain't playing around anymore. We're coming for you."

"I survived twelve years of marriage. I figure I can make it through this."

On impulse, she gave him a hug goodbye with her good arm. Before he could return it, she turned and led the girl by the hand into the church.

That hug. After so long, it felt surprisingly good.

FIFTY-EIGHT

Aubrey bicycled to the offices of the *Indy Chronicle* through cheering crowds and the distant peal of church bells. Everywhere, people hugged and leaned out apartment windows to bang pots and pans. They spotted the *Chronicle* placard on her bicycle and waved. She waved back laughing, feeling light as a feather as she zoomed past.

Yesterday, while Aubrey slept off her crushing New Year's hangover, Leftist militias destroyed the First Angels and put the Liberty Tree to flight. In the end, not much had changed. After fierce nighttime fighting, the rebels held in Fairfax, and rumors had it another rebel militia was moving in to support the line. Nonetheless, it had changed everything. A stunning victory. The rebels weren't invincible. The oppressive atmosphere of fear and dread had lifted.

She locked her bike in the lobby and tramped up the dark stairs until she reached her floor. As always, staffers shouted across the bull pen while they clacked on their typewriters, the air stale and foul with cigarette smoke. After spending the last few days with Rafael in Castle luxury, it was like returning from a great vacation, trepidation at returning to reality mixed with the comfort of coming home.

Aubrey had finished her story and saw it published in one of the world's most respected newspapers. Now she was ready for whatever came next.

"Eckert wants to see you," Garcia called from his typewriter.

"What's his mood?"

"He's got the holler tail this morning. I saw dimples."

When Eckert was pissed off, he ground his teeth, which resulted in dimples winking on the sides of his face.

"Thanks for the tip."

Garcia ignored her, already back to his story.

The editor looked up from his desk as she came in, his good eye glowering. "You don't know how to answer a phone?"

"I tried to call you back—"

"But my phone's been busy, right." The dimples winked in a steady rhythm on his stubbled jaw. "Because I've been talking to Mr. Webb trying to strategize how to contain the damage you did."

"*The Guardian* would have gotten onto it anyway."

"Are you sure you're a reporter? Because you always seem to miss my point by a mile, even when I spell it out for you in crayon. Your *name* is on the story."

"The story's out," Aubrey said. "It's done."

She thought of one of her favorite quotes, something Mark Twain once said. When the world tells you to move, you hold your ground for truth and tell the world, *No, you move.*

He sighed and ran his hands through his hair. "Grab a seat. Let's talk."

She sat across from him. "Have you gotten any blowback?"

"No," he admitted. "Not yet."

"I don't think anything's going to happen. I really don't."

"We'll see." He smiled. "I guess I should say congratulations on getting published by *The Guardian* before I let you have it any further."

"Are you firing me?"

"No, I was going to yell at you some more, but screw it." He sighed again. "What's done is done, like you said. If something's going to happen, saying we fired you won't make any difference."

"I'm sorry I put the paper at risk," Aubrey said. "I really am. But this was—"

"Please stop. I smell platitudes coming on." He fished a Marlboro from its pack and thumbed it to his lips. "You gave us some distance by getting it in another newspaper. That doesn't put *you* in the clear, though. Frankly, I'm more worried about you than the paper at this point."

"I'll be all right." Though she was no longer sure about that.

"Just watch your back. Okay?"

"I will."

"Okay, new business. What have you got for me?"

"The first UNICEF shipment is coming into the airport today."

Eckert lit the cigarette. He put his feet on the desk and inspected the cloud of smoke. "My last pack."

"Looks like I may be calling in sick tomorrow." She didn't want to be anywhere near him if he couldn't find more cigarettes.

He snorted. "Work the UNICEF story. Now that your pet project is over, I want you beating the street until you come up with more—"

Their phones rang at the same time.

He frowned at the number before answering. "Eckert."

Aubrey went out into the hall. "Aubrey Fox."

The signal wobbled but was legible. "This is Abigail Fulham with the Free Women."

"Oh." Her gut sank. The woman was calling to let her know she didn't appreciate how the Free Women were represented in the article. A courtesy heads-up the militia was coming to kill her. It wouldn't be the first death threat in her professional career, but certainly the most serious. More like a death promise.

But that was her fear talking, nothing more. Eckert had made her paranoid. Abigail had been there when she and Terry had interviewed Hannah. The story had been factual and fair. Why would she be upset about it now?

The woman said, "Hannah Miller needs to get out of the war."

Aubrey listened to the girl's story with mounting horror. The terrifying assault by the First Angels, the midnight suicide run against the rebel lines, killing her brother in a massive blast.

"The militia will use her again," the militiawoman said. "It's total war out here now. I want you to talk to Gabrielle and get her out."

"I'll do what I can."

"Whatever you can do, you need to do it now."

"I understand." The militia was going to put her back in the fight soon.

"I'm not sure you do. The other reason for my call is to warn you."

Again, that sinking feeling. She swallowed. "Warn me of what?"

"Everybody out here knows about the article. Watch your ass. Better yet, run."

Aubrey terminated the call and stared at her phone. She was trembling. She took a deep breath and called Gabrielle, who picked up on the third ring.

"I'm glad you called," the UNICEF worker said. "Everyone in New York is talking about the article. They're getting calls from American media. The story is going to spread."

"Did you get in any trouble?"

"Nothing I can't handle. You?"

"I might be in some trouble," Aubrey said.

"I can help you."

"I'm not sure you can or should."

"I can maybe—"

"There's something else I need you to focus on." She told her Hannah's story. "Can you help her?"

"I—"

Shouting erupted in the bull pen down the hall. The reporters were booing. The sinking feeling returned and wouldn't quit this time.

"I'm sorry," she said. "I didn't hear you."

"I said I'll help her," Gabrielle said. "I promise. I wish I could help you."

The shouting grew louder.

"I think it might be too late for that. I have to go. And Gabrielle?"

"Yes, Aubrey."

"Thank you." Meaning it, from deep in her heart.

She ended the call before the UNICEF worker said anything that might ruin it. She returned to Eckert's office on trembling legs.

Her editor stood behind his desk, loading bullets into a big, ugly revolver. "That was security calling. Go out the back stairwell."

"Eckert..."

His hands were shaking. "Nobody fucks with my staff."

"No," she said.

His good eye glared at her. "What do you mean, *no*?"

The Mark Twain quote about standing for truth flashed through her mind again. The exact quote said to *plant yourself like a tree by the river of truth*. Never budge or waver when you were in the right.

Tell the world, *No, you move.*

"Don't do this, Eckert. You're going to get yourself killed."

"I have to get you out of here."

"And go where? Do what? Hide? Without this job, well, I might as well give up. And I'll never let them see that."

Breathing hard, he looked down at the gun. He slapped it on the desk. "I'm going to do everything I can to get you out. I'll never stop. I'll put your arrest on the front page."

"I know you will." Aubrey mustered a smile. "You may be an asshole, but you're one of the best friends I've got. And you've never lied to me."

Before he could say anything else, she hugged him.

"It's not worth it," he said.

"You know it is."

"Not when it's somebody you love."

He leaned into her with a choking sound, and in the end it was her comforting and protecting him.

She pulled away and took his hand. "Let's go."

In the bull pen, three militiamen in dirty, ill-fitting uniforms stood with automatic rifles leveled at the crowd surrounding them. Their red-faced commander roared at the reporters to stand aside. The reporters howled back, *Shame! Shame! Shame!*

They all quieted at the sight of Aubrey and Eckert walking into the room holding hands.

She took a deep breath and said, "I'm Aubrey Fox."

"You're under arrest," the commander said.

"Who's arresting me?"

"The Progressive Leaders Committee."

The Leftist coalition, not the government, though she'd already surmised that. If it were the government, they'd have sent the IMPD. She hoped Eckert was getting all this, as he'd need it if he hoped to get her out.

"On what charge?"

"Sedition."

Treason. The penalty for which was death.

She took another ragged breath. "I'm ready."

Maybe Eckert was right, and it wasn't worth it. But it had to be.

The commander signaled his men to take her into custody. She looked around at the faces of her colleagues and smiled, hoping to comfort them as she did Eckert and in doing so comfort herself. They gazed back stricken and silent.

You're a tree, she told herself as all bravery fled.

The quote's power dissolved as the militiamen roughly bound her hands behind her with plastic cord. A tree, what did that mean? Having truth on your side didn't protect you from prison or a bullet in the back of the head. The truth didn't matter to these men the war had turned into fanatics, or rather they'd discovered their own version of truth, and they accepted no contradiction or heresy.

And the world, well, it moved for nobody. If you didn't get out of its way, it crushed you in its path. The river would go on flowing right past it, its truth ignored because nobody knew it was there. They didn't want to see it. The world was filled with men raised on shadows in Plato's cave, believing the shadows were real and denouncing and burning all who dared call them illusion.

The cords binding her hands were very real.

She felt her terror build, unsure of what form it would take when it burst from her. Crying, screaming, howling for mercy, it all crossed her mind, though none of it would do any good. She bit her lip, hoping to hold it at bay long enough to get out of the building. These men could see her scream and beg but not her colleagues. She couldn't let Eckert see, most of all. They were going to have to carry on the fight without her as long as they could while truth, dying its death of a thousand cuts, became just another of the war's many tragic casualties.

When the black hood dropped over her head and cut out the world's light, her terror became complete.

Even now, though, she didn't regret what she'd done. She had no regrets at all. Her dreams had been modest, and she'd fought for them and lived them as much on her terms as life allowed. She clung to this fact in her sudden isolation. She'd lived the job, and in its own way, the job had lived through her.

When the kangaroo court of former insurance adjusters and factory foremen and college students judged her, she'd tell them, *I could do nothing else.*

The image filled her with peace and resignation.

Aubrey stood tall as the men's hands gripped her arms. *I could do nothing else. I did no harm, and I did some good.* That was the tree. That was the light.

FIFTY-NINE

The C-130 Hercules air transport shuddered as it fought the winds over Lake Ontario. Gabrielle looked out the window and saw Canada covered in white, peaceful and unmoved.

Home.

She turned to Hannah Miller in the seat next to her. She hoped the girl, who'd lost everything, would find a home here too.

The kid was green. She'd already thrown up twice during the rough flight.

Gabrielle gripped her sweating hand.

The plane swung into its arc of descent toward Canadian Forces Base Trenton. The main hub of Canada's air operations, the base was home to 8 Wing. Planes here delivered supplies to the Arctic, staged search and rescue operations, and airlifted troops and aid to hot spots around the world. Now most of its aircraft hauled humanitarian aid to a war-torn America.

"We're almost there," she shouted over the propellers' pulsing hum.

Hannah nodded and went back to eyeing the two bored airmen sitting against the opposite bulkhead, ever vigilant in case they made a false move.

"Are your ears popping?"

Another nod.

"Do you want a piece of gum?"

Yes.

Gabrielle gave her a stick. The girl chewed mechanically. The gum had a function and nothing more. Then a smile flickered across her face as the sweet flavor flooded her mouth, offering a glimpse of the child Gabrielle had seen in the Facebook photos.

Kids are tougher than they look, she reminded herself. *They adapt.* Hannah could get through this just as Gabrielle had her own trauma. She'd forever be affected by it, but she'd survive and gain the chance to live a good life.

Maybe, like Gabrielle, she'd grow up stronger than she thought she was.

Gabrielle thought about Aubrey, the strongest woman she knew. She'd inspired Aubrey somehow, though now it was Aubrey doing the inspiring. Paul was trying to find out where the reporter had been taken. When she returned to America, Gabrielle would do everything in her power to save her friend. Another fight waiting for her in her personal war.

The Hercules slammed onto the tarmac and rolled to a stop.

Sore and tired, she grabbed her bag and took Hannah's hand. Outside, lights blazed across the airport. The night air was cold, far colder than Indy's severe winter.

The processing area was busy with airmen, military advisers, and aid workers. Gabrielle told the Canada Border Services agent that Hannah Miller was seeking asylum. Hannah's fate would be decided by a tedious bureaucratic process, but Gabrielle was skilled at moving it forward. After a battery of questions and forms, the agent took them to an empty room and told them to wait. At some point, a bus would drive them to the Interim Lodging Site at Saint-Bernard-de-Lacolle, Quebec, on the border of New York State. That would be Hannah's port of entry.

The girl curled up on the chairs and fell asleep in her tattered winter jacket and too-large army pants. She was still covered in soot and dust from the fighting she'd taken part in. Too amped up to rest, Gabrielle paced the room.

She didn't want to be here, doing this. She'd come to Indy to help all the children, not become a mother. She didn't know what to do or how to talk to the girl. Hannah Miller needed good parenting and plenty of counseling. She needed love and attention every day. She needed all the things Gabrielle couldn't give her right now.

Was she doing the right thing dragging this girl from everything she knew and dropping her in an alien land, or was she now the kidnapper?

Later, she told herself. She could wrestle with it all later. Right now, the most important thing was to remove Hannah from the war. Gabrielle would sponsor her as a refugee, while her parents had agreed to cosponsor her. After the government approved her for settlement, Hannah would stay with them while Gabrielle continued her work in America.

That was as far as her plan went. After that...It was hard to think further ahead. Hard to imagine the war in America over and coming back to pick up her life where she'd left it. She'd already gone too far to have a clear idea where home even was anymore.

Corporal Kassar entered the room, his arms full of sodas, candy bars, and potato chip bags he'd pulled from a vending machine. He was a welcome sight. Gabrielle hadn't been able to pick up any food during the pell-mell drive to the airport. Abigail had given her Hannah with a stern warning to get her out of the city fast.

"This wasn't what I had in mind for our date," Kassar said.

She smiled. "I'm glad you came."

"But can't stay long. I have an early flight. More UNICEF aid for Indianapolis."

Hannah stirred awake at the noise. She shot upright and stared at Kassar, caught between fight and run. For the last few weeks, men wearing uniforms had been her enemy. Then her eyes switched to take in the candy and potato chips.

"How is she doing?" he said.

"She hasn't said a word to me. She'll nod or shake her head if I ask her a question, but that's it."

"She's terrified." The corporal crouched to match his height to hers. "Hey, you. We're the same, kiddo. We both come from broken homes, so to speak. Like you, I grew up in war, in Syria, though I was older than you when it started."

Hannah glanced at the candy again.

"Go ahead," he said. "It's for you."

She tore the wrapper off a Snickers and took a massive bite. Her eyelids fluttered with sudden bliss. Her cheek bulged as she stared at him.

He said, "My family survived for a year before fleeing to Jordan to register with the UN as refugees. Two years after that, we found ourselves on a plane bound for Canada. I was terrified. I had no idea what Canadians were like. I looked out the window and completely freaked out. You know what I saw?"

Hannah paused in her chewing and shook her head.

"Everything was a brilliant, bright white. In Syria, it only rarely snows, and if it does, it's gone after a few hours. I couldn't believe how much snow there was here." He laughed. "I'm still getting used to the winters."

A brief smile crossed her face.

"I didn't know anybody, didn't know how things worked. Some people didn't take to Muslims coming here. It took my family months to find a place to live and settle in. But I was okay. I was safe. I had a new home, and this home wasn't going anywhere. This home was a whole country."

She lowered her eyes, still munching on her candy bar. Whatever his assurances, she obviously didn't feel safe yet, didn't feel at home.

"You don't know it yet, but you're going to be okay." Kassar looked up at Gabrielle. "What's your plan?"

"Still forming," she said. "I just wanted to get her as far from the fighting as I could. Get her somewhere she could get the help she needs. My parents will look after her. After that, I don't know. When the war ends, I'll reach out to any extended family I can find."

"And if you can't find them?"

Gabrielle let out a frustrated sigh. "I don't know. I'm running on impulse and winging it as I go. I shouldn't even be here."

The corporal tilted his head toward Hannah and pointed with his eyes. She sighed again and crouched in front of the girl.

"Hannah, look at me."

The girl's chewing came to a wary halt.

"I'm going to talk to you as one would a grown-up. And I promise I won't lie. Okay?"

She nodded. Yes, she wanted that very much.

"I don't expect you to trust me or agree how wrong it was what that militia did to you," Gabrielle said. "Me, I could never understand what you suffered, and I'm not going to pretend I do. I'm not here to replace your parents. Until you're approved to live with my parents, you'll be making most of this journey alone at a camp for refugees. What I can tell you is even when I'm not with you, I will always be working on your behalf to keep you safe and get you what you need. I swear to you I will never stop doing that. I don't expect you to trust me, but I hope you'll believe that."

Hannah absorbed all this and said her first word. "Okay."

Gabrielle choked back a sob. "Good."

The border agent appeared at the door. "Gabrielle Justine? The bus is ready."

She scooped the food into her bag. "Time to go."

"I still owe you a drink, Gabrielle," Kassar said.

She planted a kiss on his cheek. "It's a date."

Then she held out her hand. The girl took it. They walked back out into the cold, where a drab government bus idled in a cloud of exhaust.

The driver glanced at his clipboard. "Gabrielle Justine and Hannah Miller?"

"That's us."

The doors closed behind them with a pneumatic gasp. Aside from a family huddling in the back, the bus was empty. Gabrielle steered Hannah into a seat in the middle. She put her bag on the floor and stretched.

A long drive ahead. Six hours. They'd arrive at dawn.

She was tired but couldn't sleep, her mind swirling with everything she had to do. So she started to talk. She told Hannah about what happened to her as a child, the man who'd saved her, and the years she'd spent hiding from the world until UNICEF offered her a chance to make a real difference paying it forward. It took her until her arrival in Indianapolis to realize it wasn't just Ravi Patel who'd saved her, she'd saved herself by overcoming her fear.

Through it all, the child soldier listened and by the time Gabrielle was done summing up her life, the girl curled up with her head in her lap and fell asleep.

She smiled and stroked the girl's hair. Her heart stirred with protective instincts. It wasn't love, and it wasn't the desire to right a past wrong. It was something even more primal.

Its engine droning, the bus rolled on into the night.

Back in Indianapolis, the war waited for her. She'd have to make the entire trip in reverse. The UNICEF operation was gathering momentum. Aid shipments were starting to come in. Community outreach, media relations, building relationships within the IMPD and the NGOs, making sure aid got where it was needed, all of it had to be managed.

The monster who'd stolen her in her youth had affected her life and who she was, but people like Aubrey and Ravi Patel, the man who'd saved her all those years ago, influenced her far more. She'd meant her promise to Hannah that she'd watch out for her. She wanted to help all of the children, but she could make the biggest difference of all to just one, a little girl who'd suffered more than most.

Sitting in the dark while Hannah snuggled against her in sleep, Gabrielle prayed for peace. The day when all that was lost could be reclaimed. The day when all the child soldiers could lay down their arms and go home.

SIXTY

Hannah spotted the group of kids prowling the camp perimeter. She followed them. She'd been studying them for a week. Today, she'd make herself known.

She'd arrived at the Saint-Bernard-de-Lacolle refugee camp a month ago. In bewildering succession, an officer frisked her, took digital photos of her eyes, and pressed her fingers against a tablet that glowed with colors. At the next station, another officer asked lots of questions, most of which the UNICEF lady answered.

Hannah can't go back to America or risk cruel and unusual treatment, even death. My parents and I are sponsoring her. How long will it take for an asylum hearing?

Enclosed by miles of barbed wire, the camp sprawled in the middle of nowhere. Hannah didn't know how many people were here, but it was in the thousands, all living in a sea of green tents, latrines, water tankers, and prefab administrative buildings connected by footpaths and a few dirt roads. Too many people for Hannah's liking, and she knew none of them. While she shared a tent with loyalists, she didn't trust anybody.

Whatever safety this place offered couldn't last, because nothing ever did. While taking her walks around the perimeter, she pictured the camp collapsing in a series of disasters. The best way to stay safe was to keep moving or join a gang.

There were about twenty kids in the group, all wearing ratty jackets and patched military surplus pants tucked into dirty boots. They pointed at the Canadian soldiers patrolling outside the fence.

A small boy nudged the biggest, a tall, gangly kid with sandy hair sticking out from under his cap. He caught sight of Hannah and bristled.

"Get out of here, kid," he called.

Hannah shuffled her feet to keep warm but otherwise didn't budge. She didn't want to put on her war face, but she didn't want to show fear either. The truth was this was a big risk, and she was scared.

The boy marched over and glared down at her while the other kids fanned out on her flanks. "I told you to get lost."

"She thinks you're cute, Mike," one of the girls jeered.

"Give her a kiss!"

"You disrespect us, we'll kill you," Mike told Hannah. "Got it?"

"Which side were you on?" She'd studied them for the past week and knew they lived in the loyalist side of the camp, but she had to make sure.

"Congress!" the kids roared.

Hannah let go the breath she'd been holding. "What militia?"

He puffed out his chest. "Utica Street Irregulars, out of Buffalo."

"Steel City Champs," another kid said. "Pittsburgh."

The rest yelled out their unit names while a military helicopter flitted overhead on some martial errand.

"What's with the questions?" asked a girl about Hannah's age.

"Take it easy, Tanya," Mike growled. "She's one of us."

The girl said, "Yeah? Who were you with?"

"The Free Women in Indy."

Mike's eyes went wide. "Indy? You mean Indianapolis?"

"Yup."

"Were you there when they wiped out the Angels?"

"I was in that fight," she told him.

"God, I can't believe it!"

The kids crowded around clamoring with questions.

"All right, already," Mike said. "Give her a chance to talk."

"Not here." Tanya smiled. "Want to score some hot chocolate with us?"

"I'm game," said Hannah.

They marched across the snowy field and wove around the construction vehicles parked next to massive piles of earth, the work of engineers who'd begun to build a school. In the camp, they paused to allow a boxy, camouflage-painted vehicle to rumble past on the rutted road, then passed through the crowds until they reached the big mess tent.

They got hot chocolate and drank it around one of the long tables. The kids told their stories. Only Mike, Tanya, and a girl named Chloe had been fighters. The rest had worked as porters, cooks, and runners. Hannah didn't care. They were militia, people she could trust. It was good to find family so far from home.

When it was her turn to share, she took off her jacket and rolled up her sleeve to show off her tattoos. She'd added *KRISTY* and, for the bombing, an angry smiley face with a burning wick. She'd stolen a pen and touched up the ink after every visit to the shower tent. The kids leaned in to study them.

"This is my story," she said.

She'd set out to brag, but it poured out of her like a confession. It wasn't an epic adventure story but a sad tale of survival, violence, and loss. By the end of it, she was shaking, her face burning with embarrassment and a deeper shame.

The kids didn't care. They stared at her with admiration. They understood. To them, she was practically a figure of legend, one of

the few who'd survived the ferocious assault by the First Angels and
the bombing of the Liberty Tree line.

She hadn't told them about Alex. That, she didn't think anybody
would understand. If she told them, they'd see her for the monster
she was.

"I heard the Liberty Tree held the line," Hannah said. "The siege
is still going on. I really miss my sisters."

"The border's only a few miles away," Mike said. "I'll bet you're
itching to bust out of here and go back."

She wasn't sure about that but said, "Yeah."

"Maybe we could go together."

The other kids started yelling they wanted to go back too.

"Until then, we've got problems closer to home," Tanya said.

"What do you mean?" Hannah asked.

"There's a gang like ours in the camp. From the rebel side."

"Sometimes, we scrap with them until the soldiers break it up,"
Mike said. "We could use a fighter like you. You want in?"

Tanya said, "We take crap from nobody. You join us, we have
your back."

Hannah found it sad that the war went on even here, but it was a
fight she couldn't refuse.

She raised her fist. "Congress forever."

Plywood frames and heavy curtains sectioned the prefab building into rooms. Therapists worked with children one on one in
these spaces. Hannah waited her turn, then went into her allotted
room to meet with Captain Foster for her weekly session.

Foster was a big woman, strongly built. She wore glasses and an
olive-green Canadian Armed Forces sweater. Sitting in a folding
chair, she looked up from her notebook and said, "How are you
feeling today, Hannah?"

"I'm fine."

"I heard you've made some friends."

"Yup."

"Anything new you'd like to share?"

"Not really."

The therapist took off her glasses and rubbed her tired eyes. Hannah massaged a bruise on her arm, a gift from the fascist gang.

"Other kids like you act out in counseling," Foster said. "They brag about how they were big shots in the militia, how they killed people."

Hannah wondered which of her friends did that. Maybe all of them.

"You're different," Foster added. "You hardly talk at all."

"I have nothing to brag about."

"Sometimes, I wish you were more like them. At least they're an open book, even when they're feeding me a load of bull. I can't help you if you don't help me help you."

She couldn't talk her way out of the things she'd done. "You wouldn't understand."

"I might, if you let me try."

"Have you ever fought in a war?"

"No. I haven't."

"Then how could you?"

"By listening, Hannah. I've treated a lot of child soldiers from the USA. Before that, in Sudan and Mali."

Hannah said nothing.

"You know, you're romanticizing the militia you belonged to." The captain checked her notes. "The Free Women."

"Romanticize?"

"You look up to them in a way that isn't real. Militias use kids as workers, fighters, spies, even prostitutes."

"The Free Women fought for a cause that was right," Hannah said.

"A cause doesn't make people good or bad. It's people who make a cause good or bad. Does that make sense?"

She said nothing.

"In the end, people use their cause to justify doing almost anything. They dehumanize themselves and the enemy. They end up doing horrible things and thinking it's normal."

"I know normal better than you do," Hannah told her.

"Do you really think that?"

Nothing. The space heater purred in the corner.

The therapist sighed. "I'm not here to judge the Free Women's cause. What I can judge is their using children to kill people. Whatever you did is on them, not you. You have to understand it's not your fault."

Nothing.

Captain Foster closed her notebook. "Let's make a deal. If you open up to me a little, I'll rate you as ready for group. How does that sound?"

If she attended group therapy, she could be with her friends. At the last session, they'd told her, they drew pictures of the war and plotted their next scrap with the fascists.

"Okay," she said.

"Good. In one word, how would you describe how you feel most of the time?"

"Guilty."

"Anything else?"

Hannah thought about it. "Sad. Scared. Alone."

"These are all perfectly normal things to feel, though of course we want to figure out a way to feel them without so much hurt. It's important to know what you're feeling and put words to it. It's how you start to heal—"

"The last day I was fighting, the commander gave me a bag," Hannah cut in. "I was supposed to run across a street and throw the bag in a window. The bag had a bomb in it."

"Yes. Go on."

Hannah remembered the breathless dash across the street, feet pounding of their own accord. She paused to set the timer on the charge.

Seconds to go.

A silhouette appeared in the window. *That's it*, she thought. *I'm dead.* The man fired at her twice but missed, and she kept going, feeling strangely detached.

Then the figure disappeared.

"I threw the bag in the window and ran," she said. "The bomb blew up the house. I pulled my gun and shot a man coming out. Then I went inside to look for anybody still alive. I killed a man who'd forced my mom to do bad things."

Captain Foster froze with her pen poised over her notebook, where she'd been furiously taking notes. "Is that all true?"

"I wouldn't make up something like that even as a joke."

"I'm so sorry, Hannah."

"It's okay. I got him."

"Do you believe what you did was good or bad?"

She thought about it. "Both."

"Whatever you did, it wasn't your fault. None of it is your fault."

Hannah flashed to Alex lying crumpled on the floor, helpless and dying. He was the figure she'd seen standing in the window. He could have killed her to save his own life but hadn't.

If it wasn't her fault, whose was it?

Hannah's sessions didn't make the hurt go away like Captain Foster promised. They only made her angry. Angry at herself, angry at the rebels.

Sitting at their table in the mess hall during lunch, Mike promised action after they finished gossiping about the latest war news and rumors. "I talked to Thompson." The leader of the fascist gang. "We're on for thirteen hundred."

A boy they called Snowball said, "I don't know what that means."

Hannah didn't know military time either but kept her mouth shut.

"That's one o'clock for the newbs," Mike said.

"Right after lunch." Snowball grinned. They called him that because whenever there was work to do, he melted and disappeared like one. But he never shirked from a fight.

"We're meeting at the Field of Mars, behind east-side construction. No knives or broken bottles. No hitting the face or head."

Far from home, the child soldiers would go on fighting their war the only way they still could. For Hannah, it'd scratch a big itch.

"The usual star for fighting," she said. She'd become the gang's official inker, drawing stars on their arms after each fight, with extra stars for counting coup. "Extra star this time if you bring home one of their weapons."

The kids nodded, some smiling, the rest glum. Not everybody liked fighting.

"Same tactics as last time," Mike told them. "Me, Chloe, Tanya, Hannah, and Snowball in the center. We'll charge in hard. The rest of you protect our flanks."

Amped up now, Hannah fidgeted while they finished their lunch. At last, Mike stood with his tray. The gang followed his lead.

"Let's get there early," he said. "We can warm up."

Together, they trooped out to the construction site, where they'd hidden their weapons under a tarp used to cover lumber. They'd used this wood to make clubs. What a fight that had been. The fascists had fashioned their own weapons in response, creating a primitive arms race.

Hannah pulled out her club and shield, which she'd decorated with the word INDY in black marker. Then she filled her pockets with rocks, which they'd agreed to use only if the fascists did first.

"Now let's put on our war face," Mike said.

Chloe produced a tube of blue oil paint she'd lifted from the group therapy art sessions. The kids crowded around to get some on their fingers and smear stripes across their cheeks.

"Somebody's coming," Snowball said.

"Oh hell," Chloe said. "It's Captain Foster."

The kids dropped their weapons and formed a line to block the captain's view of them.

"What did I tell you kids about fighting?" the captain said.

The fascist gang swaggered onto the scene. They caught sight of the Canadian soldier and veered off toward their section of the camp.

Hannah glowered at Foster. There were scores to settle here, plenty of steam to blow off, and it was none of the captain's business how they did it. They bashed one another good out on the field, but nobody ever died.

"Hannah, come with me," Foster said.

She sighed loudly. "Okay."

The soldier led her toward the camp's administrative area. "Somebody is here to see you."

"Is it Gabrielle?"

"No, it's her father. The Immigration and Refugee Board approved your application. You're staying in Canada."

"What does that mean?"

"It means you're going to a new home today."

Hannah had been expecting Gabrielle to take her away at some point, but that possibility always seemed far in the future. Once again, everything was changing, out of her control.

She shot a look over her shoulder, but her friends were out of sight now. "I don't want to go."

"The Justines will take very good care of you. They agreed to let me continue our weekly sessions."

"This isn't fair. My family is here."

"I'm a soldier," Captain Foster said. "I understand that last part."

"Then why are you making me go?"

"Because this is the best chance you've got at having a normal life."

"There you go again," Hannah spat.

"I'll tell your friends where you went. I'll make sure you see them again. I promise."

The captain took her into an ugly prefab building crowded with Canadian soldiers and aid workers occupying tiny cubicle offices. In a waiting area, a tall man in a heavy winter coat turned as she entered.

His smile faltered as he took in her spiky hair, striped war paint, and purpled bruise on her cheek. "Hannah? I'm Ben Justine, Gabrielle's father."

"Nice to meet you, Mr. Justine," she said.

The smile returned in full force. "Call me Ben."

Ben and Captain Foster talked for a while, which Hannah tuned out, her hands playing with the rocks in her pockets.

"All right then," the man said. "Lena's waiting for us. Let's go home."

Your home, she thought. Fuming, she followed him out to his car and got in the back, where she hid behind the driver's seat.

He angled the rearview to catch her reflection. "You can sit up front if you want."

"No, thanks." She had no choice here but didn't have to pretend she liked it.

"We've got a room all set up for you at home. It was Gabrielle's before she went off to university, but you can make it your own. It's been a long time since we've had a girl your age in the house, so I hope you'll bear with us."

Hannah said nothing.

They drove through monotonous woodland until they reached a city called Saint-Jean-sur-Richelieu. Ben pointed out the sights, but she wasn't listening.

A different world appeared.

At a traffic light, she looked over at a restaurant. Past intact window-panes, families ate with their coats off and without any fear of snipers or bombs. No bullet holes blemished the walls, no smoke fouled the air.

Cars crossed the intersection in front of her.

Hannah closed her eyes against sudden vertigo. Just miles from America's endless war zone, people lived in an entirely different reality.

And she remembered: *This is what peace looks like.*

Hannah shot upright in bed and gripped the soft mattress beneath her. The nightmare dissipated, though its terror lingered. Drenched in sweat, she looked around the unfamiliar room.

"Hannah!" Lena called again from downstairs. "Breakfast!"

"Okay," she yelled, at last remembering where she was.

The room had a bed, dresser, vanity, and writing desk. Movie posters and paintings decorated the walls. Sunlight flooded the room through the window.

Hannah got out of bed still wearing her ratty T-shirt and army surplus pants. After her long, hot bath last night, she'd put them back on before bed. She felt in her pocket for her pens. They were still there.

Lena had laid out a dress for her to put on. Hannah ignored it just as she'd ignored the pajamas last night. Instead, she pulled on the oversized Canadian Armed Forces sweater that Captain Foster had given her. Then she went downstairs slowly, taking in every detail and scanning for threats.

Dishes clattered in the dining room. The antique grandfather clock ticked. Ben puttered in his and Lena's bedroom upstairs.

"Hi," she said.

Lena's smile faltered at the sight of Hannah in her militia uniform. "I put out something clean for you to wear."

The woman looked like an older version of Gabrielle, beautiful but with the same fragile quality, as if she were a rare glass artifact.

Hannah didn't want to hurt her feelings. "I'm sorry."

"It's okay. I didn't know what to get you. I have no idea what girls your age are wearing these days."

"That makes two of us."

Lena winced as she realized she'd said the wrong thing. "Oh."

"We could find out together, maybe."

The woman brightened. "Why don't we go shopping today?"

"Okay." Hannah wasn't sure how she felt about putting aside her militia uniform, but she didn't want to let Lena down. The woman was so nervously attentive, she didn't know whether she found it irritating or adorable.

Dressed in a suit for work, Ben took his seat at the table. "Good morning."

Hannah sat and fidgeted while he cracked open the newspaper and Lena went to get breakfast. The woman returned with a plate of bacon, eggs, and buttered toast. She set it down along with a glass of orange juice.

Hannah gaped at the meal, which was as wonderful and expansive as dinner had been last night. "Is this all for me?"

Ben put his paper aside and picked up his coffee cup. "Go ahead and eat."

She smiled at her food, unsure where to even begin. Then she began to wolf it down, cheeks bulging.

Lena took her own seat and frowned at the show. "Hannah, eat slowly or you're going to choke."

Hannah closed her eyes and chewed, savoring the rich flavors.

Ben said, "When was the last time you had a meal like this, Hannah?"

She shot him a wary look and shrugged. He echoed her shrug and tucked into his eggs. After breakfast, Hannah tried to help clear

the table, but Lena wouldn't have it. Ben excused himself to join
Lena in the kitchen. Hannah heard them talking.

I don't know how to speak to her, Lena was saying.

We need to let her be herself until she feels safe.

I just want to help her.

I know.

Should I let her help with the dishes? She's our guest. I didn't know.

Maybe it's a good idea, Ben said.

I don't want to ask her to work. I can't imagine what she went through.

Hannah sighed with shame. This wasn't her home. She didn't fit
in here. She didn't deserve any of this. She just wanted to go back to
her friends, people who understood her.

Lena returned to the dining room. "Would you like to help me
do the dishes?"

"Okay." Hannah wanted something to do.

"I'll be off to work then." Ben kissed Lena. "Have a good day,
you two."

Hannah grunted, already starting the dishes. She enjoyed the
work. Work was honest. It wasn't confusing. She didn't feel caught
between worlds. She didn't want to smash something.

After they'd finished, they went out to the car.

She buckled up. "You don't work?"

Lena tensed a little behind the wheel. "I work at home. I'm
a technical writer. I'm taking a hiatus so I can spend some time
with you."

Hannah sank lower in her seat. "You didn't have to do that."

"Nonsense. I wanted to do it. Business is slow anyway, with the
economy."

"What does Mr. Justine do?"

"Ben works in insurance. He doesn't have the flexibility I have,
and frankly, his profession makes more money than mine, especially
right now."

Hannah found her accent adorable. *Frankly*, she thought, saying it in her mind the way Lena had. *Flexibility.*

They pulled into the mall lot and found a spot to park. Inside, some of the stores were either closed or having going-out-of-business sales. Canada had its own troubles because of the war.

Hannah got to pick out what she wanted at the clothing stores, favoring plain, dark outfits that were warm and looked like they'd last. Her only nod to fashion was a big scarf that was blue, the Congressional color.

At the food court, Lena bought her a cheeseburger, fries, and a Coke for lunch. They sat in the middle of the dining area, which made Hannah nervous, but she went along with it. She didn't want this woman to see her as a freak.

"What's going to happen to me?" she asked.

"Ben and I were thinking you should go to school. What do you think?"

A new school, kids who spoke French as their primary language, catching up on all the lost time and work. "I think I'd rather be back in Indy getting shot at."

Lena smiled. "You're strong. I can see that. You'll find your way."

"It's hard to think about. I guess I'll just go and see what happens. I still can't believe I'm here. It's like a dream."

"There's just one thing I'd advise you about school."

Hannah reached for more fries. "What's that?"

"You might not want to tell the other kids about being in a militia."

"Why?"

"You'll impress them, but they may end up shying away from you because they won't understand. It's hard enough to make friends at a new school."

Hannah considered it. "Okay."

"Good. It's up to you, of course."

"What about after? When Gabrielle comes back, will I live with her?"

"We'll talk about that later."

"It's okay if you want to send me back to the camp."

"Oh, Hannah, that's not going to happen. Whatever comes next, you have a home here. I hope you'll see it as a fresh—"

An explosion erupted at the end of the foot court, impossibly loud, its colossal force ripping through the open space—

"Hannah! Hannah, are you okay?"

She lay curled up in a ball under the table, barely breathing, her body clenched, her heart racing in panic. *Get down! Mortar!*

Lena was on her hands and knees, staring at her with worry. "Somebody dropped a glass jar or bottle. It was just a noise. You're perfectly safe."

Hannah barely heard her, shaking uncontrollably, still in the grip of terror as the explosion tore at her nerves and wouldn't stop.

The school buzzed with news of the spectacular Congressional victory in California at the Battle of the Palm Desert. Aside from die-hard guerillas camping out in the national forests, the rebels had been purged from the state. Congressional forces now held the coast all the way from San Diego to Seattle.

In response, the rebels had stepped up attacks all over the country in an effort to give President Marsh a win as the peace talks ground on in Ottawa.

In the cafeteria, Hannah sat at an empty table with her back against the wall. She scanned the room while she ate her bag lunch. The kids' chatter washed over her.

The war news made her happy but not as much as it would have two months ago. At night, she revisited the horrors she'd suffered, but in daylight, the war grew distant as she acclimated to her new calm life with the Justines. She hadn't scrubbed off her tattoos, but she'd stopped reinking them. Every day, they faded just a little more.

Spring had arrived. The world was starting to turn green again. Soon, summer would come, and she'd go back to wearing short-sleeved shirts without any trace of her story showing.

Her eyes settled on three girls who were looking around for a place to sit. She tensed as they made a beeline for her table.

She sank lower into herself.

The only thing Hannah wanted was to be left alone. From her first day at the school, her classmates hated her. They said Americans had ruined everything, wrecked the economy, and were taking Canadian jobs.

The more she tried to hide and be left alone, the more they bugged her.

When a boy called her *Yankee* like it was an insult, she'd punched him and got sent to the principal's office. She'd promised Lena and Ben not to do it again.

The girls arrived at her table. One said in accented English, "Can we sit here with you?"

Hannah shrugged to say it didn't matter.

"I'm Olivia," the girl said as she sat down with her lunch tray.

"Rosalie."

"Romy."

Olivia said, "You're Hannah Miller, right?"

Hannah nodded.

"We're grade six."

"I would be but got held back," Hannah said. "I missed a whole year."

"Poor you," Romy said. "The grade fives are all a bunch of jerks."

Hannah smiled and bit into her sandwich. She was right about that. "After summer school, I hope to catch up."

"We were curious about you. About the war."

She could tell the girls had been talking about her for a while, working up the courage to ask her about it.

Rosalie lowered her voice. "Did you know anybody who got killed?"

"My parents."

"What happened to you?"

She shared the story she'd made up in case anybody asked. Her parents killed in a mortar attack, shuttling around refugee camps, sponsorship by the Justine family to live in Canada. The girls were impressed anyway.

"That's so sad," Olivia said.

"Maybe what happened in California will end the war," Rosalie said. "You could go home and pick up your old life. You must miss all your friends."

"Canada is my home now," Hannah said.

The girls seemed pleased by this. "It's a really great country."

"The winters kind of suck, though."

They laughed.

"I have an idea," Olivia said. "We'll be your friends. If you want."

"We can help you with your French," Rosalie chimed in.

"Yeah, your French is terrible," Romy said.

They were plain and probably not popular themselves, but Hannah didn't mind at all. She pictured sitting here with them every day at lunch hearing about their crushes and favorite movies and clothes they wanted to buy. The kids they didn't like based on prejudices they'd made up and believed important. All of it meaningless to her. They were like a movie themselves, bittersweet theater filled with childhood drama that both mimicked and avoided the real world.

She smiled and said, "I'd like that."

Yes, she'd like that very much. After everything, she was ready to smile now and then, have a conversation that wasn't about survival and death.

"Did you see any fighting during the war?" Olivia asked her.

"Between the militias? On TV, it never looks like anything is happening."

Hannah offered to share her dessert, a slice from a chocolate cake Lena had baked for her. "Let's talk about something nice. So who do you like?"

Olivia turned scarlet while the other girls howled.

They talked about boys for the rest of lunch, inventorying them as cute or nice or just annoying, and Hannah found herself smiling more and more.

She'd wanted to become lost again, and this was a good way to do it.

Hannah was ready when Captain Foster pulled into the driveway. Looking out the window, she zipped up her spring jacket with trembling fingers. "She's here."

Lena hugged her. "You'll do great, I'm sure. I'm proud of you."

Hannah went outside and got in the car. "Good morning."

The captain backed out of the driveway. "How was your week?"

Hannah looked out the window at the world that once seemed so alien but now felt more and more like home. "I'm really nervous about doing this."

"I know," the woman said, as always giving a simple acknowledgment that whatever she was feeling was normal but shouldn't control her.

"I made some friends at school," Hannah said.

Foster pulled onto the road that would take them to Saint-Bernard-de-Lacolle. "That's a big step for you. How is it going?"

"I don't know what to talk to them about, so I just listen. They like that."

"You're doing everything right. You're reclaiming your childhood."

Every day, she woke up, brushed her teeth, ate breakfast, went to school, came home, watched TV or read, ate her dinner, did her homework, went to bed. Her new life was still strange, but she now remembered this, not the war, was normal.

The woman added, "You're a role model for what these kids can become. They need to hear it. You need to show them what's possible."

The number of kids at the refugee camp had skyrocketed in the past month. UNICEF was pushing a model treaty forbidding the use of child soldiers, and it was spreading throughout the states. UNICEF next partnered with the Canadian military to expand the rehabilitation programs at the camps.

"Ben and Lena said they want to adopt me," Hannah said.

The captain grinned. "That's very good news."

"I don't know."

"You still don't think you deserve it?"

"Maybe." Being a kid again, living the way the people thought of as normal, it was all meant for Maria, not her.

"Whatever you did, it wasn't your fault," Foster said.

The camp came into view. A lot had changed in the months since she'd lived here and run with the Congress gang. The sun had melted all the snow and turned the fields green and the roads into mud. There were more tents, more buildings.

Hannah got out of the car and looked around. Nearby, a family lived in a trailer that had a vegetable garden growing on a small plot next to it. Smoke wisped in the air from a small fire. A man was hanging diapers on a clothesline.

She'd thought her return would be a homecoming, but the camp now seemed alien and hostile. What a horrible place.

"This way," Foster said.

"Wait." She took off her jacket, which was Congress blue, and left it in the car. The marks on her arms were gone. Only a small scar on her left temple remained to tell her story.

The tables had been cleared from the southeast mess tent. A crowd of kids sat on the ground, buzzing with conversation. Empty space separated the Congress and President gangs. Captain Foster tapped the microphone and launched into her introduction, talking about how kids were the future, how they'd be the ones to rebuild America after the war.

Hannah's stomach flipped as she picked out Mike, Tanya, Chloe, and the rest of her gang, who grinned and pointed at her.

She smiled back. This part felt like a homecoming.

Then it was her turn to talk. Blushing furiously, she walked up to the microphone. "Hi. My name is Hannah Miller. I was a soldier with the Free Women militia in Indianapolis. I was a fighter."

One of the kids called out, "Congress forever!" The rest roared. Some of the President gang shouted back, "Executive power!"

Hannah raised her hands for quiet. "I'm here to talk to everybody, not just my old comrades." She smiled. "I see Gary Thompson out there."

"You come back for more?" the kid yelled to laughter.

Hannah said, "Not today."

The kids quieted as she told them about her brother disappearing at the truck stop, her parents murdered, training with the Free Women, fighting the First Angels, bombing the Liberty Tree line, taking revenge on the giant.

"My old comrades know that story," she said. "But I never told them or anybody else the real reason why I left the militia. In that battle—"

Her voice hitched. She steeled herself by taking a deep breath.

"In that battle, I killed my own brother with my bomb. I killed Alex."

Saying it aloud unleashed a torrent of pent-up grief. She burst into tears. Her cheeks turned hot with embarrassment and a deeper shame that was always there.

"I didn't care what happened to me after that," she said in a stronger voice. "But I was very lucky. An enemy soldier brought me to UNICEF, and UNICEF got me out of Indy. The Justines gave me a home. I have a new family who love me regardless of what I did. I go to school and live a life a lot like the one I had before the war."

Hannah didn't know how to continue. The kids all gazed at her with a fierce longing. She *was* lucky. Only one in a hundred refugees was granted permission to live in Canada, and she'd won the lottery. She had a new family that wanted her and gave her everything she needed. These child soldiers, these orphans and lost children, all they had was one another and Captain Foster.

"Whatever you did in the war, whatever you saw, it wasn't your fault," she said. "And you should know there are people who love you. I love you."

Hannah's war was over.

After her speech ended, Captain Foster placed her hand on her shoulder and squeezed. "You did good."

"I don't see how I changed anything."

"You showed them what's possible, that they can live a normal life again," the captain said. "You told them they're loved even if they don't think they deserve it. And they heard it from one of their own. Believe me, you did good."

"Okay." Hannah hoped it was true.

"You never told me about your brother. I'm sorry."

"I'm never going to fight again."

"You ready to go home?"

"No." Hannah wiped her eyes and walked into the crowd to find her old gang.

Tanya and Chloe cried and hugged her. They all sat on the floor to talk. A lot of other kids stayed too, kids she didn't know, even Thompson and most of his gang.

They talked about the war, comparing commanders and weapons and combat experiences, but the kids were far more interested in Hannah's life outside the camp. They asked her about her family, house, school, friends, what she ate, what movies she watched.

They didn't resent her. To the child soldiers, she lived an exotic life full of wonder, and by hearing her talk about it, they were able to taste it themselves.

At last, it was time to go. Hannah promised she'd come back.

While it wasn't home anymore, she'd always have family here.

A typical school night, dinner followed by family time in the living room with the radio playing softly. Hannah sat cross-legged on the rug working on her decimals. The old math, but she didn't mind.

She looked up at Lena, nestled on the couch with her book, and Ben, newspaper on his easy chair, and felt something that might have been love. One day, they'd die like everybody else she'd ever loved, but not for a long time.

Lena caught her staring and smiled. "How are you feeling?"

"Good."

"*En français, s'il vous plaît?*"

"*Je vais bien.*"

"Very good," Lena went on in French. "You work so hard."

"I want to catch up."

"You need to have fun too. Any big plans this weekend?"

"Well. Olivia asked me to a sleepover at her house Saturday night."

"That is a wonderful plan."

Hannah wanted to go but wasn't sure she was ready to leave the safety of her home and its comforting routines. "I'm not sure I'm ready."

"We'll be just a phone call away."

She thought about it. "Okay. I'll tell her yes."

Ben lowered his newspaper. "Listen."

Lena cocked her ear toward the radio. "What is it?"

He grabbed his TV remote and turned it on. "Armistice!"

Cheering crowds filled the screen, which carried the caption TIMES SQUARE. New York City, the other capital of the United States.

"Oh, God," Lena said, choking back a sob. "It's real."

"What does that mean?" Hannah said. "That word?"

He smiled and said in English, "It means there's a truce."

She swallowed hard. "The war's over?"

"The shooting is over. It's the first step to peace."

The screen cut to a reporter in front of Americans roaring and flashing victory signs. On the right side of the screen, a crying militia fighter hugged her comrade.

Hannah stared at this woman until her own eyes stung with tears. She remembered Grace Kim telling her on the rooftop, *Some of us don't get to go back*, and prayed that wasn't true. Everybody deserved to go back, even the rebels.

The reporter said the states had agreed to a convention in Columbus, where delegates would rewrite the Constitution. After that, new elections. Both sides were calling for a general amnesty for the militias.

Ben stood. "Come with me to the dining room. Both of you. Please."

Hannah followed him to the big wood table, where he opened a bottle of red wine and poured out three glasses.

He smiled. "I've been saving this bottle for just this occasion."

The adults raised their glasses and waited for Hannah to do the same.

"To peace," he said.

To my family, my friends, my comrades: Namaste, Hannah thought and sipped the wine. She'd expected it to be very bitter, but it wasn't.

They returned to the living room to watch the coverage of the celebrations. The President of the Senate would address the nation in an hour. After that, President Marsh would take his turn.

"This feels real," Ben said.

"Gabby must be so happy." Lena beamed. "She'll be home soon."

Hannah nodded, sleepy from the wine and excitement.

"Bedtime," Ben told her. "Tomorrow is another day."

She went upstairs to brush her teeth and put on her jammies. Usually, she sat on the toilet reading until Lena came in to tell her to quit stalling, but this time, she got ready quickly.

She slid between the covers, luxuriating in their softness. Lena and Ben tucked her in and kissed her good-night. For Hannah, this was always a moment of safe smells and the wonderful feeling of being a child again.

The lights went out, and that's when the war came back, as it always did.

Dad reached for her in the smoking car. Mom toppled to the asphalt. Her friends died in battle one by one. She killed enemies, shot the giant. And she hugged Alex again and again and again.

These images would plague her dreams until the sun returned to burn away the night's terrors. In the dark, she could never forget, but in the light of day, she could forgive. One day, she might even forgive herself.

On that day, she'd heal, find herself rather than get lost, and learn the magic of making something out of nothing. Her memories of her family, who'd died helping her survive, would fill her only with love and not emptiness and anger and guilt. That was her cause now.

Until then, Hannah would pray with all her heart for those she left behind. She'd pray that all the child soldiers would forever wake to sunlight instead of gunfire.

Return to childhood and, being children, learn to play again.

ACKNOWLEDGMENTS

It was impossible to write a novel about love and hate without reflecting on the people I care about most. I'd like to thank my children and my partner, Chris Marrs, whose love keeps me going.

I'd also like to express my gratitude to those who shaped my journey as a writer: Eileen DiLouie, Chris DiLouie, John Dixon, Peter Clines, David Moody, Timothy W. Long, Ron Bender, Ella Beaumont, Randy Heller, Chris Arnone, Jim Curtis, Anthony McCurdy, all my IFWA and HWA friends, and many others.

To you all, I'd like to say: "May you live in interesting times." But only the good kind of interesting.

Another hearty thanks goes to Jean-François Bissonnette, who was kind enough to help a friend of a friend on Facebook with some French-Canadian translations.

Finally, I'd like to thank David Fugate, my amazing agent, and Bradley Englert, the best editor I could hope for, who always knows how to get the best out of me.

extras

meet the author

Photo Credit: Jodi O

CRAIG DILOUIE is an acclaimed American-Canadian author of literary dark fantasy and other fiction. Formerly a magazine editor and advertising executive, he also works as a journalist and educator covering the North American lighting industry. Craig is a member of the Imaginative Fiction Writers Association, the International Thriller Writers, and the Horror Writers Association. He currently lives in Calgary, Canada, with his two wonderful children.

Find out more about Craig DiLouie and other Orbit authors by registering for the free monthly newsletter at www.orbitbooks.net.

if you enjoyed
OUR WAR

look out for

ONE OF US

by

Craig DiLouie

"This is not a kind book, or a gentle book, or a book that pulls its punches. But it's a powerful book, and it will change you."
—Seanan McGuire

Known as "the plague generation," a group of teenagers begins to discover their hidden powers in this shocking postapocalyptic coming-of-age story set in 1984.

They've called him a monster from the day he was born.

Abandoned by his family, Enoch Bryant now lives in a rundown orphanage with other teenagers just like him. He loves his friends, even if the teachers are terrified of them. They're members of the rising plague generation. Each bearing their own extreme genetic mutation.

The people in the nearby town hate Enoch, but he doesn't know why. He's never harmed anyone. Works hard and doesn't make trouble. He believes one day he'll be a respected man.

But hatred dies hard. The tension between Enoch's world and those of the "normal" townspeople is ready to burst. And when a body is found, it may be the spark that ignites a horrifying revolution.

One

On the principal's desk, a copy of *Time*. A fourteen-year-old girl smiled on the cover. Pigtails tied in blue ribbon. Freckles and big white teeth. Rubbery, barbed appendages extending from her eye sockets.

Under that, a single word: WHY?

Why did this happen?

Or, maybe, why did the world allow a child like this to live?

What Dog wanted to know was why she smiled.

Maybe it was just reflex, seeing somebody pointing a camera at her. Maybe she liked the attention, even if it wasn't the nice kind.

Maybe, if only for a few seconds, she felt special.

The Georgia sun glared through filmy barred windows. A steel fan whirred in the corner, barely moving the warm, thick air. Out the window, Dog spied the old rusted pickup sunk in a riot of wildflowers. Somebody loved it once then parked it here and left it to die. If Dog owned it, he would have kept driving and never stopped.

The door opened. The government man came in wearing a black suit, white shirt, and blue-and-yellow tie. His shiny shoes clicked across the grimy floor. He sat in Principal Willard's creaking chair and lit a cigarette. Dropped a file folder on the desk and studied Dog through a blue haze.

"They call you Dog," he said.

"Yes, sir, they do. The other kids, I mean."

Dog growled when he talked but took care to form each word right. The teachers made sure he spoke good and proper. Brain once told him these signs of humanity were the only thing keeping the children alive.

"Your Christian name is Enoch. Enoch Davis Bryant."

"Yes, sir."

Enoch was the name the teachers at the Home used. Brain said it was his slave name. Dog liked hearing it, though. He felt lucky to have one. His mama had loved him enough to at least do that for him. Many parents had named their kids XYZ before abandoning them to the Homes.

"I'm Agent Shackleton," the government man said through another cloud of smoke. "Bureau of Teratological Affairs. You know the drill, don't you, by now?"

Every year, the government sent somebody to ask the kids questions. Trying to find out if they were still human. Did they want to hurt people, ever have carnal thoughts about normal girls and boys, that sort of thing.

"I know the drill," Dog said.

"Not this year," the man told him. "This year is different. I'm here to find out if you're special."

"I don't quite follow, sir."

Agent Shackleton planted his elbows on the desk. "You're a ward of the state. More than a million of you. Living high on the hog for the past fourteen years in the Homes. Some of you are beginning to show certain capabilities."

"Like what kind?"

"I saw a kid once who had gills and could breathe underwater. Another who could hear somebody talking a mile away."

"No kidding," Dog said.

"That's right."

"You mean like a superhero."

"Yeah. Like Spider-Man, if Spider-Man half looked like a real spider."

"I never heard of such a thing," Dog said.

"If you, Enoch, have capabilities, you could prove you're worth the food you eat. This is your opportunity to pay it back. Do you follow me?"

"Sure, I guess."

Satisfied, Shackleton sat back in the chair and planted his feet on the desk. He set the file folder on his thighs, licked his finger, and flipped it open.

"Pretty good grades," the man said. "You got your math and spelling. You stay out of trouble. All right. Tell me what you can do. Better yet, show me something."

"What I can do, sir?"

"You do for me, I can do plenty for you. Take you to a special place."

Dog glanced at the red door at the side of the room before returning his gaze to Shackleton. Even looking at it was bad luck. The red door led downstairs to a basement room called Discipline, where the problem kids went.

He'd never been inside it, but he knew the stories. All the kids knew them. Principal Willard wanted them to know. It was part of their education.

He said, "What kind of place would that be?"

"A place with lots of food and TV. A place nobody can ever bother you."

Brain always said to play along with the normals so you didn't get caught up in their system. They wrote the rules in such a way to trick you into Discipline. More than that, though, Dog wanted to prove himself. He wanted to be special.

"Well, I'm a real fast runner. Ask anybody."

"That's your special talent. You can run fast."

"Real fast. Does that count?"

The agent smiled. "Running fast isn't special. It isn't special at all."

"Ask anybody how fast I run. Ask the—"

"You're not special. You'll never be special, Dog."

"I don't know what you want from me, sir."

Shackleton's smile disappeared along with Dog's file. "I want you to get the hell out of my sight. Send the next monster in on your way out."

TWO

Pollution. Infections. Drugs. Radiation. All these things, Mr. Benson said from the chalkboard, can produce mutations in embryos.

A bacterium caused the plague generation. The other kids, the plague kids, who lived in the Homes.

Amy Green shifted in her desk chair. The top of her head was itching again. Mama said she'd worry it bald if she kept scratching at it. She settled on twirling her long, dark hair around her finger and tugging. Savored the needles of pain along her scalp.

"The plague is a sexually transmitted disease," Mr. Benson told the class.

She already knew part of the story from American History and from what Mama told her. The plague started in 1968, two years before she was born, back when love was still free. Then the disease named teratogenesis raced around the world, and the plague children came.

One out of ten thousand babies born in 1968 were monsters, and most died. One in six in 1969, and half of these died. One in three in 1970, the year scientists came up with a test to see if you had it. Most of them lived. After a neonatal nurse got arrested for killing thirty babies in Texas, the survival rate jumped.

More than a million monster babies screaming to be fed. By then, Congress had already funded the Home system.

Fourteen years later, and still no cure. If you caught the germ, the only surefire way to stop spreading it was abstinence, which they taught right here in health class. If you got pregnant with it, abortion was mandatory.

extras

Amy flipped her textbook open and bent to sniff its cheesy new-book smell. Books, sharpened pencils, lined paper; she associated their bitter scents with school. The page showed a drawing of a woman's reproductive system. The baby comes out there. Sitting next to her, her boyfriend Jake glanced at the page and smiled, his face reddening. Like her, fascinated and embarrassed by it all.

In junior high, sex ed was mandatory, no ifs or buts. Amy and her friends were stumbling through puberty. Tampons, budding breasts, aching midnight thoughts, long conversations about what boys liked and what they wanted.

She already had a good idea what they wanted. Girls always complimented her about how pretty she was. Boys stared at her when she walked down the hall. Everybody so nice to her all the time. She didn't trust any of it.

When she stood naked in the mirror, she only saw flaws. Amy spotted a zit last week and stared at it for an hour, hating her ugliness. It took her over an hour every morning to get ready for school. She didn't leave the house until she looked perfect.

She flipped the page again. A monster grinned up at her. She slammed the book shut.

Mr. Benson asked if anybody in the class had actually seen a plague child. Not on TV or in a magazine, but up close and personal.

A few kids raised their hands. Amy kept hers planted on her desk.

"I have two big goals for you kids this year," the teacher said. "The main thing is teach you how to avoid spreading the disease. We'll be talking a lot about safe sex and all the regulations about whether and how you do it. How to get tested and how to access a safe abortion. I also aim to help you become accustomed to the plague children already born and who are now the same age as you."

For Amy's entire life, the plague children had lived in group homes out in the country, away from people. One was located just eight miles from Huntsville, though it might as well have been on the moon. The monsters never came to town. Out of sight meant out of mind, though one could never entirely forget them.

"Let's start with the plague kids," Mr. Benson said. "What do all y'all think about them? Tell the truth."

Rob Rowland raised his hand. "They ain't human. They're just animals."

"Is that right? Would you shoot one and eat it? Mount its head on your wall?"

The kids laughed as they pictured Rob so hungry he would eat a monster. Rob was obese, smart, and sweated a lot, one of the unpopular kids.

Amy shuddered with sudden loathing. "I hate them something awful."

The laughter died. Which was good, because the plague wasn't funny.

The teacher crossed his arms. "Go ahead, Amy. No need to holler, though. Why do you hate them?"

"They're monsters. I hate them because they're monsters."

Mr. Benson turned and hacked at the blackboard with a piece of chalk: MONSTRUM, a VIOLATION OF NATURE. From MONEO, which means TO WARN. In this case, a warning God is angry. Punishment for taboo.

"Teratogenesis is nature out of whack," he said. "It rewrote the body. Changed the rules. Monsters, maybe. But does a monster have to be evil? Is a human being what you look like, or what you do? What makes a man a man?"

Bonnie Fields raised her hand. "I saw one once. I couldn't even tell if it was a boy or girl. I didn't stick around to get to know it."

"But did you see it as evil?"

"I don't know about that, but looking the way some of them do, I can't imagine why the doctors let them all live. It would have been a mercy to let them die."

"Mercy on us," somebody behind Amy muttered.

The kids laughed again.

Sally Albod's hand shot up. "I'm surprised at all y'all being so scared. I see the kids all the time at my daddy's farm. They're weird, but there ain't nothing to them. They work hard and don't make trouble. They're fine."

"That's good, Sally," the teacher said. "I'd like to show all y'all something."

He opened a cabinet and pulled out a big glass jar. He set it on his desk. Inside, a baby floated in yellowish fluid. A tiny penis jutted between its legs. Its little arms grasped at nothing. It had a single slitted eye over a cleft where its nose should be.

The class sucked in its breath as one. Half the kids recoiled as the rest leaned forward for a better look. Fascination and revulsion. Amy alone didn't move. She sat frozen, shot through with the horror of it.

She hated the little thing. Even dead, she hated it.

"This is Tony," Mr. Benson said. "And guess what, he isn't one of the plague kids. Just some poor boy born with a birth defect. About three percent of newborns are born this way every year. It causes one out of five infant deaths."

Tony, some of the kids chuckled. They thought it weird it had a name.

"We used to believe embryos developed in isolation in the uterus," the teacher said. "Then back in the Sixties, a company

401

sold thalidomide to pregnant women in Germany to help them with morning sickness. Ten thousand kids born with deformed limbs. Half died. What did scientists learn from that? Anybody?"

"A medicine a lady takes can hurt her baby even if it don't hurt her," Jake said.

"Bingo," Mr. Benson said. "Medicine, toxins, viruses, we call these things environmental factors. Most times, though, doctors have no idea why a baby like Tony is born. It just happens, like a dice roll. So is Tony a monster? What about a kid who's retarded, or born with legs that don't work? Is a kid in a wheelchair a monster too? A baby born deaf or blind?"

He got no takers. The class sat quiet and thoughtful. Satisfied, Mr. Benson carried the jar back to the cabinet. More gasps as baby Tony bobbed in the fluid, like he was trying to get out.

The teacher frowned as he returned the jar to its shelf. "I'm surprised just this upsets you. If this gets you so worked up, how will you live with the plague children? When they're adults, they'll have the same rights as you. They'll live among you."

Amy stiffened at her desk, neck clenched with tension at the idea. A question formed in her mind. "What if we don't want to live with them?"

Mr. Benson pointed at the jar. "This baby is you. And something not you. If Tony had survived, he would be different, yes. But he would be you."

"I think we have a responsibility to them," Jake said.

"Who's we?" Amy said.

His contradicting her had stung a little, but she knew how Jake had his own mind and liked to argue. He wore leather jackets, black T-shirts advertising obscure bands, ripped jeans. Troy and Michelle, his best friends, were Black.

He was popular because being unpopular didn't scare him. Amy liked him for that, the way he flouted junior high's iron rules. The way he refused to suck up to her like the other boys all did.

"You know who I mean," he said. "The human race. We made them, and that gives us responsibility. It's that simple."

"I didn't make anything. The older generation did. Why are they my problem?"

"Because they have it bad. We all know they do. Imagine being one of them."

"I don't want things to be bad for them," Amy said. "I really don't. I just don't want them around me. Why does that make me a bad person?"

"I never said it makes you a bad person," Jake said.

Archie Gaines raised his hand. "Amy has a good point, Mr. Benson. They're a mess to stomach, looking at them. I mean, I can live with it, I guess. But all this love and understanding is a lot to ask."

"Fair enough," Mr. Benson said.

Archie turned to look back at Amy. She nodded her thanks. His face lit up with a leering smile. He believed he'd rescued her and now she owed him.

She gave him a practiced frown to shut down his hopes. He turned away as if slapped.

"I'm just curious about them," Jake said. "More curious than scared. It's like you said, Mr. Benson. However they look, they're still our brothers. I wouldn't refuse help to a blind man, I guess I wouldn't to a plague kid neither."

The teacher nodded. "Okay. Good. That's enough discussion for today. We're getting somewhere, don't you think? Again, my goal for you kids this year is two things. One is to get used to the plague children. Distinguishing between a book and its cover. The other is to learn how to avoid making more of them."

Jake turned to Amy and winked. Her cheeks burned, all her annoyance with him forgotten.

She hoped there was a lot more sex ed and a lot less monster talk in her future. While Mr. Benson droned on, she glanced through the first few pages of her book. A chapter headline caught her eye: KISSING.

She already knew the law regarding sex. Germ or no germ, the legal age of consent was still fourteen in the State of Georgia. But another law said if you wanted to have sex, you had to get tested for the germ first. If you were under eighteen, your parents had to give written consent for the testing.

Kissing, though, that you could do without any fuss. It said so right here in black and white. You could do it all you wanted. Her scalp tingled at the thought. She tugged at her hair and savored the stabbing needles.

She risked a hungering glance at Jake's handsome profile. Though she hoped one day to go further than that, she could never do more than kissing. She could never know what it'd be like to scratch the real itch.

Nobody but her mama knew Amy was a plague child.

if you enjoyed

OUR WAR

look out for

A BOY AND HIS DOG AT THE END OF THE WORLD

by

C. A. Fletcher

"This un-put-down-able story has everything—a well-imagined post-apocalyptic world, great characters, incredible suspense, and, of course, the fierce love of some very good dogs." —Kirkus (starred review)

When a beloved family dog is stolen, her owner sets out on a life-changing journey through the ruins of our world to bring her back in this fiercely compelling tale of survival, courage, and hope. Perfect for readers of Station Eleven and The Girl With All the Gifts.

My name's Griz. My childhood wasn't like yours. I've never had friends, and in my whole life, I've not met enough people to play a game of football.

My parents told me how crowded the world used to be, before all the people went away. But we were never lonely on our remote island. We had each other and our dogs.

Then the thief came.

And there may be no law left except what you make of it. But if you steal my dog, you can at least expect me to come after you.

Because if we're not loyal to the things we love, what's the point?

Chapter 1

The end

Dogs were with us from the very beginning.

When we were hunters and gatherers and walked out of Africa and began to spread across the world, they came with us. They guarded our fires as we slept and they helped us bring down prey in the long dawn when we chased our meals instead of growing them. And later, when we did become farmers, they guarded our fields and watched over our herds. They looked after us, and we looked after them. Later still, they shared our homes and our families when we built towns and cities and suburbs. Of all the animals that travelled the long road through the ages with us, dogs always walked closest.

And those that remain are still with us now, here at the end of the world. And there may be no law left except what you make it, but if you steal my dog, you can at least expect me to come after you. If we're not loyal to the things we love, what's the point? That's like not having a memory. That's when we stop being human.

That's a kind of death, even if you keep breathing.

So. About that. Turns out the world didn't end with a bang. Or much of a whimper. Don't get me wrong: there were bangs, some big, some little, but that was early on, before people got the drift of what was happening.

But bangs are not really how it ended. They were symptoms, not cause.

How it ended was the Gelding, though what caused that never got sorted out, or if it did it was when it was too late to do anything about it. There were as many theories as there were suddenly childless people—a burst of cosmic rays, a chemical weapon gone astray, bio-terror, pollution (you lot did make a mess of your world), some kind of genetic mutation passed by a space virus or even angry gods in pick-your-own-flavour for those who had a religion. The "how" and the "why" slowly became less important as people got used to the "what", and realised the big final "when" was heading towards them like a storm front that not even the fastest, the richest, the cleverest or the most powerful were going to be able to outrun.

The world—the human part of it—had been gelded or maybe turned barren—perhaps both—and people just stopped having kids. That's all it took. The Lastborn generation—the Baby Bust as they called themselves, proving that irony was one of the last things to perish—they just carried on getting older and older until they died like people always had done.

And when they were all gone, that was it. No bang, no whimper even. More of a tired sigh.

It was a soft apocalypse. And though it probably felt pretty hard for those it happened to, it did happen. And now we few—we vanishingly few—are all alone, stuck here on the other side of it.

How can I tell you this and not be dead? I'm one of the exceptions that proves the rule. They estimated maybe 0.0001 per cent of the world population somehow escaped the Gelding. They were known as outliers. That means if there were 7,000,000,000 people before the Gelding, less than 7000 of them could have kids. One in a million. Give or take, though since it takes two to make a baby, more like one in two million.

You want to know how much of an outlier I am? You, in the old picture I have of you, are wearing a shirt with the name of an even older football club on it. You look really happy. In my whole life, I haven't met enough people to make up two teams for a game of football. The world is that empty.

Maybe if this were a proper story it would start calm and lead up to a cataclysm, and then maybe a hero or a bunch of heroes would deal with it. I've read plenty of stories like that. I like them. Especially the ones where a big group of people get together, since the idea of a big group of people is an interesting thing for me all by itself, because though I've seen a lot, I've never seen that.

But this isn't that kind of story. It's not made up. This is just me writing down the real, telling what I know, saying

what actually took place. And everything that I know, even
my being born, happened long, long after that apocalypse had
already softly wheezed its way out.

I should start with who I am. I'm Griz. Not my real name. I
have a fancier one, but it's the one I've been called for ever. They
said I used to whine and grizzle when I was a baby. So I became
the Little Grizzler and then as I got taller my name got shorter,
and now I'm just Griz. I don't whine any more. Dad says I'm
stoical, and he says it like that's a good thing. Stoical means
doesn't complain much. He says I seemed to get all my complaining out of the way before I could talk and now, though
I do ask too many questions, mostly I just get on with things.
Says that like it's good too. Which it is. Complaining doesn't get
anything done.

And we always have plenty to do, here at the end of the
world.

Here is home, and home is an island, and we are my family.
My parents, my brother and sister, Ferg and Bar. And the dogs
of course. My two are Jip and Jess. Jip's a long-legged terrier,
brown and black, with a rough coat and eyes that miss nothing. Jess is as tall as he is but smooth-coated, narrower in the
shoulders and she has a splash of white on her chest. Mongrels
they are, brother and sister, same but different. Jess is a rarity,
because dog litters seem to be all male nowadays. Maybe that's
to do with the Gelding too. Perhaps whatever hit us, hit them
too, but in a lesser way. Very few bitches are born now. Maybe
that's a downside for the dogs, punishment for their loyalty,
some cosmically unfair collateral damage for walking alongside us all those centuries.

We're the only people on the island, which is fine, because
it's a small island and it fits the five of us, though sometimes

I think it fit us better and was less claustrophobic when there were six. It's called Mingulay. That's what its name was when you were alive. It's off the Atlantic coast of what used to be Scotland. There's nothing to the west of it but ocean and then America and we're pretty sure that's gone.

To the north there's Pabbay and Sandray, low islands where we graze our sheep and pasture the horses. North of them is the larger island called Barra but we don't land there, which is a shame as it has lots of large houses and things, but we never set foot on it because something happened and it's bad land. It's a strangeness to sail past a place so big that it even has a small castle in the middle of its harbour for your whole life, and yet never walk on it. Like an itch you can't quite reach round and scratch. But Dad says if you set foot on Barra now you get something much worse than an itch, and because it's what killed his parents, we don't go. It's an unlucky island and the only things living there these days are rabbits. Even birds don't seem to like it, not even the gulls who we never see landing above the wet sand below the tideline.

North-east of us are a long low string of islands called the Uists, and Eriskay, which are luckier places, and we go there a lot, and though there are no people on them now, there's plenty of wildlife and lazy-beds for wild potatoes. Once a year we go and camp on them for a week or so while we gather the barley and the oats from the old fields on the sea lawn. And then sometimes we go there to do some viking. "Going a-viking" is what Dad calls it when we sail more than a day and sleep over on a trip, going pillaging like the really ancient seafarers in the books, with the longships and the heroic deeds. We're no heroes though; we're just scavenging to survive, looking for useful things from the old world, spares or materials we can strip out from the derelict houses. And books of course. Books turn out to be pretty durable if they're kept away from damp and rats. They can last hundreds of years, easy. Reading is another way we survive. It helps to know where we came from, how we got here. And most of all, for me, even though these low and empty islands are all I have ever known, when I open the front cover of a new book, it's like a door, and I can travel far away in place and time.

Even the wide sea and the open sky can be claustrophobic if you never get away from them.

So that's who I am, which just leaves you. In some way you know who you are, or at least, you knew who you were. Because you're dead of course, like almost every single human who ever walked the planet, and long dead too.

And why am I talking to a dead person? We'll get back to that. But first we should get on with the story. I've read enough to know that I should do the explaining as we go.

Chapter 2

The traveller

If he hadn't had red sails, I think we'd have trusted him less.

The boat was visible from a long way off, much further than white sails would have been against the pale haze to the north-west. Those red sails were a jolt of colour that caught the eye and grabbed your attention like a sudden shout breaks a long silence. They weren't the sails of someone trying to sneak up on you. They had the honest brightness of a poppy. Maybe that was why we trusted him. That and his smile, and his stories.

Never trust someone who tells good stories, not until you know why they're doing it.

I was high up on Sandray when I saw the sails. I was tired and more than a little angry. I'd spent the morning rescuing an anchor that had parted from Ferg's boat the previous week, hard work that I felt he should have done for himself, though he claimed his ears wouldn't let him dive as deep as I could, and that anchors didn't grow on trees. Having done that, I was now busy trying to rescue a ram that had fallen and wedged itself in a narrow crack in the rocks above the grazing. It wasn't badly injured but it was stubborn and ungrateful in the way of most sheep, and it wasn't letting me get a rope round it. It had butted me twice, the first time catching me under the chin sharply enough that I had chipped a tooth halfway back on the lower right-hand side. I had sworn at it and then tried again. My knuckles were badly grazed from where it had then butted my hand against the scrape of the stone, and I was standing back licking my fist and swearing at it in earnest when I saw the boat.

The suddenness of the colour stopped me in my tracks.

I was too shocked to link the taste of blood in my mouth with the redness of the sails, but then I have little of that kind of foresight, none at all really compared with my other sister Joy, who always seemed to know when people were about to return home just before they did, or be able to smell an incoming storm on a bright day. I don't much believe in that kind of thing now, though I did when I was smaller and thought less, when I ran free with her across the island, happy and without a care beyond when it would be supper time. In those days I took her seeming foresight as something as everyday and real as cold water from the spring behind the house. Later, as I grew and began to think more, I decided it was mostly just luck, and since she disappeared for ever over the black cliff at the top of the island, not reliable luck at all.

If she'd really had foresight, she would never have tried to rescue her kite and fallen out of life in that one sharp and lonely moment. If she'd had foresight, she'd have waited until we returned to the island to help her. I saw the kite where it was pinned in a cleft afterwards, and know we could have reached it with the long hoe and no harm need have come to anyone. As it was, she must have tried to reach it by herself and slipped into the gulf of air more than seven hundred feet above the place where waves that have had two thousand sea miles to build up momentum slam into the first immoveable object they've ever met: the dark cliff wall that guards the back of our home. She wouldn't have waited for us to help though. She was always impatient, a tough little thing always in a hurry to catch up with Ferg and Bar and do what they did even though she was much younger. Bar later said it was almost like she was in such a hurry because she sensed she had had less time ahead of her than the rest of us.

We never found her body. And with her gone, so was my childhood, though I was eight at the time and she only a year more. Two birthdays later, by then a year older than she would ever be, I was in my mind what I now am: fully grown. Although even now, many years after that, Bar and Ferg still call me a kid. But they are six and seven years older than us. So Joy and I were always the babies. Our mother called us that to distinguish us from the other two.

Though after Joy fell, Mum never called any of us anything ever again. Never spoke at all. We found her halfway down the hill from the cliff edge, and we nearly lost her too. Far as we could make out she must have been careering down the slope, running helter-skelter, maybe mad with grief, maybe sprinting for the dory with some desperate doomed hope that she could get it launched and all the way round the island against the tide to rescue a child who in truth could not have survived such a fall. She never spoke because she all but dashed her brains out when she stumbled forward, smacking her head into a rock as she fell, temple gashed and watery blood coming from her ears.

That was the worst day ever, though the ones that followed were barely lighter. She didn't die but she wasn't there any more, her brain too wounded or too scarred for her to get out of herself again. In the Before she'd have been taken to a hospital and they would have operated on her brain to relieve the pressure, Dad said. But this is the After, so he decided to do it himself with a hand drill: he would have done it too, if he had been able to find the drill, but it wasn't where it should have been, and then the bleeding stopped and she just slept for a long, long time and no more fluid leaked out of her ears, so maybe it was best that he didn't try and drill a hole into her skull to save her.

I hope so, because I know Ferg hid the drill. He saw me see him, but we've never, ever spoken of it. If we did, I'd tell him I admire him for doing it, because Dad would have killed Mum and then would have had to live with the horror of that on top of everything else. And, even though she's locked away inside her head, you can sit and hold her hand and sometimes she squeezes it and almost smiles, and it's a comforting thing, the tiny ghost bit of her that remains, the warmth of her hand, the skin on skin. Dad said that day was the darkest thing that ever happened to us, and that we're past it, and that now we have to get on and live, just like in a bigger way the worst thing happened to the world and it just goes on.

He holds her hand sometimes, in the dark by the fire, when he thinks none of us notice him doing it. He does it privately because he thinks we would see it as a sign of weakness, a grown man needing that moment of warmth. Maybe it is. Or maybe the weakness is hiding the need, which is something Bar said to Ferg one evening when she was upset and no one knew I was listening.

Follow us:

f /orbitbooksUS

🐦 /orbitbooks

▶ /orbitbooks

Join our mailing list
to receive alerts on our
latest releases and deals.

orbitbooks.net

Enter our monthly
giveaway for the chance
to win some epic prizes.

orbitloot.com